THE
HARLAN
ELLISON
HORNBOOK

BOOKS BY HARLAN ELLISON

THE HARLAN ELLISON HORNBOOK

PENZLER BOOKS · NEW YORK

Penzler Books, 129 West 56th Street, New York, N.Y. 10019

Printed in the United States of America

Mirage Press limited edition/September 1990
Penzler Books edition/November 1990

10 9 8 7 6 5 4 3 2 1

Library of Congress Cataloging-in-Publication Data

Ellison, Harlan.
  [Hornbook]
  Harlan Ellison's hornbook / Harlan Ellison.—Penzler Books trade ed.

    p.   cm.
  ISBN 0-89296-239-9
  I. Title.
PS3555.L62H67   1990
813'.54—dc20

89-40520
CIP

Acknowledgments

One tries to be punctilious. No writer does it unassisted. Every one of us says the same thing, book after book. And sometimes the thankyous run for pages. Often, it is the only recognition the excellent typesetter or editorial assistant gets for the uncounted hours of labor in aid of a single book getting through the labyrinth. But because twenty years have elapsed since these columns were written, memory fails and time carries away the names of those who were there, indispensably, at a special moment. I apologize to those who read this and know their efforts were important. They are no less important than these few who *are* noted.

And so, in the name of *all* good friends, those who were, and are gone . . . those who are, and remain . . .

Thanks to Brian Kirby, Art Kunkin, Tim Kirk, John Heidenry, Leo and Diane Dillon, Jack Chalker, Otto Penzler, Bill Malloy, Robert Crais, Dr. Sidney Coleman, Stanislaw Fernandes, Gahan Wilson, Mariana Hernández, Lynn Lehrhaupt, Ed Bryant; and a slug on the bicep to Gil Lamont; and a kiss on the puss to my *much* better half, my wife Susan.

This one is for

EDDIE LONDON

more than just a friend
for twenty-seven years

and for

BILL DIGNIN

whose camaraderie stretches
back through thirty-eight years
to days of youth in Cleveland

Table of Contents

→

NOTE: Many of the numbered installments, and some of the Appendixes, are
preceded by *Interim Memos*, written for this volume, updating or
providing background for the selection.

THE
HARLAN
ELLISON
HORNBOOK

Author's Note

What that is, the little mortarboard representation above, is something typesetters call a *dingbat*. These are ornamental slugs of type that are used by book designers, publishers, academics, and others involved with putting books together, as borders, decorations, separators, that sort of thing. They can also be used in place of what those who create type fonts call "bullets." A bullet looks like this • usually, but sometimes it even looks like this ● ; but if it's much larger it's probably a smear of ink from the printing press and has no esoteric meaning whatever. Dingbats can be in any shape. They are intended—when used as a surrogate for a bullet—as a kind of asterisk, to draw your attention to something usually explained or amplified in a footnote at the bottom of that page. Dingbats can look like anything; like these:

I once saw a dingbat in the shape of U Thant having an animated conversation with Mae West at the now-defunct Steuben Tavern in New York City. Well, you can just imagine.

Anyhow. The little mortarboard dingbat—selected to connote wisdom—appears here'n'there throughout this book. *Why* it appears is this: after the Author of this excellent volume had submitted the final manuscript, the Publisher and his Sanhedrin of dark-cloaked esthetes raised a number of queries about one or another minor matter. Such as, "In your review of the restaurant El Palenque in installment 8, you suggest starting dinner with a *chi-chi cocktail*. What the hell is a *chi-chi cocktail*?"

Well, how the devil should *I* know what a *chi-chi cocktail* is? In the first place, I don't drink. In the second place, I wrote that damned column eighteen years ago. In the third place, it was on the menu and someone I was with ordered it and said it was excellent, which is as close to finding out what it was made of as I ever got. And in the fourth place, who gives a damn?

Now most of the queries the Sanhedrin raised were more pertinent than that, but the bulk of them went to clarifying cultural tropes and contemporary references readers of today might not recognize. (Bearing in mind that for much of today's reading audience, anything earlier than The New Kids on the Block or *America's Funniest Home Videos* falls into the category of Ancient History, if it's recalled at all.) So that meant, if I was to satisfy the Publisher and his Sanhedrin, that I would end up littering the bottoms of pages throughout this book like Fifth Avenue after a Ronald McDonald Testimonial Parade. Footnotes up the gi-gi. (Incidentally, the cocktail is pronounced the same way: *cheee-cheee*. Even as gi-gi is *geee-geee*. See what I mean about explaining all this stuff?)

So it seemed far more rational simply to use a dingbat to indicate a footnote sort of comment, and to put all the comments and explanations at the back of the book, following the last actual essay, but just before you hit the wonderful Index done by Gil Lamont. And so it came to pass that 🎓 appears hither and yon as you wend your way from front to back. When you see it, you can either ignore the damned thing, or anal-retentively scurry to the penultimate section of the HORNBOOK for some basically wiseass remarks. The choice is yours.

You think this Author business is easy? As S. J. Perelman said, "The muse is a tough buck."

Robert Crais is considered the fastest rising new star in the mystery field. His novels *The Monkey's Raincoat* and *Stalking the Angel* receive widespread popular and critical acclaim, as does his work for television. He has written and/or produced such series as *Hill Street Blues*, *Cagney & Lacy*, and *Men*. Crais has been nominated for such awards as the *Emmy* by Academy of Television Arts and Sciences, the *Edgar* by the Mystery Writers of America, the *Anthony* by the membership of the World Mystery Convention, the *Shamus* by the Private Eye Writers of America, and the *Macavity* by the Mystery Readers of America. He has won both the *Anthony* and the *Macavity*. Currently, Crais is developing prime time series pilots for NBC, CBS, and ABC, as well as writing his new novel, *Lullaby Town*. His four-hour miniseries, *Cross of Fire*—an examination of the rise to power of the Ku Klux Klan in 1920s America—aired, to killer ratings, last fall on NBC.

Foreword

The Cricket Beneath the Hammer

by Robert Crais

Here is one of the ways in which I met Harlan Ellison:

I was down to Eddie Dipente's dojo just below Crenshaw, here in Los Angeles, trying to work off the cloudy mind and soft body I get from too much writing. It's always the same that way. I'll get wrapped up in a project, spend twelve, fifteen hours a day on my butt, eating poison and wrecking my body until finally I can't stand it any more, just about go nerve-snapping crazy with it, and I run down and let Uncle Eddie straighten me out.

You've got to know Eddie. Six-one, one ninety-five, some-thing like that, a rich mocha color with a sprinkling of gray in whatever tight-packed hair he has left. For twenty-two years he taught hand-to-hand down at Pendleton until he bailed out of the Corps and set up shop here in "Laz Anglas," teaching actors and cops and imitation tough guys some of the nifty things he knows how to do with and to the human body. For the record, he also plays a fine jazz piano, can't sing worth a stick, and is one of the warmest, most caring human beings I've ever met. Go figure.

Anyway, I was down at Eddie's dojo, off in a corner by myself, struggling through a couple of katas that Eddie had set up for me, just stuff of his own, not the formal stuff, a little *tae kwan do*, a little *kung fu*, when he came up with the big blind-you-it's-so-white smile and said, "Got a little treat for you. Got a friend coming in you gonna like. Another writer." Eddie takes much joy in knowing writers, and can quote at embar-rassing length from Kipling and Twain and Raymond Chan-dler and I think he must know every haiku ever written by Matsuo Bashō. Eddie said, "I've been trying to get this guy back to the mats for years, and he's gonna give it a shot again, so you guys can work out together."

I said, "Uh-huh," a little pissed, because I like working out alone and Eddie *knew* I like working out alone, and he could tell I was pissed and I knew he could tell because of the way his eyes were enjoying the hell out of it.

Harlan Ellison came out of the locker room.

Eddie made the introductions, told us what he wanted us to do, then walked away. It was hot and sweaty, there in our corner of Eddie's world, and we grunted and puffed and strained, and you could tell that Harlan had not done these things for many years. A long time ago he had been through Ranger School at Fort Benning, and had studied *jeet kun do* with Bruce Lee, but in recent years he had been ill with some sort of bizarre *Andromeda Strain*-version of Epstein–Barr Disease and he was . . . is there a sensitive way to say this? . . . an abso-lute wreck.

I watched him struggle to work through the tight hamstrings and the frozen lower back and the stiff shoulders and the Achilles tendons like dried leather and I thought, Christ, if this guy throws a head-high roundhouse kick we'll have to call an ambulance. Eddie would drift over, watch a while, then try to look encouraging and say stuff like, "Good effort, man. Take it slow, Harlan. You've got all the time in the world." That kind of thing. You see?

I'm not sure why now, but we barely said a word, Harlan with his pain and me with mine, though about halfway through we stopped for a breather and he looked at me, sweat running into his eyes and down his nose, and said, "Man, if I ever had to use this shit, I'd get killed." He looked sort of sad when he said it.

An hour and a half later it was over, Harlan gray-pallored and hurting, unable to raise his arms above shoulder height even to dress. We said our goodbyes, mumbling the sort of things two guys who'd just met in a gym and worked out together say, *good workout, man, get together next week, grab some lunch or something.* I left first, heading out to my car, thinking I would never see Harlan Ellison again.

Half a block down the street, five pseudo-humans jumped out of a 1968 Chevy Impala and tried to shake me down. It was not a smash&grab. It was the "hey, don't I know you?" number. You know the drill. Pretty soon you're getting shoved and the knife or the Special comes out and then your keys and credit cards are gone along with whatever dignity you might've had in your back pocket. Only it had been a rough week, I didn't much feel like handing over what was in my pocket, and I pushed back. Okay, so sometimes I'm dumb. It was getting bad fast and the Korean guy in the little fruit market was doing everything he could not to see what was going on right in front of him and I was wondering if I was going to die for forty-two bucks and some plastic when Harlan came down the sidewalk and I yelled, "Get Eddie." Harlan took in the scene in a microsecond and started back for the dojo. The sub-humans, displaying their quota of rationality for the decade, saw Harlan headed for help, began to back off . . . and I went for them. Call it spring fever. Here they were, backing off, going away, leaving me alone, and I was so damned blind-furious *ANGRY* that all I could think was, "You fuckers ain't gettin' away from *me!*" Okay, so sometimes I'm *really* dumb. I grabbed the nearest cretin, pulled him backward, and the others converged like piranha at a chum line. I thought, oh, jesus, I am dead.

Then Harlan was there, Harlan who could barely move and who knew that if he had to use this stuff he would surely die, there he was, showing Crane technique from the Kung Fu, arms thrusting and windmilling as best they could, a Jack-Haley-as-the-Scarecrow movement out the corner of my eye. . . .

They kicked our asses.

I got slammed backward into the car, caught a knee in the groin, and then I was covering up on the street, trying to survive. When I looked up again, after what seemed like years, Harlan was sitting on the sidewalk, feet out in front of him and legs locked like some kind of Raggedy Andy, hands in his lap, and I said, "Your nose is bleeding."

He said, "There's a cut over your left eye. Can you see okay?"

I touched at the eye and saw the red on my fingers. "Yeah."

He said, "I think I tore a couple of muscles in my left shoulder."

"Uh-huh."

We sat like that awhile, a couple of dopes, him on the sidewalk and me in the gutter, big deal Hollywood writers out on the town. He wasn't yet married to Susan, but I was married to Pat, and would have to explain, and it would go hard. The Korean guy came out, swatted flies away from his fruit, and went back inside. Didn't see us, I guess. I said, "Hey, Harlan?"

"Huh?"

I ever have to use this shit, I'm gonna get killed. "You shoulda went screaming for Eddie. You shouldn't'a come tried to help."

He cocked his head and gave me genuine honest-to-god confused. "What else could I do?"

Being into the zen of martial arts, I look for lessons in the world around me and, in Harlan and his work, find them.

There are lessons here: "One's bad karma defies space-time equations; a continent is no thicker than a membrane when one carries the misery inside; there is no escape, no place to hide." Read of Valerie, and learn of duplicity and betrayal. Read of Ahbhu, and learn the harsh responsibilities of love and friendship. There are lessons here: "Surround yourself with joyful people." Read of Don Epstein, and learn of the singular importance of individuality and strength. Read of the deaths of Harlan's mother and father, and the lesson is this: rush home *now*, tell your parents what you need to tell them *now*, ask the questions that your childhood demands you ask *now*, hug them or hit them or kiss them or shriek at them and *risk* that they will hug *you* or hit *you* or reject *you* but do it *now*, because when death knocks it is too late. There are lessons here. Read of Ronald Fouquet, the child killer, and learn of rage and fear. There are lessons here. . . .

Harlan denies this. He says, "I'm simply a writer, a story-teller; if you read this column expecting to learn great lessons about life, or expect me to explain the Natural Order of the Universe, forget it." He's wrong, of course. He often is. Take Christmas. A perfectly wonderful, nifty, heartwarming time of the year, yet Harlan loathes it. You see? Wrong.

Even though Harlan may deny that he is a teacher, or be uncomfortable with having an influence on the lives of other people (see his essay concerning his friend, the wonderful writer Herbert Kastle), the facts speak for themselves—Harlan is, and does. He might rail that young people at a lecture he gave did not know of Dachau, but they know *now*, because Harlan told them about it. And I'd bet heavy sugar that somewhere out there, a kid who has never heard the name will read Harlan's essay in this volume on the death of Lenny Bruce and, because of that essay, track down the sides to *Religions, Inc.* and *Fat Boy* and *How to Relax Your Colored Friends at Parties*. Man, that kid is in for a kick.

Harlan Ellison writes about the physics of being human and, whether he knows it or not, accepts it or not, these are the lessons he offers. Not by way of lecture (though he does), but by example. Harlan Ellison does not tell you how to be; he tells you how *he* is and by so doing provides a measure with which you might gauge yourself. *Here is how a specific man comports himself. Does it make sense? Is it ethical and good? What would I do in that situation? Would my actions cause shame or pride? Where does my responsibility end, and where does it begin, and what do I want to see when I look in the mirror?*

Since these columns are better than fifteen years old, one might wonder if they can possibly be relevant to today's experience. (In point of fact, there are things in here that, not to kick it bloody while it's down, we couldn't give a shit less about. Say, the dubious culinary qualities of long defunct restaurants, the lineage of Harlan's *marabunta* horde of house-keepers/assistants/secretaries, and Harlan's aforementioned [and wholly incorrect] views on Christmas. But Harlan is a master showman, and whether writing about things as obscure and mind-numbing as the vocal stylings of Buddy Greco or the vagaries of microcephalic science fiction groupies, you will be entertained and pleased. As he says, he is not above tossing in a flying fish or a troll to make the story more interesting, and Harlan can sling fish faster than a Japanese trawler at Marine-land. But back to relevance. . . .) Read his column on the apathy of college students, and of how their only interest in him as a lecturer was in how much money he makes, and you will think he wrote it this morning after a run-in with a truckload of Harvard Business School yuppies. It was written in 1973. Courage, honor, responsibility, joy, love, friendship, pain, out-rage, anger, trust—the things of being human—are always relevant.

Harlan Ellison is Jiminy Cricket to our Pinocchio. But did you know there were *two* talking crickets? Walt Disney based his cute, lovable creature Jiminy (as well as the rest of the movie) on a book, *The Adventures of Pinocchio* by Carlo Collodi. In the book, the talking cricket wasn't named Jiminy and wasn't cute and lovable. Collodi referred to it simply as the Talking Cricket. In the film, Jiminy spoke the truth as he saw it to Pinocchio and the two of them lived happily ever after. In the book, the Talking Cricket spoke the truth to Pinocchio, and Pinocchio smashed it to death with a hammer.

Spreading the truth is neither safe, nor easy.

Herein, there are lessons. Open your eyes and take advantage of them. Harlan the Fish Juggler will make you laugh and cry and snigger and giggle and probably pee in your pants. High entertainment is at hand. Harlan the Cricket offers larger opportunities.

You will be tested, from time to time throughout your life, and if you pay attention here your point score will be higher than it otherwise might be.

Introduction

The Lost Secrets of East Atlantis

by Harlan Ellison

*T*here are seismic temblor authorities who contend it all began with the *tsunami* that resulted from the sub-sea earthquake in the Taiwan Trench that inundated Japan and took Tokyo out of the international financial community permanently.

Whatever sequence of major upheavals proceeded from that disaster—referred to by survivors, to this day, as The Divine Hiccup—within four months the interlocking temblors had latticed the Earth's crust, finally building up a pressure directly under the Tropic of Cancer at 23°30′N 38°7′15″E— about one hundred kilometers due south of the port city of Yanbu' in Saudi Arabia—below the Red Sea, Al-Bahr al-Ahmar.

When the mantle exploded, the fissure slithered north northeast beneath the mountains of the Harrat al-'Uwayrid where some unknown impediment forced the massive energy toward the surface, shattering the mountains, severing a gigantic chunk of the Madyan, leaping the Straits of Tiran and Jubal, taking out the southern tip of the Sinai Peninsula, and racing across the Arabian Desert.

When the juggernaut reached the 27th Parallel approaching the 32nd Meridian, it just said t'hell with it, and blew out nine hundred kilometers of Egypt, reducing everything between Cairo and the Aswan Dam to a fine powdered ash that made for spectacular sunsets for decades to come.

And there, in the caldera that had been the Valley of the Kings, all supposition surrounding the myths of Atlantis came to an end as the lost continent thrust up its highest mountain. For thrice thirty thousand years The Spire of the Sun had lain hidden beneath the desert. A mountaintop sheathed in solid gold; at its apex, hewn from the basalt, the House of the Heavens; a temple whose underground levels fell dizzyingly for a mile *inside* the mountain; prayerhouse to deities so arcane and ancient that not even the sigh of their names had come to us through antiquity.

When the archeological teams from Thule and Brasilia and Sydney landed their huge choppers in the sea-washed plazas of the House of the Heavens, and the scientists entered the three great triangular portals that swung open at the touch of a finger on center-pivots, they roamed far and deep, and they came, at last, to the central nidus of the Atlanteans. And it was there, on a golden tabulary, they found—perfectly preserved as if waiting for the light of the stars to fall upon its inscribed pages of thinnest beaten silver—the lost manuscript of *The Harlan Ellison Hornbook.*

No?

You're not going for it?

Well, okay, so it isn't eons, it's only twenty years—give or take a cardiac arrest or two—since this book was put under contract. But it *seems* like eons, to hear Jack Chalker and Otto Penzler tell it. And tell of it they have, in Jack's case for two decades, which could, I suppose, be considered reason enough for *kvetching*; but in Otto's case it's only been about three years, even though I promised to deliver the manuscript in thirty days.

So, *okay*, I admit it. I'm running a little late this century. But I've been sick.

The forty-six columns (and ancillary material) that constitute the raw, 484-page manuscript of the *Hornbook* have awaited assemblage between hardcovers more than fifteen times as long as it took to write them. With the exception of the final three columns—written for a long-defunct periodical called *The Saint*

Louis Literary Supplement in 1976—all of this 120,000 word volume (including a complete, hitherto-unpublished motion picture screenplay) was written in one unbroken fourteen-month burst of journalistic activity.

Between the essays on television contained in my books THE GLASS TEAT (1970) and THE OTHER GLASS TEAT (1975), and the cultural ruminations that make up AN EDGE IN MY VOICE (1985), lie the essays of the *Hornbook*, written between 26 October 1972 and 13 December 1973.

I don't need anyone to tell me that this "trove" of "lost writings" is not as important as, say, locating buried scrolls from the Great Library at Alexandria, pre–first burning. But in the twenty years since the *Hornbook* columns appeared in the pages of the *Los Angeles Free Press* and the *L.A. Weekly News*, some decent measure of literary celebrity has come my way; and if what has been published under my name has any lasting merit—one hopes, but it's never anything better than a crapshoot—then this substantial chunk of prose is certainly (at least) another measure of ultimate worthiness. Posterity needs all the help it can get. Ask John Fante or Frederic Prokosch or Shirley Jackson. We all need a pat on the back, even unto the grave.

(Quentin Crisp has written: "Artists in any medium are nothing more than a bunch of hooligans who cannot live within their income of admiration.")

At least one full generation of readers has grown up since

Original column logo by Gahan Wilson

I wrote these wonky little essays on the passing parade. The concerns of those years near the end of the Vietnam war, near the end of the reign of Nixon, near the end of a period of heightened social consciousness, now seem like musty, if amusing, reminiscences of ex–Flower Power advocates bent on boring their yuppie-in-training offspring. Nonetheless, voices of yesterday speak in these pages and, for kids to whom nostalgia is breakfast, there may yet be a few bemusing stories to recount.

Had this book been published when it was first signed up, it would have spoken directly to the times. Twenty years after the fact it offers itself in a different language entirely. But whether in Urdu or Serbo-Croat or Cockney, the stuff that really counts never changes. Courage, friendship, integrity, passion, idiocy, and the variegated pratfalls of just folks translate easily.

From East Atlantis, the lost *Hornbook* is delivered from the House of the Heavens, situated conveniently near the new Atlantis Marriott, the Trump Trylon and Perisphere, the Taco Bell Shopping Mall and Driving Range, and the spectacular MGM-Sanyo HundredPlex Theater, straight to you.

Be kind. We've had a long journey, and we're sorry we kept you waiting.

HARLAN ELLISON
8 July 1989

When I was a little boy, they called me
a liar, but now that I'm grown up, they
call me a writer.

ISAAC BASHEVIS SINGER

God gave us memory that we might
have roses in December.
JAMES M. BARRIE

Writing is an occupation in which
you have to keep proving your talent
to people who have none.

JULES RENARD (1864–1910)

Everything I Know About My Father

26 October 1972

As if emerging from a dark dream, it suddenly occurs to me that I've spent at least half my life looking for my Father.

No, don't get it wrong: I'm not a bastard. I was born in University Hospital in Cleveland, Ohio, at 2:20 P.M. on 27 May 1934, to Louis Laverne Ellison and Serita Rosenthal Ellison . . . so I know who my Father was. And right here on my birth certificate, which I'm looking at, it asks in a little box: *Legitimate?* (Which is about as chill shot a way of asking it as I've ever seen.) But, happily for my Mother and unhappily for my biographers, it says right back, and snappishly: *yes.*

So when I say I've spent half my adult life looking for my old man, I don't mean it like something out of Victor Hugo. (Though it now occurs in the wake of the first realization—and how strange that one awakening of curiosity firecrackers into other awarenesses, *seriatim*—that I've written a number of stories in which kids are looking for their fathers, for one reason or another, to suit the plot. The one that pops to mind foremost was called "No Fourth Commandment," and it was about a kid who was looking for his father, whom he'd never

My father, Louis Laverne Ellison

known, to kill him for fucking-over his mother. Sold the story after its magazine publication to *Route 66*, where it was adapted into a teleplay by a guy named Larry Marcus, and was retitled "A Gift for a Warrior." It aired on January 18th, 1963, almost a year to the day I arrived in Los Angeles from Back East, and years later Marcus and the producer of *Route 66*, Herbert Leonard, did it as the basis of their film *Going Home*, without paying me for its second adaptation, but that's another story and my attorney is in the process of talking to them about it, so let's get back to the point.)

My Father died in 1949, when I was fifteen. And I'd lived with him and my Mother, off and on, for those fifteen years, but I never really knew him, or even much about him. It wasn't till my Mother was very ill, three or four years ago, and she thought it was all over, that she spilled some very heavy data about Louis Laverne.

There's a lot of it she won't be happy if I relate. It is silly, of course, it's all forty and more years gone, but family skeletons rattle loudest in the minds of those who live in memories, which is where my Mother's at. Today is nowhere nearly as important as all the yesterdays with my Father. So I won't go into the circumstances of how my Father practiced dentistry in Cleveland for eleven years. That's a story for another time, years from now.

For openers, like me, my Father was a short man. Even shorter than I, as I recall. I'm 5′5″, for the record. He was incredibly gentle: I remember once, when I'd done something outstandingly shitty as a child, he was compelled to take me into the cellar and use the "strap" on me. His belt. Now perceive, please, that there is no faintest scintilla of hatred in this recollection. He was *not* a brutal man, and about as given to corporal punishment as Albert Schweitzer. But it was a time in this country when such things were expected of a father. "You just wait till your father comes home!" was the maternal cry, and one feared with only half a fear, because I knew my Dad just couldn't do such things.

But, as I say, on one occasion the punishment fit the crime—perhaps it was the time I shoved Johnny Mummy off the garage roof while we were playing Batman and Robin—and my Dad took me down into the cellar at 89 Harmon Drive in Painesville, Ohio, and he walloped me good.

I got over the stinging in about an hour, though there was a dull remembered pain for weeks thereafter.

My Father became ill. He went upstairs into his bedroom and he cried. He wasn't himself for several weeks after. Of course, I knew none of that at the time.

He was gentle, and he looked like, well, the closest way I can describe him was that he resembled a short Brian Donlevy. If you're not hip to who Brian Donlevy is, check out the *Late Late Show.*

When he was a little boy, my Father worked on riverboats, as a candy butcher. From that job he got into working minstrel shows. He sang. Really fine voice, even in later years. In fact, he had his photo on the sheet music of "My Yiddishe Momma," a song Al Jolson made famous; the song was written by a friend of Dad's, who dedicated it to my Father's mother . . . whom I never met. Never met my paternal grandfather, either.

Dad wanted to be a dentist, and he wound up practicing in Cleveland. Around Prohibition time. He was such a sensational dentist, I'm told, that the mob used to come to him for their mouthwork. My Mother worked as his receptionist after they'd been married a while, and she tells me when the gangsters came to get drilled and filled, my Dad insisted they check their heat with Mom. There were times, she says, when her desk drawer was difficult to pull open, so filled with guns was it.

Anyhow, you may wonder why I'm talking about all this here, the initial offering of a new column. Well, I wanted to talk about something important for openers, and almost all of this I never knew until a few days ago when my Mother came to visit from Florida. I don't see much of her, and we've never really talked to each other; but she got onto the subject of my Father, as she usually does, and I started prying the *real* truth out of her about him. Not the bullshit they feed kids about their parents, but who he *really* was. In all of the things I've ever written, I've said virtually nothing about my Father, you see, and that's because I simply didn't know the man. We were in the same house, but we were strangers. It was as though we vibrated on different planes of existence, passing each other and passing through each other, like shadows.

But when my Mother got around to telling me my Father had done time in prison, in some strange and perverted way I started to realize I'd been searching for "Doc" Ellison almost all my life.

Because of the stuff I'm not allowed to tell, he had to give up the D.D.S. practice. It was Prohibition time, it was Depression time, and my Dad had to support my Mother and my sister and me. So he got into the selling of booze.

Most of this is unclear because my single source of information, my Mother, chooses to blur it all. But as best I can tell, my Dad had friends in Canada, and he would make auto runs up through Buffalo into Toronto to pick up the hootch. Then he'd drive it back down to Cincinnati and Cleveland and thereabouts. After a while, things got easier, and my Dad gave work to a guy he met, a guy who was as down on his luck as Dad had been. And one night, on a run, the guy got busted while transporting the alcohol. So my Dad took the rap, and let the other guy get off. As my Mom tells it, the driver had a family and, well . . .

My Dad was a gentle man.

So he went to the can. Fairly stiff sentence, from what I can gather, but he didn't do it all. (And years later, when *I* wound up in jail, I was always amazed at how facilitously and soberly my Mother took it, and how competent she was at bailing my ass out of the slammer. Now I understand.)

After that, my Dad went to work for my uncles in Painesville, in their jewelry store. I was a little kid at the time, and knew none of what had gone down.

Years went by, and my Dad thought he owned a piece of the store—Hughes Jewelry on the corner of State & Main in Painesville. I was too busy fighting for my life to pay much attention, and I was always running away, but then in 1947, after my Uncle Morrie had come back from the War, it turned out my Father *didn't* own anything. He had been the manager of the store, had built up the clientele and won friends all through town—he was the only Jew ever taken into the Moose lodge in Painesville, a town famed for its anti-Semitism—but when the crunch came down, my old man was out on his ass. But it had been my Mother's brothers, you see, and so there wasn't much he could do about it. Jewish families hang tight that way. So at close to the age of fifty, my Father had to open his own store.

He couldn't get ground-floor space on Main Street, so he took an upstairs suite, and sold from there. In his off-hours he sold appliances by personal contact. It was a grueling existence. The fucking climb up those stairs alone was murder. That staircase went almost straight up, and he had to make that climb twenty times a day.

Well, it killed him a year later.

May 1st, 1949, a Sunday, I came downstairs from my room, to see my Dad sitting in his big overstuffed chair by the fireplace, the Sunday edition of the *Cleveland Plain Dealer* around his feet, his pipe in his mouth. I was still on the stairs, about to ask him for the funnies when suddenly he began to choke.

I watched, helpless and with a kind of detached fascination as he died right before my eyes. Coronary thrombosis. It was all over in seconds. My Mother was mostly stunned, but somehow we managed to get him onto the sofa; the pulmotor squad arrived too late. They couldn't have done anything. He was gone the minute he started to choke.

All through the next days, I moved like some kind of somnambulist. I was into baseball in those days, and I had a fuzz-less tennis ball that I bounced against the house. For the next month all I did, from morning till night, was stand outside on the front lawn under the maple tree, and bounce that ball off the wall, and catch it in the trapper's mitt my Dad had bought me. I threw the ball and caught it, threw it and caught it, over and over and over . . .

It must have been hell for everyone inside the house, the sound of that ball plonking against the wood, again and again, without end, till it got too dark to see it.

We moved away from there soon after, and I went from

straight A's in school to failing grades in everything. I became a trouble kid of the worst sort. But it worked out.

Ever since then, I now realize, I've been looking for my Father. I've tried to find him in Dad-surrogates, but that's always come to a bad end. And all I ever wanted to tell him was, "Hey, Dad, you'd be proud of me now; I turned out to be a good guy and what I do, I do well and . . . I love you and . . . why did you go away and leave me alone?"

When I lived in Cleveland, I used to go to his grave sometimes, but I stopped doing that fifteen years ago and haven't been back.

He isn't there.

Valerie, Part One

2 November 1972

H ere's one I think you'll like. In this one I come off looking like a *schmuck*, and don't we all love stories in which the invincible hero, the all-knowing savant, the omnipotent smartass is condignly flummoxed? It's about Valerie.

About 1968 I knew this local photographer named Phil. He wasn't the world's most terrific human being (in point of fact, he was pretty much what you'd call your garden-variety creep), but he somehow or other wormed his way into my life and my home—I believe *wormed* is the right word—and occasionally used my residence as the background locale for sets of photos of young ladies in the nude. Phil would show up at my house in the middle of my work-day, all festooned with lights and reflectors and camera boxes . . . and a pretty girl, whom he would usher into one of the bathrooms and urge to divest herself of her clothing, *vite vite!*

Now I realize this may ring tinnily on the ears of those of you who spend the greater part of your off-hours lurching after your gonads, but having edited a men's magazine in Chicago some years ago, the sight of a lady in dishabille does

Photo of Valerie

not cause sweat to break out on my palms. What I'm saying is that after two years of examining transparencies framed in a light-box, while wearing a loupe to up their magnification, all said transparencies of the world's most physically-sensational women, all stark naked . . . one develops a sense of proportion about such things. One begins looking for more exotic qualities—such as the ability on the part of the ladies to make you laugh or cry or feel as though you've learned something. (As an aside: nothing serves better to kill ingrained sexism than an overdose of flesh in living color; very quickly one differentiates between images on film and living, breathing human beings. I commend it to all you gentlemen who still use the words *broad* and *chick*.)

Consequently, it was not my habit to skulk around the house while Phil was snapping the ladies. When they'd take a break, I'd often sit with them and have a cup of coffee and we'd enter into a conversation, but apart from that I'd generally sit in my office and bang the typewriter. This may seem to have been the wrong thing to be banging, but, well, there you are. (Because of this attitude, Phil drew the wholly erroneous conclusion that I was gay, and had occasion, subsequently, to pass along his lopsided observation, sometimes to young ladies with whom I had become intimate. What a nasty thing to say, particularly from a man who lures six-year-old boys into the basements of churches and then defiles, kills and eats them, not necessarily in that order. Isn't idle gossip a wonderful thing!)

This use of my home and myself by The Demon Photographer went on for about a year, and I confess to permitting the inconvenience because on several of these shooting dates I *did* meet women with whom I struck up relationships. One such was Valerie.

(Of *course* I know her last name, you fool. I'm not giving it here out of deference to her family and what comes later in this saga.)

The Demon Photographer—squat, ginger-haired, insipid—arrived one afternoon with her, and I was zonked from the moment I saw her. She was absolutely lovely. A street gamine with a smile that could melt jujubes, a warm and outgoing friendliness, a quick wit and lively intelligence, and a body that I would have called *dynamite* during my chauvinist period. We hit it off immediately, and when Phil slithered away at the end of the session, Valerie stayed on for a while.

It didn't last all that long, to be frank. I can't recall all the specifics of disenchantment, but attrition set in—it's happened to all of you, so you know what I mean—and after a short while we parted: as friends.

Over the next few years, Valerie popped back into my life at something like six-month intervals, and if I wasn't involved with anyone we'd get it on for a few days, and then away she'd fly once more. There was always a kind of bittersweet tone to our liaisons: the scent of mimosa (and mimesis, had I but known), dreams half glimpsed, the memories of special touches. There was always the feeling that something lay unspoken between us, and a phrase from Sartre's THE RE-PRIEVE persisted: "it was as if a great stone had fallen in the road to block my path." In a way, I believe I was in love with Valerie.

Time passed. In mid-May of 1972 I was scheduled to speak at the Pasadena Writers' Week, and early the day of the appearance, I received a call from Valerie. I hadn't heard from her in almost a year.

After the hellos and my unconfined pleasure at hearing her voice, I asked, "What are you doing tonight?"

"Going out with you," she said.

(Witness, gentle readers: the desiccated ego of The Author, suddenly pumped full of self-esteem and jubilation, merely refractions of adoration at the perceptivity and swellness of a bright, quick lady saying, "You're fine." What asses we *machismo* buffoons can be.)

"Listen, I'm slated to go out and speak in Pasadena to a gaggle of literary types. Why don't you go with me and watch how I turn the crowd into a lynch mob."

"That's where I *am*," she said. "In Pasadena. At my mother's house. You can pick me up and I'll stay with you for a couple of days."

"I'll buy that dream," I said, and we set up ETA and coordinates.

That evening, in company with Edward Winslow Bryant, Jr. (dear friend, sometime house guest, outstandingly talented young writer, author of AMONG THE DEAD, CINNABAR, and co-author of PHOENIX WITHOUT ASHES) I drove out to Pasadena to pick up Valerie. When she answered the door she paused momentarily, framed in the opening, wearing a dress the shade of a bruised plum; as said, a body that should have been on permanent exhibition in the Smithsonian; wearing nothing under it.

Oh, Cupid, you pustulent twerp! One of these days some nether god is going to jam that entire quiver of crossbow bolts right up your infantile ass!

I went down like a bantamweight in an auto chassis crusher.

Carrying her overnight case, her hair dryer and curlers, her suitcase, her incredibly sweet-smelling clothes on wire hangers, I took her to the car, and was rewarded by the sight of Ed Bryant's eyes as they turned into Frisbies. Not to mention the unsettling memories of the hugs and kisses and liftings off the floor and spinnings around I'd just received inside the house.

We did the speaking gig, and Valerie sat in the front row displaying a thoroughly unnerving expanse of leg and thigh. I may have fumfuh'd a bit.

Afterward, Valerie, Ed and I went to have a late dinner at the Pacific Dining Car. Sitting over beefsteak tomatoes and the thickest imported Roquefort dressing in the Known World, Valerie started whipping numbers on me like this:

"I've always had a special affection for you. I should have moved in with you three years ago. Boy, was I a fool."

I mumbled things of little sense or import.

"Maybe I'll move in with you now . . . if you want me."

The next day, a girl from Illinois was to have flown in for an extended weekend. "Give me a minute to make a phone call," I said, and sprinted. I made the call. Bad vibes. Harsh language. Dead line.

"Yeah, why don't you move in with me," I said, slipping back into the booth. Everyone smiled.

When she went to the loo, Ed—whose perceptions about people are keen and reserved—leaned over and said, "Hang onto this one. She's sensational."

Opinion confirmed. By a sober outside observer.

So I took her home with me. The next day, Ed split for his parents' home in Wheatland, Wyoming, beaming at Harlan for his good luck and prize catch. That left, in the household, myself, Valerie, and Jim Sutherland: young author of STORMTRACK, occasional house guest and ex-student of your humble columnist at the Clarion Writers' Workshop in SF & Fantasy.

Later that day, Valerie asked me if she could use the telephone to make a long distance call to San Francisco. I said of course. She had told me, by way of bringing me up to date on her peregrinations, that since last she'd seen me she had been working in San Francisco, mostly as a topless waitress at the Condor and other joints; that she had been rooming with another girl; that she had been seeing a guy pretty steadily, but he was into a heavy dope scene and she wanted to get away from it; and she loved me.

After the call, she came into my office in the house and said she was worried. The guy, whom she'd called to tell she was not coming back, had gotten rank with her. The words bitch and cunt figured prominently in his diatribe.

She said she wanted to fly up to San Francisco that day, to clean out her goods before he could get over there and rip them off or bust them up. She also said, very nicely, that if she went up, she wanted to buy a VW minibus from a guy she knew. It would only cost $100 plus taking over the payments, and she'd need a car if she was going to come back here to live. "I want to work and pay my way," she said.

Or in the words of Bogart as Sam Spade, "You're good, shweetheart, really good." Remember, friends, no matter how fast a gun you are, there's always someone out there who's faster. And how better to defuse the suspicions of a cynical writer than to establish individuality and a plug-in to the Protestant Work Ethic.

She asked me for the hundred bucks.

Unfortunately, I didn't have the hundred at that moment, even though I said credit-card—wise I'd pay for her plane ticket to San Francisco.

She said that was okay, she'd work it out somehow. Then she went to pack an overnight bag, leaving all the rest of her goods behind, and promised she'd be driving back down the very next day.

Jim Sutherland offered to drive her to the airport—I was on a script deadline and had to stay at the typewriter—and she left with many kisses for me and deep looks into my naïve eyes, telling me she was all warm and squishy inside at having finally found me, Her White Knight.

It wasn't till Jim returned, young, innocent, a college student with very little bread, that I found out she had asked *him* for the hundred bucks, too. And he'd loaned it to her, with the promise of getting it back the next day.

The worm began to gnaw at my trust, but I decided to wait and see what happened.

. . . as *you* will have to wait, till next week, when I conclude this two-part revelation of gross stupidity and chicanery, under the general title: VALERIE, COME HOME!

Valerie, Part Two

9 November 1972

*V*alerie, the Golden Girl, the Little Wonder of the Earth, having fundanced her way into my life again, had now cut out for San Francisco with a hundred dollars of *Jim's* money. But she'd said she could manage somehow *without* the hundred . . .

If she'd needed it *that* badly, after I'd said I didn't have it, why didn't she ask me again, rather than come on with a kid she'd just met a day earlier? How the hell had Jim come up with that much bread on the spur of the moment?

"We stopped off at my bank on the way to the airport," he said. I was very upset at that information.

"Listen, man," I said, "I've known her a few years and she's not even in the *running* as the most responsible female I've ever known. I mean, she's a sensational lady and all, but I don't *really* know where she's been the last few years."

Jim suddenly seemed disturbed. That hundred was about all he had to his name. He'd earned it assisting me in the teaching of a six-week writing workshop sponsored by Immaculate Heart College, along with Ed Bryant; and he'd worked his

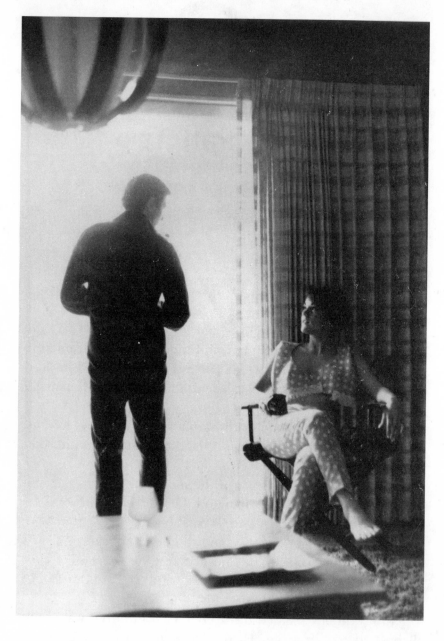

Photo of Ellison with Valerie

ass off for it. "She said she'd borrow it from a friend in San Francisco and get it back to me tomorrow."

"You shouldn't have done it. You should've called me first."

"Well, I figured she was your girl, and she was going to live here. And she said there wasn't time to call if she was going to make the plane, so . . ."

"You shouldn't have done it."

I felt responsible. He'd been trusting, and kind, and I had a flash of uneasiness. The old fable about the Country Mouse and the City Rat scuttled through my mind. Valerie had been known to vanish suddenly. But . . . not this time . . . not after her warmth and protestations of love for me . . . that was unthinkable. It would work out. But if it didn't . . .

"Listen, anything happens, I'll make good on the hundred," I told him.

And we settled down to wait for Val's return the next day.

Two days later, we reached a degree of concern that prompted me to call her mother. The story I got from her mother did not *quite* synch with what Valerie had told me. Valerie had said she'd told her mother she was moving in with me; the mother knew of no such thing. Valerie had told her she was working in Los Angeles; Valerie had told *me* she would try and get a job when she returned from San Francisco. The worm of worry burrowed deeper.

Using the phone number of Valerie's alleged apartment in San Francisco, I got a disconnect. No word. No Valerie, no word of any kind. Had her ex–boy friend murdered her? Had she bought the VW bus and run off the road?

Students of the habit patterns of the lower forms of animal life will note that even the planarian flatworms learn lessons from unpleasant experiences. I was no stranger to ugly relationships with (a few, I assure you, a very few) amoral ladies. But *homo sapiens*, less intelligent than the lowest flatworm, the merest paramecium, repeats its mistakes, again and again. Which explains Nixon. And also explains why I was so slow to realize what was happening with Valerie. It took a sub-thread of plot finally to shine the light through my porous skull. Like this:

In company with Ray Bradbury, I was scheduled to make an appearance at the Artasia Arts Festival in Ventura, on May 13th. That was the Saturday following Valerie's leavetaking. Ray and I were riding up to Ventura together, and though I'm the kind of realist who considers cars transportation, hardly items of sensuality or beauty, and for that reason never wash my 1967 Camaro with the 74,000 miles on it, I felt a magic man of Bradbury's stature should not be expected to arrive in a shitwagon. So I asked Jim to take my wallet with the credit cards, and the car, and go down to get the latter doused. I was still chained to the typewriter on a deadline, or I would have done it myself.

Jim took it to a car wash, brought it back, and returned my wallet to the niche in my office where it's kept at all times. Aside from this one trip out of the house, the wallet (with all cards present) had not been out of my possession for a week.

The next day, Saturday, Ray came over and I drove us up to Ventura. After checking in, we went to get something to eat. At the table, I opened my wallet to get something—the first time I'd opened the wallet in a week—and suddenly realized some of the glassine windows that held my credit cards were empty. After the initial panic, I grew calm and checked around the table, covered the route back to the car, inspected the map-cubby where I always keep the wallet, looked under the seats . . . and instantly called Jim in Los Angeles to tell him I'd been ripped off.

Since the wallet had only been out of the house once in the last week, the cards *had* to have been boosted at the car wash. Do you see how long it takes the planarian Ellison to smell the stench of its own burning flesh?

I called Credit Card Sentinel, the outfit that cancels missing or stolen cards, advised them of the numbers of the cards (I always keep a record of this kind of minutiae handy), and asked them to send the telegrams that would get me off the hook immediately. There's a law that says you can't get stuck for over fifty bucks on any one card, but there were *five* cards missing—Carte Blanche, BankAmericard, American Express, Standard Chevron Oil and Hertz Rent-A-Car—and that totaled two hundred and fifty dollars right there; with Sentinel, the effective lead-time for use of the cards is greatly reduced.

Having deduced *à la* Nero Wolfe that the thief had to have been the dude who swabbed out the interior of the car at the washatorium, I called the West L.A. police, detective division, the area where the car wash was located, and put them on to it. I called the owners of the car wash and relayed the story, and tried to coordinate them with the detective who was going to investigate, advising them that they should check out the guys who'd worked interiors that previous Friday, noting especially any who hadn't shown up for work.

My detective work was flawless . . . aside from the sheer stupidity of my emotional blindness.

You all know what happened.

But *I* didn't, until five days later, when I received a call from the BankAmericard Center in Pasadena asking me to verify a very large purchase of flowers sent to Mrs. Ellison in the Sacramento, California Medical Center. I assured them there *was no* Mrs. Ellison, I was single, and the only *Mrs.* Ellison was my aged mother, in Miami Beach.

The charge, of course, was on my stolen card.

Then the light blinded me.

The next day, I received a bill for forty-three dollars from the Superior Ambulance Service in Sacramento, a bill for having carted someone from a Holiday Inn to the Sacramento Medical Center on May 13th. The name of the patient was Ellison Harlan and the charge had been made to my home address.

In rapid succession came the BankAmericard reports of huge purchases of toilet articles, men's clothing, women's sportswear, hair dryers, and other goodies. Of course, I knew what had happened. At this point, pause with me, and join in a Handel chorus of *O What a Schmuck Is Thee!*

Care to relive with me the last time you were fucked over? The feeling that your stomach is an elevator, and the bottom is coming up on you fast. That peculiar chill all over, approximated only by the morning after you've stayed up all night on No-Doz and hot, black coffee. The grainy feeling in the eyes, the uncontrollable clenching of the hands, the utter frustration, the wanting to board a plane to . . . where? . . . to *there!* . . . to the place where something that can be hit exists. It's one thing to be robbed, it's quite another to be taken. Okay, no argument, it's all ego and crippled masculine pride, but God it burns!

I pulled my shit together and dropped back into my Sam Spade, private eye, mode. First I called the Sacramento Medical Center and checked if there was a Valerie B. checked in. There wasn't. Then I asked for a Mrs. Ellison Harlan. There wasn't. Then I asked for Mrs. Harlan Ellison.

There was.

Then I called the Security station of the Sacramento Sheriff's Department, there at the Medical Center. I spoke to the officer in charge, laid the entire story on him, and asked him to coordinate with Officer Karalekis of the West L.A. Detective Division, as well as Dennis Tedder at the BankAmericard Center in Pasadena. I advised him—and subsequently advised the Administrative Secretary of the Center—that there was a fraud in progress, and that I would not be held responsible for any debts incurred by the imposter posing as "Ellison Harlan," "Harlan Ellison," or "Mrs. Harlan Ellison." Both of these worthies said they'd get on it at once.

Then I called Valerie. She was in the orthopedic section. They got her to the phone. Of course, she answered: the only one (as far as she knew) who had any idea she was there was the man who had purchased the flowers.

Is the backstory taking shape finally, friends? Yeah, it took me a while, too. And I'm dumber than you.

That was May 23rd, ten days after the ambulance had removed her from the Holiday Inn and she'd been admitted to the Center.

"Hello?"

"Valerie?"

Pause. Hesitant. Computer running on overload.

"Yes."

"Harlan."

Silence.

"How's San Francisco?"

"How did you find me here?"

"Doesn't matter. I get spirit messages. All you need to know is I found you, and I'll find you wherever you go."

"What do you want?"

"The cards, and the hundred bucks you conned off Jim Sutherland."

"I haven't got it."

"Which?"

"Any of it."

"Your boy friend has the cards."

"He split on me. I don't know where he is."

"Climb down off it, Princess. If I'm a patsy once, that makes me a philosopher. Twice and I'm a pervert."

"I'm hanging up. I'm sick."

"You'll be sicker when the Sacramento Sheriff's Department there in the hospital visits you in a few minutes."

No hangup. Silence.

"What do you want?"

"I said what I wanted. And I want it quick. Jim's too poor to sustain a hundred buck ripoff. I can handle the rest, but I want it all returned *now*."

"I can't do anything while I'm in here."

"Well, you're on a police hold as of ten minutes ago, so figure a way to do it, operator."

"God, you're a chill sonofabitch! How can you do this to me?"

There is a moment when one watches something beloved sink beneath the waves, and resigns oneself. There is a moment when one decides to cut the devil loose, to let the fire consume the holy icons and the fucking temple itself.

"I'm the only one who can press charges against you, Valerie. Try and wriggle and I'll chew on your eyes, so help me God."

There was silence at the other end.

And silence, I now realize, till next week, when—because I've run over again—I'll conclude VALERIE, COME HOME.

Valerie, Part Three

23 November 1972

Sorry about missing my deadline last week, avid readers. Hope none of you succumbed to withdrawal. I was pressed on a deadline with my partner Larry Brody on the pilot script for the occult/fantasy series we sold to Screen Gems/NBC, *The Dark Forces*; and though I hates to keep y'all waiting, it was a matter of something like ten grand and, well, *you* understand. In point of fact, I called Chris Van Ness at the *Freep* and asked him to insert a block with the column art by Gahan Wilson, and an explanation that I'd died of cancer of the lymph glands, or somesuch, and would return next week (if they rolled aside the rock in time), but for some inexplicable reason Chris Van Ness didn't do what he'd said he'd do, so please address all letter bombs to the culpable party. In any case, here we all are, gathered together around the campfire once again, and I'm prepared to finish off this last of three parts about Valerie the Vamp and how she ripped me off. When last we saw Harlan the Dumb . . .

Valerie was ensconced in the Sacramento Medical Center, orthopedic section. As best I could piece together the off-camera action, she had either met up with her boy friend at the

Burbank Airport—a guy described in the police report from his purchase of the flowers sent to Valerie as "Mrs. Ellison" in the hospital as a "dark, swarthy guy," a description that tallied with Valerie's mother's recollection of him as "a Latin of some kind, maybe Cuban"—or had had him fly to Sacramento from San Francisco. They had shacked up at the Holiday Inn and *something* had happened to Valerie. Something serious enough for her to have to be rushed by ambulance to the Medical Center, at which point the boy friend had checked out on her, with my credit cards.

Now I had her on (I thought) a police hold. I'd contacted the Sacramento Sheriff's station at the hospital, and they said they'd check her out and keep her there for the action of either the Sacramento or Los Angeles police. I'd gotten her on the phone and told her I wanted the $100 she'd mooched off Jim Sutherland returned, and the cards as well.

"I can't do anything while I'm in here," she said, finally.

"You're not getting out." I was firm about that.

"Then I can't get the money."

"Then you'll go to jail. I'll press charges."

"Why are you doing this?"

"I'm just a rotten sonofabitch, that's why."

A few more words were exchanged, then she rang off. I turned to Jim Sutherland and said, "I may have to fly up to Sacramento. It looks resolved, but I've got bad feelings about the sloppy way the BankAmericard people and the cops are going at this thing. Besides . . . I want to look at her face."

What I was saying was that I wanted to see if I could detect the stain of duplicity in her expression. What I was saying was I'd become a man with an ingrown hair that needed digging and tweezing; like all self-abuse, I needed to put myself in the line of pain, to relive the impact, to see what it was that had made me go for the okeydoke, what had made me such a willing sucker, so late in my life of relationships, making a mistake of placing such heavy emotions in such an unworthy receptacle. I was consumed with the need to *understand*, not merely to stumble on through life thinking my perceptions about people were so line-resolution perfect that I could never be flummoxed. She had taken me, and with such perfection that even after I had spoken to her in the hospital, even after I *knew* I'd been had, some small part of my brain kept telling me her expressed affection and attention could not *all* have been feigned.

Thus do we perpetuate our folly.

Fifteen minutes later, she called back, collect.

"What did you tell them?" she demanded.

"Tell who?"

"The cops. A cop just came up to talk to me."

"I told you what I told them. That you were a thief and you were registered under an alias and I wasn't going to be responsible for any bills you ran up and they'd better hold onto your pretty little ass till the laws had decided what to do with you."

"Are you going to press charges?"

"Give me reasons not to."

"I'll get the money back for Jim."

"That's a start."

"I can't do anything else."

"The cards."

"I don't have them." And she named her boy friend, who she said had kited off with them. That didn't bother me; I'd already had the cards stopped. Larry Lopes (pronounced LO-pez) was his name. It comes back to me now.

"Okay. You get the hundred back to Jim and as far as I'm concerned you can move on to greener pastures."

She rang off, and I sat in the dwindling light of the sunset coming over the Valley to my hilltop, thinking furiously. Getting no answers.

I heard nothing further for several days, and when I checked with Dennis Tedder at the BankAmericard Center in Pasadena, I was informed Valerie was no longer at the Sacramento Medical Center.

They'd let her skip on the 23rd of May.

She was gone, leaving behind a bill, in my name, for over a thousand dollars' worth of treatments.

My feelings toward Mr. Tedder, Officer Karalekis of the

West L.A. porker patrol, and the nameless Sacramento Sheriff who had not only spoken to me, but had confronted Valerie and gotten an admission of guilt . . . were not particularly warm. Kindly note, I have just made an understatement.

Things progressed from miserable to ghastly. The Superior Ambulance Service in Sacramento, despite several long letters explaining what had happened, and backing it up with Xerox documentation of the fraud, continued to dun me for the forty-three bucks Valerie's passage from the Holiday Inn to the hospital had incurred. They finally turned it over to the Capital Credit and Adjustment Bureau. My attorney, the Demon Barrister Barry Bernstein, sent them a harsh note, and they finally cleared the books of my name. But the time spent, the aggravation when the nasty little pink notes came in the mail . . .

And the hospital bill. It kept getting run through the computer and kept bouncing back to me. Finally, I called the head of the business office at the hospital and laid it all out (again) in detail. As of this writing, *that* goodie is struck.

And Valerie was gone.

In speaking to Tedder at BankAmericard, I discovered, to the horror of my sense of universal balance, that Bank of America really *didn't* care about bringing her and Mr. Lopes to book. They apparently don't expend any effort on cases under five hundred dollars. BofA can sustain innumerable ripoffs at that level without feeling it. (This I offer as incidental intelligence on two counts: first, to permit those of you who are planning scams against BofA to understand better the limits of revenge of that peculiar institution, a limit that scares me when I think of how much they must gross to *permit* such a cavalier attitude; and second, to slap BofA's pinkies for their corporate posture on such matters; at once similar to that of the great insurance conglomerates that permit ripoffs, thereby upping premiums, a posture that *encourages* dishonesty and chicanery. A posture that has aided in the decay of our national character. It occurs to me, when I say things like that—though I genuinely believe them—that they sound hideously messianic, and I blush. So ignore it, if you choose.)

Valerie was gone, as I said. When I called her mother, to inform her of the current status, she sounded very upset and offered to give Jim back his hundred dollars. I thought that was a helluva nice gesture. Yet when the check arrived, it was only for fifty. Poor Jim. I would have made good the other fifty, on the grounds that he'd laid the money on her because he thought we were a scene, but it never came to that.

Two or three months later, Valerie called again.

I had tracked her through my own nefarious contacts, to Pacifica, a community near San Francisco. She had been hanging out with a ratpack of losers and unsavory types, and I knew where she was virtually all the time. But I'd told her mother if the money came back to Jim and the cards weren't used again, I would have no further interest in seeing her cornered, and I held to that.

Then she called. Out of the blue, to snag a fresh phrase.

"Hello?"

"Who's this?"

"Valerie."

Terrific. What're you selling this week, cancer?

"Are you there?"

"I'm here. What do you want?"

"I want my stuff. My clothes and electric curlers and stuff."

They were all packed in the bottom of Jim's closet . . . waiting. For what, we'd never stopped to consider. Maybe the Apocalypse.

"Sure, you can have your stuff," I said.

"How do I get it? Will you drive it out to my Mom's in Pasadena, she doesn't have a car."

I have heard of *chutzpah*, I have witnessed incredible gall and temerity, but for sheer bravado, Valerie had a corner on the product.

"I'll tell you how you get it," I said. "We're like a good pawn shop here. You come up with the fifty bucks for Jim, the fifty you still owe him, and we release your goods. Just redeem your pawn ticket, baby."

"I don't have fifty."

"Ask Larry Lopes for it."

"I don't know where he is."

"Ah, but I know where *you* is. Have your friends boost somebody's hubcaps and get the fifty."

"Go to hell!" And she hung up.

I shrugged. Ain't life teejus, mah baby.

Later that day, Valerie's mother called and offered to unhock Valerie's goods for the fifty remaining. She made it clear she had no idea where Valerie was on the lam, but I don't think anyone will consider me cynical for believing that may not have been the strict truth.

So Jim took the clothes out to Pasadena, picked up the fifty, and the Sacramento Medical Center canceled the bill as unrecoverable, and that's as much as I know, to this point.

Well . . . not quite.

I know one more thing. And it's this:

In every human being there is only so large a supply of love. It's like the limbs of a starfish, to some extent: if you chew off a chunk, it will grow back. But if you chew off too much, the starfish dies. Valerie B. chewed off a chunk of love from my dwindling reserve . . . a reserve already nibbled by Charlotte and Lory and Sherri and Cindy and others down through the years. There's still enough there to make the saleable appearance of a whole creature, but nobody gets gnawed on that way without becoming a little dead. So, if Cupid (that perverted little motherfucker) decides his lightning ought to strike this gnarly tree trunk again, whoever or whatever gets me, is going to get a handy second, damaged goods, something a little dead and a little crippled.

Having learned that, all I can advise is an impossible stance for all of you: utter openness and reasonable caution. Don't close yourself off, but jeezus, be careful of monsters with teeth. And just so you know what they look like when they come clanking after you, here is a photo of one. The package is so pretty, one can only urge you to remember Pandora. Be careful which boxes you open, troops.

Photo of Valerie

Interim Memo

RATHER THAN WRITING AN EXPANSIVE GENERAL INTRODUCTION to the HORNBOOK, and missing this or that sidebar anecdote, I've opted for this device, the Interim Memo. From place to place in these pages, when some updating information is needed, I'll drop in on you and do one of those numbers like the pre–end credit explanations in a movie, telling you what happened to the principal characters, or passing along whatever dubious wisdom I've accrued in the twenty years between.

Take for instance this column.

I was thirty-eight years old. I was dating a marvelous young woman named Lynda who went on to get her degree and Master's in psychiatric medicine. Last I heard, she had married one of her professors at UC, Berkeley and was in practice. I may have some of this wrong, she may be a psychologist and not a psychiatrist, but I seem to recall she went to medical school, as well, so probably the latter. Haven't heard from her in years, and that makes me mildly sad. We were good friends, she was a fine person, and now, at age fifty-five, I recall those kids and pets, men and women, friends and lovers, who have gone past and don't keep in touch.

But when I *do* cast back in reflection on the women I knew, one thing comes sharply into focus: they were all a kind of getting-ready for meeting and marrying Susan. And I lament the thirty-five years I spent without her.

Getting Stiffed

30 November 1972

*T*urned around—widdershins—
the other day, and realized I'd been writing professionally for
seventeen years. Holy shit! When I sold my first novel, I was
barely twenty-one, and for the last decade and a half I've gotten
used to being called "brilliant young writer" or "*enfant terrible*"
or other useless appellations guaranteed to lull an egomaniac
into believing he can eternally bear a banner emblazoned
NEW! NEW! NEW! like some detestable margarine advertise-
ment. But I'm *not* new no more, and the next sound you hear
will be the Whey-Faced Child Author heaving an adult sigh of
relief. (Permitted on the grounds that Lynda, who is eighteen
and incredibly lovely, realized that she had read my first novel
when she was in grade school. And if you don't have the sense
to realize the woman on the other side of your bed was one year
old when you started selling stories, and that time passes, and
growing up is a delight, and getting older is a joy, then you
ought to go over to Baskin-Robbins and have them scoop out
your head for the flavor of the month, Adolescent Brainpan
Ripple.)

So I'm thirty-eight, thank god, and at least chronologically
no longer a tot, thank god, and enjoying the hell out of playing
at being an adult, thank god, and looking forward to gray hair,
I wish already, and from that lofty pinnacle of advanced
wisdom I am now permitted, after seventeen years as a professional writer, to give advice to younger writers.

The trouble with young writers, however, is that they are amateurs, many of them, and amateurs are all paranoids. They believe myths and legends passed on by generations of other amateurs who never made it as professionals, and they never get to check out the accuracy of the myths, so they react to the legends as though they were reality.

Well, today, kiddies, Unca Harlan will set to rest one of the great untrue myths of the writing game: that editors steal stories submitted for publication.

Amateurs frequently ask me, "How do I keep *Them* from stealing my story or story idea when I send it in to a magazine with a stamped self-addressed envelope in case it's rejected?" By *Them*, I presume they mean the faceless, nameless *Powers* the uninformed think of when they refer to editors and publishers. I seldom deign to honor such questions with anything more than a cursory, "Don't worry about it." Not only because the question-asker's manuscript is probably on an intellectual level with the question itself, but chiefly because: in seventeen years as a free-lancer, I have *never* known a reputable, or even semi-reputable editor to cop someone's plot. There are cases where it *looked* like theft or plagiarism, but when investigated it always turned out to be an extenuating circumstance compounded of lousy office procedure, righteous circumstance, inept communications with the author and that aforementioned healthy dose of paranoia on the part of the one who submitted the manuscript. Again, to the last item, usually an amateur.

Oh, there are endless instances of a writer sending in a story similar to one an editor had already bought, and thinking, when the other appeared, that the editor had ripped off the idea and farmed it to another contributor, and I choose to think that's just rotten timing, but in all the years I've worked for, submitted to, hustled after and been rejected by magazines from the best to the worst—and pay-scale or reputation frequently did not decide which was which—I've found the men and women behind the editorial desks to be scrupulous about such matters to the point of anal retention.

Your ideas are safe. At least ninety-nine point something

infinitesimal percent of the time. I won't say it *can't* happen (this being a big and constantly-surprising universe), but the chances are so slim it ain't worth fretting over.

On the other hand, getting robbed outright is quite another matter. I don't mean just losing an idea, I mean actually having your manuscript stolen, filched, purloined, palmed, spirited away, published. And you did not receive a penny. Not a sou. Not a krupnik. Not even Blue Chip stamps. To which situation applies Ellison's First Law of Literary Brigandry:

If your manuscript was stolen and published and you didn't get paid, it was not the fault of the editor, it was solely and wholly the fault of the publisher.

Editors are good people. Some are cranky, and some are cavalier in their treatment of writers; some are inept, and some have no talent; some are out of touch with the times, and some were never in touch. But *all* of them are honest. Most of them were writers at one time or another, so they *understand*. Their reasons for leaving the honest life of the writer and entering the damned brotherhood of the blue pencil are multitudinous, but none of them are crooks.

Publishers, on the other hand, are frequently not only *schlockmeisters* of the vilest sort, upon whom used car dealers would spit, but they are equally frequently ex-manufacturers of piece goods, gadget salesmen off the Jersey Turnpike, defrocked carnival pitchmen, garment center *gonifs* whose idea of creativity is hiring a pistolero to break not just someone's tibia, but fibula as well. While this cannot be said for Saints like Nelson Doubleday or Charles Scribner, there are at least half a dozen guys I would gladly name right here (were it not for the *Freep*'s adolescent fear of lawsuits) whose connections with The Mob, whose pokey-pocked pasts, whose absolute lack of even the vaguest scintilla of ethic or morality or business decency marks them as men unfit for human congress. They are, truly, the Kings of the Pig People. And they operate some of the biggest publishing outfits in New York. 🎓

I will, however, tell you a fascinating story about how I got stiffed once during those seventeen years that may provide a few moments of horrified distraction while you work out the ending of that short story for *Ellery Queen's* (a *very* reputable periodical, I hasten to add).

All in all, I've been rather lucky. Also damnably cunning and persistent, which is the key to how to avoid most of what I'm about to lay on you here. I've only been taken half a dozen times in seventeen years, with sales upwards of eight hundred in magazines, and something like twenty-five in books. That isn't the worst batting average in the world, but each one of those six sticks in my craw like a boa constrictor trying to swallow the Goodyear blimp.

The only time it mattered, though, was with a short-line publisher who used to have his offices on lower Madison Avenue, in the Mosler Safe Building. Along about 1960, when I'd been released from the Army with relieved sighs (theirs *and* mine), when I was just starting to get back into free-lancing and was hurting for money, a dear friend who was working as editor on the chain of seamy periodicals with which this Jesse James of the Publishing World festooned the newsstands, called me and asked if I had a story for one of their detective magazines. The only unsold manuscript I had at the time—and there was some urgency to the request—was an absolutely dreadful piece of *dreck* (and I use the ethnologue specifically) about a guy who murders another guy and disposes of the body by grinding it up like a pound of ground round and flushing it down the toilet . . . all but the teeth and suchlike, which he threw in the Hudson. He gets caught when the toilet backs up. It was titled (and I trust you'll forgive me for this: I was younger and less a credit to my race in them days) "Only Death Can Stop It."

Despising myself for even submitting it, I sent it on over to the editor and was mortified, chagrined and delighted when he called the next day to say he'd buy it. Thirty-six hundred words, thirty-six dollars, a penny a word. At that low ebb of financial tide, I was overjoyed to take a penny a word. Particularly for that specific thirty-six hundred words, arranged abominably in that fashion.

I was supposed to have been paid on acceptance, but when the money didn't materialize in a few days, I called my friend the editor and made mewling sounds. He was genuinely unhappy about having to tell me the "policy" of the magazine had changed slightly: they were now paying on publication. He wasn't happy about it, but he said the Publisher was adamant on the point. I swallowed hard and said, "Wow, I really needed that money." My friend (who remains a dear friend to this day) offered to pay me out of his own pocket, but I'd heard through the Manhattan jungle telegraph that the Publisher hadn't paid *him* in several weeks, so I refused the offer. Like a jerk, I decided to wait. People in the Publishing Industry are all gentlefolk, right? Till that time, I'd never had cause to think otherwise.

Two weeks later, my friend was "let go." Sans a month's wages.

Still I waited, feeling certain no Publisher could actually *print* something he hadn't paid for. I mean, after all, there *is* a law in such matters!

From afar, even today, come the sounds of the Muses, wailing, "Naïve child, gullible waif, *moron!*"

Finally, the magazine hit the stands, and I waited very patiently for three weeks for the check. No such creature surfaced. I began calling. The Publisher was invariably 1) out to lunch, 2) in conference, 3) out of town, 4) at a distributors' convention, 5) in the bathroom, 6) tied up with affairs of state or 7) none of the above, under the general heading "unavailable."

I talked to my friend, the ex-editor, who was also starving, who advised me sadly that we'd both (and many others) been taken, and he was truly sorry he'd ever hyped me in the first place. I could not find it in my heart to blame him, or conceive of redress where he was concerned.

The Publisher, however, was another matter.

So one afternoon, I put on my one and only suit, a charcoal gray item in those days, and I took the IRT down to the Thirties, from whence I sojourned forth to the Mosler Safe Building. When I reached the offices of The Great Cosmocockik Publishing Corporation, I was confronted by a cubbyhole arrangement of open-fronted offices known in the trade as a "bullpen." In each cubby a young woman sat madly blamming away at a typewriter or adding machine. It seemed to me that surely in *one* of those dingy cells some bright young lady might have been put to productive use typing up my lousy thirty-six buck check. But by then the cunning of the beast had come to the fore, and I knew such was not the case. I also knew, from the unflagging regularity with which calls from "Mr. Harlan Ellison" had been refused, that I would get no action if I used that name.

"May I help you?" asked the receptionist.

"Yes," I replied, giving her a steely, no-nonsense look. "Mr. Attila B. Hun is the Publisher here, is he not?"

"Uh . . . yessir."

"Fine. Would you please tell him Mr. George Knowlton of the Manhattan Central Division of the Bureau of Internal Revenue would like to speak to him." It was an order, not a question. It was also a name I had made up on the spot, as is Mr. Hun's at this moment.

The young lady blanched, shoved back her caster chair and careened into Hun's lair. In a moment she was back, pressing the buzzer to release the gate that afforded me entrance, and she ushered me into the sonofabitch's office.

He started to get up, and I leaned across the desk and blathered, "I'm Ellison, you eggsucking thief, and you owe me thirty-six bucks, and if you don't lay it on me right now I'm gonna strangle you with that Sulka tie around your wattled neck!"

He started screaming for help instantly.

I panicked.

I saw a door at the side of the office, and bolted through it, just as the office help came crashing through the other door. They were all going in one direction and I was going in the other, around into the corridor, around behind them, and past all those little cubbies . . . now empty. In a blind stagger, but still possessed of a demonic singularity of purpose, I grabbed an enormous L.C. Smith typewriter—five thousand pounds, one of those old office standards, impossible to lift, much less carry, much lesser at a full gallop, for anyone save a madman on the verge of being apprehended and thwarted in his revenge—and I bounded down eighteen flights of fire stairs without even seeing the EXIT door through which I'd burst.

I hit Madison and ran like a kindergarten teacher who's mistakenly answered a casting call for a porno flick.

Sometime later, and many blocks farther crosstown and uptown, I hocked the behemoth for seventy-eight dollars.

A clear profit of forty-two bucks.

So, like I said, don't worry about it.

Interim Memo

IMMEDIATELY FOLLOWING THIS COLUMN, YOU WILL FIND THE text of a letter written to the *Los Angeles Free Press* (heretofore and hereinafter abbreviated to *Freep.*) It takes me to task for bad behavior. Throughout this book, and with the permission of the journals in which such letters were first published, I've included pertinent reader reaction. What I *haven't* included, usually, are all the letters of praise. That's self-serving and doesn't throw much light. Hell, there are even people who admire the manifestos of skinheads or Phyllis Schlafly. There's no accounting for taste, however warped. So what you'll encounter are those followup comments by strangers that savage me. And any reply I made to such letters.

For those who get itchy when they confront others' "dirty linen," I have to declare as follows:

The tradition of "confessional writing" is a long and honorable one. Washington Irving, Cervantes, Thomas De Quincey, Shaw, Henry Miller, Charles Bukowski, Mailer . . . all of them, like Virginia Woolf, Anaïs Nin and Mark Twain, were driven to write of the human condition as viewed through the most perfect lens available to them: their own experiences.

It makes people uncomfortable, this public exposure of the moist throbbing within. But as Mario Vargas Llosa has said, "The writer is an exorcist of his own demons." And I have seen more clearly than often I wished to see it, that those who write so glowingly and passionately of love, truth, honor, courage and friendship do not necessarily demonstrate such a passionate glow in real life. There are columns to come in this book that deal precisely with this dichotomy. There are writers who lie to themselves, and to their readers. Lying to readers in fiction is probably okay, because what *is* fiction but the well-constructed lie? Yet I believe to the shoe-tops that a writer should not lie to him/herself. Because that corrupts the writing.

Because of the kinds of fiction I choose to write, I feel the necessity to examine every facet of my life, my actions, what I've experienced and what I believe. In that way, I can write absolutely without restraint, without self-censoring that is usually only a dodge to keep hidden that which I fear to reveal. We are all flawed, and we rearrange the past to make ourselves look better in the retelling.

The poet Olin Miller wrote, "Of all liars, the smoothest and most convincing is memory."

I cannot do that. It isn't any great nobility on my part, it is an inescapable dedication to the Work. And that means that when I write essays, introductions, comments on the Work, I tell it all.

Any number of writers now include introductions to their stories, but when I started doing it back in the Fifties, it was looked on as an egomaniacal intrusion. (In England, they still insist on dropping the introductions when they republish my books. They contend—and I think they're correct in their appraisal of the U.K. readership—that a more reserved nation is affronted by such confessions.) I think it's necessary to commit such material to print. It keeps the reader aware to the simple truth that writers are just men and women, with a certain talent, but nowhichway different from other men and women, and subject to the same fears. It creates, I believe and I hope, a bond between the artist and the audience.

Apparently, it works. The introductory material in my books seems to fascinate and edify the readers, and I get too much mail that says something like, "Gee, I like your introductions better than the stories." Well, that doesn't *actually* drive me coo-coo with joy, but I get the sense they're trying to convey.

And so, columns such as this one.

Which *does*, as I admit in my reply to the letter that came after the publication of the column, demonstrate at least questionable ethics on my part. I don't try to weasel out of it, but the column *was* sent to the subject in plenty of time prior to its publication, for her approval or cease&desist. She allowed it to appear in print, and I submit that I extended exactly the right courtesy, however ill-advised may have been the writing of the column in the first place.

What the piece says about those who brutalize us with their weakness, however, stands unaltered. I am nailed to that theory and not twenty years under the bridge alters my position. Last week one of those leaners tried to eat up several days of precious time I was spending with old friends I hadn't seen in ten years. They are ever with us.

And one last note.

The recipe for *café ellison diabolique* mentioned *en passant* is as follows:

Café Ellison Diabolique

10-oz. coffee mug
mortar and pestle
Maxim freeze-dried instant coffee
El Popular Mexican-style cake chocolate
Ferrara Italian anisette sugar
granulated sugar
water (boiling)
cream

Into a 10-oz. coffee mug spoon 1½ teaspoons of Maxim freeze-dried instant coffee, 3 teaspoons of granulated sugar, and ¼ teaspoon of Ferrara Italian anisette sugar.

With a mortar and pestle break off and hand-crush sufficient El Popular Mexican chocolate from the brick cakes in the 15-oz. package to produce 3 full tablespoons of finely-crushed chocolate grind. Add it to the coffee mug's contents.

Add boiling water to mug's contents, leaving one-sixth of the mug empty for cream or half-and-half. Stir well.

This is my personal coffee recipe, refined over the last ten years to produce a balance between the harsh, often oily and unpleasant taste of regular coffee and the cloying sweetness of hot chocolate. While it bears lineal ties with Russian Coffee and *Café Chocolat,* the bite of the newly-developed freeze-dried coffees (*never* use standard-ground instants of the powdered variety) and the addition of anisette sugar give it a special piquancy all its own. I find that coffee prepared in this way, first thing in the morning, soothes the jangled stomach lining yet furnishes the push to get to work at whatever's in the typewriter from the night before. In the evening, coffee prepared in this way can have salutary effects as an aphrodisiac. Thus the adjective of its title.

The Tyranny of the Weak, and Some Foreshadowing

7 December 1972

Quite a lot lately, I've been accused of being a rotten sonofabitch. Well, actually, the parties relaying the appellation haven't called me that, they've merely said they've heard me *called* that by others. Now I don't mind people *thinking* I'm dumb . . . what I resent is when they *talk* to me as if they think I'm dumb. It's like the woman who confronts the psychiatrist at a cocktail party and says, "I have this friend who wants to have an extra-marital affair, and she . . ." Up front, the shrink knows she's talking about herself; or more accurately, about her *other* self, her secret self, her wish-fulfillment self.

So, up front, I know when Janet Joiner of San Diego writes me and says I'm supposed to be a rotten sonofabitch—which she's heard through the jungle telegraph—what she's saying is: *I* think you're a rotten sonofabitch, but I'm afraid you'll cut me up verbally if I step out and tell you to your face.

Which would have derived for her more pleasure, had she done it without hypocrisy, because the penalty of talking to me as if she thinks I'm too dumb to understand the obfuscation, is that I'll cut her up right here in print, rather than writing a letter. And in the process, because this is a relatively lightweight indictment against me, I'll make some generalized comments about the benefits of being a rotten and thoroughly calloused sonofabitch with strangers.

The background is quite simple, actually. Ms. Joiner is a young woman who bopped into my life one day many months ago, wholly uninvited. She had read my work and wanted to meet me. Now that's terrific for my ego, and I hardly discourage such worshipful pilgrimages, but sometimes I'm busy writing, or I'm feeling generally all-around shitty and rude, and when a body manifests itself on my doorstep I'm as likely to bury a Viking battleaxe in the visitor's head as I am to invite the waif in for *café ellison diabolique* and whatever else might develop.

Well, Ms. Joiner spent some small amount of time (judged on the cosmic scale) with me, and we parted friends. She went back to San Diego with my best wishes and that, as the OXFORD DICTIONARY OF QUOTATIONS puts it, was that.

Came the night of the KROQ concert, a Saturday night, I believe, and I was home alone working, thoroughly enjoying the solitude and the flow of backlog mail being cleared off my desk. (As a societally-crippled child of the Puritan Work Ethic, there are times when I really jubilate behind the act of working my ass off). The phone rang, and it was Ms. Joiner, in town with her gentleman friend. He had gone off to do some sort of football spectator number, and she was looking for diversion. Without pejorative, both Ms. Joiner and I (and certainly you, gentle reader) knew what form of diversion she was seeking. She advised me she was in for the concert but it looked to be a charnel house scene, festooned with fuzz, and having called out from beneath every slippery rock in the Southern California landscape a full complement of the Lizard People. She said she was holding some prescription medicines but didn't have them in the legit bottles with physicians' labels thereon, and she was twitchy she'd get busted.

"Well," said I, being polite, "if you want to go to the concert and call me when it's over, I'll see how caught up on work I am, and maybe we can have a cup of coffee later, but frankly, I'm not too hot for any company tonight." I went on in that vein for a few more beats, making it abundantly clear that I was enjoying my ascetic retreat from the hurly-burly world of social intercourse. The call was terminated, but a short time later she called back and told me again that she was holding. I advised her if she was nervous, to get the hell out of there, but that I'd decided I was one with Greta Garbo, that I vanted to be alone. She seemed bugged by that information, and rang off. Frankly, in two minutes Ms. Joiner was out of my mind as I threaded my way through the intricacies of a series of letters from an English solicitor I'd engaged to sue the London publisher of one of my books.

Today, I received the letter. On orange stationery. Four space-&-½'d, elite-typed pages of rebuke and condemnation. On what grounds? Well, I'll copy off some of it for you, and then we'll get into the subject of who should have a claim on your emotions and guilt as you trudge down Life's foggy highway.

Ms. Joiner says, in part:

"Don't panic . . . I realize that you don't give even the tiniest shit, I just want to tell you anyway. . . . Okay, I assume you have probably heard more about the incredible fiasco of the KROQ concert than I [*an Ellisonian aside: take note of the many assumptions Ms. Joiner makes; on these assumptions hinges the totality of her accusations*]. I assume that you can imagine the scene . . . little Miss (Almost) Innocent, scared out of her wits, tearfully pleading with the Yellow Cab dispatcher to please make an exception, finally having her agree to send a unit, but that it would be about fifteen minutes. Since you knew how exceedingly frightened I was, naturally all I wanted to do was get the hell *out* of that place. Twice stopped by The Man, who dumped out my sack of tangerines and cheese, then passed on. All I had in my (stupid, unknowing) mind was getting my young ass the *other* side of that goddam cyclone fence.

"Now here is where I get just a leedle pissed: it seems to me that, being such a great cosmopolite, the ultimate Angeleno, that you would think to tell an out-of-town Dodo . . . that this was not, absolutely no way, the sort of place where unescorted white chicks stand around on curbs."

Ms. Joiner then diverged for a page and a half to relate how she had once been raped by some black men while stationed with her husband-at-the-time at a military base. It was a particularly ugly story and one she related in the letter with more rationality and understanding of what had happened than I think I'd be capable of summoning had it been someone close to me. It is a story Ms. Joiner tells, free of racial prejudice but understandably filled with horror at what happened, and how her life was demolished as a result of it. One cannot read the story without feeling her panic at being set adrift on a street corner in Los Angeles in an area where she felt threatened. Had I known *any* of this, I'm sure her situation that evening would have impinged more acutely on my consciousness. Being gang-raped and brutally beaten is about the ugliest fate I can think of, even from a man's viewpoint, or maybe *particularly* from a man's viewpoint. Scenes in Dickey's DELIVERANCE do not go unnoticed. But I knew none of this, and contrary to Ms. Joiner's assumption I *didn't* perceive her terror. Perhaps her attempts during our telecon to sound cool succeeded better than she might have wished.

In any case, on to her letter again.

"Okay, it was probably a naive assumption that LA would be similar [to San Diego's "safer" concert areas], but surely if the area were that dangerous, and an unsuspecting chick called a resident and talked for awhile, and indicated her intention of leaving, and of leaving by cab (which an Angeleno would know always involves a certain curbside wait), and that if this were not a safe thing for her to do, that a knowledgeable resident of the city would at least have the basic decency to tell her, right? I mean, if it is so bad out there, don't you warn people? Or were you chuckling as you hung up, 'Well, that silly bitch won't annoy me again! They'll fix her ass. Tee hee . . . etc.' Was it that I am so goddamned dumb that I deserved it or something? If so, you are a worse bastard than they all say you are. (Hah! Chew on *that* one a while . . . T. Hee.) I choose not to tumble my idol just yet, however, and have managed to convince myself that you either a) didn't know what the streets around the Coliseum are like at night (which I very much doubt) or that b) the dangers are so well known to you that you assumed they were well-known to all, even out-of-towners."

I've skipped most of the personal vilification in the letter, but I think this sums it up on Ms. Joiner's part:

"What I'm talking about is just the kind of concern which one ordinarily manifests simply by virtue of his humanity toward another human simply by virtue of *his*. So I'm puzzled, and kinda sad, and well . . . your halo has slipped just a little."

Well, Ms. Joiner, and all of you out there waiting to find out what this is in aid of, I'm gonna solve the puzzle for you. And you can stuff that halo up your nose.

First of all, I've never, to my recollection, been to the Coliseum. Now I may have been, but if I ever was, nothing happened in the vicinity to conjure up the dark and Jack-the-ripper–like visions Ms. Joiner derived from the locale. In point of fact, to demonstrate just how disinterested in her call I was, I thought she was calling from the Hollywood Bowl, which is where I've attended most concerts. If this tells you I wasn't aware of what was happening, so be it. I knew very little about the KROQ concert, then or now, and I couldn't have cared less. Rock concerts are uniformly downers, as far as I'm concerned, and I would sooner take a bath in lye than go to one. Shit, I have trouble dragging myself to snake pits like the Troubadour when I have passes and there's someone I want to see.

Second, I *am* a man, and try as I may, even with my belief in, and support of women's liberation, I *still*, dammit, think like a man. I don't think of people standing on a well-lit street corner of L.A. in peril of being raped by hordes of slavering Mamelukes or Ethiopians. Now maybe that's divorced from reality, living in the times around us, but L.A. hasn't *yet* become New York, as far as I can tell, so . . . no, it never crossed my mind.

Further than that, I won't defend myself against what is a clearly paranoid fantasy-trip on Ms. Joiner's part. I find it impossible to conceive of myself as kin with, for instance, the people who watched Kitty Genovese getting knifed to death in New York streets, and did nothing to help her. For my own sleeping benefit, I have credentials as one who gives a damn, as well as scars to attest, so I won't take on *that* bum rap.

But the deeper issue here is one deserving of comment.

To be unwittingly elevated to the role of "hero" by a

stranger is to have one's humanity denied almost as specifically as ignoring another human's plight in moments of stress and danger. I never asked to be your goddam hero, Ms. Joiner! I am *no one's* fucking hero. I am merely a writer who sets down some stuff, usually from the gut, occasionally from the head, and that doesn't make me Simón Bolívar or Jomo Kenyatta or Richard Motherfuckin' Nixon! Lautrec once said, "One should never confuse a writer with what the writer writes." That is as true of me as it was with Scott Fitzgerald or Fyodor Dostoevsky, both of whom were failures as human beings.

By what right do you presume to drop into my existence, puddle around on a superficial level, and then make demands of my time or emotions? And when I politely choose to ignore those demands, try to whip guilt on me? This was your trip, from start to finish. There's nothing wrong with building dream castles in the air, lady; the derangement comes when you try to move furniture into them!

Rotten bastard? You betchum, Red Ryder. The world is filled with two kinds of people, basically: those who can sustain themselves, and those who sustain themselves by sucking on others. That's called vampirism.

Jewish mothers do it, ex-lovers do it, employers do it, losers do it, and those who live lives they detest do it. And theirs is the tyranny of the weak.

As a published writer I receive hundreds of letters and phone calls from people imposing on my life and my work-time with demands that I find them agents, read their novels for comment, tell them where conventions are being held or—most hideous of all—merely that I notice their letters and write them a response to let them know they've been heard. Sure, we all want to be noticed, we all want to stand on some far peak in Darien and scream into the wind, "I'm here! I exist! I'm important, I live, I breathe, I need!" And in our own ways we all do it incessantly. My way is this column and my books. Your way is to dream a dream of heroes, and then slide into hatred and paranoia when the call goes unheeded.

Rotten bastard? Try tough bastard. It fits better. If "they" say I'm rotten, I smile. If "they" say I'm a mean and selfish sonofabitch, I jubilate. There is love in me, Ms. Joiner, and there is caring, but *I* will pick the receptacles into which to pour it, if they are willing; *I* will say with whom I spend my days and nights and moments of meaning.

And not strangers or relatives or charisma-hustlers will get a drop of it, not a speck of it, if I'm unwilling to give it.

My advice to all of you out there, and to all the Janet Joiners swilling the cheap muscatel of hero-worship, is to find your *own* reality and cease these vampiric attempts to suck meaning from wish-fulfillment and pointless fantasy.

Harlan's linen . . .

Dear Editor:

Why must the readers of the *Freep* be insultingly subjected to writer Harlan Ellison's airing of his dirty linen in matters of his private sex life quarrels which should be handled on a strictly personal, confidential level?

While I sympathize with his need for freedom, independence, his rejection of the role of hero or superstar, and his commendable rejection of would-be or real vampires, hero worshippers, or groupies, must he mention the *name* of the young lady who presumably wrote to him in confidence and deserves the common courtesy of a *confidential* reply?

Mr. Ellison could have discussed the subject of human parasitism and exploitation, and made his quite valid points, without publicly embarrassing the young lady in question. After all she did not write her letter to the *Free Press* and publicly slander Mr. Ellison. She wrote directly to him.

Does the Editor of the *Freep* write articles detailing his intimate sex life at home with his wife and publish such deeply personal matters for mass public consumption? No, the Editor has better judgment, discretion and taste! It is most unfortunate that Mr. Ellison's sense of privacy and confidence is demanded rightfully for himself, but apparently the same rights are not respected by himself for others.

The Golden Rule, if it is to have any validity, must be mutually applicable, violations of which are not mutually permissible for vengeful or spiteful purposes.

Respectfully yours,
Carl Michael Vrooman
Pasadena, Calif.

Harlan Ellison replies

Dear Art:

. . . As to Mr. Vrooman's letter, I can only agree. The gentleman has written a rational and kind letter, pointing up a flaw in my character that I would be a hypocrite to deny. Perhaps the name of the young lady who wrote the letter that formed the basis for last week's column should have been omitted. Perhaps not. The point of the column was that one should defy attempts by strangers to whip gratuitous guilt on us. It seemed to me at the time I wrote the column— and still does—that the only way to de-fang such vampirism is to bring it out into the light of day. A personal letter in response to the lady in question would only have permitted her more room to rationalize the situation. Public disclosure is final, even though it may serve to tarnish my personal courtliness. But to disabuse Mr. Vrooman of the idea that I am a stranger to good manners, he should know that before the column was published, a copy of same went to the lady, with my urgings that if she wanted to rebut the pages of the *Freep* were open to her.

As to the "airing" of private lives, that is a more basic carp, and one I cannot remove from Mr. Vrooman's view short of ceasing to write the column. On that score, if the tenor of the *Hornbook* columns continually affects others as strongly as it did Mr. Vrooman (who admits, it seems to me, the rightness of the position I took), and affects them with negativity, then readers should most certainly write the Editor of the *Freep* and tell him so. He is no fool. If he's publishing something that annoys his buyers, he will dispense with it. But the *Hornbook* is clearly a "journal," in many ways a memoir, for better or worse . . . and that's the way I intend it.

Harlan Ellison

Interim Memo

I WENT. I FINALLY PICKED UP AND WENT TO SCOTLAND. AND came back sadly knowing I was not meant to live in that fine place. It had nothing to do with Scotland; it was me. I was by that time a thing unfit for peace and solitude.

But I found the dream. Not as I expected, and perhaps only in a way that borders on some psychic foreshadowing that led me there, that prevented me from summoning up the self-examination that would have told me to stay home.

I went to Scotland; several times; and it was there that I found the dream.

I met my wife in Glasgow in 1985. She isn't Scottish, she's English, but she came north to hear me lecture, and I came a long way east to intersect my destiny.

Could I have known that? Well, not unless I'm also ready to believe that Shirley MacLaine is the reincarnation of Ankhese-namun (as opposed to some slave who schlepped stones up a ramp building the Great Pyramid of Cheops), that Elvis frequents 7-Elevens after midnight, that space-traveling aliens have nothing better to do with their time than butcher cows and give Whitley Strieber a hard time, and that "pro-lifers" actually give a shit about the value of life. But it sure is poetic, ain't it?

With Bloch and Bormann in Brazil

14 December 1972

One of these days, as I've been saying for the last year or two, I'm going to pick up my ass and move to Scotland. My friends refuse to accept the statement at face value. They live in a universe where the natural forces don't change. It has held me in it, since the dawn of memory, and they seem unable to conceive of it without me. They are wrong. I will go. And soon.

Don't ask why Scotland, I can't give you rational answers. I know Ireland will admit me, as a writer, free of taxes, and that is a situation greatly to be admired, but something in my blood and bones draws me to Scotland. I've never been there, but I've read about it, and it sounds like precisely what I'm looking for: a country of the mind that is quiet, far, free of complications, chill and distant. In my fantasy-eye I see myself sitting before a fireplace, smoking my pipe and reading one of the millions of books I've never had the time to read. In that wonderful eye I'm wearing a turtleneck sweater and there's a shaggy dog lying somewhere nearby. Of late, sadly, since the death of my dog Ahbhu, the vision grows misty at that part. Maybe I won't have a dog. But it's Scotland, I'm in no doubt about that. Somewhere far North, near the Lochs, where no one will erect a missile base, or carve out a freeway; somewhere devoid of McDonald's greaseburgers and lacquered ladies; somewhere out of touch where phones won't ring with offers I can't refuse; a place where letters will be slow in arriving, bearing their nickel-and-dime messages of involvement and emotional need (see last week's diatribe in this space); a place where I can sit at my typewriter and put down all the stories that movies and television prevent me from writing now.

Dreams. How we live in them. How they make the days of keeping appointments and spending time in the company of people who say things we've heard in just those same words a thousand times . . . just a little more bearable. Without them, what an utter desolation of predictability and frustration. Even for the best of us. Even for the most unstructured of us, the freest of us. Dreams. Without them, the suicide statistics would be catastrophic.

And yet, the best dreams of all are not the ones we carry with us for years or the ones we realize or the ones we never turn into reality. The best dreams are the ones that come upon us suddenly, startling us like fauns in a forest. The ones we never knew we had, till we were living them.

I'll tell you one that happened to me.

Despite my hunger to live in Scotland, I'm not much of a world traveler. I've been all over the United States, god knows, but I've never been to Europe. The farthest I've been is to Brazil.

In 1969 I was invited—along with such luminaries as Roger Corman, Josef von Sternberg, Roman Polanski, Diane Varsi plus a gaggle of science fiction writers including Heinlein, Bester, Harrison, Sheckley, Van Vogt and Farmer—to be a guest of the 2nd International Film Festival of Rio de Janeiro. In company with a redheaded screenwriter named Leigh Chapman, I made the trip, and was rather thoroughly depressed. The gap between wealthy and poor in Brazil is even more marked and cataclysmic than here in the States. I've written about it elsewhere, and it has nothing to do with the dream that came to me while in Rio. But it was the overlying patina of awfulness that marked the journey.

The dream came to me in this way:

As "notables," we received invitations to endless embassy

receptions. Rio went bananas over the film/sf folk. Everywhere we went, we were cheered as though we had somehow contributed to the advancement of Western Society, when, in point of fact, we were only a *divertissement* for the Leblon billionaires; the twentieth century version of bread and circuses.

After the first couple such social orgies, staged with incredible opulence in settings of art and grandeur (and so painful to me personally, when matched against the sights that had been burned into my mind: the *peons*, in their hillside *favellas*, feeding a dozen family members, children, animals, from one big kettle in the front "yard" of their tin-roofed hovels . . . going without food so they could buy candles to burn on the steps of the glorious Catholic churches . . . the women wearing themselves down working in the factories so their shark-thin young men could hustle wealthy American and German widows on the Copacabana beach), I could attend no others.

Yet my hideous sense of gallows humor urged me to make one special reception. We received an invitation to the Polish Embassy's shindig.

I confess to an ugliness of nature that demanded I see what the Polish Embassy was like.

We were advised it was black tie, and that we should be assembled in front of our hotel at 5:00 to be transported by limousines. It was 120° in Rio that Summer, and even the air conditioning in the hotel was gasping. So at quarter to five we found ourselves decked out in elegance, standing on the restaurant patio, waiting for the limousines that were promised.

In Rio, time comes slathered with molasses. When they say 5:00 they mean 5:30 if you're lucky, 6:00 if they're on time, 6:30 if they're running true to form, and 7:00 if they're a little late. At 7:30 we were all wilted and swimming in our tuxedos. And finally, the "limousines" arrived: four old buses. We were sogged aboard and driven to the Polish Embassy.

Understand this: in Rio, the embassies outdo one another for sumptuousness. The Spanish Embassy is in a renovated villa, festooned with ancient tapestries, stained glass windows, antiques, reeking of history. Harry Harrison told me about it. He went, I didn't. The American reception was held in an art museum, with three rock bands, light shows and old movies being flashed across the walls, champagne flowing, all free-form and glass walls. One could expect no less from the Polish Embassy. Unless one had a gallows sense of humor.

The Polish Embassy was like a bad Polack joke. It was on the third floor of an apartment building, a huge empty series of rooms devoid of furniture. No air conditioning. No music. The refreshments consisted of cornucopial flowings of *slivovitz* and a species of *vodka* Brian Aldiss assured me could be used to launch a Soyuz rocket into Lunar orbit. (Not being a drinker, I have to rely on the opinions of experts in these matters.)

The Polish attachés were sensational. To a man they were all short, round, cherubic and clothed in heavy wool suits that were fashionable around 1938. Miraculously, even in the humid, dripping atmosphere of the apartment, suddenly jammed with several hundred sweating aliens, all babbling in various tongues, with droplets of moisture condensing on the walls, even in their wool suits, none of them perspired. Maybe that's why the Soviets do so well in the Cold War. Sorry about that.

I wandered around with Robert Bloch (the novelist who wrote, among other things, PSYCHO; the scenarist who wrote, among other things, *Asylum*) while the Poles had their picture taken with the stunning Leigh Chapman, who could not convince them she wasn't a movie star. On one wall in what we took to be the living room of the empty apartment, we found a painting. Bob and I looked at it, then looked at each other. A chill ran up our spines. "Does that look to you like what it looks like to me?" I asked. He nodded.

The painting was a hideous green and yellow smash of disturbing alienness. It looked like something straight out of a Lovecraft story; the unnameable and unspeakable Elder God named Yog-Sothoth, or maybe Yig, or a close relative. We shuddered and walked away, and neither of us went back into that room throughout the reception. We pressed our way into the farthest corner of the "dining room," trying with equal vigor to get as far away from that painting as possible and to get next to the one open window in the place.

And here's where I fell into the dream.

Or maybe it was a nightmare.

I tell it *precisely* as it happened, without comment. It is true. You can ask Robert Bloch, a man who does not lie.

I was looking out the window, frankly bored, when my eyes traveled across the narrow street to the apartment building across from us. One floor above us, across the way, the curtains were parted, revealing the interior of an apartment. I stared in to that apartment for several seconds before my mind would accept what I was seeing:

On the wall was an enormous red flag with the Nazi swastika emblazoned in the center. The flag was torn and frayed at the edges, as though it had been ripped suddenly from the wall of a building going up in flames. But perhaps I dramatize. It may just have been old and weathered.

On another wall, there was a huge framed photograph of Adolf Hitler.

And marching back and forth in front of the window was a gentleman whose face I could not see, dressed in the black leather and livery of an SS officer. He was marching stiffly, in what newsreels have always advised me was a "goose-step."

I stared, dumbfounded, for a minute or two. Then I nudged Bob Bloch. "Take a look out the window," I said, softly, fearing for my sanity. "Into that apartment across the street. And tell me if I see what I see."

Bob bent around me and looked. He was silent for some time. Then he looked around at me and tried to say something several times. When he finally got it out, it was a breathy kind of, "Oh, my God."

We called several other people's attention to it, and they all seemed chilled by the sight. But they all saw it. After a few minutes, the fellow in the other apartment saw us staring, and he pulled the curtains.

Further, deponent sayeth not, save to comment that Ladislas Farago and his stories of Martin Bormann being in Argentina may be accurate, and that at moments like that, sweltering in a sudden dream, one realizes how much closer to reality fantasy is than we would like to believe.

Interim Memo

THE COLUMN, APPEARING WEEKLY IN AN INFLUENTIAL LOS
Angeles newspaper, provided a fine dodge for cadging free
meals. At least, that was my despicable intention. But I discovered, when I had dinner on "professional courtesy" at a joint
that damned near poisoned me, that if I was to retain my
integrity I had to pay for the meals, and even go for a look-see
incognito.

From this reevaluation of my purposes, I came to the belief
that there is no point in acquiring power, position, vast wealth
or influence unless one can use it for self-serving ends. *Having*
those things is a genuine pain in the ass. Takes a *lot* of time,
makes people try to bump you off, narrows your choices and
surrounds you with people you can't trust. So if you plan to be
the next Kingfish or Supreme Ruler, you'd better get started
right now corrupting yourself. Otherwise, shine it on.

Oh, and sadly, El Palenque is long gone.

Last I heard, the Bambi Bakery was doing nicely with
Roberto's brother Rudy still at the helm; but Roberto Rivera—a
sweet man—was managing something called Myron's Disco-
theque. That was three years ago. Damn! He ran a *swell* eatery!

The First of Three Culinary Comments

21 December 1972

*T*he adage goes, "Americans eat to live; the French live to eat." Somehow, I don't think that's either entirely accurate or all-encompassing; but as one who was a gourmet reporter for a number of years, I've come to appreciate the joys of good dining. Granted, in this land of McDonald Shitburgers and the revolving fans atop Kentucky Colonel Chicken Cesspools blowing the ghastly stench of rancid cooking fat across the freeways and for miles thereabout, it is more and more difficult to get a meal that doesn't leave one with a case of Montezuma's Revenge . . . even so it behooves me, as a man of conscience, to refer you to an incredibly fine restaurant here in Los Angeles: one that serves exemplary food, charges reasonably, offers a pleasant ambience and whose owner treats his customers with respect and affection. As opposed to the hordes of subdued-lighting, plastichromed, expense account writeoff lunch-counters that have developed terminal cases of acromegaly-*cum*-pomposity and stiff you a week's wages for food a lemming would rather dive over a cliff than eat.

(Actually, the realities of dining in Los Angeles are only reflective of the freeway/Howard Johnson/Taco Bell/Jack inna Box/Co'Cola/frozen french fries idiom into which all Amurrica has been lured over the past thirty-five years. To my certain knowledge there are people between the ages of fifteen and thirty-five who have never tasted real food. From their lips, Trilby-like, the phrase, "Gimme a jumboburger an' frenchfries anna coke," leaps unbidden whenever their stomachs toll trough-time. For those miserable unfortunates no uplift or enrichment, such as one derives from the zucchini florentine at Musso & Frank's Grill, the beefsteak tomatoes and onion slathered with *real* chunky Roquefort at the Pacific Dining Car, the hot dogs at Pink's, the moussaka at Greektown . . . for them only the dark tunnel of heartburn and pseudo-beef patties immolated in yak butter, or whatever it is Pup 'n' Taco uses. And it's their own fault, of course. As Jefferson said, "People get pretty much the kind of government they deserve." Which explains Nixon, Reagan and, by extension, the kind of food they permit to be shoved at them. Again, by extension, the dining scene runs a parallel to the situation with hookers in L.A. as opposed to the rest of the country. A young lady of my acquaintance, a professional woman in the field of *amour*, came out here from New York and was both delighted and amazed at the parameters of prostitution. She commented that the johns out here are so timorous and corrupted by Angeleno life that all they expect for their money is a blowjob. In Manhattan, she mused, a hooker wouldn't last a day with that kind of sole stock in trade. She settled down in Laurel Canyon, happy as an Australian cuscus; the working hours were better, the pay higher, and the wear and tear on her private parts infinitely less. But . . . I digress.)

So in what will probably be a vainglorious attempt to wrench your culinary habits out of the slough of despond into which they have sunk, let me tell you about *El Palenque*.

To begin with, it's an Argentinian restaurant.

In the best traditions of that special kind of cooking.

Where Mexican cooking is spicy and aggressive, Argentinian food is solid and masterful without reaming your sinuses. It is primarily meats . . . steaks and sausages and other proteins that fill your belly with substance and your mouth with heavenly tastes. Side-dishes are similarly unfrightening, but bold.

El Palenque (pronounced puh-*lenk*-ay), means the hitching post. It can be found at 660 N. Larchmont, on the corner of Melrose Avenue; one block west of Gower, well within spitting distance of Paramount Studios.

It's a small place. If you worked at it, you could probably cram in about half a dozen automobiles . . . about that size. There's a bar, though beer and wines are all you can get; if it's booze you want, go to the Luau. Food is what El Palenque offers, in abundance, and at prices that will gladden your heart.

The owner is Roberto Rivera, round and pleasant, and possessed of a mild Latin charm that is happily light-years away from the cloying toadiness of most *maître d*'s on Restaurant Row. If pressed, Mr. Rivera will tell you he is from Honduras and, with his brother Rudy, opened the Bambi Bakery on Santa Monica in 1964. (It is from Brother Rudy's bakery that El Palenque gets the amazingly delicious bread it serves; it comes in small rolls the size of your hand, and is served at table warm enough to melt the butter without great clots falling in your lap.) Because of Mr. Rivera's peripatetic background, the menu is not *strictly* Argentinian, though all the favorite Gaucho dishes can be found therein. Lynda tried the *Lomito Saltado* the other night ($2.35 à la carte, $2.75 on the full dinner), and I won't say she raved about it, but when she had eaten all there was on the plate, she began to whimper. When I asked her why, she told me that she was sad there was no more to eat. When I offered to get her another order she added that she was stuffed full, there'd been more than enough to bulge the sexy space where her top and slacks left naked belly, but she was distraught to think there was no more of that goodness to be force-fed. *Lomito Saltado*, for the two or three of you out there who don't know it, is a Peruvian wonder containing chunks of sirloin steak, cooked with tomato and onions, mixed with golden brown french fries and served with rice.

Argentinian, Peruvian . . . and the side orders of *Platano Fritos* are Cuban. Again, for the uninitiated, platanos are the exquisite green bananas called plantains, fried till they assume the color of Spanish doubloons. They are served in a heaping jumble with sour cream. I can assure the gourmets in the audience that I have not tasted such well-prepared and oil-free plantains since one remarkable dining experience in the Irish Channel in New Orleans several years ago.

Preparation of these Central and South American dishes is effected by two stalwarts: Vidal, the night chef (with a sure assist from Roberto), and "Toyi", who has been with the Rivera family for more years than they can count. "Toyi" prepares most of the dishes earlier in the day, setting them up in such a way that Luis, the waiter, can hustle them to your table steaming hot from the kitchen. Luis, by the way, is one helluva waiter. Though I can't swear to it, I'm sure he must have tiny wings on his feet . . . for the service at El Palenque is not merely fast, it is virtually instantaneous.

And when it comes, ah! What happiness. Let me give you a suggestion for a typical dinner:

Begin with either a Chi-Chi cocktail or a marguerita. Then a small salad, crunchy and fresh and nicely accoutered with bleu cheese dressing. It isn't a big, or even an elaborate salad, the usual staples, but it rests lightly in the stomach and doesn't cloud the main issues, yet to come.

For the appetizer course, try the meat turnovers, the *empanadas*. They're akin to *kreplach*, but the pastry shell is crisp and brown, and the meat inside is handsomely spiced, but not hellish.

The main course ranges from familiar dishes like soft beef tacos (for those who venture into unknown lands toe-first) and traditional T-Bone and New York steaks; to the full gaucho dinner, the *parrilla mixta*, which includes ribs, skirt steak, sweetbreads, kidneys, plain and black sausages, and comes served crackling on its own hibachi. The mixta, I must warn you, is a *big* meal. Though I've seen one person *almost* finish the selection, he had not eaten all day and was ravenous . . . and even so, he had to have help to the car afterward. But despite his bloated appearance, he wore a beatific smile.

For first-timers, I would recommend the marvelous *entraña*, a char-broiled 12–14 ounce skirt steak. The skirt is something like a London Broil, the way Raquel Welch is like Kate Smith; they're both women, even as both edibles are related cuts of meat. But after the name, all similarities cease.

The skirt comes in a long, thinnish slab with a tender middle and a crunchy outer shell. It is one of the universe's special gifts. It comes with french fries, which are absolutely correct and as crunchy as the steak itself. When consumed in company with an order of plantains, the diner is offered a range of tastes, sweet and pungent, that make the dinner hour a pleasure.

For dessert, a cup of El Palenque's excellent coffee (with refills that keep coming endlessly and without charge) laced with fresh milk; and "Toyi's" incredible *flan*, a caramel custard pudding that will make your eyes roll up in your head.

Then sit back and try to get your hands locked across your stomach. You will know what satisfaction is, at last.

El Palenque has other things to recommend it, as if what has been set down already weren't enough:

A lively and variegated group called Rocky and The Latin Image, a five-piece percussion and piano operation, plays every night but Monday and Tuesday. With vocals by a gentleman announced as "the internationally-famous Velasquez," the mood of the restaurant is constantly one of life and exuberance. A small dance floor adjoins the bandstand and the clientele—a wild mixture of South and Central American–born residents of the Los Angeles *barrio*—move on and off the space with that willowy grace and zest for life that can only be captured in dances of Latin origin. On a recent evening, the hypnotic oneness of several couples swaying to the mambo almost drew our attention from the pursuit of stuffing our stomachs. Almost.

But on Monday and Tuesday when The Latin Image is silent, El Palenque makes up for the short-changing by lowering its dinner prices. It is possible to sock away a meal for two, with wine, such as the one I've outlined here, for less than seven dollars. Similar dining bargains are few and far between in Los Angeles.

El Palenque is open Sunday from 2:00 in the afternoon till 2:00 in the morning. Monday through Thursday: 11:30 A.M. till 2:00 A.M. Friday and Saturday: 11:30 A.M. till 4:00 A.M.

And if the sheer improbability of those hours doesn't bring you up short, just stop to think of how hard it was to find a restaurant open late enough after a movie to give you a good meal, the last time you were caught out in the city after eleven o'clock. El Palenque burns with life till well after the rest of provincial L.A. shuts down.

So. Go have a good meal. But don't tell your friends about the place unless they can be trusted. The only drawback to my sharing this wonderland with you is the fear that it will be invaded by the Strip rats, the talent agency phonies and the bores. It's happened with other good, small restaurants. I'd hate to see it happen to El Palenque.

But Rivera's paradise is too special and too worthwhile a treasure to keep to myself. So I share it with you, in hopes your taste buds will return to life; I share it with you as an act of camaraderie; please don't abuse the privilege.

And tell Roberto Rivera that Harlan Ellison sent you. If you do, he might sit down a while and tell you what goes into the black sausage.

Interim Memo

AFTER YOU'VE EITHER CHEERED YOURSELF HOARSE OVER THIS one, or purged your outrage at my perfidious disrespect; after you've sighed with relief that the secret hatred you've had to keep to yourself for years is not ideopathic, or dropped to your knees in prayer that some malevolent deity pan-fry my innards for such loathsome heretical awfulness, carry away from this column (and its update in Installment 43) only one Jot of Accepted Wisdom:

Send me an Xmas card and I will hunt you down.

Flee to the jungles of Bolivia, I'll hunt you down.

And when I get you, I'll nail your head to a coffee table.

With dripping fangs I look forward to the consummate idiot who thinks s/he will be smartass clever by doing it. There're always a few. Killing them slowly and painfully, gleefully and sloppily, is no act punishable under law.

No Offense Intended, But Fuck Xmas!

28 December 1972

*F*irst of all, let's exclude the Prince of Peace. None of what I'm about this week has anything to do with him. From what I've read, he was an okay sort of guy on whom has been laid more superhero tripe than any one social malcontent should have to cope with.

What I'm concerned with here is how much I, and most of you, whether you will cop to it or not, have come to hate, loathe, despise and revile Christmas.

Not even the obvious cliché Scrooge anti-commercialized Christmas denigration that berates greedy shopkeepers for stringing plastic holly in the middle of August, that castigates even worthwhile charities for their shameless whipguilt hustling for funds, that chides average citizens for falling for the okeydoke and going in hock to BankAmericard to buy gifts they can't afford for people they don't give a damn about. *That* facet of the problem is so much an obviousness that everyone has learned to live with it, pays it lip-service the way lip-service is paid to horrors such as "everyone knows politicians are crooked," and does nothing to revise the situation. Amazing how much shit folks can learn to eat.

No, I'm finally going to come out of the closet and openly state in print how much the entire concept of the "holiday" horrifies me. If I touch a shuddering chord here that resonates in tone with what you've been concealing in your heart of hearts, then consider me only as the fatmouth willing to suffer the brickbats of Jesus Freaks, et al., who'll surely burn a cross on my lawn for putting down their be-all/end all's natal day. I'm willing to stand the gaff, gentle readers, if you will merely turn to the East and say to the sunset, "God forgive me, I've had the same thoughts."

Consider: the following items came over the news on December 24th and 25th: four men in San Francisco abducted two young girls off the streets in broad daylight; a young woman whose estranged husband showed up at her door with presents for their kids was shot to death by the wife, who then put the pistol in her mouth and blew her head off; a 65-year-old man in Manhattan threw himself off the Brooklyn Bridge with a note (apparently written with a ballpoint so it wouldn't smudge in the water, which is really forethought of a high order) saying he couldn't make it through another Christmas alone and unloved; a sniper in downtown Chicago knocked off four people on Christmas Eve, and was never located; a noted psychologist released a statement that suicide rates go up to triple normal during the holidays; police in Los Angeles and San Francisco agreed, with some consternation, that crime doubles during Christmas. There's more, much more, but why belabor the point? The only *good* news during Christmas this year was that Harry Truman, that indefatigable old curmudgeon, was still holding on with filled lungs, failing kidney, stuttering heart and deep in a death coma.

Christmas is an awfulness that compares favorably with the great London plague and fire of 1665–66. No one escapes the feelings of mortal dejection, inadequacy, frustration, loneliness, guilt and pity. No one escapes feeling used by society, by religion, by friends and relatives, by the utterly artificial responsibilities of extending false greetings, sending banal cards, reciprocating unsolicited gifts, going to dull parties, putting up with acquaintances and family one avoids all the rest of the year . . . in short, of being brutalized by a "holiday" that has lost virtually all of its original meanings and has become a merchandising ploy for color tv set manufacturers and ravagers of the woodlands.

Look: I dig my privacy. 364 days out of the year I can think of nothing more pleasant than being left alone of an evening, working at writing a story, watching some television, making a small meal, smoking my pipe, just swimming along softly behind an ambience of aloneness. There is nothing of *loneliness* in all that, but *aloneness*, which is something else altogether, something fine and rewarding filled with restoking the internal fires, coming to grips with myself, perceiving my directions and my place in the universe.

But on Christmas Eve I was alone, and I wanted to slash my carotid artery. (And when I read the foregoing to the two young ladies who are secretarying for me, they stared at me with undisguised loathing for my rottenness and countered with the arguments that a *lot* of people *like* Christmas a bagful, and they offered as their reasons that many people dig it because they don't have to work, and others adore it because they get bonuses.

(Had I the sense of a maggot, I'd rest my case right there.

(But for the sanctimonious few who would revile the ladies for their opinions, only slightly less than they will me for mine, I press forward, bearing in mind Dickens's remark that ". . . every idiot who goes about with 'Merry Christmas' on his lips should be boiled with his own pudding, and buried with a stake of holly through his heart."

(And did you ever notice, the only one in A CHRISTMAS CAROL with any character is Scrooge? Marley is a whiner who fucked over the world and then hadn't the spine to pay his dues quietly; Belle, Scrooge's ex-girlfriend deserted him when he needed her most; Bob Crachit is a gutless toady without enough get-up-and-go to assert himself; and the less said about that little treacle-mouth, Tiny Tim, the better. No, Dickens knew what he was doing when he made Scrooge the focus of the story. My only disappointment in him is that he let himself be savaged by those three dumb Ghosts. God Bless Us, Every One *indeed*! Not even at Christmas would I God Bless Nixon or the terrorists who machine-gunned the Olympic athletes or the monkey-trial reactionary fundamentalists who bludgeoned the California State Board of Education into stating in all future textbooks that Darwin's Theory is an "unproved theory" as valid as the "special creation" nonsense. Bless 'em? I'd like to boil them in their own pudding and bury them . . . but you know.)

Christmas is constructed and promulgated in such a way that to defy it or ignore it makes one a monster. To refuse to send cards, to toss the ones received in the wastebasket, to refuse to accept gifts and refuse to give them, to walk un-touched through the consumer-crowds and never feel the urge to buy Aunt Martha that *lovely* combination rotisserie-&-bidet, to maintain one's sanity staunchly through the berserk days of year's end makes one, in the eyes of those who lack the courage to eschew hypocrisy, an awful heretic, a slug, a vile and contemptible thug.

But consider the millions who are alone on Christmas. All the divorcees, all the kids on the road, all the septuagenarians in the Fairfax retirement homes, all the parents who lost kids in 'Nam, all the truck drivers who take Christmas schedules so they won't have to sit around and brood on how miserable they are. Think of the poor sonofabitch glimpsed through the front windows of an Automat, sitting there by himself eating the $1.79 Xmas Special w/giblet gravy.

And don't give me any of that bullshit about how we must take these poor unfortunates to our Christian bosoms and make them welcome at this wonderful time of the year.

Half of them are rapists and ax murderers, and they'll eat your dinner, knock you in the head with a candlestick and steal all the presents from under your tree.

What they want, flat truth, is to be left well alone, to get through this horrendous sorrow-show as quickly as possible.

And when I read all *that* to one of my secretaries—the other having resigned and stalked out of the house muttering *Antichrist*—she snottily advised me she didn't mind anyone's not liking Christmas, what she resented were loudmouths like me who *talked* about it. Which is a terrific Silent Majority attitude, paralleling the Administration's attitudes about civil disobedience and vocal dissent. They don't mind your *thinking* it (at the moment), but god forbid you should try to *do* something about it.

It never occurs to her that the pro-Christmas lackeys bombard the rest of us through every possible medium of mass communication from Muzak wassail wassails in the elevators to *White Christmas* and *Miracle on 34th Street* all over the tube for two weeks prior and a week post. That every nit one encounters in banks or bakeries, who snorted and snarled and dealt you inept service all the rest of the year suddenly blossoms forth with a phony "Merrrrry Christmas" in hopes of a Yuletide giftiepoo. That even the blasphemy blasphemy curse blasphemy telephone company answers its phones with, "Merry Christmas, may I help you?"

"Yes, I'd like you to check out an address for me, please."

"Merry Christmas, we are not permitted to check addresses."

"Yes, but, er, I'm a paraplegic cancer victim in an iron lung and the house is on fire and I'd like you to check out my address because I'm blind and the fire department needs it to locate me before I'm incinerated."

"Merry Christmas, I'm sorry, sir, but you'd better fuck off."

"Thanks. And a Merry Christmas to you."

What I'm saying, in sum, dear friends, is that it is all hopelessly artificial. That people are no better at Xmas time than any other time, and by spouting platitudes in the name of a scrawny prophet who got hammered in place for saying stuff a lot more radical than what I'm saying here, none of those Yule-nuts become brighter or more sanctified or even a tot kinder.

And weighed against the people who suicide out of loneliness and misery, all the sales of Timex watches don't mean a goddam thing.

So next year, to all my friends, and particularly to my enemies, take your pointless and money-wasting Hallmarks and jam them up your pantyhose.

Next year, time and finances permitting, I will cause to have erected on the roof of my home, a ten foot high neon sign that blinks on and off in blood-red and cash-green, BAH! HUMBUG! and any little clown who comes caroling at my door is going to have boiling pitch dumped on him.

And fuck you, Tiny Tim!

Interim Memo

JUST FOOLIN' AROUND, FOLKS. NOT REALLY MORBID, JUST KINDA streetcorner riffing on a theme. Most of the dates in this next column has come and went, and I'm still pulling oxygen. Well, you know: the good die young. Noriega will live forever. Nixon'll haunt our great-great-grandchildren. And ALL THE LIES THAT ARE MY LIFE actually got published in 1980, and I'm still waiting for the goddam Book-of-the-Month Club to accept *any*thing I've written.

The Day I Died

4 January 1973

*D*riving home from Norman Spinrad's New Year's Eve party at which I finally met Cass Elliot—as invigorating an experience as one could wish for the dawn of a new year—skimming the crusty '67 Camaro with its 56,000+ miles of dead years in its metal bones through Beverly

Hills. KFAC was working Ravel's *Bolero*. Not tired, it was still early for a New Year's Eve, something like one o'clock.

Thinking.

No. Woolgathering. (THE AMERICAN HERITAGE DICTIONARY OF THE ENGLISH LANGUAGE, p. 1473, col. 2: woolgathering *n.* Absent-minded indulgence in fanciful daydreams.) That's what I was doing: woolgathering.

Frequently, that's how my writer's mind conceives plots for stories, or more accurately, concepts for stories. The unconscious computer makes a storage bank search of idle thoughts looking for linkages, cross-references, points of similarity. When it finds something interesting, it checks it against all the muddle and mud swirling around in the cortex, and comes up with something that makes a story.

The elements this time were these:

1972 is gone. It's a new year. 1973. Another year.

One year older. Moving on up the road toward the grave just the way old Camaro is moving on up the road to Beverly Glen. Traveling the road.

Harry Truman is gone. I miss him. Salty old Harry who told them all to go fuck themselves. Ten years ago he said he wouldn't die for at least ten more because he had ten years' work still to do in the Truman Library in Independence, Missouri. Ten years later, all the work done, almost to the month, he died. Did he know?

Could I know when I'm going to die?

Will I get to finish all the stories I have to write?

Will I suddenly get rammed by a Pontiac Grand Am at the next light, centerpunched into an early oblivion?

When will I die?

New Year's Eve is a good time to think about it.

So. This column.

Thinking about when I'll die. Mortality is the subject.

I will die in 1973. Here is how it happened.

I went to New York to be guest of honor at a science fiction convention called the Lunacon. To amortize the cost of the trip I accepted several lecture gigs in surrounding areas. So I went into Manhattan two weeks before the convention. I had just returned from speaking at Dartmouth, and was staying with my friend Max Katz, the *Sesame Street* segment director, in his Penthouse G on East 65th Street. Max and Karen were out when I taxied in from Kennedy International, and after putting away my overnight case I found the note they'd left for me: *We went to dinner at The Proof of the Pudding. If you get in by nine, join us. Love, M&K.*

I looked at my watch. It was 9:28. Still time to meet them for a piece of Key West lime pie. I left the apartment and took the elevator to the lobby. The street was quiet and pleasant with an April breeze. I started to walk down 65th to First Avenue, carefully avoiding the piles of dog shit.

Two guys in Army field jackets were coming toward me, up the street. I instinctively tensed. I was in New York and could not forget that Karen had had her purse ripped off her shoulder in broad daylight in front of Bloomingdale's, in front of hordes of people who would not help her as she struggled with the snatcher. New York was not what it had been when last I'd lived there, in 1961.

As they came toward me they parted so I could walk between them. I guess I knew in my gut what was about to happen. They swung on me and jammed me against the brick wall of the poodle clipping joint down the street from Max's building. They both had knives.

"Gimme your wallet," one of them said, not even lowering his voice. He pushed his knife against my collarbone. The other one smelled of fish.

I remembered a way I'd confounded a mugger many years before. I began mumbling unintelligibly in what was supposed to be a foreign tongue, waving my hands feebly as if I didn't understand English.

"Your money, motherfucker . . . I'll shove this in your fucking throat!"

I rolled my eyes wildly and continued babbling.

A group of people had come out of Max's apartment building, were turning toward us. "Come on," said the one who smelled of fish. "You cocksucker!" the one with the knife at my collarbone said.

They let go and moved off. I took two steps and felt the pain. I tried to turn, and saw the one who had done all the talking had spun and come back at me. The pain was in my back, below my right shoulderblade. It got worse. Doors slammed in my head. Everything went silver. I fell to my knees.

The group from Max's building walked past me. I fell down and lay there. In a little while I died.

Max and Karen came home from dinner and didn't find out I'd been killed outside their building till the next afternoon. Karen cried, the Lunacon had a minute of silence for me, and my replacement, Isaac Asimov, said dear good things about me, better than I deserved.

I died on April 19th, 1973.

I will die in 1981. Here is how it happened.

I was living in Perthshire, in Scotland. I had had a bad cold for weeks. I was living alone. The girl who had been staying with me had gone away. I was writing DIAL 9 TO GET OUT at last. My big novel. The one that would finally break my name into the memory books of great writers. It had taken me ten years to get to it. I was deep in the writing. I didn't eat regularly, I've never been one for cooking for myself. I developed pneumonia in that handsome old farm-house.

It killed me. I never finished the book. My stories were read for a few years, but soon went out of vogue.

No one in that little Scottish town understood that as I lay there, doped up and dying, that the pathetic movements of my hands were my attempts to convey to the nurse or the doctor that I wanted my typewriter, that I wanted more than anything, more than even life, to finish that book.

I died on December 11th, 1981.

I will die in 1986. Here is how it happened.

ALL THE LIES THAT ARE MY LIFE had been published in March. Book-of-the-Month Club had taken it as its April selection. The film rights were being negotiated by Marty. It looked to be the best year I'd ever had.

I was on a publicity tour for the book, fresh from a talk show over holovid. Oh, yes, I should mention holovid. After two-dimensional depth television, Westinghouse developed "feelie," a rather euphemistic name for projected video, giving the vague impression of the actual presence in your living room of the actors. Then the cable people in conjunction with LaserScience, Ltd. of Great Britain combined holograms with 3–D projection techniques and came up with holovid, in which the viewer actually became a part of the show or studio audience.

I was in Denver, preparing to be choppered over to the studio, when I fell ill. I was using depilatory on my beard in the hotel suite's bathroom when I felt dizzy and suddenly keeled over. The publisher's rep and the PR woman heard me crash and came running. They got me to the hospital where the phymech took readings. (A phymech is a robot physician, used primarily for running physicals and determining the nature of the illness. Lousy bedside manner, but they've cut down the incidence of improper analysis by eighty percent over their human counterparts.)

The judgment was cancer of the stomach.

I went into surgery the next morning. It had spread, running wild, not even the anti-agapic drugs would work. I was listed as terminal. Perhaps two weeks, the last five of those days heavily sedated against the pain. It was a shame: the Cancer Society was on the verge of a major breakthrough. Had I lived another five years, I'd have seen cancer become no more serious than the flu.

I spent the last two weeks in a hospital bed, a typewriter propped on a little table. The newspapers come and did their interviews briefly . . . I was abrupt with them, I'm afraid. I didn't have too much time to talk, I had things to write.

I finished my last novel in that bed, but the final twenty thousand words were rather garbled, I was so drugged, going in and out of consciousness. But I finished it, and was saved the horror of having another writer complete the work from my notes.

When I died, I was not unhappy. I rather regretted being denied those last twenty years, though. I had *such* stories to write.

I died on my birthday, May 27th, 1986.

I died in 1977 when a right-winger shot me because I'd done an article in *World* Magazine on President Agnew, and how he should be indicted as a criminal for the war in Brazil.

I died in 1979 in a plane crash in Sri Lanka. I was on my way to see Arthur Clarke. We were going to go scuba diving off the coast of coral. The plane exploded; I never knew what hit me. My fourth wife got the flight insurance.

I died in 1982 during the worst blizzard the East Coast had ever seen. I froze to death in my car on a lonely Connecticut road where I'd run out of gas. Some asshole suggested that because I'd been frozen, they might try to preserve me cryonically for restoration later. Fortunately, he was ignored.

I died in 1990 from a sudden, massive coronary. I was sitting at home on a Sunday afternoon and felt the slam of it, and had just a moment to realize I was dying the same way my father had died. But he never had a U.S. postage stamp commemorating his achivements.

I died in 1998 from ptomaine poisoning in a sea food restaurant in the undersea resort city of Cayman. They had to wait three weeks to ship my carcass out; it would have been simpler to turn me into fish food and let my soul wander the Cayman Trench. I always hated the lack of imagination of Those in Power.

I died in 2001 on my way back from Sweden. I died very peacefully, in my sleep, onboard the catamaran-cruiser *Farragut,* somewhere in mid-Atlantic. I died with a smile on my face, lying in bed, holding the Nobel Prize for Literature to my chest like a teddy bear.

I died in 2010 from weary old age, surrounded by grandchildren and old friends who remembered the titles of my stories. I didn't mind going at all, I was really tired.

Hey! You! The skinny sonofabitch with the scythe, I'm over here . . . Ellison. I saw you looking at me out of the corner of that empty socket in your skull-face, you sleazy eggsucker. Well, listen, m'man, understand this: since I know I'm going straight to Hell anyhow, and since I've always lived with the feeling that Heavens and Hells are sucker traps for the slowwitted and one should get as much goodie as one can while one is breathing, you'd better get used to the idea that you're going to have to come and get me when my time's up. Kicking and screaming, you blade-boned crop-killer. Hand to hand or at gunpoint, you're going to have to fight me for my life.

Because I've got too much stuff yet to do, too many stories yet to write, too many places I've never seen, too many books I'ver never read, too many women to admire, and too many laughs yet to cry. So don't think I'll be a cheap acquisition, clatterframe! And if you *do* get me, I'll be the damnedest POW *you* ever saw. I'll try and escape, and if I can't, I'll send back messages.

And it'll drive your boney ass crazy, Mr. D., because I'll be the first one to write about what it's like over there in *your* country.

INSTALLMENTS

Harlan Ellison's Movie

11 January through 15 March 1973

Interim Memo

ONE OF THE FRIENDS WITH WHOM I WAS HAVING A ROUGH patch, as discussed in this column, read this piece when it was first published, and recognized himself. We had a long talk. More than one long talk. We cleaned it up. We're still friends.

Fair Weather Friends, Summer Soldiers, and Sunshine Patriots

29 March 1973

"**N**owhere are we commanded to forgive our friends," said Cosimo de Medici (1389–1464). Today I'd like to dwell with morbid attention on friendship.

It occurs to me that this column has evolved in some ways into a debunking platform, from which I cynically shoot holes in the balloons of motherhood, Christmas cheer, New Year's resolutions, childhood memories . . . all the ratholes of the soul into which we crawl to avoid ugly realities. I don't mean it to be that. I never intended it that way. But oddly enough, I find others who shamefacedly admit that, yes, they had always believed in their darkest core that the things I've written were so. And I suppose confronting these truths can't be a bad thing; the human animal has a virtually limitless capacity for rationalization, an uncanny talent for ignoring lessons learned. So these little candles lit in the darkness don't do any lasting damage, and if they codify universal feelings . . . well . . . then I suppose the job was worth doing.

I say all this upfront because what I'm about to venture on the subject of friendship is depressing as hell, but—at least to me—inescapable.

Most of the people we call "friends" are merely passersby in our lives; acquaintances with whom for a short time we have something in common. A mutual club membership, a commonly shared lust, a project, a cause, a crusade, an accident of blood relationship, a physical closeness of habitation . . .

What Kurt Vonnegut calls a "false karass."

Yet *friendship* seems to me something else again. Something far nobler, vastly more enriching and warming, something purely succoring. It's there, whether you need it or not, whether you ever make a call on it or not, even if you don't want it. There is a guy I know (and it's going to be hard in this column not to name names, though I'll try my best), and I am his friend. He loathes me. Wants nothing to do with me. Would punch me out if I offered friendship. But I am his friend. He ain't mine, but I am his. I would do anything for him. He did me a good turn once, and I put such high value on that favor that forever I am on call for him. Times have passed and we no longer talk, he thinks he has a gripe against me—and he may be correct in that belief—but I'm *still* his friend. That's the way it is with me.

It defies reason or common sense, even good sense. But I am a creature who lives by rules and ethics and moralities I've honed and winnowed and pruned through the years till they suit me, so I can do no other. It fills me with sadness that he is no longer my friend; for him *I* was merely an acquaintance.

Friends are those into whose souls you've looked, and therein glimpsed a oneness with yourself. They are a part of you, and you a part of them. They own a piece of you.

And when it goes sour, it makes you want to go blind.

I'll tell you about one of those in a moment, but first I want to talk about what it feels like when you're in the middle of losing a friend. Having been through three divorces I can tell you the situations are not at all dissimilar.

What is it that makes a friendship go sour?

For me, it's the realization, usually after many small disappointments, that the person in whom I've placed my trust and camaraderie, is not the person I thought him or her to be at all. Usually it's in the area of ethics. Not one of us is as clean as we would have the world believe. We cheat a little, fudge a little, lie a little, cut a few corners, and occasionally even do something that fills us with self-loathing and guilt. Most of the time we lose very little sleep over the minor gouges we rip in the flesh of honesty; it's too busy a world, and we move so fast we've skimmed past the moment of recognition in which we face ourselves and understand that we've sold out our souls. But our friends see. And though they may not comment on it, because they *are* our friends, it diminishes them because it means they have put their faith and trust in some creature less grand than they'd at first imagined. It makes our friends less, and we can only steal from them for so long before they turn away. It has gone sour.

I feel this most acutely at the moment, because I'm in the process of losing one of my closest friends. A fellow writer, I've known him for ten years and have felt more brotherly toward him than almost anyone I've ever known. I am short on family; most of my relatives are clowns I wouldn't associate with if they weren't related, so I see no reason why accidents of blood should bind me to human beings who, but for their familial relationships, are detestables or bores; my friends are my family; I never had a brother; so this friend means a great deal to me.

But over the years I've seen his attitude toward me sicken and turn ugly. He feels a sense of competition: in writing, in career success, in notoriety, in women, in even the day-to-day minutiae of conversation. If I say night, he says day. If I say good, he says bad. If I say fried rice, he says steamed rice. We have reached a point where we avoid each other's company, because we cannot talk. I cannot blame him entirely; I am by nature a competitive animal, even when I'm relaxed and unaware of the pressure I'm applying. But I've recognized it and now—for a long time now—have laid back when in his company. I don't *want* that kind of scene with him. But in some special part of his heart, he hates me. He loves me, as well; but that worm of hatred gives him no rest.

But that's only part of it. That's the part that has soured him against me . . . even though he refuses to admit it, and we still dance the friendship dance with one another, a hideous rigadoon of spastic movements and terrible lies. The part that has soured me against him is in the area of ethics. He is a back-stabber and a weaseler and a guy who will rationalize himself into some very ugly situations.

I remember one time, a few years ago, when I met a girl who was interested in me, and I (at first) in her. She was throwing a party the night I met her, but I had a previous appointment and couldn't go. She knew the name of this other writer, my friend, and I suggested he might like to attend the party. She told me to invite him. There were to be many unattached ladies present.

So I called my buddy and told him; and *en passant*, with a laugh, suggested he hustle any other fine female he saw, but to kinda sorta leave *that* one because I wanted to get to know her myself. So he went to the party.

Guess which one he bedded down with that night?

Out of an apartment filled with females he'd never met before, and with whom he could have formed a liaison without contretemps, guess which one he beelined?

That wasn't the first time I had my moment of doubt about my friend's fidelity, but it *was* a bit of a shocker. I'm not even dealing with the silliness of my "staking out" the girl—she was a free agent and could choose whomever she wanted, of course. Nobody owns anybody. What I'm crawling toward is that he *sought her out specially.*

To what end, I must ask. To the end of chopping me, comes the answer. Chill shot.

Recently, he did it again. Same situation, different cast of characters. Except this time it was a girl I'd brought in from far out of town. And this time I chose to absent myself from the play. I suggested they go off together and just not bother to bother me. It was with a sigh of relief from me that they split my house. But I liked him a lot less. His girlfriend wasn't too happy about it, either.

But what has gone down in the past two weeks, during the Writers Guild strike, has been the most souring.

For those of you who don't know what the strike's all about, or who have been confused by the stupid articles in *The Hollywood Reporter* (a simpleminded puff-sheet for the Producers Association that has traditionally bumrapped writers), be advised we are out on the bricks to get wage increases that have been substandard since 1951, plus many other areas where we who create the dreams feel we are entitled to a taste, seeing as how everyone else is getting fat. It's too complex to go into here, but suffice it, if you trust me at all, that it's a necessary strike and the Guild is on the side of the angels. (A few of whom, I'd love it a lot, should flap down and carry picket signs in front of Universal just to scare the piss out of Wasserman.)

My friend doesn't work much in tv, or films, but when he does, he reaps the benefits that other Guild members struck for and sweated for and negotiated for in years past. The Guild doesn't ask much of its members, actually. Years go by without any call on their time or efforts. But in a strike it's *got* to be solidarity or the pavement-pounding and out-of-work can go on for months. So *everyone* is called on to picket, or work in the Strike Action office, or drive a car to pick up people or *somedamnthing* . . . *any*thing!

The strike has cost a great many good men and women their incomes, their jobs, their reputations. Doug Benton, who was producing *Columbo*, and George Eckstein, who was readying a pilot project, have both been canned by Universal and each have received threatening letters from Lew Wasserman—one letter says they're going to be sued for breach of contract, another says they're going to be held to the terms of the contracts—but even if we settle the strike next week, and all of us start working for the higher compensations that have been negotiated, those writer-producer hyphenates who've been loyal to their union will *still* never regain the lost wages their striking has cost them. Hell, Wasserman can meet the new increases in compensation using just the money he's withholding from Benton and Eckstein and other hyphenates. Liam O'Brien was supposed to fly to London to write a film for one of the struck studios. He didn't go. God knows how much he lost. People who've created tv shows and sold them for the first time in long years of struggling, have struck and been aced out of the Fall schedules.

My friend called me, the first morning of the strike, hysterical, and asked me, because I am on the Board of Directors of the Guild, to get him off picket duty, because he was writing a book. Well, shit, I'm writing a book, too, and I have work stacked to the ceiling on my desk, but we're both freelancers and I *know* he can knock off for three or four hours once a week, to carry a picket sign, without seriously hindering his work schedule. I told him I couldn't and wouldn't do it, not even if I had the power, which I didn't. He thinks I'm a fucked-up friend. I think his ethics suck.

He's called me several times on the same subject. He ain't happy out there in the rain with that pole over his shoulder. I feel for him. But not much. He wants the gravy, even when he says he never asked to be a member of the Guild, that he was forced to join write for tv (which, surprise, surprise, is the *nature* of a union), but he won't give even a few hours of his life in the common cause.

So it goes sour.

I see him as a man who can't be depended on when the crunch sets in. And if he trembles in a lightweight breeze like this, how dependable can he be when a hurricane hits?

What kills a friendship? Seeing the flaws in someone you

thought was golden, and knowing those same flaws are in yourself; but knowing that having seen them *there*, they will not be permitted *here*.

The terrible part of losing a friend, the *most* terrible part, is seeing one you loved turn, like Jekyll into Hyde, from a friend into a hideous example.

Beware, I warn you, between meeting and parting, of confusing an acquaintance with a friend. They are two very different species. And for pete's sake, learn which *you* are!

Interim Memo

THIS ESSAY AND INSTALLMENT 24 POSE THE GREATEST PER-
sonal problems for me, of all the material in this book. These
columns were written twenty years ago. Things have changed a
lot. I reread this installment and cringe at the self-serving
arrogance and unvarnished, indefensible rudeness of many of
the throwaway remarks I made. Perhaps it is because marriage
to Susan has made me a more decent, (I hope) more gracious
person. Perhaps it just took me longer than it should have, to
shuck off the posturing of the smartass adolescent. Whatever.

And I thought long about how I presented myself here,
and about how I presented someone else in Installment 24; and
for a time I wrested with the decision to drop these two. But for
bad or good, this was what I was in 1973; and what I wrote I
believed. Much of it I still stand by. But things have changed.

Nonetheless, if this *Hornbook* is to be taken as an accurate
diary of the period, then I cannot comfort myself with the ease
of just letting these two pieces "vanish." I may, as often as any
of you, be deluded, but I struggle mightily against being a
hypocrite. I've talked about that in an earlier Interim Memo.

Installment 24 will bear its own Interim Memo, so I'll
address the second part of these ruminations on "godhood"
there; but in this installment two things need to be addressed:

The first is a sense of chagrin at the posturing of the twerp
who wrote these words in 1973.

The second is to report that Herb Kastle died on October
19th, 1987; and to report that the end of his life was not the
note of triumph I wished for him.

He wrote many more books in the years following this piece. Some were good, some were slightly less than that. None were bad. He wasn't capable of writing badly, so they were just less worthy than others. But his vogue passed, he found it hard to get work, he had a number of cruel relationships that took the starch out of him, some leaners got to him financially, and he sank deeper and deeper into a crushing, solitary depression.

He stopped calling. Not just me: anybody. He became a kind of hermit up there in the Hollywood Hills; and one day in '87 he died. It got to me so much that I didn't really want to hear the details, particularly after I heard he'd been dead some days before anyone found him. It may have been his heart, or his heart in that other way we used to call broken-hearted, but he's gone, and he can't update himself as these columns finally reach print.

But after I wrote this piece, Herb and I spent a lot more time together, after he read it and we could declare our friendship on a more realistic level. I made the mistake of buying the new BRITANNICA (that virtually useless thing with the Macropedia/Micropedia setup that makes it impossible to find *any*damnthing) and I sold him my 11th edition—which was the last really wonderful edition of the BRITANNICA—for something like forty bucks, because he coveted it. And when he died, I tried to buy it back—at *any* price, because it had been mine, and it had been his, and we were still linked by those volumes—but the woman who answered the phone at the last number I had for him, gave me such a vague, such a hard, such a flat affect time about it, that I said ah t'hell with it.

So Herb is gone now, and if he found peace anywhere along the way, it certainly didn't come during those last isolated years. I keep thinking that if I'd been able to track him down (because he kept changing his phone number and never replied to bread&butter notes suggesting dinner), if I'd been able to get to him, to let him know how much he was still admired and loved, that it might have come out differently.

But then, we *always* think that, don't we?

Troubling Thoughts About Godhood, Part One

6 April 1973

*T*hey're truly touching, the little fools. They can't seem to differentiate between the stories they admire and the writer who wrote them. No, you bright-eyed little students and fans of Greatness, *not me*! It's not me you love, it's the talent. I have nothing to do with that: I'm the vessel into which the wine was poured, but the crockery has no sweetness, it merely suffers itself to be carried about and used, at the whim of the talent.

I stand up there and tell them, over and over again, "Toulouse-Lautrec once said, 'One should never meet an artist whose work one admires; the artist is always so much less than the work.'" I tell them that in lectures at high schools, in rap sessions at colleges, in essays accompanying my short stories, in person and in print. They refuse to listen. *You* refuse to listen!

Dan Blocker, who died, who used to be on *Bonanza*, once told me of a woman he encountered when he was putting in a personal appearance at a rodeo.* She was a sweet, motherly old lady who came up to him and began talking to him as though he were Hoss Cartwright. "Ma'am," Dan said, stooping down to

---

* This anecdote is repeated in Installment 46, dated June–July 1977. I could plead deterioration of cerebral matter, but the simple truth is that four years had elapsed, a similar context presented itself, and I automatically reached for the proper emblematic anecdote, having forgotten I'd employed it here. You're not experiencing *déja vu*. —he, '89

smile at her, "Hoss Cartwright is just the character I play on teevee; I'm Dan Blocker."

She smiled at him with one of those aw g'wan with you smiles, as though charmingly chiding him for thinking she was such a penny fool. And then she went on, "Yes, I know. Now . . . Hoss, when you get home to the Ponderosa tonight, you tell your daddy, Ben, to fire off that old Chinese man who's been doing your cooking! You and your brother Little Joe need a good woman in there to cook you some *dec*ent food . . ."

Nothing strange. Nothing out of the ordinary. She was a product of her times, her culture, and her inability to separate fantasy from reality; precisely because everything is done, every waking and sleeping moment of the day, to eradicate that important boundary from your minds. Where does shadow and image leave off and substance begin. None of us can tell any more. We really believe it matters what the car we buy looks like. We really believe there is "honor" in what happened in Vietnam. We really believe growing old is terrible.

You believe it. I don't.

And you really believe that there are living gods whom you can elevate to pedestals—famous writers, talented actors, adroit painters, dissembling politicians, slick columnists, guitarists and Fender bass players and mumblers of doggerel you delude yourselves into thinking are poets merely because their soggy images are shouted at 350 decibel amplification, their right hands grip a microphone, they sweat a lot, their bellies are flat, their clothes are sequined, and they're so hip they won't rhyme "June" and "Moon," but the banality of their lyrics is as awful as a bulbous-eyed Keane waif, as empty of depth of originality as the iconography of Elvis on black velvet.

You cannot separate a talent from an individual. And so you raise to godhood those who, were they not gifted with that special ability, you would deride and pillory and cast into prisons for their selfishness, evil, rapacity and lack of humanity.

This week: the subject is godhood. I suppose, in some ways, an extension of last week's thoughts on friendship. And since I'm clearly the only one among you pure enough, noble enough to discuss the subject critically, I'll cop to having been

on both sides of the godhood scene—as god and worshipper—
and tell you about two famous men I've known.

The first one is Herbert Kastle. He may not be famous to
you nits who don't even know the names of the actors who strut
for you, or the writers who scribble for you, or in fact the names
of anyone failing to appear on the Johnny Carson Show, but
around Dell and Avon paperbacks' publishing offices, around
the money coffers of Great American Literary Houses like
Bernard Geis and Delacorte, Herbert Kastle is famous as hell.
You don't make $150,000 from THE MOVIE MAKER, $100,000
from MIAMI GOLDEN BOY and $100,000 from MILLIONAIRES
(with the total far from registered) without becoming famous as
hell. Not to you mud-condemned slugs who read books and
never look at the names of the authors, but to the fat old tigers
and their sleek editorial cubs who give out one hundred and
fifty grand 🪙 advances to authors who can come away from
their own books with hundred thousand dollar royalties. (As a
comparison, ninety percent of the writers in the world never
make a dime beyond the advance money they receive for a
book, and the advances are usually about three thousand
dollars. Now lay those figures against what Kastle carts off, and
you'll realize how much greater must be the slice of the pie
enjoyed by the publishers.)

Herb Kastle is famous. He's also likeable. He looks like a
cuddly Jewish teddy bear, all the best kinds of character lines in
his face, San Andreas crinkles radiating from the corners of his
eyes, no-shape comfortable body in which one could easily live
if one's head was straight.

More important, Herb Kastle is a fine writer. His first few
books, KOPTIC COURT (1958), CAMERA (1959), COUNTDOWN TO
MURDER (1960), THE WORLD THEY WANTED (1961), THE
REASSEMBLED MAN (1964) and HOT PROWL (1965), drew him to
my attention as a man who wrote in that special cathartic style
that spoke to Irwin Shaw's contention, "He is on a journey and
he is reporting in: 'This is where I think I am and this is what
this place looks like today.'" A writer does not write one novel
at a time or one play at a time or even one quatrain at a time.
He is engaged in the long process of putting his whole life on

paper. For Herb Kastle—who, when he started, was a nice Jewish boy with a wife and a family and all the middle-class twitches to which we are all heir—writing was clearly a way of purging his soul, and the struggles with his identity were clear in every novel he wrote.

(That struggle is nowhere more evident than in his new novel, ELLIE, published by Delacorte Press on March 21st. It is very likely Kastle's finest work to date; a searing and unrelenting study of a man obsessed by that sex object most destructive to his nature. It will sell like orangeade at the final truck stop before the Gobi Desert. In publishing circles it is the *Last Tango* of the contemporary sex novels. I strongly urge you to slither out and buy it. It is guaranteed to mess your mind.)

The other day, Herb Kastle wandered into my house and finally, after fourteen years of what I'd taken to be a casual acquaintanceship, laid on me the crushing data that I had been a profoundly important influence on his life and his success. In some strange Vonnegut *karass* way, we are linked, and I'd never realized it. And in the moments after he blurted that linkage, I understood that I had been elevated to godhood.

And could not handle it.

I first met Herbert D. Kastle in New York, in 1959. We met in the offices of Theron Raines who, at that time, was agenting for both of us. But I'd already (apparently) had an effect on Herb. I'd been writing professionally for three years, was at that time in the Army and had come into New York on leave, to try and scare up some money. My first wife had run off again, for the millionth time, taking with her the furniture, all my clothes, and every cent in the bank account. I had decided to divorce her and was desperately trying to find the pennies to get back into civilian life.

I'd read KOPTIC COURT the year before and, without knowing Kastle, had fired off a letter to him through his publisher, enthusing about the vigor and honesty of the book. (It's recently been reprinted by Avon in paperback, and I re-read it a while ago; miraculously, it holds up as well as when I first came to it. It's another one I commend to your attention.)

The letter had been a casual thing for me. I'm inclined to

revel in the utter craftsmanship of other writers, and like to let them know about it when it so seldom occurs. But for Herb, I learned later, it was a seminal communication. One of the things I'd talked about in glowing terms was that the novel had a last line punch like a short story, a very rare and difficult thing in this universe. I couldn't have known of it, of course, but Herb had worked on that ending for a week. He was justifiably proud of the effect it had produced, and usually it's not the sort of thing readers notice. So here came my letter, out of nowhere, fastening on that certain special act he had performed with clean hands and dedication and composure . . . and someone had noticed.

When we met in Theron Raines's office, we immediately liked each other: I was thrilled to meet a man who'd given me hours of fine reading, he was pleased to meet a writer who had been deeply-enough affected by his life's work to send out a cry across the emptiness in which most writers work.

I can't recall meeting Herb again until almost ten years later, when I was already an established Hollywood writer, and his life and writing had taken a different, to me ominous turn. (Although we almost shared a book once. Walter Fultz, the man who bought my first novel, back in 1956, was editing for the now-defunct paperback house, Lion Books. He wanted to put together a co-authored volume of stories by Herb and me: my stories of the street gangs of Brooklyn, Herb's stories of the uptown young Jewish thugs. It never came off, and Lion Books had to close down when they got caught in a distributors' crunch. And Walter Fultz, just a few years ago, died suddenly and under mysterious circumstances; one of the finest men I have ever known. As a sidelight to tragedy, Walter's emotional problem is one that, today, would be acceptable. Had he lived today instead of fifteen years ago, he would never have had to exist in the shadows of closets, would never have had to struggle with his life; to seem to be that which he wasn't; would never have had to be ashamed of what he was; and he would be with us today. I miss him.)

Ten years later, I was working on *The Oscar* at Paramount for Joseph E. Levine. Herb had come out to California for a visit. His marriage of many years was on the rocks and he was putting a continent between himself and his pain; yet another foolishness: the shimmering interface between oneself and one's bad karma defies space-time equations: a continent is no thicker than a membrane when one carries the misery inside: there is no escape, no Cloud-Cuckoo Land, no place to hide; literally no doors and no windows.

Herb came to have lunch with me at the Paramount commissary. We were never alike. He was always subdued, cool, interiorly-directed, polite, charming. I was always a street urchin, quick to anger, quicker to cool down, rabidly enthusiastic about everything, flaming, loud, crude. Each has its merits and flaws. But we weren't alike. And it was the difference between us that drew us together. He liked my raw style, I envied his ease in moving through the world like a phantom cat burglar turned novelist. But there was no competition between us. Writers who are good are never in competition; each has a corner on the market for the special product each produces; no writer can write another's book, not really.

Yet I think only in the most recent past has Herb come to know something about me that functions as my driving force: I consider myself an Artist, not merely a scribbler. When we sat across from each other in the Paramount commissary, with actors and producers waving and me digging the shit out of it—a little kid from Painesville, Ohio playing at being in the magic land of Hollywood—Herb clearly saw me as a surrogate Sammy Glick, a moderately-talented writer who had used charisma and drive to cash in on the big time. He was wrong about that, but he had no way of knowing it.

And again, without my knowing I was doing it, I steered Herb's life in a direction that would shape all the rest of his days. Or so he tells me.

I had been offered a job writing a B flick for Bert I. Gordon, a very decent and charming man who made low-budget thrillers that could always be counted on to do well at the saturation booking level. I didn't have time to do it, I was scheduled for another Levine film after *The Oscar*, and so I suggested to Herb that I recommend him to Bert Gordon for the project. It was, again, a casual thing, and I didn't even remember having done it until Herb reminded me the other day. It's the sort of kindness one does for one's friends without thinking in terms of coin returned.

I lost track of Herb; but what happened is that he got the assignment, wrote the screenplay for *The Museum of Dr. Freak* (which was shelved and never filmed for reasons probably having nothing whatever to do with the script), and from there moved on to scripts for the *Bonanza* and *Honey West* television series.

But from that lunch meeting, and from the tunnel vision through which Herb saw me . . . saw what he *thought* was me . . . he began to make notes on a Hollywood novel. He called before he flew back East with the outline for the book, and told me that he was about to change his life, that for the space of three books he was "going into business" and that he'd keep in touch. Then he went away.

In 1968 Herb sold THE MOVIE MAKER to the Mike Todd of the publishing world, Bernard Geis—he who gave us Jacqueline Susann—and it was an instant financial success. It was a splash book.

I bought a copy but didn't get around to reading it. On looking back, I think there was an ambience to the work that put me off, made it easier for me to rationalize why I didn't have the time to read the latest book by a writer whose every word had been absorbed minutes after coming into my possession. It had the unsavory feel of something left too long in the greenhouse. The scent of decaying orchids came off that book. It was probably my imagination.

A year later, when it was in paperback, a friend called me and said, "Hey, did you know there's a character in this cheap sex novel, THE MOVIE MAKER, who's a dead ringer for you? Do you know a guy named Herbert Kastle?"

I sat down and read THE MOVIE MAKER.

Yes. Herb Kastle had taken me as the model for Lars Wyllit, the driven, feisty, cunning, moderately-talented sexual profligate with hangups about his height. As I've said in this column many times, none of us care to cop to our true faces.

Eichmann never thought of himself as a human monster, merely as a man doing his job. Capone never sat beside a swimming pool in Miami Beach, his brain rotting away from tertiary syphilis, saying to himself, "I'm a gangster." He surely thought of himself as a businessman. I've never known a hooker who thought of herself as anything different from a clerk in a Woolworth's. The image of me that had been filtered through Herb's mind struck me as being too blatant, too shallow, too easily-dismissed, too cartoony, really to touch anywhere near the complex wonderfulness that I knew was my real self. (He said, humbly.)

Even so, Lars Wyllit was the only character in the book for whom the author showed any genuine love or caring. Cheap as that little fucker was, Lars Wyllit comes off well in the novel. A lot better than the Herb Kastle–surrogate, the ostensible hero of the novel, Charley Halpert, in whom Kastle displays a sort of pity and hopeless nobility.

I called Herb in New York, we talked, he asked if I was pissed-off at the way he'd portrayed me, I said no, he was more than entitled to write it any way he saw it . . . and we promised to get together when next he came West.

Some time later, he did, and we got together at MGM where I was working. At that time, Herb talked about having done the Geis novel, and I ventured the opinion that it was not a particularly healthy book, from the outlook of a writer's self-analysis. It was a book of self-loathing. Herb didn't talk about that too much.

But the money was rolling in, the book had freed him of the rigors of his past and his unsuccessful marriage, and he was now in the process of reaching maturity; adjusting to a life style that included fame, money and women. Lots of women. In a strange sort of way, I think I now see, Herb Kastle had come relatively late to success, and he was trying to live the life he thought *I* lived. In some ways he had perceived correctly about me, for I, too, have always been cannibalistically hungry for serious recognition, but he had overlooked a core truth. I had *always* been poor and driven, he had had critical acclaim and middle-class comfort; when I began to "make it," it came slowly, in gradual stages, like taking immunization shots of rattlesnake venom so when the big bite came, I sickened, but did not die. Herb, on the other hand, was trembling with the venom from a massive overdose all at once.

On the inside cover of my Bantam paperback copy of CAMERA, he wrote this, in 1969: "Harlan: Here are a few beasts who cried sex at the heart of love. You could say this novel was the first step away from KOPTIC COURT toward MOVIE MAKER & the three Bernard Geis novels that will follow. Wonder if I'll ever turn back again. Best wishes, Herb Kastle."

It *was* a turn away from the heart of love about which Herb Kastle had written so feelingly. THE MOVIE MAKER had a raw and bloody fascination, but it was a book of self-hate and the horror of self-discovery. I could only hope Herb would find his way out of the swamp.

We didn't see each other again for some years. His next novel, MIAMI GOLDEN BOY, was published with the same hoopla as THE MOVIE MAKER and, the wheel turns, the wheel turns, it came my way as a review assignment for the *Los Angeles Times* Book Review Section. I read the book, and thought it was rather undistinguished, the sort of thing one comes to expect from Bernard Geis sexploitation writers, hardly the gleaming jewel Herb Kastle had proffered in years past. I reviewed it honestly, but not harshly. I did a full takeout on "schlock" novelists, rating them from the best of the species—with Herb, James Michener and David Slavitt (Henry Sutton) at the top, down through Irving Wallace, Herman Wouk, Leon Uris, Harold Robbins and others in the mid-rank to "troglodytes" like Jacqueline Susann and Taylor Caldwell in the sub-cellar—and apparently, again without meaning to do it, I influenced Herb's life because the review caused MIAMI GOLDEN BOY to sell better in Los Angeles than anywhere else in the nation. Pickwick could not keep it in stock.

And Herb read the review. He read it and he heard the tone of sadness for the Kastle-who-had-been.

We talked of it on several occasions. And he told me MILLIONAIRES, the third of the big-money books he'd "gone into business" to write so he could break free of his old life, was a better book. He hoped I'd like it.

I did. It was strong, determined, honest, and yet held all the commercial elements that mean big paperback reprint sales, movie deals, attraction for the under-the-hair-dryer set.

He had taken a direction with his talent he knew was dangerous, but apparently he had come back from the edge at the final tick of midnight. Herb Kastle has always seemed to me a writer who possessed that rare inner vision to know truly what he's writing, how good or bad it is, what its worth to posterity and to his own self-esteem is, and to thank god not even the $100,000 rolls in the hay of success could take that from him.

Now it's 1973, and Herb lives out here. He's writing movies, he's living in a beautiful home, he has the life style his adolescence demanded and his maturity finds supportable. He went into and came out on the other side of a mutually destructive love affair with a woman who forms the model for Ellie in the new novel. He wrote the book with ferocity and the need for purification of system one gets from a sauna bath, and it reads with the drive and fire of a man who has glimpsed a personal hell and decided not to burn.

But he walks in here and tells me I'm the one who brought him to this place, at this time; and I shudder to think he genuinely believes it.

I am not his god, or his mentor, or his stalking horse. I did whatever was done without even thinking of the life and soul of Herb Kastle. And that's the bottom line about elevating mere mortals to godhood: gods are as liable to hurt as help, and because they do not understand the enormity of their power, they make no distinctions between the two.

And so, even as Herb wrote ELLIE as an open letter to be read by that one woman, as I wrote last week's column on friendship for that one friend to read, so I write these words about the folly of ever letting oneself be totemized by one's friends or fans or acquaintances. And I tell you to your face, Herbert D. Kastle, I reject the office. Keep it for yourself.

And since I've run out of space this week, I'll resume the chronicle of godhood, and about how I made the mistake Herb made in worshipping another human being, the week after next. Next week I want to talk about the animated film festival at the L.A. County Museum of Art, since it opens next week and if I wait it'll be dated. But come back for some light chatter next week, and the week after that I'll tell you how my personal god shoved a flaming stick up my ass.

Bless That Pesky Wabbit

19 April 1973

Sitting in a screening room at the L.A. County Museum of Art several weeks ago, I had this swell time. I'm out on the road as I write this, explaining the ethical structure of the universe to college students from Wisconsin to Hanover, New Hampshire—students who couldn't give a shit—and since I don't even understand how to operate my ten-speed, you can imagine how perceptive and pithy are my observations about the universe—so the students are absolutely correct in their apathy—and my thoughts keep pulling back to that darkened screening room and the swell time I had, so I'll tell you about it, in hopes you'll go to the Museum and have a swell time yourself. Watching cartoons.

Perhaps, for a fantasist, which I like to call myself, the Eighth International Tournée of Animation at the Museum (13 April–5 May) transcends the massmind definitions of animated film: escapist entertainment for children and the bored. Perhaps I'm a fantasist today *because* of the cartoons I saw when I *was* a child. Perhaps neither is strictly true, only partially . . . and the real truth is that as an observer of the film medium I adore the animateds because they seem to me the products of delightfully fevered brains, that they display a much freer sense of imagination than movies as a whole, that they are a kind of adytum of the mind's secret lusts and peculiarities, that at core the basic nature of comic art is to inform a special deranged rigadoon of Freudian/Jungian catharsis. Or perhaps it's just that I love cartoons a whole lot.

The nice thing about animated films is that even if they're esoteric images laid end-to-end, you don't have to worry about understanding what's happening, the way you do with live-action films, because you are permitted by history to dig them solely as cartoons. Thus, the intellectual pressures are removed; Sisyphus can, for once, not only let the boulder roll assovertea-kettle down the hill, but can lounge around chucking pebbles after it.

Something occurs to me. Before I get into the lovely specifics of the Tournée (as run for me in extract by Ron Haver of the Museum), I'd like to pounce back on that offhand remark about who I am today being at least partially (but probably significantly) as a result of cartoons. And therein, to find a "meaningful" reason why you should scamper like a roadrunner to the Museum to catch the festival of animation.

I've written about it elsewhere, in stories and essays and suchlike, but never really in this column . . . but my childhood was singularly fucked. (Which should come as no surprise to those who view me today as singularly fucked.)

We lived in Painesville, Ohio, a dreadful little hamlet thirty miles northeast of Cleveland, my Mother, my Father, my sister Beverly and myself. I was always alone. (Beverly, with whom I no longer have even minimal human congress, is eight years older than I and represents virtually everything in this life I find detestable in human beings. She married and went away from Painesville pretty quickly, so much of my childhood was spent without even *her* shrike presence in my *Weltansicht*.)

There were very few Jews in Painesville. For the initial, formative years of my youth at Lathrop Grade School there were no other Jewish kids my age. It made a helluva difference in the way I grew up; one wouldn't expect it, necessarily, but anti-Semitism was an ingrained attitude in Ohio in those days, the Forties. Kids really believed what their parents told them: that Kikes Killed Gentile Babies and ground them up to make matzohs for Passover. (Not true.) (Or if we do, we *always* remove the U.S. Keds before cooking them.) So the kids were ruthless to me. Utterly bestial. Of course, I didn't help engender much affection in them, I was a snotty punk of a kid who thought he was infinitely brighter than even the best of them. (True.) (With or without U.S. Keds.)

So I had no friends: was always alone. And when they got around me, they liked nothing better than to beat the shit out of me. Some time in this column I'll go into the specifics of all that, and I'll tell you about Kenny Rogat and Jack Wheeldon and my friend Tony Brown and Leon Miller and the birthday party no one came to, and the big pond down behind the Colony Lumber Company, and the nature of revenge . . . don't forget to remind me to tell you about that one day real soon.

But anyhow, I had no friends. Not for the first six or seven years in Painesville, till other Jewish families either moved in or began copping to their Semitic origins. So I was alone. In a world that I felt hated me, that held nothing but animosity for me. Add to that loneliness the random factors that I was a very tiny kid, a Munchkin really, that I was already reading the classics and AN INTRODUCTION TO GENERAL SEMANTICS by Lord Alfred Korzybski (introduction by S. I. Hayakawa) while the rest of my classmates were heavy into LAD: A DOG and STAR THIRD BASEMAN by John R. Tunis, and you can easily perceive that I had need to find a better world into which I could flee.

The world I made for myself was bounded on all four sides by fantasy. On the North, it was old-time radio programs—*Jack Armstrong*; *The Shadow*; Lux Presents Hollywood; *Quiet, Please*; Fred Allen; *Land of the Lost*—on the South it was pulp magazines—*G-8 and His Battle Aces*; *The Avenger*; *Doc Savage*; *Blue Book*; *Argosy*; *Startling Stories*—on the East by comic books—*Airboy*; *Plastic Man*; The Spectre; Hawkman; The Pie-Faced Prince of Pretzleburg; *Capt. Marvel*—and on the West by movies—Val Lewton's terror films; Wild Bill Elliott as Red Ryder with Robert Blake as Little Beaver; Laird Cregar as *The*

Lodger; William Eythe and Veda Ann Borg and June Preisser and Don "Red" Barry and Lash La Rue . . . that whole crowd.

And very particularly, the cartoons.

No week was complete without a Saturday afternoon matinee marathon of two "B" features, a singalong, a newsreel ("the eyes and ears of the world"), an Edgar Kennedy or Pete Smith specialty, maybe a James Fitzpatrick TravelTalk and . . . six cartoons. Popcorn, a Sugar Daddy and a Tootsie Roll the size of a massage parlor cordless vibrator (not the shriveled weenie they offer for 25¢ today, mere adumbration of the glories of old) . . . those were my staples through the wondrous worlds populated by Bugs Bunny, Mickey Mouse, Yosemite Sam, Daffy Duck (who was my particular favorite) and an endless pride of shrieking, scuttling, mayhem-prone cats and mice. Not to mention (from later, from 1956) that sensational frog who was entombed in the cornerstone of a Warner Bros. cartoon building till the day he was released by a poor *schlep* of a construction worker and leapt forth singing, "Hello mah honey, hello mah baby, hello mah ragtime doll . . ." His name was Michigan J. Frog.

Cartoons were a universe wherein the natural laws of physics did not apply. They were a pre–Tolkien Middle Earth in which the lesson could be learned that if you walked out over the edge of a cliff, you could continue walking or even stand suspended in midair, as long as you didn't look down, suddenly realize there was nothing under you, and didn't panic. In its cockeyed way, it was an unforgettable lesson about the nature of fear; I always knew, in the Abbott & Costello films, that as long as Lou Costello didn't know he was afraid, the monster killer would not attack him; from the moment of having learned that lesson in movies, I have always known nothing could hurt me if I wasn't afraid of it—street thugs, mad dogs, poisonous snakes, intimidating salesmen, the whole gamut of terrifiers who can reduce us to jelly.

They were a Narnia, an Erewhon, a Lilliput of bright colors and simple ethics. They made clear and telling points about greed, venality, courage, friendship, self-sacrifice, casual injustices of regimented systems and, for better or worse, they helped form the exoskeleton of my attitudes toward life, success, my friends and myself. Cartoons, the animated morality plays of my childhood, helped forge me in the furnace of escape from a bitter and unsupportable reality.

Is it any wonder, then, that I plead with you to go to the L.A. County Museum, to the Leo S. Bing Theater (Fridays at 8:00 P.M., Saturdays at 2:00 & 8:00 P.M., Sundays at 3:00 P.M.), to witness in all its magnificence and lunacy just how far the genre of the animated fantastical has come since I sat in the darkness of the Lake Theater in Painesville, Ohio . . . is it any wonder indeed?

(Admission is $2 a throw for kids, students and both Museum and American Film Institute members, $2.50 for anyone else coming in as general audience, and worth every krupnick of it.)

For the record, the fact sheet Ron Haver gave me says this: "The International Tournée of Animation is a non-profit endeavor on the part of film makers involved in various aspects of producing animated films. Their goal is to expand the audience for this art form and to provide the bridge between the public that wants to see new horizons in film and the film maker who wants his ideas seen and heard. . . .

"The nature of conventional film exhibition stacks the cards very much against short films. The full-length single feature consumes all the program time in theaters. The double-feature squeezes the short film out as well. What shorts do survive in theatrical exhibition are too often innocuous trivia, sports exhibitions, travel and adventure provided by travel and tourist agencies.

"The serious film, the experimental film, the way-out art film are left adrift in a confused distribution sea."

So if you're a lover of the animated film—and only a soulless beast could be otherwise—the Museum offers an opportunity to climb into that beautiful pea-green boat adrift on the confused distribution sea, to squiggle down in a comfortable musty seat in Mr. Bing's theater, to delight and revel in a twenty-film program of 101½ minutes duration, to view again with the eyes of a child, yet the mind of an intellectual, the splashcolors and freak images of the animators, before the Tournée end its run here in May and goes on the road (American Film Institute Theatre in Washington, D.C., Walker Art Center in Minneapolis, Chicago Film Society, San Francisco Museum of Art, Stanford University and the Pacific Film Archive in Berkeley).

Merely to lure and totally capture me, merely to turn me into a slobbering prosyletizer, Haver ran 65 minutes out of the total 101½, and I commend to you the following:

The Mad Baker (USA, 9½ minutes) by Ted Petok; an unforgettably hilarious send-up of all Frankensteinian mad scientist films. "They said I was deranged at Escoffier when I tried to graft a chocolate chip cookie on a hot cross bun . . . they said there were things Man was never meant to know . . . experiments better left to God . . . well, I'll show them . . . have a Girl Scout cookie . . . I don't think you need to ask what they're made from . . . heh heh heh . . ." If I get back to Elay before the Tournée ends, I'm going back to see that one: I was laughing so hard through most of it, I missed half the funnies. Oh, *do* see it, it's worth the price of admission all by itself. Petok is a goddam certifiable furry-eared madman with a talent for transmogrifying cliché to his own nefarious purposes that borders on genius—a border separating the nations of genius and berserkdom. In the future, I would walk a mile, scamper two miles, drag myself on broken and bleeding stumps *ten miles*, not to miss a Petok cartoon.

The Candy Machine (USA, 4 minutes) by George Griffin; a paranoid trip into subway surrealism with a lurking figure who is the archetypical molester, a carnivorous candy machine, a brilliant technique of animation that looks like crazed Crayolas run amuck, and a subcutaneous ominousness that pervades whole areas of the Tournée.

Tup Tup (Yugoslavia, 9 minutes) by Nadjelko Dragic & Zagreb Film; which is *The Candy Machine*'s paranoia hyped to a breathtaking degree. This Oscar nominee is a nightmare vision that seems to say modern society drives one mad as a mudfly and that one's toad-self can only be Princed by anarchy & suicide. Very sexual, very phallic, very odd, very frightening, hardly a Saturday morning teevee slip-in between *The Banana Splits* and *Scooby Doo*.

Propaganda Message (Canada, 14 minutes) by Barrie Nelson; capturing in animation the utter stupidity of regional chauvinism and the false karasses of ethnic bigotry, all whipped at you in a kind of bilingual Lou Meyers cartoon look.

There's an 8½ minute *précis* of the Oscar-winning *A Christmas Carol* from Great Britain, based on the original steel engravings from the Dickens classic; a 40-frames per foot smashcut image-trip called *Frank Film* by Frank Mouris that leaves one sense-blind for minutes after it's faded; another of the hilarious and lecherous Murakami–Wolfe adventures of the Amorous Jean Navarro, based on a fable by Chaucer; a first film by a student at the San Francisco Art Institute that combines "surrealism, metamorphosis, dimensional change, absolute control of image and design in motion." And that's only the jive *I* saw. There's so much more it would take another column to talk about it.

But if I haven't wooed you sufficiently with what I've set down already, surely nothing can send you off to the Museum, to your everlasting sadness: if you never learned the life-lessons the animated films have for you, there is a dead place in your soul that can never be irrigated by the laughter and wonder of cartoons. And I feel soooooo sorry for you.

For the rest of you . . . GO! And to Ron Haver, the Museum, and all the wondermecks who brought these films forth from their individual lunatic asylums of imagination . . . thanks a lot. It was nice to flip back to kidhood again, even while staying an aching adult.

Interim Memo

IF WRITING THE INTERIM MEMO FOR INSTALLMENT 22 WAS tough, this one has been a serial killer.

The events related in this essay happened in 1961. I wrote this column in 1973. It was a long, hard twelve years between. It is now 1989, and when I came to this place in the manuscript, I realized I had to do something about it.

Because, in the last few years, the man I call Scarff in this piece and I have drifted back into each other's company. It isn't the way it was in 1952 or '53, when we were a high school kid and a young New York writer. Nor is it the way we were when I was an editor and he was coming in to take over my job, in 1961. But we're talking again, and seeing each other every once in a while, and I guess that's a different degree of friendship.

The point is: I couldn't just run this piece the way it had first appeared, with these patched-up circumstances. I had to either drop the installment, or send it to him to refresh his memory, and ask his permission.

Which I did, today. We talked, I FAXed Installments 22 and 24, and just waited for the word. Here is the totality of his response:

Dear Harlan:

I hated reading it. I hated reading it the first time.

I never declared bankruptcy. If I had, putting "everything in my wife's name" wouldn't have done the slightest good, since everything has always been in both our names.

Billie found out about the other woman by some other path, not from me.

I made more money as a freelance that year than Bill paid me in salary. I even lent you some of it.

Bill told me I was the editor and you were being done the favor of an extra month's salary, but you were NOT to do any business whatsoever; you were there to fill me in on things in progress, period. He told me you knew that.

Go ahead and run the damned thing. I'm friends with you now, as usual.

Troubling Thoughts About Godhood, Part Two

26 April 1973

*T*wo weeks ago, before I left on the lecture tour that finds me tonight, writing this in Philadelphia, I was talking about friendship and the perverse ways in which we raise friends to godhood, and expect from them a nobility we do not ourselves possess; and then how we bleat and cry when they turn out to have feet of fecal matter.

I talked about how it had happened to me, how I'd been put in that position of obligation, and how I hated it. At that time I promised to tell you about the reverse, about the time I raised a friend to the holy state and how he fucked me over. From this story, one would hope, you will derive a valid object-lesson that will save you from the same pain. Maybe not. None of us excels in remembering our mistakes. We keep making them over and over, like brute beasts, somewhichway in this area dumber than the lowest paramecium that, if burned, will shy away from fire for the rest of its brief life.

It begins in the early Fifties, when I was a high school student in Cleveland, having just discovered science fiction and realizing that all the other gigs at which I had played—acting, singing, stealing—all of them were five-finger exercises for me, that I wanted to be a writer, wanted very little else than to be a writer, would settle for no other life than that of a writer. A number of professional writers became my friends, and several of them were extraordinarily kind to me, "taking me under their wing," so to speak.

One of those writers became a close friend, in the way an acquaintance of nearly the same generation can best become a close friend: as an older brother. As I had no brothers, and my Father was dead by that time, the guy filled a very particular need in my life. Someone older, more experienced, kind but watchful, someone who was a perfect role model. He was a fine writer, in the early stages of his career but already widely-published and highly-respected. He had a fascinating family background, had been on the road and adrift in the world long enough to be street-wise, yet cynically optimistic. And he seemed to love writing as much as I did. He talked writing, lived the life of a writer (as I'd always seen it in my fantasies), and wrote like a demon. He was clearly on his way to a brilliant and long career. But he was only a few years older than I, and so I was able to relate to him not as a distant and Olympian literary figurehead—the way I viewed the imposing literary bulk of a Salinger or a Hemingway—but as, well, what I said: a knowledgeable and witty older brother.

He came to visit in Cleveland and we chummed around; I went to New York to visit him and stayed in his apartment and was introduced to other writers, even attending a gathering of the now-legendary Hydra Club, New York's professional sf society. I met the late Willy Ley and Robert Sheckley and Fletcher Pratt and Katherine MacLean and H. L. Gold, who was at that time the editor of *Galaxy* magazine, and Phil Klass, who is "William Tenn," and Harry Harrison. It was a stellar crowd, and I confess to feeling that I had at last found *my* people. I was hooked; it was the life of a writer for me, just as soon as I could get through college and blah blah blah.

You may be wondering why I haven't used the name of my friend thus far. Did it on purpose. Shadow of bad things to come. Let's call him Scarff, just for the sake of convenience: those who knew us then, and know me personally now, will know to whom I refer. The rest of you need never know. He's still around, and as the finale of this epic will demonstrate, there is no further need for either of us to know the other, so there's no purpose served in offering him up as gossip.

Well. I went off to college, still writing, still pulling rejection slips from editors. But Scarff was handy when I needed reassurance. I'd write a story and send it to him and he'd do a heavyweight criticism of the attempt, and not once did he reply with a letter from which I failed to gain some sensible, workable data. Not silly literary theory, but hardcore *writing* information, like "You can't cheat a reader's need to feel you've actually created a whole character by describing him as 'looking just like Cary Grant, except with bigger ears.'"

I've saved those letters. They are some of the best teaching I ever had.

Is it any wonder, then, that I worshipped him? He was the perfect role-model. His ethics were unshakeable—he told me so himself. His skill and talent were obvious. His kindness was second only to his personal strength and willingness to share what he knew with a rank novice. He was, to me, an heroic figure. Competent as a Heinlein protagonist, knowledgeable as an Asimov technician, warm and funny as a Sheckley character, handsome and charismatic as one of Chad Oliver's pipe-smoking archeologists. And his girl friend was sensational.

Things went badly for me in college. I was a restless and distracted student, garnering grades so low they made a .083 average; the creative writing classes at Ohio State were virtually nonexistent and what there was, was so out of touch and off the wall it bore no relation to the real world of writing and selling. When I would be at my lowest ebb, I would call Scarff and he'd try to cheer me. And finally, when it became clear to both of us that college held no light for me, nor that it could inform in any way the career I had chosen for myself, he advised me to split and come to New York.

Shortly thereafter I did just that. I was thrown out of OSU for several good reasons—which I'll detail another time—and after a few months of regrouping my emotional forces, I went to New York. To become a writer, yuk yuk.

I mooched room and board for a while from Lester del Rey and his late wife Evelyn, two of the kindest people I have ever known; and stayed a while with Scarff in his tiny bachelor apartment in the West 30s. But he was pressed for space and so I moved out, moved uptown to West 114th Street off Broadway, and for the next few years we saw each other only intermittently.

His writing had slowed. Both in total output and in number of product. He had always been close to poverty—despite the excellence of his work—and he was forced to take on other kinds of jobs to keep going.

Time passed rapidly for both of us. I got married the first time in 1956, he married his sensational girlfriend somewhat earlier, I got drafted in 1957 and wound up in Chicago in 1959, working for a publisher who oddly came to have an almost Satanic hold on me. I didn't see or communicate with Scarff very much. I had been a selling professional for almost five years at that point, though I'd hardly begun to write what I've come to think of as my "serious" work; to that time, I'd been merely a journeyman, writing hundreds of thousands of words of pulp stories, learning my craft, finding my own voice. Scarff had virtually ceased writing. An occasional piece would surface, but nothing very long or very unified or very startling. It was sad-making, but hardly my place to pass any value judgments about the reasons he had slowed and stopped. He was working in advertising at that time, I believe.

Chicago was a bad time for me. My four-year marriage to my first wife, Charlotte, was coming to a terrifying and lunatic conclusion. I divorced her, went through six months of pure effort in an attempt to flush myself down a toilet, got my head straightened by a friend named Frank Robinson, himself a good writer, and returned to New York to pick up the pieces. Not yet sane, I met a lady, married her on the rebound, and found myself in 1961 back in Evanston, Illinois, working for the same publisher; but this time as editor of a line of paperback books I'd created.

When I finally came out of the fog Charlotte's descent into the maelstrom had visited on me, I looked around, found myself working for a man I despised, married to a marvelous woman whom I did not love, father of a thirteen year old son from her first marriage many years before, desperately unhappy with myself, and simply desperate to free myself so I could put myself back together.

I had, shortly before this point, come back into contact with Scarff. As editor of the Regency Books line, I felt an obligation to certain writers whose work I'd admired and felt had not been widely-enough circulated. To the end of providing good books to a wide audience by these writers, I published B. Traven, author of TREASURE OF THE SIERRA MADRE, Philip José Farmer, Lester del Rey, Clarence Cooper and, naturally, myself. And I contacted Scarff. He was living in dire financial straits in New Jersey with his wife and several kids, scuffling to make ends meet. He had declared bankruptcy and everything was in her name. I called him one day and reminded him of two books he'd done. The first was a realistic novel that had predicted the fall of the cities within the next fifty years. It had first seen print in a small edition from Lion Books, a now-defunct paperback line, in the mid-Fifties. I suggested he add the several subsequent stories that he'd written in the same world-scene, pad it with some new linking material, and I'd publish it as a new novel. The second I'd only seen as the first thirty pages of a manuscript about a prison break. It had haunted me for years. I offered him contracts on both books, at the top figure my publisher would permit.

He was effusively grateful, saying I was a godsend, and had come along at just the right moment. His family was hungry, the rent was unpaid, he was bogged down and disconsolate. I felt wonderful! I was able to help out the man I most respected and admired in the world. It was like paying back some of the joy and help he'd given me when I'd needed it.

He said he was coming out to Evanston, to see me, and he'd put the first book together before my very eyes. I felt that was a salutary attitude on his part. Perhaps at my house, seeing work and life going on apace, he would start writing again. I sent him the advance for the first book, and he came to Evanston.

Scarff stayed with me for many weeks. We assembled the first book and started to put it into work for the printer. He talked the second book. I pried the advance for the second book loose from the publisher, with great effort.

Then the fog lifted, and I decided I not only had to divorce my second wife, but had to flee Chicago–Evanston entirely. I arrived at that conclusion secretly, but during a long bus ride to Seattle, with my second wife, Billie, asleep some rows in front of us, during the darkest hours of the night, I confided the decision to Scarff. (We were on our way to the World SF Convention, 1961; Scarff had taken only part of the money I'd thought was "desperately needed by his family to live on" and sent it to them; the rest he was to spend at Seattle, using it to fete fans and strangers in an act of profligacy that unsettled me enormously, though my thoughts, clearly, were elsewhere. But it was then, cloaked in darkness aboard a Greyhound rushing through silence, that I set out the lures that were to show me how foolish I had been to visit on merely another flawed human being the responsibilities of godhood.)

I told Scarff of my intentions, and set about convincing him that he should take over my job at Regency Books. It was a well-paying job, several thousand dollars a month, a steady kind of artistically-connected work that could provide for him not only a stable and financially-solid situation for his family, but the kind of scene that might get him back to writing with self-assurance. He seemed reluctant, and tried to dissuade me. But not very hard, I realized later. He finally said if I could convince the publisher to accept him in my place, he would take the job. He then admitted that he thought my leaving Billie was a good idea. I swore him to secrecy, particularly from my publisher, because I knew I would need at least one month's wages to sustain both Billie and myself through whatever was to come in the next few months. He promised to say nothing. I felt secure; now I had a way out, a friend whom I could trust, a plan that would minimize hurt all around, and I was repaying my friend with a secure future for the help he had proffered in my past.

So I will not look like a bad guy, I will gloss over what next happened to me.

I was committed to severing the marital ties with Billie, and I became involved with a woman from my past. It was a stupid and weak thing to do, and I bear the guilt for it with little pleasure. But Scarff knew about it, because I told him, and when Billie came to him, he told her, precipitating a series of scenes and passion plays that came close to destroying Billie and myself.

While trying to handle that aspect of the separation—and I freely admit I handled it badly—I was trying to convince my publisher to hire Scarff as my assistant. He didn't want any part of it. He didn't like Scarff, felt Scarff had the wrong back-ground for the job, was irresponsible . . . in short, it was an uphill fight.

Finally, I got him to agree.

At that point, I feared Billie might tell my employer that I was planning to leave in a month. Scarff spent quite a lot of time playing to that paranoia. So I went to tell my publisher that I was going, that I had brought Scarff in to take over for me so there would be no break in the publishing schedule, and that I wanted a month on the job to train him. My publisher agreed.

I was slow coming to this conclusion, but I now feel I was handily manipulated by Scarff. From the moment he knew I was jumping out, from the moment he realized he might at last have the financially and prestigiously secure future that had eluded him all his days, he set about running me through a series of mazes, like a frantic rat. Telling Billie about the other woman; playing on my fear of being fired before I had the funds to cut out and still provide for the needs of Billie and her son; staying sweetly out of it save to move me closer and closer to the final decision.

And when it was all settled, that Scarff would take over for me in a month, I was clubbed with just how far he would go to secure the position for himself:

The Regency Books office was one room in a professional building in downtown Evanston. I had set up a small table on which Scarff would work during that month. When I came into the office the first working day of the week after I'd told my publisher, I found Scarff had moved all my papers off my desk, to the little table.

He had set up the editorial desk for himself. Phone calls would come in and be greeted as follows, by him: "Is this a business call or a personal call for Mr. Ellison? I'm the new editor here now, my name is Scarff." If it was a personal call, I was permitted to take it, if it was business—even if Scarff had no idea what it was about—he intruded himself and handled the call. All of my projects were re-shaped to his own designs.

For those who ask, why did you put up with it, I can only suggest that I was in a state of shock that he had even *done* such a thing, was rewarding my friendship with such a blatantly anarchistic maneuver, that I was being fucked over by someone I'd treasured and loved as a man of high ethic and purpose. Add to it that I was in a personal quandary about my wife and the other woman, and there was much of the somnambulist about me. Also, much of the weak and cowardly. It isn't always possible to look good when retelling the pivotal incidents of one's life.

I took it for less than a week, and quit.

Because of not having the money I needed, four years of bitter struggling and poverty lay ahead for me, and for Billie. I arrived in Los Angeles with her and her son, with ten cents in my pocket. It was a period of pain and scuttling like an animal to keep her in decent surroundings (we had separated and I had to come up with the rent on two separate apartments), while trying to break into films and television.

Everyone survives. Somehow, even if they suicide, everyone survives 🎓. I came through it and made a career for myself in the visual media, Billie remarried, to a fine man who has made her happy, and Scarff went on from Regency Books to a job at *Playboy* and then on into public relations work. He still lives in Chicago, with his family.

There's a punch line, however. It keynotes what happens when a god turns to a monster for one who stupidly worships.

Many years later, when editing an anthology, I contacted Scarff for a story. Though I despised him, I had lost no respect for his work as a writer (Again, I reiterate, one should never confuse the artist with the artist's work.) He promised to do a story for the book, said he needed some money, and if I'd send him an advance of $100 he'd write the piece in the next few weeks and I could send the balance of the payment when I accepted the story. It had been so long since Scarff had written *any*thing except PR puff for a pickle manufacturer, I sent the $100 immediately.

He never wrote the story.

The book went to press and he never returned the $100, money that was taken from the pockets of other writers who could have realized greater advances on the work they *had* produced for the book. Again, I was bitterly disappointed, and again I felt like a patsy.

I never worked very hard at trying to get the hundred back. I confess to a sickness of soul that made me turn away from all thoughts of Scarff, who now loomed as large in my world as a detestable example of a man who would sell out his friends for security as he had loomed in godlike adoration.

I did hold back some small royalties on a story we had written together, many many years before, a story published in a book of collaborations I'd done with fourteen other writers, but it was pennies and would never total the hundred he'd taken. And besides, it was too late to use the money for the other writers in the anthology.

That was the way it stood till several weeks ago.

A writer of my acquaintance contacted me for Scarff's address. Said he wanted to buy one of Scarff's earlier novels for a possible movie deal. I told him to hold off for a few days, that

I'd get the address to him but I had an old score to settle and wanted to use the deal as a lever.

Then I called Scarff and told him about the movie deal, about the potential money involved, and told him if he wanted me to make the connection he had to write the story he'd promised me years before, to be included in the final volume of the anthology, that had grown out of proportion into three big books.

He said I was blackmailing him. I said he was correct.

There was a protracted silence on the line between Los Angeles and Evanston. And then that familiar bemused snicker I knew so well.

"This is really ugly," he said.

"Isn't it?" I said.

"I really can't believe you'd do this," he said.

"I learned from the master," I said.

Then he began talking about the first fifteen pages (or some lie like that) of the story he'd started for me, years before. He said he'd go down into his basement office and dip the dust off them, and try to finish it for me. I was very polite, I think. I said that was swell, and I'd be happy, on seeing and accepting the story, to pay him at a handsome rate, any amount beyond the initial hundred he'd already gotten, so he'd make the full advance payment.

"Why don't I just send you the hundred back?"

"Because I don't want the hundred, Scarff. Money isn't what's between us and you know it. I want you to have to anguish to write that story."

(Now I wonder if I wasn't still trying to save him from pickle publicity . . . but that's a nobler instinct than I care to ascribe to what I was doing. I wanted revenge, and I wanted him in pain.)

"I'll get back to you," he said, and hung up.

I was both sickened and joyous. It was one of the ugliest things I'd ever done.

Several hours later he called back.

"I don't want any part of this; it stinks," he said.

"That's right, it does."

"I'd rather pass on the movie deal . . . if he wants the book badly enough he'll find me," he said. "I'm sending you a check for a hundred dollars."

"Very noble," I said. "Floating ethics serve you well."

I hung up.

The check came in last week. I'll cash it and put it to work on the anthology Scarff would have appeared in. It'll pay some other writers who *can* write. I don't take Scarff's revulsion at the blackmail proposition as an act of purity on his part. I take it as a reluctance on his part to assume responsibility for the monster he created in me that would permit such a ghastliness even to be considered.

But the lessons I've learned—that I hope this story teaches you—are many. And valuable. Incredibly valuable. They've made me, in some ways, a tougher and less likeable fellow. They've made me become very realistic about what it takes to buy someone's soul. They've strengthened my resolve never to sell out a friend, no matter *what* the price.

And the sad part about it is that Scarff still doesn't know what kind of a human being he was dealing with. I *never* would have kept him from that deal. I never intended to, not for a moment. But I knew he would *think* I would. Because that's where *his* gut is at.

The writer who wants to buy your book is Stephen Kandel, Scarff. He can be reached either through my agent, Martin Shapiro of the Shapiro–Lichtman Agency in Los Angeles, or through the Writers Guild of America, West, in L.A. I gave him *your* address after I spoke to you the first time.

Good luck, little godling; because god knows you'll need it. I'm going to take a shower.

Interim Memo

THERE WAS AN EVEN BETTER STORY THAT CAME OUT OF MY TRIP to Billings, Montana—where this installment was written. Exactly the kind of berserk life-experience about which I speak in this piece. But it hadn't happened as I sat in a Holiday Inn (or whatever it was) writing this column. It happened later that night, and when I tell people about it they get the special look I describe herein, that look of *This guy is lying in his teeth.*

You see, the night of the day I wrote this, I gave an evening lecture at Eastern Montana University, and someone in the audience took a shot at me. It's a long story, and one I'll save for another book, some other time. But I've recounted it hundreds of times since it happened; and every time I tell it, someone gives me a hoot for making up bullshit.

Now, when I married Susan, and she commenced traveling with me to my lectures, and she began hearing these seemingly berserk episodes from my past, her eyebrows went up. She loves me, so she never once said, *Oh, c'mon, gimme a break!* but I could tell that I was stretching her credulity.

Until—and this happened again and again—I'd tell some wild experience, and unbidden, someone would jump up in the audience—just as I described it in the essay—and yell, "He's not lying! I was there when The Hole In The Wall Gang, all one hundred of them, came charging at him with six-guns blazing!"

And Susan came to understand that yes, this lunatic stuff had, in fact, honest-to-spinach, happened. But the one story she found a little dicey, was the Billings, Montana episode where someone got off a shot at me while I was in the middle of my lecture, right there in an auditorium jammed to the walls with Montanans.

Until we made a pit stop at the International Superman Exposition in Cleveland, last year, 1988. I was standing with Susan in the hall of the Cleveland Convention Center, middle of June, talking to Tony Isabella and Bob Ingersoll, and up walked a woman I didn't recognize at first, and she smiled and said, "Hi, Harlan, remember me? Sue Hart, I brought you to Billings for a lecture and they took a shot at you on the stage. Remember?"

And my wife, Susan (not the Sue who'd walked up to us), gave a hoot-hoot-hoot of *eureka!* and squealed, "Ohmigod, it *did* happen!"

I rest my case as to veracity. For the record.

Where Shadow Collides with Reality: A Preamble

11 May 1973

*F*or the record. One of the dumb expressions. For *whose* record? Who the hell is keeping track? What a paranoid phrase: as if one day we'd be called on to make an accounting. Shades of Joseph McCarthy and Reagan's subversive list (whereon your gentle correspondent's name appears). Also a grotesque manifestation of ego run mad. As if anyone gave a damn where someone stood on the smallest issue. God (or whoever's in charge) knows we ignore the "record" most of the time; we continue to elect thieves and reprobates and moral salamanders; truth to tell, most of the nits who use the phrase, "for the record," a hundred times a month, would re-elect Nixon tomorrow, in defiance of the "record." So. It's a stupid phrase, and I hereby move we stop using it in our daily speech as though it had some significance, and further, that we cease to allow politicians and other mainliners to use it. Now that I've gotten *that* off my chest . . .

For the record, I'm writing this in Billings, Montana. I'm on my way home from the lecture tour, and by the time your beady little marmoset eyes read this in the *Freep*, I'll have been home for a day or two, recuperating, and thanks a lot I had a nice time, but don't bother to call, I've got work to catch up on.

Perhaps one day soon I'll do a column or two on what it's like being on the road for a month, lecturing at colleges, hustling business at publishing houses in New York, riding the Amtrak Metroliner between N.Y. and Philly, the joys of Dartmouth, the anguishes of science fiction conventions, the pains of knowing you lost not one but *two* Nebula awards *a priori* and then having to be a cheerful and witty toastmaster at the banquet where others get the goodies, the rain in Wisconsin which is seldom on the plain; I'll write about Max and Karen and Bettina and the Countess Von Sternberg from Brooklyn and Susan and Denny and Ann and Stephanie and Andrea and Dana and Doxtater and the loons at Dartmouth who had a "Harlan Ellison Look-Alike Contest" and a "Nubile Co-Ed Availability for Dinner with Ellison Contest" before I ever got there, thereby making it a foregone conclusion that I was a sexist swine and effectively putting me beyond the pale of any human relationships. Perhaps I'll write about that, one day. Perhaps not. I wouldn't want to bore you.

And besides (and here we come to the nubbin of this week's ruminations on the state of the universe), when I rather matter-of-factly relate the weird and fascinating experiences that seem to happen to me in carload lots, I keep being accused of making up stories out of whole cloth to perpetuate some deranged charisma myth about my loveable self. And it's that I want to talk about today: shadow and reality, witnesses, and all the lies that are my life.

Look: I lead this really dynamite, interesting life. I tell you that not merely to make you miserable in your own wretched existences, but to set forth what I've come to believe is the mark of success in life:

You're a success if you live a life that brings you as close as possible to the dreams you had when you were a kid. Whether it's to be a cowboy or a movie star or the best goddam milkman in the world, if it's what you dreamed of being when you were a tot, and you're doing it now . . . you've made it.

I always wanted to be a world-famous writer. Well, I'm a world-famous writer, and I love it, and I'll be damned if I'll dig my toe in the dirt and do an aw shucks number. Or, as Zero Mostel said in *The Producers*, "When you've got it, baby, flaunt it!"

And *because* I'm living the best possible kind of life I can lead, I have adventures. Now maybe my adventures aren't as wild as Cousteau's or Lawrence of Arabia's, or even Mailer's, but because I'm a good storyteller, I can see the plot-line in the daily occurrences of my life, and when I retell them, I try and put a punch line to them, to tie them up dramatically the way I would a story. Now I'll grant you that this kind of minor rearrangement of the time-sequences, emphases and insights is akin to lying, but that's what I get paid to do: lie professionally. And it sure beats the bejezus out of the dull, random manner in which life feeds us our experiences. So, in a very special way, everything I ever relate about how I live my life is a lie. Or maybe "lie" is too harsh a word. "Fib" is closer, but I suspect Vonnegut's "foma"—harmless untruths—is the best. 🎓 I never change the facts, just the way they are colored or arranged. I'll never tell you I won if I lost, I'll never tell you I was a good guy if I was a bad. But there's a bit of the imp in me, and if I add a flying fish or troll to an otherwise ordinary tale, it's only to make you a little sunnier and happier as you move toward the grave. How can you condemn a man for such a noble and humanitarian activity?

On the other hand, there are times when truly amazing

adventures befall me, solely due to my fearless wonderfulness and the core truth that I have more charisma than even the Pillsbury Dough Boy. And when I later go back and recount such exploits, there are bound to be those who say, "That crazed fucker is lying in his teeth."

At which point I say, "Just ask Avram Davidson. He was there when I stood off an entire Italian street gang in Greenwich Village." Or I say, "Just ask Bob Silverberg. He was there when the drunken Puerto Rican came at me with a busted Rheingold beer bottle, quart size." Or I say, "Just ask Mariana Hernández—she's my secretary—because she was there the morning I fell face-first into my bowl of chocolate Malt-O-Meal."

And it's those witnesses whom I adore, because they rig the line between my fantasies and my reality. Truth to tell, friends, I've long since given up trying to differentiate between the two. My fantasies seem so much a part of my world, I can't tell where the shadow leaves off and the substance begins.

And since I intend to launch off on a series of these tales, I wanted to lay the ground rules this week, so you'd know what to expect. And to offer witnesses who can be contacted to prove that what I say is pretty much the truth.

I do this not so much because I really give a shit, but because Chris Van Ness at the *Freep* tells me he's had a few complaints about the column. People writing or calling in saying, "Who the hell cares about this Ellison schmuck and whether or not he was a pimp in Kansas City." Well, to begin with, I was never a pimp in K.C. Or anywhere else for that matter. But I *was* a hired gun for a wealthy neurotic in Cleveland, when I was a teenager, and it's a pretty good story, which I'm going to tell you next week, and I simply feel the time is ripe for us to understand what this column is all about, and what it's *not* all about.

Maybe I should have done this twenty-four weeks ago when the *Hornbook* started, but it never occurred to me that there would be people who objected to being entertained.

That's what this column is all about. Entertainment. I'm not a political columnist, nor a literary critic, nor a historical analyst. I'm simply a writer, a storyteller; if you read this column expecting to learn great lessons about Life, or expect me to explain the Natural Order of the Universe, forget it. Jack Margolis, poor Jack who's getting his ass kicked by various and sundry because he's a sexist, *that* poor Jack who never copped to being anything *but* a sexist so how can you revile him, friends, well, he's into saying meaningful things from time to time . . . but I try not to. It's long been my feeling that a writer who sits down to write The Great American Novel usually winds up writing The Great American Shitpile. Too self-conscious. You can read great pronouncements about the condition of life in our times by Reagan and Unruh and all sorts of others from Ann Landers to Billy Graham, and maybe that's what you need to enrich you; but as for me, all I want to do in these little journals is entertain. Make you laugh, make you cry, make you wait. As the English novelist Charles Reade said.

If that isn't good enough for you, why simply turn to another page of the *Freep* and get uplifted or informed. But I'm confounded by readers who can't be amused by foma, who want every stick of type in this paper to be heavy, redolent, *festooned* with import. It's like a female editor I met in New York, whom I referred to as an "Editrix," for a gag. It was to giggle, but a feminist in the crowd hissed and made a nasty to-do about it. Well, shit, friends, anything that can't be made fun of, *anything*, *any*damnthing, is doomed to sink of its own humorless weight. You've got to *laugh*, dammit! You've got to find giggles throughout the day or simply fucking *die*! Why the hell do you think so many deep-thinking intellectuals watch re-runs of *Gilligan's Island* on the sly? Because they've got to lighten up.

Well, that's what this column is. A lighten up.

And if you find that an ugly, or a waste of space, well, just consider that the space might be used for rectal suppository ads or as promo for The Clint Eastwood To Replace John Wayne As Reactionary Sex Image American Patriot Hero Figure Committee. On the other hand, it might be used to run something worthwhile, so *that* argument doesn't hold.

All of which brings me with very little linear sense to the end. This week. Oh, I'll be back all right. Until the shrieks outnumber the sighs of joy. But as long as Kunkin & Co. permit me to journal out my days in small parcels, the *Hornbook* will continue to try to outrage, tickle and lie to you.

But *next* week I'll tell you about how I packed this .25 Beretta for Al Wilson when I was seventeen years old, and if you don't want to laugh, then you can either go fuck yourself or read Chris's record reviews.

And if you need a witness, call Ben Jason in Cleveland. He was there. So was I. And next week, so will you.

When I Was a Hired Gun, Part One

25 May 1973

*T*o be read in the style of a Dashiell Hammett story, featuring Sam Spade, "the hardest-boiled private eye of them all." Move it.

I was once a hired gun.

Restrain mirth, and zipper your pudding-trough, and I'll lay it on you how it came to pass that a seventeen-year-old kid wound up packing a .25 Beretta for a pseudo-wealthy neurotic paranoid. (Yeah, that's right, it's the same model Beretta that Bond packed in the early Fleming books, till armaments experts pinned him to the wall with the skinny that that particular model automatic is a "ladies' gun" about as effective in stopping a determined thug as a hatpin, which I didn't know at the time, or I'd have crapped with terror.)

It was 1951, Cleveland. I was going to East High School, a pretty tough school even for those *Blackboard Jungle* days, and I was into science fiction. I was a charter member of the Cleveland Science Fiction Society, calling ourselves The Terrans. We'd gone from one member's house to another with our meetings, until one week an *outré* dude named Al Wilson showed, and offered us his pad for a regular meeting place.

It was a converted dentist's office over a supermarket, on the second floor of a building somewhere around East 125th Street and St. Clair Avenue. Some of the facts blur, it's over twenty years ago; but the substance is precise.

Wilson looked like a Martian to me. At least, what I had always seen represented in sf magazines as a Martian: skinny, large head, receding hairline, big eyes. He was, to me, a weird and fascinating man. He was into the Fortean Society and all its unexplained phenomena, Korzybskian General Semantics, heavyweight physical sciences, occultism, and he filed his socks under "S" in the filing cabinet. His place was a rabbit hole for me, and I fell down that hole willingly because my Dad was recently dead, I was lost and miserable, doing rotten in school, relating only to science fiction and the emerging world of sf fandom. So Al Wilson came around at just the right time. He wasn't close enough physically or emotionally to be a father image for me, but he was the guru I needed at just that time.

So I started hanging around Al's place all the time. He had a Multilith machine right in the middle of the floor, a Varityper for typing up issues of the club newsletter, and stacks of erudite and obscure books, like Tiffany Thayer's novels, Fort's studies of "excluded facts," what they called "a procession of the damned," James Branch Cabell, Lord Dunsany, Lovecraft, Lincoln Barnett . . . that whole crowd. There was a cot in the middle of the "apartment." No sheets. Al slept whenever he felt like it, ate whenever he felt like it, operated off no known clock.

One day, after I'd been playing Roo to his Kanga for some months, Al sat me down and asked me if I wanted a job.

I was seventeen, my Dad had died leaving my Mother and myself not too well off, we were living in a resident hotel on East 105th Street, The Sovereign (where Joel Grey also lived when he was Joel Katz), and the best job I'd been able to get was in a bookstore. "How much and what do I have to do?"

"Two hundred a month and you'll be sort of a bodyguard for me. Run errands. Be around when I need you."

I looked at him. Weird eyes looked back.

Al Wilson worked on the assembly line at Thompson Products—or maybe it was Fisher Body in East Cleveland, I don't remember exactly—and I knew he made a good wage, but *two hundred a month* for a gopher?

I said okay, and went to work for Al Wilson.

I didn't tell my Mother. She was always a little leery about those oddball sf people I was hanging out with, and if I'd told her I was making fifty a week, without deductions, for body-guarding a Martian, she'd have . . . well, she'd have done what she did later. So I kept it quiet and slipped a few bills into her purse when she wasn't looking. Made up in a small way for all the money I'd stolen out of her purse when she was sleeping.

I ran peculiar errands for Al Wilson. Food, sometimes, which wasn't peculiar, but books of a *very* peculiar nature other times, and strange messages to even stranger people. Then one day, Al brought home a package and unwrapped it on the feeder ledge of the Multilith. I came over and watched; it was a gun. And a shoulder holster. "What's that for?"

He looked at me with those weird eyes and said, "You'll need to wear this from now on when you're running errands for me."

"To the supermarket?"

"You'll be flying out this week. Other things."

So I started packing the heat. I thought it was funny; and I dug playing pistolero. Sue me.

He also said, "From time to time I want you to scare me." It was in one of those moments when Al wasn't goofing or being weird. It was one of his pathetic moments. He was a lonely man leading an isolated life, he'd been married and divorced long before—even though he was only in his thirties—and now he was all alone inside his skull, thinking things no one else could understand, making friendships slowly, trusting no one. I didn't ask him what he meant, I *knew*. He wanted me to feed his strangeness, whatever that was.

So I would leave, during the dark of the evening, and I'd go down the long hall and down the stairs and go outside and around the side of the building and there, where they'd rolled up the awnings that shaded the big display windows of the supermarket, I'd climb up the ratchet bar that raised and lowered the canvas awnings, and I'd stand on the rolled-up awning, which brought my face to just the level of the second storey window, and I'd make hideous sounds and tap on the windows and scream and scare the hell out of him.

Did he know it was me? Of course he knew. He'd asked me to do it, hadn't he? Move it.

Peculiar errands. "Take this briefcase and go to a man in Cincinnati whose name I'll give you, and hand it to him and tell him the key to unlock it will come under separate cover by another route. If he asks you your name tell him it's Roger Conroy, and spell it for him with two 'y's'."

Peculiar errands. "I have this canister of fulminate of mercury," he said to me one day, showing me a large canister of fulminate of mercury, which explodes on the slightest friction or shock.

"Jesus Whirling Christ!" I said, with a decibel count that could have gotten me a booking as the PA system for Madison Square Garden. I jumped eleven feet nine inches and came down running. Eventually he collared me and said I had to dispose of it. "You're outta your meso-po-tam-i-an mind," I said, feet still running, body held aloft, "no way I'm gonna get near that stuff. That's *dangerous*, Al! If it goes off there won't be enough of me left to slip into an envelope and mail back to my Mummy."

So we did it together. We took a bus out Euclid Avenue to what used to be called the Nottingham area beyond East Cleveland. There was this idyllic little pastoral setting, all trees and low hills, right near a shopping area, and running through it, about three hundred yards from Euclid Avenue, which was the main thoroughfare bisecting the heart of Cleveland, was Euclid Creek. Pre–pollution time, it was a sort of park where people went to lie out under the trees and read, play with their children, walk their dogs, nice place.

Al and I got down from the bus, walked down the slope to the Creek, and Al uncapped the canister he'd been carrying in a paper bag. Those of you who know what fulminate of mercury does on contact with water will know what happened next. You will also understand that I had (and have) a *very* inadequate grasp of chemistry.

But Al should have known! (That has always been one of the big mysteries about him: he clearly *did* know a whole hell of a lot about science . . . why *didn't* he know what would happen? Or *did* he?)

He tossed the protective canister into the Creek and we turned to go, when the GODDAMNEDEST FUCKING GIGANTIC CATACLYSMIC KRAKATOAN EXPLOSION!!! (East *or* West of Java!) went off and that bloody canister came erupting out of the Creek with a waterspout that drenched us both. And hurled the canister right back at us as if King Neptune had got it right in his kisser. Al grabbed for it, and chunks of mercury were all over the grass, sputtering and exploding and sparking and banging away with a million tiny reports like the Lilliputian militia on maneuvers. He grabbed the canister and *flung it back in!*

"No, no!" I screamed, but Al was busy picking up the bigger chunks of mercury with his bare hands, burning the shit out of himself, and whipping the exploding chemical back into the Creek.

This time it went off with a series of explosions like giant firecrackers, and the canister came up out of the depths skipping across the water like a spasming submarine. I ran like a thief.

Behind me, last thing I could see, was Al Wilson, a deranged Martian elf, scampering around grabbing up burning mercury with his hands throwing it into the Creek . . .

In the distance I could hear police sirens . . .

I didn't see him for a week, but when I went back to his pad, he made no mention of the event, and I didn't comment on his bandaged hands. Peculiar errands.

Then Al fell in love. Oh god.

He came home one night after working the swing shift, and his face was almost beatific with light. Seems there was this girl working a couple of lathes down from him, and he hungered for her soul as no one had hungered since Paolo and Francesca were condemned to an eternal fuck in THE DIVINE COMEDY. He set me to the task of shadowing her, to finding out where she lived. So I went to work with him one day, he pointed her out to me, and I came back when his shift was ended, and followed her. On the bus. I don't remember where it was now, this many years later, but it was one of the suburban tract house areas. I tracked her for a week till I was pretty sure I knew her habits, and then I asked Al what he wanted to do about it.

"I don't know."

"Well, why don't you just go up to her and ask her for a date?"

"I can't. I'm afraid."

"Oh, Al, for Christ's sake!"

"I can't. I need you to make an introduction for me."

"*Me?!?*"

"Sure. I'll send her a gift, and you'll be my John Alden."

"Oh, Gawd! Miles Standish was an asshole, Al. No wonder Priscilla Mullins flopped for John Alden. Do it yourself."

"No, no. I've made up my mind. I'll send her a special gift and you'll carry it for me and you'll tell her all about me. She'll like you."

Seers, savants and soothsayers will perceive what came next.

So will dummies.

I came waltzing up to this girl's house one evening, carrying Al's "special gift." All set to make the big pitch for the Martian. Now, you may ask, what special gift did Al Wilson, who thought like none of us, maybe not like anyone else who'd ever lived on the Earth, select for the girl of his sex dreams? A brooch, an amethyst necklace, flowers, a five-pound box of cherry-filled chocolates, an ermine cape, a complete set of the works of the Brontë sisters, a gift certificate for a year's worth of McDonald hamburgers, a diamond ring . . . ?

Al Wilson had bought her an eleven-pound steak, had it wrapped in plastic, and had mounted it on an expensive Swedish serving tray.

Don't ask and I won't have to talk about it.

"Al," I'd said, "what the hell kind of a gift is *that* to make an introduction?"

He insisted that was what he wanted her to have. Today, that might be a wild gift, the cost of meat being what it is, but this was in the early Fifties and a slab of meat was just plain *crazy*. But I took it. I was working for him.

Up to the door of the house, rang the bell, waited. She came to the door, opened it, and looked at me. Did I bother to tell you she was a sensational-looking girl?

"I was wondering how long it would take you to say hello," she said. "I've been watching you follow me home for a week."

Dwell on that for a while. I'll finish this next week.

Interim Memo

THE CONCLUSION OF THE STORY ABOUT AL WILSON TAKES CARE of itself; but a month elapsed between the original publication of parts one and two. And I make reference to intervening events. Here's what happened to *those* sidebars:

1. *The Starlost* went on the air, over the NBC owned-&-operated stations. 20th Century–Fox screwed me, screwed the production, didn't have it filmed by Sir Lew Grade in England, but rather laid it off on a Canadian company. It was a *terrible* series, and I talk about what happened in an essay titled "Somehow, I Don't Think We're in Kansas, Toto" that originally appeared as the introduction to PHOENIX WITHOUT ASHES, a novel based on my Writers Guild Award–winning pilot teleplay. The novel was published as a paperback original by Gold Medal in 1975, and was excellently written by Edward Bryant. It is now out of print (but may return soon). The essay, updated and expanded, can be found in two places: STALKING THE NIGHTMARE (1982) and the thirty-five year retrospective THE ESSENTIAL ELLISON (1987). So I won't take up space reprinting it again here. If you're curious, you can find it. A nightmare.

2. The novel based on *The Dark Forces* didn't get finished. Pinnacle didn't publish it. The tv series went through script development—another year out of my writing life—and the network gave it a pass. "We don't think the audience wants to see sf or fantasy," they said. That was 1973–74. They knew, with the intelligence best capsulated by critic John Simon in the phrase ". . . as vast and mysterious as the inside of a noodle . . ." that the American audience was turned off by sf and fantasy. And they were proved as absolutely correct as they always are, by the utter disinterest of the American audience in *Star Wars*, three years later; as they have been by such films as *Alien*, *Close Encounters*, *E.T.*, *Brazil*, *Roger Rabbit*, the *Star Trek* films, *Batman* and maybe a hundred others since 1973–74; such unarguably immutable disinterest that brought back *The Twilight Zone* and has become even more concretized, to the extent that sf and fantasy films now hold almost all the boxoffice records. How could I have ever doubted their keen insights and informed extrapolations?

3. My mother died. I write about that later.

4. Not only were the charges of strike-breaking against me dismissed, but in the extensive hearing set up according to Writers Guild rules (chaired by the famous Christopher Knopf), an unprecedented censure of the Board of Directors was handed down. Much of the background of this incident— mentioned so casually in my column, as it was just unfolding at that time—is related in the essay about *The Starlost*. Suffice to say, in this life, the two most despicable things you could call me—that I would sooner put a bullet through my head than *be*—are scab or plagiarist. I had not, in any way, hindered our strike. I had, in fact, resisted all blandishments and threats on the part of the studio, had even gone so far as to thwart their machinations to get *another* writer to do the work I refused to do; and had gone to Canada at the direct instructions of the Board of Directors (hence the investigatory committee's censure), and with grave misgivings.

5. And "Catman" can be found in my collection AP-PROACHING OBLIVION. And so much for updating. My, how time flies.

When I Was a Hired Gun, Part Two

28 June 1973

Since the June 1st edition of the *Freep*, wherein I told the first part of the story of how I was a hired gun for Al Wilson, back in 1951 when I was seventeen . . . many strange and wearying things have happened to me. My sf tv series, *The Starlost*, goes on NBC in September, and I've been commuting between L.A., N.Y. and Toronto, writing scripts and working with Canadian writers who'll write *other* scripts; I've written half a new novel that Pinnacle Books will release in October, the first of *The Dark Forces* series featuring my sorcerer Kraiter and based on yet another tv series I've sold (in collaboration with Larry Brody); there was a writers' conference in the wilds of the Michigan woods; there was the news of my Mother's near-death in Miami Beach (and I'm still sweating *that* one out); I've been brought up on strike-breaking charges by my own union, the Writers Guild—and I'd as lief not go into *that* one, friends, it makes me too angry to articulate, but it'll work out, never fear—I am secure in my own ethical behavior—and I wrote two new stories, one 15,000 words long and the other 5,000. The former is in response to an assignment to write the "ultimate futuristic sex story." It's called "Catman" and you'll find it in a forthcoming anthology titled FINAL STAGE. So. All of that is the reason I haven't been able to tell you what happened with Al Wilson and my being a hired gun.

But I'm back now, and here we go again.

If you recall, last time, I told about how I'd been hired by Al, a wealthy neurotic, to pack a Beretta for him, be his errand boy and general all-around companion. Al was a tot weird, if you recall, and when he fell in love with a girl who worked the same shift at Fisher Body in Cleveland, he decided I would be his John Alden to the swing shift Priscilla Mullins. His "love gift" was a huge slab of meat on a wooden platter. I'd been following her for days, to find out where she lived, and to give you an indication of how suave a secret agent/shadower I was, when I rang the doorbell and she answered, she said, "I was wondering how long it would take you to say hello. I've been watching you follow me home for a week."

Then she invited me in. She introduced me to her Mother. "Oh, you're the one," her Mother said. "We were going to call the police about you." I guess I giggled nervously.

"What's with the steak?" the girl said.

"Ah-hmm. I am a messenger for Mr. Al Wilson, who works with you at the plant. Mr. Wilson, who is a very shy man, but a very nice man, would like to come calling. He has sent me and this small token of his respect and admiration as a calling card."

They looked at the steak, then they looked at me, then they looked at each other.

"I think we should call the cops," her Mother said.

"No, no!" I said, my voice rising. "This is strictly legit. Al is just, well, you know, really quiet and bashful about women, and he's seen you every day at the plant and he didn't know how to strike up an acquaintance."

"You related to him?" the girl asked.

"I work for him."

"Doing what?"

How the hell do you tell two total strangers that you are a hired gun. I mean, for chrissakes, I had *zits* . . . I didn't look a *thing* like Dick Powell or Bogart or even, god help me, Audie Murphy. I was just a kid with a dumb steak in my hands.

"I run errands for him. He has money."

That seemed to brighten both of them. "We'll cook it for

dinner," the Mother said. "Why don't you stay?" said the girl. So I stayed. The night.

We talked through most of the night, the girl and I. It is not by chance that I keep calling her "the girl." After twenty-some years, I can't recall her name. What I do recall is that she tried to get me to take her to bed, and I was a virgin, a *scared* virgin, and most of that night was spent in consummate horror of being deflowered. You must grasp that I was seventeen, had never even *kissed* a girl, and the idea of that lush creature and myself in a bed filled me with nameless terrors H. P. Lovecraft never imagined.

I fled the next day, in company with the girl, with whom I rode the bus back into Cleveland. When she got off at Fisher Body, I kept going and would gladly have motored right out of the state if it hadn't been for having to report back to Al.

He wasn't home when I got there, so I guess I went off to school. But at the end of the academic day I took the streetcar out to his apartment on St. Clair Avenue, and waited for him. When he showed, I thought the first thing he'd ask me was what had happened on his love mission. But he didn't. He told me he had a *vital* errand for me to run, that he'd been out getting me plane tickets, and I was going to Cincinnati.

"Don't you want to know what happened with the girl and the steak?"

"Oh, sure. What happened . . . but be brief."

So I told him she seemed like a nice girl (I didn't mention that she wasn't terribly bright, as far as I could tell) and that she seemed responsive to his overtures (I didn't mention that she had spent the better part of the night trying to reap the dubious benefits of my post–puberty tumescence) and that he should call her.

I wish I could tell you they got married and had nine kids, or that she had spurned him in a flamboyant scene, or that he had killed her, or she killed him . . . but the truth of the matter is that I never heard another word from Al about The Great Love Affair of the Century.

Instead, I readied myself to go to Cincinnati.

(An Author's Note: after the first section of this reminiscence was published, I received a call from an old friend of twenty years' standing, Roy Lavender, formerly of Ohio, now living in Long Beach. Roy remembered Al, remembered the period I had been working for Al, remembered, in fact, things *I'd* forgotten. You can perceive with what joy I took that call after the long preamble I had written about people thinking the weird things that happen to me are fever dreams made up on the moment. Roy is a living verification of what I've set down here, and he gave me some facts about Al I never knew. He also pointed out that the contents of the container Al threw into Euclid Creek—as reported last installment—was not fulminate of mercury but, rather, metallic sodium. Hence, the explosions. Roy also reminded me of the time Al was beset by a group of juvies from the area, who came up over the grocery awning to rip him off and beat him up in the apartment, and how Al beat the shit out of them, at one point using the handle from the Multilith press to slam a kid so hard it lifted him off through the window into the street below. Stay healthy and live long, Roy Lavender: you are my last touch with proof in this important life-experience.)

Anyhow. Al handcuffed an attaché case to my wrist, gave me a hundred bucks, and sent me off to the airport. I made a mistake, however. It was a school day, and I stopped off at the optometry shop of my brother-in-law, Jerry, at East 9th Street and Prospect in Cleveland, to tell him I was going out of town and would be back the next day. Now, my family has always considered me something of an irresponsible, not to mention a dreamer who might as easily come home for dinner as show up ten hours later with a story that I'd been kidnapped by puce-colored aliens from Proxima Centauri who had kidnapped me and taken me for a ride in their motorized garbanzo bean through the reaches of deepest space. So when Jerry saw the attaché case handcuffed to my wrist, he thought I was into another big lie, and he instantly called my Mother, to tell her to stop me at the airport.

Thus, when I got there, I was greeted by cops and airport fuzz who yanked me off the flight, searched me—they couldn't search the case, they didn't have a key—and finally had to release me, because I was legitimately ticketed.

I went to Cincinnati, really pissed at my Mother, and ambivalent as hell about my role in life. Was I, in fact, Ashenden the secret agent, or was I a punk kid who needed his Mommy's approval before he could have an adventure? Not in the least ameliorating my feelings was the memory of Al's words as he'd handcuffed the case to my wrist:

"Be careful. There are people who will try to take this away from you." At that moment I decided to leave the Beretta with Al. Good thing I did: can you imagine the looks of lively interest on the faces of the airport cossacks?

When I got to Cincinnati, I took a cab to the address Al had given me, where I met Don Ford, a science fiction fan (now, sadly, deceased) I knew casually, but whom I knew to be a friend of Al's. He unlocked the cuffs, took the case into the next room, and came back to offer me the hospitality of his home for the rest of the day and that night. I had no idea what was in the case, but Roy Lavender advises that Al Wilson, for all his weirdness, was a man who had invented a method for producing steel directly from iron ore without going through the pig iron stage. He had contacts in South America and in Newfoundland, and apparently there *were* big business interests that were willing to stop at very little to get the secret.

None of this did I know.

But when, the next day, I went to board the plane back to Cleveland, someone took a shot at me.

Okay, okay. I'm dreaming. Have it your way. All I know is that as I crossed the tarmac to board the plane—in the days before those access tunnels that take you from the plane's passenger cab straight into the terminal—I heard what *sounded* like a gunshot, and a hole appeared in the fuselage of the plane. I may be making that up. I didn't wait around to ponder the equation. I bolted past everyone else, shoved me widdle way up the gangway and was inside that liner before that pre–Sirhan Sirhan could get off another.

When I got back to Cleveland, I tendered my resignation.

It had been a brief but fascinating sojourn in company with

the mysterious Martian, Al Wilson, but I suddenly realized I had a deep-seated aversion to bullet holes in my as-then-sexually-unexplored cuteness.

Al reluctantly let me off the hook, said he would miss me, and we went our separate ways.

There is a memorably resonant afternote, however.

I never saw Al Wilson again, save once.

I was in Philadelphia in 1953, there for a sf convention, and on a dead Sunday morning, while everyone else slept off the effects of having drunk themselves into stupors the night before, I went looking for an open breakfast nook. You may have heard how dead Philly is on a Sunday morning. The reports are hardly exaggerated.

But as I walked the street seeking a breakfast counter, I saw a man walking toward me. As we neared each other, I recognized him as Al Wilson. I stopped. He came straight up to me, as though he'd known I would be there, and had hurried to meet me. There was no preamble, no greetings between two people who hadn't seen each other in years. He merely came in close, looked straight at me with those faintly protruberant eyes, and said in an undertone, "When you see Stan Skirvin, tell him to examine pages 476 to 495 in T. E. Lawrence's THE SEVEN PILLARS OF WISDOM."

Then he walked past me and was gone.

I have read those pages in every hardcover and paperback edition of Lawrence of Arabia's book ever printed: I have never found the slightest clue to what mystery may be therein hidden.

But I'll tell you this: Al Wilson walked out of a chill Philadelphia morning in 1953 to *tell* me that, and I'll be damned if I don't believe that if I can ever unravel what he meant, I'll be *rich*, Willy Loman, *rich as Croesus*!

And that's the story of how I was a hired gun.

Honest.

A Rare, Kindly Thought

12 July 1973

Waxing philosophical is not one of my favorite pastimes. Ever since I was let down by Eric Hoffer, I've realized virtually any clown with a sesquipedalian command of the English language can write a book of "philosophy" and get a following of dregs to chant his or her brilliance to the academic skies. Look at the Skinnerians. Saddening, really, how easy it is to dupe a large contingent of lames and wearies, get them to accept a "philosophy of life" *in toto*. The no-neck nits who followed Senator Joseph McCarthy into the witch-burning arena; the millions and millions of Americans who refuse to accept the responsibility for their own existences and follow Nixon even when they know he's a thief, a liar and a self-server; all the poor bastards who are into Jesus Freakism because they can't face the world as it really is and haven't the stamina to change it for the better; Existentialists, Solipsists, Berkleyites, Sybarites, believers in Atlantis, flying saucers, reincarnation, Catholics who clap their hands in adolescent delight at the Reaffirmation of the Doctrine of Papal Infallibility, crazed reactionaries who cling with unsupportable paranoia to the Threat of the Communist Menace; and all the phonies who went from dope to Zen to the Maharishi to Baba Ram Dass to macrobiotic dining to astrology and don't know where their next savior is coming from. All of them, the poor fuckers, washed here and there like flotsam on the inexorable tide of Life. Believing. Having nothing to succor and recommend them *but* their beliefs. Proselytizing and chanting and stumbling ever forward toward lightless deaths in which they will certainly find *none* of it carries the spark.

One guy even wrote *me* a letter telling me I had The Word and he wanted to be my Follower. Sooner would I have the clap for a thousand years than stalk about spouting The Word. On him I wish a plague of toads in his bathroom.

However, I did have an idle thought the other day, which I guess comes under the heading of "philosophy."

I'll probably have to wash my mind out with Lava for even venturing that this idle concept is philosophical, but it seemed to me a particularly gentle and humanistic thought, so I'll share it with you. It's not often I have these damned things, and while it probably isn't profound in the Nietzschean sense, it may permit you to love a few more of the walking-wounded around you than you'd thought possible; and if it serves no other end . . . well, the time is well spent.

What it was, was this:

Those we call "phonies" may not, in fact, be phonies at all. They may merely be poor suckers who don't know who they are. They may not be trying to "put on airs" but may simply be lost souls who haven't established their own personal ambiences. The universe lets us know it ain't easy; these days especially. Everywhere you look, someone is telling you how to dress, what to wear, who to associate with, what to listen to, how you should think and react and feel . . . and that's an ugly pressure many people can't handle. Whether you call it Future Shock, or Cultural Ambivalence, or Alienation, what it means is that most of the people you meet in a day—and probably the both of us, if we'd but cop to it—are spinning. They don't know what to believe, or how to act to be "cool," or what is currently in or out. If that weren't the truth, how do you account for the hypes of "acts" like Johnny Winter or Nazareth or Alice Cooper, none of whom can hold a moment of fascination for an intelligent human being with taste, while Bach and Scarlatti go on and on and on?

I will cop to having been a phony so long, it's become my real skin. Now. That out of the way, I can point out that there are people who are so confused as to their true nature that they *seem* phony because they're never the same two days running. Take a joker like Buddy Greco. Good singer. Nice voice. The poor slob is so confused about who he is, has *always* been so confused about it that instead of getting his own sound, he emulates other, more successful singers.

When folk singing was in, he sounded like a solo Kingston Trio. When Sinatra was hot, he sounded like a surrogate. When Bobby Darin was popular, Greco dropped all the "g's" off his words (grammatically, it's called apocope) and ran that number. Now he's into country-rock. He isn't a phony, despite the Sicilian cufflinks and the white-on-white shirts. He's merely confused. He hasn't got enough personal strength to find out his true name and go with it; for good or ill.

The same for several dozen friends of mine, nice people all, who move from apartment to apartment and change their phone numbers so often they have permanent deposit on file with Pacific Telephone. When it was drug culture time, they came around and espoused the joys of honking kitchen cleanser; when flower power was preeminent they were seen on The Strip with garlands of hollyhocks, festooned with beads; when it was Dissent Time, they always saluted with a balled fist from their freshly-coral-waxed cars; now that greed and taking care of number one are the in-trips, they have become the most venal and despicable slugs in the garden. They're turning Republican.

For the most part, I can't bring myself to hate them. Forgive them, Father, they know not who they am.

They are searching for a skin to wear. For a hat that fits them comfortably. For a scene that won't reject them in six months when it ain't chic no more. In the truest sense of the word, they are seekers.

Formerly, a great number of those tagged "phonies" were gay. That was their lot. They were forced to play at roles that didn't suit them. Things are a little better now. They can declare and find life-niches that joy them. I wish them God-speed and good luck. The same for many women I know. Shoehorned into socially-acceptable sets, they railed and wept and felt strictured. Now, for them, things can be different, too. But for the mass of men and women who don't know what they want, have no idea what they're capable of doing, conceive of no enrichment beyond that which is programmed by their society, there is no way of coming out of the closet. They must search and search, stay a while in this scene, stay a while in that scene, and if they get very lucky, they find a face behind which they can hide with security.

So I have to separate the "phonies" into two major groups. Those who know who they are and find something loathsome in the self-image, and so *consciously* adopt another mien. I know a writer who, if left to his own devices, with no one peeking through his curtains at night, would live a life of television, bowling, McDonald's hamburgers and *Mad* magazine. He's a sentimental person who secretly digs the effusions on Hallmark cards and cries at movies about dogs, God and paraplegics. But he knows the world he wants to move in would label him a square, so he watches only educational programming on the Living Arts of Japan, has learned to play backgammon (which bores the *ass* off him) in Beverly Hills, studies the wine list at Scandia and orders the correct vintage straight out of a supplement in *Esquire*, and actually *reads Esquire*, something I haven't been able to do in years, though I have five years remaining of a twenty-year subscription. He has confided that he is dismally unhappy with his lot in life, that he doesn't know where he's going or what he eventually wants to be, and when I suggested that he is playing a mugg's game by trying to emulate life styles not his own, he shrugs off the answer as too simply structured, and continues looking for The Holy Grail. It's a no-price life.

The other group, and larger by far, is comprised of those who aren't phony at all, who are simply trying to find a way to get through all the days and nights of their lives without suffering too much. They believe what is told them, they wear those gawdawful platform shoes that make them look like clubfoots, they read Jacqueline Susann or Kurt Vonnegut with equal aplomb because they're #1 on the *Times* list, they laugh at Rodney Dangerfield or George Carlin and make no distinctions for originality or imagination, and the dreams they dream belong to others who have had them first and deserve them. They are the Wandering Jews of our Times.

Someone said to me, the other day, about a woman we both knew, "She's such a phony." And I started to agree, and just as suddenly stopped, because the thought—the "philosophical" thought, if you will—I've explicated here hit me. She isn't a phony. She's just spent all her formative years trying to be the kind of woman one guy after another with whom she's been involved *wanted* her to be. It's made her sly, cynical, unhappy, undependable, giddy, a thing of bits and pieces. She isn't phony, she just doesn't know who she is.

And when I thought that, it was as though someone had drained all the dislike out of me for that person.

Try it. Maybe it'll work for you.

Obituaries are terrible things, and I hate them more than I can say. But yesterday, Sunday the 8th, Gene L. Coon died. He was a writer. He was the Producer of *Star Trek* for a while, and we served together on the Board of Directors of the Writers Guild, and he was as good a man as I've ever met. He was enormously kind to me personally, and he was a rarity in this cesspool of an industry: he was an honest, caring human being with taste and discretion and imagination and vast pools of love. He spent much of his life unhappy, and only got happy during the last few years. That his joy should have been cut off so suddenly, so without warning, merely causes those of us who knew and admired him to rail at a Thug God whose list of motherfuckers and thieves ought to be so filled he wouldn't have time to gather away from those of us who treasure them, one of the few good guys walking around. For those who knew him, who even met him once and drew pleasure from his existence in a frequently loveless world, this is a lousy week. As Dorothy Parker once said of someone else, we will not soon see his like again.

Interim Memo

REFERENCE IS MADE IN THIS PIECE TO A TEN-THOUSAND-WORD essay I did on the films of Val Lewton, and the uses of fear in films of terror. If you have a copy of my collection OVER THE EDGE (1970), you'll find it reprinted from its original publication in *Cinema* magazine, 1966. Chances are, you don't have OVER THE EDGE, because it's been out of print quite a while; and the new edition—which has been under contract to Stuart Schiff for some time—though not as long as the *Hornbook* has been hanging fire—is still being revised. (I'd have handed in OVER THE EDGE: *The Revised Edition* a long time ago, but Stuart is holding out for the new centerpiece of the book to be a novella I've been working on for many years, a story called "Bring on the Dancing Frogs," which may well be the pinnacle achievement of my storywriting. But it is an extremely complex and challenging piece of writing, and not until this year have I had the time to sit quietly, without a million distractions—such as earning a living—and painstakingly think it through to completion.) So you can either read an abbreviated version of the piece in AN EDGE IN MY VOICE (1985) or wait till next year when Stuart Schiff publishes OVER THE EDGE.

The Swigart bibliography noted herein . . . well, it's long out of print. But rumor has it that a 1000-page updated edition is working its way toward publication sometime early in the '90s.

3 Small Pleasures for a More Endurable Existence

19 July 1973

From time to time, I like to share with you some special things that make life a little more pleasant to endure. Books, films, places to eat, people you ought to know, a strange thought or two. This week, I'll go for your senses of sight, taste and imagination with a new movie, a sensational Castilian restaurant, and a new publishing venture that came to me as a birthday present.

First, the movie.

Elsewhere, in print, I've raved about the films of terror produced by the legendary Val Lewton at RKO between 1942 and 1946. (And for those who know little more than that about Lewton, I recommend VAL LEWTON: THE REALITY OF TERROR, by Joel E. Siegel, Viking Press, 1973, $6.95.) I once did a long critical essay in *Cinema* magazine about Lewton and how his films captured the essence of *terror*, an emotion quite different and infinitely nobler than that snared by *horror* films or monster epics. Terror is a difficult feeling to evoke on film—usually it turns laughable—and only Lewton (regularly) and a few others (occasionally) have managed it. For every sillyass *Night of the Lepus* or *Frogs*, there have been a dozen *Creature That Gnawed on Pittsburgh* abominations, and neither group shows much imagination or intelligence.

And "intelligence" is the operative word for classics in the genre of terror, because the evocation of terror entails the drawing on subliminal and ancient fears in an audience. Universal symbology, universal fears, Jungian memory, disquieting imagery, these are all passports to the land of terror for the scenarist concerned with doing more than jumping out of a secret panel and shrieking "Boo!" at Mantan Moreland.

The horror and monster flicks go for the cheap shot; they are on the Erich Segal level of competence and they leave no residue of fear. They are the sort of nonsense used by boys with terminal horniness to get equally as simple-minded girls to cuddle close in Chevys at drive-ins. For the *cognoscenti* they are a bore, if not an affront. But a well-wrought and intelligent film of terror is a delight to behold, a shiverful experience that never quite leaves you. *Repulsion, Psycho, The Haunting*, the original *Dracula*, Pinter's *The Servant, Séance on a Wet Afternoon* and Lewton's *Cat People, The Leopard Man* and *Isle of the Dead* are all classic examples of what I mean. They tread the thin line of tolerable terror and touch common tones in the psyche that cannot fail to immobilize even the most jaded horror movie–goer. Their ilk is rare. Not since Lewton has any single creator been able to bring it off regularly. Polanski comes closest, but even there I find a soul-sickness that repels as much as attracts.

Yet one man has been working in this idiom for years and is only now coming to be recognized as a master of the form. The reason is a fairly simple one. For many years he wrote films of "horror" for American–International and was hamstrung with wretched casting, inept production, low-budget and wholly unimaginative budgets and the interference of exploitation moneymen. Even so, several of his early films remain high water marks of the genre, and at a recent L.A. County Museum retrospective in conjunction with the Writers Guild and the American Film Institute, there was sufficient material to put on a three and a half hour show that brought a standing ovation from the audience. Just this year, for the first time in all the years he has worked in film and television, this splendid writer received a Writers Guild award for Most Outstanding Teleplay. And long overdue, I might add.

This is beginning to sound like one of those banquet

introductions where you try painfully to conceal the name of the guest speaker whom everyone knows, till the last two words. I will end your suspense. He is the man who wrote *Duel* and *The Night Stalker* for television, the man who wrote *The Raven* and *The Comedy of Terrors* for AIP, the man who wrote the novels THE SHRINKING MAN and I AM LEGEND, and the man who has written the most truly terrifying film of the past ten years, and his name is Richard Matheson.

His latest film, which you *must not miss*, is *The Legend of Hell House*. It will scare you as nothing since *Repulsion*, *Psycho* and *The Haunting* scared you. In a season when *Scream, Blacula, Scream!* and *SSSSSSS* and *The Boy Who Cried Werewolf* are released to no notice whatsoever, *The Legend of Hell House* emerges as one of the most brilliantly conceived and executed films of menace ever put on celluloid. Matheson wrote the script from his novel, HELL HOUSE, and under the direction of John Hough it becomes such a potential winner for the ailing 20th Century–Fox Studios that one hopes they will not cast it out merely as another exploitation sleeper.

With absolutely stunning performances by Pamela Franklin (whom you may remember as one of the children in the film version of Henry James's "The Turn of the Screw," *The Innocents*), Clive Revill, Roddy McDowall and even Ms. Gayle Hunnicutt—who, previous to this, demonstrated roughly as much thespic ability as a rutabaga—a gorgeous rutabaga, granted, but a vegetable nonetheless—the film trembles from moment to moment with an unbearable tension that cannot possibly leave you unmoved.

Every sneaky and scream-inducing craft trick of the terrorist has been used by Matheson, and unless you have been lobotomized you will not be able to escape the fright and helplessness of immobility brought on by scenes such as the poltergeist dinner party, the attack of the cat, the ghostly rape, the discovery of Belasco, the sexual sleepwalk of Ms. Hunnicutt, the shadow in the shower sequence, the discovery of Dr. Barrett by his wife . . . oh, it is to go on detailing every incident. This is, in short, a film of superlative measure. One of those twitchers that will live in the dark spaces of your imagination for years to come.

And what a delight to see Matheson turned loose after all the years of his work coming forth at only half-speed because of circumstances over which he had no control; to see him on tv and in film, finally unleashed. I predict that if the Powers That Purchase hire Matheson and let him do what he does best, unfettered, in the next decade we will see a body of works of terror that will ultimately rival the best of Lewton.

Second, the restaurant.

Juan Jose's La Masía (9077 Santa Monica Boulevard, 273-7066) is a treasure. It is easily on a par with the last smash dining spot I recommended, *El Palenque*, the Argentinian restaurant on Melrose. This time, I offer you the exquisite wonders of Continental Castilian cuisine, and if you've come to trust my palate from your encounter with *El Palenque*, you will perceive I mean no hype when I say this *boîte* can't possibly stay uncrowded for long. So go there, and tell them I sent you, but keep it to yourselves otherwise. Because if the Scandia crowd hears about the quality and the prices, *we'll* never find seats.

La Masía looks like a garden doorway between Tana's Restaurant and The Troubadour, but once you enter you are pulled gently into an ambience of dark woods, low beamed ceilings, hanging plants of almost Rain Forest lushness, graceful and facilitous table service, and food that is brought to your table so hot that it steams. This last may not seem like such a telling point in the restaurant's favor, if you are one of the debased creatures raised on McDonald's slopburgers that come to you tepid from under the infra-red heating lamps, but for those of us who savor cuisine prepared with love and craft, the concept of a cheese sauce still bubbling when it reaches the table is enough to cause almost orgasmic tremors. All this, however, is serendipity.

For it is the brilliance of the menu itself that will draw you again and again to La Masía. Dishes prepared with those minute extra touches of culinary imagination, variants on staple and familiar dishes that have paled in lesser dining spots, creativity in areas where only the chefs and the owners could know that care and *lagniappe* have been considered.

Let me tell you of a typical meal I had there last week. It was shortly before Lynda and I were to go see a screening of *The Legend of Hell House* at the Academy Theater (which is just across Santa Monica Boulevard from La Masía) and I'd decided I would eat lightly. So I ordered a bowl of gazpacho, the Andalusian cold salad soup, and a glass of iced tea. I thought I'd get away cheap and calorie-free that way. Lynda loathes shrimp, so, in my never-ending campaign to introduce her to the exotic foods of the universe, I cajoled her into ordering an appetizer of Scampi a la ajillo, figuring if she turned green (as she is wont to do), I would polish off the little dears myself. I ordered no main course, Lynda requested the Besugo al Horno, baked red snapper, seasoned, and topped with cheese. I loathe red snapper. The only thing we agreed on was the two glasses of iced tea.

My gazpacho came to the table quickly, and it was nicely chilled . . . none of this semi-cool nonsense that meant it had been left standing on the serving sideboard for an order to come in. Topped with several twists of ground pepper, it had the coral color of diced pimientos and tomatoes mixed in just the right proportions. Not too cucumbery, not too eggy, not too tomatoey, it was semi-thick and utterly memorable. I dipped my face into the bowl and actually licked off the residue. Lynda turned the other way. It was one of the two best bowls of gazpacho I've ever encountered.

Lynda went at the Scampi with caution, prying the tender flesh out of the shells with a look on her face that surely duplicated that worn by Saint Joan at the stake. Not even the bubbling sauce of butter, wine, tomatoes, garlic and herbs in which the shellfish languished served to allay her fears. But one bite later, when the scent of that miracle hit me, and I leaned over to taste and convince her she was correct in her hatred of shrimp, she bared her fangs and struck out at me with the shrimp fork, threatening me a grievous mischief if I put my pudding-trough near her beloved Scampi.

From the Tugboat Annie of the dinner table, no greater recommendation can be obtained. I rest my case.

Suffice it to say, I was not able to avoid the pleasures of the variegated menu. At a nearby table I saw diners having at a dish that looked splendiferous, so I asked our waiter to do the same to us, and he brought me a dish of stuffed mushrooms, each one the size of a hockey puck with a thyroid condition, absolutely surface-tensioned with crabmeat. They were so rich I could only eat three of the five monsters.

Lynda's red snapper came in a wok dish and was covered with a topping of cheese that was crispy at the edges, still malleable in the center. I arm-wrestled her for several bites. I will never again badmouth red snapper. It was an epiphany.

For dessert, the *flan* was out of this world.

And all of it came to under ten dollars. In a similar Castilian restaurant in New York, such a meal would have been over thirty dollars, and we'd have been insulted into the bargain. I was able to tip handsomely and still get away cheap, a delight to cheapskates like me.

In case you can't tell, I recommend La Masía without reservation. Which is what you should have if you plan to eat there on a busy night of the week.

Third, the publishing event of the century.

Before I get into it, let me assure cynics in the crowd that I am involved in this affair merely as subject (which is the rationale for mentioning such a self-serving ego trip in my own column), not as recipient of financial benefits.

Ms. Leslie Kay Swigart, a librarian and bibliophile, has compiled a 124-page book titled HARLAN ELLISON: A BIBLIO-GRAPHICAL CHECKLIST. It is the end-result of three years' work by Ms. Swigart, and has been published by Joe Bob Williams of Dallas. They are charging three bucks for it, and it is sorta kinda my thirty-ninth birthday present. It includes a listing of every single story, article, movie, television script, column, book review, movie criticism, book, interview, published letter and assorted miscellania I've ever had in print. And all of them illustrated with photographs of the book covers or artwork, including foreign editions and paintings by the Dillons that have graced my meager efforts.

There are over 870 entries, seventeen years' work as a professional.

In addition, the book has a cover by the Dillons, a great gaggle of photos of your humble columnist from his youth to the present (a span of six weeks), specially-written appreciations by such as Isaac Asimov, Robert Silverberg, Ben Bova, Joanna Russ, Edward Bryant and James Sutherland. I wrote a new Afterword for the volume.

There were only 1000 copies printed, each one is numbered, and they are available for $3.50 (the 50¢ covers postage and mailing envelope, etc.) from: Ms. Leslie Kay Swigart, PO Box 8570, Long Beach, California 90808.

I would not lie to any of you. This is the biggest head-sweller I've ever had, and if you give even the tiniest shit about what I've written or where it was published, this is a massive and exhaustive work. I would be flattered if you wanted one for your library. But beyond that, if Joe Bob and Leslie don't sell that thousand white elephant run of this monster, they'll be thrown in the poorhouse.

And on that note of reticence, I leave you till next week, at which time I'll be writing from Seattle.

And by the way, make sure Ms. Swigart sends you the version of the bibliography with the photo of me exposing myself in front of Kate Smith and Art Linkletter on *You Bet Your Life*.

Interim Memo

THIS WAS SIXTEEN YEARS AGO.

We still have friends in and out, the door as close to revolving as sanity permits. But we discourage it now. I'm a happily married man, I have a full-time staff that comes in five days a week in hopes of assisting me toward clearing the long-standing obligations (such as the *Hornbook*), and Susan and I give a heavy sigh of relief when the last voyager goes out the door.

Even so, in the past couple of months (as I write this in July of 1989) we've had the following sharing Ellison Wonderland:

Leo & Diane Dillon, the longtime friends who taught me most of what I know about integrity and personal courage; the same Dillons who have won the Caldecott Award for their book covers; same Dillons who've done the covers for so many of my books. For the first time ever, they came to my home—though I had lived with, and off, them in New York years ago—and got to see all their wonderful art framed on my walls.

Ken Steacy, whose artwork was turned to my Kyben war stories in the wonderful graphic novel NIGHT AND THE ENEMY. He came to visit, and gave me a swell gift: a model he'd constructed from scratch, of Blackhawk and his plane.

Gil Lamont. David Morrell. Dan Simmons. The memory blurs. It just keeps on keeping on. Good friends. Estimable talents. Ah, hell, maybe life ain't such a bowl'a mush, after all.

Notice: do *not* call us from East Weewah, asking if you can live here for a while. I will just insult you.

Varieties of Venue

9 August 1973

I've always said being Jewish doesn't necessarily make a person eligible for 2000 years' retroactive persecution, but recent events are just too *come on, world, gimme a break!*

No sooner do I cease writing *The Glass Teat* for the *Los Angeles Free Press* and get set to start writing *The Harlan Ellison Hornbook* for that outlet, when Brian Kirby and all the people I knew split, and started *The Staff*. So I held off with this column's inception and did some writing for *The Staff*. For which I never got paid. When it became apparent to me that my love of the "Movement" is only twice as strong as my love of being paid for what I write—even if it is only a token sum—when it became clear to me that in the name of "love" I (like many others) was being ripped-off by the Movement—I stopped writing for *The Staff*. Then Judy Sims of *Rolling Stone* was assigned to put together the *L.A. Flyer* insert section for *Stone*, and she asked me if I'd revive *The Glass Teat*. I was less interested in going back to a column that I'd mined for 2½ years than starting a fresh one, but Judy is a friend and the pay was nice, and I'd always wanted to be in *Rolling Stone*, so I did it. After three issues under Judy's superlative editorship, the far-seeing *Stone* entrepreneurs in San Francisco killed what had become a fascinating section, Judy became L.A. Bureau Chief, and *The Glass Teat* was dead again after a two-installment revival. Peace and quiet and an absence of deadline-scurrying reigned in Ellison Wonderland

Second *Hornbook* logo
by Tim Kirk

till October of 1972 when Art Kunkin and I agreed that I'd return to the *Freep*, this time with *The Hornbook*. Through trial and tribulation and the ineptitude of various production personnel, the column went 29 installments over nine–plus months of *Freep*. I missed a lot of deadlines because of lecture tours, the serious illness of my Mother in Florida, and the horrors of getting my NBC series *The Starlost* ready for airing next month, but I returned to L.A. at the end of July and was getting settled down to a regular schedule again . . . when Kunkin was fired.

Which is why, gentle readers, you find Installment 30 of *The Harlan Ellison Hornbook* in something called *The Weekly News* (which ain't nearly as dramatic a title as, say, *The Daily Planet* or *The Underground Crusader* or *The Illustrated Press*, but since Kunkin isn't Morgan Edge or Perry White or even Steve Wilson, and since L.A. isn't Metropolis or even Big Town, I suppose it'll suffice). It is my hope and fervent desire that you all support the hell out of *The Weekly News*, because I've worn holes in my soles *and* my souls, lugging this farrago of peripatetic reportage and reminiscence from scandal sheet to scandal sheet.

For the nonce, in any case, here is home. I have a new, bright piece of logo art done for the column by Hugo award–winning fantasy artist Tim Kirk, I have my scatterdemalion self together, my act ready to display, and I hope those of you who read me in other printed media will let your friends know where I am now. Whenever I missed a few weeks in the *Freep*, a flood of ugly and berserk letters washed over the *Freep* desks, and it would only be a kindness to advise those maniacs that their connection and supply can now be found nestled in these pages.

In short, we've all suffered enough, so let's settle down to a smooth time of regular columns and *please!* don't nobody make no sudden moves. Hello, again.

What my house is like, is a big elephant flophouse. I moved out of the tree house in Beverly Glen in March of 1966 when I married The Carnivorous Plant, Lory Patrick, my third ill-starred attempt at being A Nice Married Person, and moved in here, to what has come to be known as Ellison Wonderland. (I will not apologize for the play on words.) The Asp, Ms. Patrick, lasted forty-five days and was sent on her pillaging way, and I've been living here "alone" in these nine rooms and two-and-a-half baths for seven years. Some other time I'll describe the joint room by room—they tell me it's a rare playpen that *Better Homes and Gardens* would greatly desire to photograph— and when I recover my sanity from those 45 days of horror with The Dragon Lady Patrick, I'll do a novel about it (to be titled TAKEN, as in "patsy")—but at the moment, what I want to illuminate is the procession of friends, writers, lady friends (which is a more weighted term than simply "friends," if you ken my meaning), deadbeats, criminals, revolutionaries, neurotics, flippos, random psychopaths and celebrities who use this house as a way-station on the underground railroad or as a brief stopover in the erratic progress of their spotty lives.

Because the truth of the matter is that during my seven years here in Ellison Wonderland I've lived strictly *alone* for only five months.

There are always at least two or three other residents in the house. I'm told it is a happy place (except when I'm behind deadlines and being pressured by lunatics from 20th Century–Fox, at which time, I'm told, the place bears a closer resemblance to the locale described by Dante Alighieri) and the Blue Bedroom has marked residence for such notables as Norman Spinrad, Theodore Sturgeon, Daphne Davis who started the N.Y. newspaper *Rags*, Edward Bryant, Charles Platt of *New Worlds*, Prof. Darko Suvin, Bantam Books editor Sharon Delaney, ex–Doubleday editor Judith Glushanok, English writer Mary Ensor, Ben Bova who edits *Analog*, novelist Richard Hill, sf author Keith Laumer, feminist Vonda McIntyre, an ex-con who is currently doing smashingly well as a novelist, Bill Wyman of the Rolling Stones, and so many others I go into Cheyne–Stokes breathing when I try computing the numbers of the horde.

And that's just the *blue* bedroom.

Not a week passes in which other parts of the house are not festooned with sleeping bags, sheets and blankets on the sofa, pishy-pads on the waterbed, dining room carpet set up with pillows as mattress. Come summer, and the requests pile in from my ex-students at the various Clarion Writers' Workshops for snooze space whilst they pass through the City of the Angels. I just got rid of Robert Lilly, Gus Hasford, two young women whose names I never learned, and Arthur Byron Cover, well-known Tazewell, Virginia layabout and incipient novelist. Tim Kirk will be living here next week while he completes the illustrations for my Harper & Row anthology, THE LAST DANGEROUS VISIONS; Lisa Tuttle is supposed to be coming from Dallas or Houston or someTexaswhere; Ben Bova will be back so we can work on our ABC-TV Movie of the Week, *Brillo*; Susan C. Lette has wangled a couple of weeks off from her husband and kids so she can come here to write; Judith Glushanok will be returning from London and need a place to flop; and when David Wise returns from Seattle I'm terrified to learn that Arthur Byron Cover will be back here with his mismatched argyle socks and his nine hundred and seventy-two thousand comic books. My milk bill is staggering.

My attitude toward all this is an oddly ambivalent mixture of feelings ranging from joy and pleasure at being surrounded by quick, clever and witty people whom I love and admire . . . to utter loathing of their presence when I want to work or be alone with a woman. From moment to moment it changes: my soul leaps with pride that I'm able to repay some of the kindnesses that were visited on me by writers and friends when I needed help, when I was getting started . . . and my brain burns with unreasoning annoyance that they take up space, kill my privacy, eat me out of house and home, and break my Looney Tunes drinking glasses. I vacillate between affection and gratitude that they are around to help me out when the workload gets unbearable or watch the house when I'm on tour . . . and rage when they don't take out the garbage or wash the dishes and I have to spend valuable writing time being a housekeeper. My philosophy of life is that the meek shall inherit nothing but debasement, frustration and ignoble deaths; that there is security in personal strength; that you *can* fight City Hall and *win*; that any action is better than no action, even if it's the wrong action; that you never reach glory or self-fulfillment unless you're willing to risk everything, dare anything, put yourself dead on the line every time; and that once one becomes strong or rich or potent or powerful it is the responsibility of the strong to help the weak *become* strong. In this way, opening my home to those who—in my view, because I'm a selfish sonofabitch and I have no time for lames and whiners—have strength that merely needs time and circumstance to ripen, is a way of paying back dues to a world that has been very good to me. I am seldom disappointed in my choices of those helped in this way. Once or twice I've had people I loved dearly, who lived here, slip away into lives that creamed them: doping to destruction, running with killers of the soul, demeaning their talent, living lightless days and nights of sorrow and hopelessness. But for the most part, everyone who came here has gone away strengthened, their wings repaired, their egos inflated and toughened, and from those enrichments I've sustained my own feelings of worthiness. It's a selfish practice, hardly one of nobility and humanitarianism.

So even when I bitch about returning home from a month on the road to find a freezer full of steaks eaten, I know in a special part of my heart that it was money well spent.

Which doesn't keep me from pissing and moaning about it, of course. If you want consistency, look for it in the graveyard; I'm a flawed, miserable human being and I'm not responsible for my lunacy or my contradictions.

Nor am I responsible for the madness that goes on in this house. Steve Herbst from Chicago going out one day and coming home with an electric piano which he set up in the living room and on which he drove us all mad playing the six repetitious barrelhouse riffs he thought would make him a rock star. For *days*!

Deborah Kenworthy writing from Buffalo that she wanted to get away from her family and she'd work as secretary for me in exchange for room and board, and then driving me up the wall with a personal manner that was a cross between Queen Victoria and Ilse Koch. (Ilse Koch was the lady who made lampshades out of Jews at Buchenwald.)

Ed Bryant coming for a weekend and staying three years, off and on, hoarding away cookies and peanut butter in the Blue Bedroom against, I suppose, the Apocalypse; squirreling away so many cases of diet cola that poor Jim Sutherland (about which loon more at another time) fell over them and banged his head on the wall, knocking loose the framed portrait of Ellison the Good, inscribed, "From your friend and mine, God."

(I can't resist.) Jim Sutherland, current resident of Blue Hell, who goes out early in the dawn and crouches by the rear wall of the garden, waiting to catch breakfast of fresh gecko as the little lizards come out to sun themselves. You should see his tongue. Ukh. Sutherland, turning himself into a turnip for the delight of Roz's children. Sutherland, killing my tropical fish; Sutherland, swearing his bedroom is occupied by a giant chicken.

Oh god . . . Sutherland!

Gus Hasford, refusing to bathe. Cindy Dwan being saved from death by a mad dash to UCLA Emergency. Phil Mishkin appearing at the door in the wee hours, needing a bed till Julie would let him back in the house. Thirteen kids and their teacher from the Dayton Living Arts Center appearing with sleeping bags in a van that blocked the entire street. Robert Sheckley hiding out from publishers. Ted Sturgeon making *paella* with his hands. Sutherland's Sure Death chili. Carol Botwin and her imbroglio with Adele Davis, right before my very eyes.

Yes, life here at Ellison Wonderland is a constant joy.

Something like traveling through Transylvania in the company of Genghis Khan, the Marquis de Sade, Little Nemo and Conan the Musclebound. I don't want anyone to get the wrong idea . . . that I don't *like* all this company, but if you want a clearer, more detailed picture of what life is like here in these nine rooms and two-and-a-half baths, I refer you to "The Persecution and Assassination of Jean-Paul Marat as Performed by the Inmates of the Asylum of Charenton under the Direction of the Marquis de Sade."

God, and Arthur Byron Cover, willing, I'll return next week for another report from the Country of the Blind.

Interim Memo

IT'S WORSE NOW. HORRIBLY WORSE. IT'S BEEN EIGHT YEARS OF Reagan. That drove the spikes home. Susan and I were doing a lecture gig at State University of New York, Stony Brook, oh, maybe a year ago. And during a midnight session—packed to the walls—I was babbling on about something or other, and I said:

"Blah blah blah blah Dachau blah blah blah somethingor-other." And I went on. But after a few seconds, a young woman—maybe nineteen, twenty, like that—raised her hand. I said, "Yes?" She said, "Who was that person you named?" I was confused; I hadn't named any person. "Which person?" I asked.

"That dak-ow person."

(To their holy credit, about half the students in the auditorium turned around and stared at her, their hair on end, disbelief on their faces.)

"Do you mean Dachau?" I asked. She nodded, bewildered at the stares of the assembled. The *other* half of the audience kept quiet, but it was apparent they didn't know who that "dak-ow" guy was, either.

Utterly unmanned, I sighed, and felt such a pain in my chest that tears started to well up. I said, very softly, "Dachau wasn't a person, Miss. It was a death-camp where they cremated millions of people. World War Two."

It's worse now. I know it's not *all* students, it's not *all* teenagers. But it's oh so damned damned *many* of them. They seem to know nothing earlier than last week. And they're smug about it. As if the essence of cool is to be *tabula rasa*. I've made gags out of it: they listen to rap music . . . which is an oxymoron; for them, nostalgia is breakfast; they're the clone-children of Dan Quayle, the first Stepford Wife vice-president in the history of the United States. But the tears well up.

I am hardly the model of moral exemplar. More the crank, if truth be known. But I live by pride in reason, even when reason makes no practical sense. David Denby wrote a sentence in a film review in *New York* magazine last year, that says it best: "He can be petulant and whiny, a hero who is also a pain in the ass."

And Hunter Thompson summed up my kind of fool when he referred to ". . . the dead end loneliness of a man who makes his own rules."

So I don't hold myself up as the intellectual conscience of rats and mice, much less the human race.

But the tears do, yes they do, they do well up.

Why I Fantasize About Using an AK-47 on Teenagers

16 August 1973

When I go out to lecture at colleges, I'm constantly amazed and saddened at the crippling apathy and lassitude of the vast majority of the student populations. They come slouching in to classrooms where they unexpectedly find me perched like a troll on a desk, their dulled and passive expressions momentarily raised to the level of disinterest. I'm not talking about lecture halls or auditoriums where I've been publicly announced as a guest lecturer, but classrooms where my appearance has been at the whim of a professor who has read my stories and thinks I'd be a treat for his students. So I'm sprung on them without warning. Most of them have never read anything I've written. (That doesn't distress me. Most of them have read *nothing* beyond that which is forced on them as classroom fodder; the obligatory porno-backs; LOVE STORY, THE OTHER; a little Tolkien or Heinlein's STRANGER so they can carry their end of the conversation or, if it's a guy, get laid; THE HAPPY HOOKER, something by Harold Robbins; a surfeit of Marvel comics.) So they wander in, find this creature recently fallen off the Moon, and they slump into seats, staring out from under lowered lashes, wary, semi-surly, daring me to bore their asses off, as do many of their professors.

No, I'm not disturbed that they've never read my work, most of them: go into the street and buttonhole any random dozen pedestrians, and ask them to name ten writers and, if you're lucky, they'll name Mickey Spillane, John Steinbeck, Ernest Hemingway and William Shakespeare. If you're un-lucky, they can't even remember *those* bestselling names. The American reading public seldom notices that books are *written*; they seem, to them, to be artifacts that magically appear on newsstands, in Greyhound waiting rooms, left on top of the dryers in laundromats, underfoot in university common rooms. They don't seem to realize there are human beings that sat in front of typewriters, even as I do now, and *wrote* those books. Even popular trash is all of a piece: zip, they just happened! THE GODFATHER, THE LOVE MACHINE, THE BETSY, LOVE STORY. Were it not for the manifest wonders of late night talk shows, bombarding us with the likes of Jacqueline Susann, Erich Segal, Rex Reed and whatever "movie star" has recently had a biography ghost-written, they would not even know *those* names as being attachable to living (?), breathing (?) human beings. I take it in stride, truly. My teeth grind only occasionally. Just a little. My lectures draw large audiences and there is a sizeable group of people who actually look for my name on

books. I'm hardly unknown. It's an easily supportable existence.

But, with rare exceptions, a few minutes into my "presentation" and they come awake, watch, listen, ask questions, join
in with the gags, the insults, the random bits of proffered
information, and I do very nicely in classrooms, thank you.

Now if you've never attended one of my public gigs, you
will have to take this on faith (or ask a friend who had been
there when I've run my demented thought-processes past a
crowd), but my "lectures" are enormously successful. As proof,
just to get you on my side in this discussion, and to lay a
groundwork of trust for what I'm about to say here, if I *weren't*
a good and stimulating lecturer, I wouldn't be called on to play
all the college dates I handle every year . . . something well
over 200 speaking engagements in the last five years. And I
wouldn't command the speaking fees I get, which are usually
many thousands a night, plus expenses.

So, if you'll accept that I do happy numbers on a college
audience, and do those numbers effectively, you'll understand
my sadness at the disenchantment engendered by the weary
demeanor and dulled sensibilities of vast hordes of college
students I confront annually. Please excuse my unbecoming
modesty.

I used to be utterly gung ho behind the belief that: "the
Youth of America" will save us. Boy, did I learn my lesson. They
are no better or nobler than my generation, which was the
Silent Generation of the Fifties that scraped its hind legs
together like Buddy Holly and the Crickets, served their time in
the post–Korea ROTC, polluted the ecology without regard to
the future and in general sat by and let Senator Joseph
McCarthy spread his pall of paranoia, fear and Commie-hatred
across the land. Kids today are just as fucked as we were. Maybe
more so, because kids today at least had ten years of the Sixties
to see what significant changes could be wrought by a tenor of
revolution. (Case in point: yesterday morning, driving over to
Warner Bros., I saw a girl about seventeen, wearing the
"uniform," pre-faded jeans, bare-midriff shirt permitting her
protruberant gut to bulge visibly, capacious shoulder bag, deck

platform hooker shoes . . . *an ecology patch on the seat of her ass* . . . standing a foot and a half in front of a litter basket on the corner of Ventura Boulevard and Laurel Canyon . . . hitchhiking . . . *throwing filter-tip cigarette butts onto the sidewalk.* When I yelled, "Litterbug!" at her, she gave me a killing look: how *dare* I put her down! Flipped me the bird. Nobler than my screwed-up generation, and all the ones who pummeled the world before me? Hell, no, Sunny Jim. Just as selfish, thoughtless, grungy and hypocritical.)

Maybe it's because they *do* come out of those ten years of riot and carnage, Kent State and Jackson State, Vietnam, LBJ, Nixon, the assassination of King, the ecology awakening, the monstrousness of the political conventions, the supersonic jet boondoggle, the marching, the demonstrating, the Chicago Conspiracy Trial . . . all of it. Maybe they're *entitled* to be apathetic, deadass uninvolved, sluggardly and concerned with Number One. Maybe all they have to look forward to each day is gutless rock, bad dope, inept sex, vegetarian astrology and the time-clock boredom of their classes. Maybe.

But maybe not.

I'll tell you why I think *maybe* not.

When I'm lecturing, inevitably some clown gets personal and wants to know how much bread I make a year. I try to be very candid when I speak publicly—I'll answer *any* question, to the best of my recollection, Senator—and I tell the pinhead I make in the neighborhood of a hundred grand a year.

That often draws a gasp from the assemblage.

Then I tell them what I'm about to tell *you.* My deep, dark secret of success in this life: you can have anything you want. *Anything Every*damn*thing*! All you have to do is go and get it. All you can have in this life is what you grab and hold onto with both hands. But you got to go and *do*!

Some of them will stare at me with disbelief. They live behind their eyes and they suppose some fairy tale that I was born to wealth and indolence, that I use voodoo or murdered a wealthy relative to achieve my present position of relative financial comfort. So I tell them two short stories about HOW IT IS IN THE REAL WORLD. *These* two stories I tell you now:

When I got my tail thrown out of Ohio State University after a year and a half, and went to New York to try and make a career as a writer, I'd been on my own—pretty much—since I was thirteen. I'd worked at all kinds of jobs, eking out an existence on the road, moving toward goals only vaguely identifiable.

I had to get a job, to live. I got myself a ratty little room at 611 West 114th Street, off Broadway, uptown, across from Columbia University. It cost $13 a week, and the only thing that could be said in its favor was that Bob Silverberg—who was a year ahead of me in writing professionally—lived in the building. But even that $13 a week was rough to come up with. That was 1954.

My Mother, who was convinced at that point that I'd wind up either in jail or the gutter (and she had good cause to wonder such a wonder, I assure you), came to New York on her way to Europe. Before you draw any wild conclusions that my Mother was a frenetic jet-setter who spent all her time, like Auntie Mame, dashing hither and yon, permit me to disabuse you. For twenty-five years my Mother had lived in Cleveland and Painesville, Ohio, by the skin of her and my Father's teeth, and when my Dad died in 1949, my Mother had to make do the best way she knew how. Now, five years later, she had scrimped and saved sufficient pennies to go for a couple of weeks to visit family she hadn't seen in a quarter century, in England. It was a poor folks' journey, I guarantee. But she had treated herself to two posh nights at the St. Moritz Hotel on Central Park South before going abroad, and I went to see her. Even as hard up as she was, she had stretched her finances so she was able to give me five postdated checks for $13 each . . . my rent for the next month . . . postdated so I wouldn't blow the money on books or something else less immediate than shelter. I took the gesture as an insult, of course. I was then, and frequently am now, an utter asshole about accepting compliments, largesse, kindness, charity or pity.

I stalked out of the St. Moritz—it was a Saturday afternoon—vowing I'd get a job immediately. I was not going to accept one of those checks!

(As it turned out, from what follows, I *did* use the checks to keep the rain off my head. Did you ever notice how we all try to appear as Pillars of Strength and Self-Sufficiency, only to rationalize our weakness when we do precisely what we said we wouldn't do?)

I decided right then and there, on Seventh Avenue and Central Park South, in the middle of a Saturday afternoon, that I was going to get a job *that day.* I started walking downtown on Seventh Avenue, and with no direction in mind, no destination at hand, I turned left into W. 57th Street, walking crosstown toward the East River. I walked for a long block and, between Sixth Avenue—known to all but tourists who call it the Avenue of the Americas as Sixth Avenue—and Fifth, I turned into an office building. For no damned good reason except it was the first one I turned into.

I checked the listing of residents in the building, on the lobby directory, and the one that caught my eye was Capitol Records. I walked through the narrow and dingy lobby to the elevator, in semi-darkness. It was a standard upper midtown sweatshop office building lobby, faintly redolent with the scent of dirty pushbrooms and Pine-Sol.

I took the elevator up to whatever floor it was (that's almost twenty years ago, there are small details I don't recall) and got out. There was a reception desk. A man was sitting behind the desk, reading a newspaper. It was a Saturday, the regular receptionist was off, and this was some minor office manager type who'd been assigned to keep the place on skeleton alert.

"Yeah?" he asked, lowering the paper an inch.

"I want a job," I said, flat and direct. I knew he would say nothing doing, and I was ready to turn around and walk down to the next floor and try the next office, and the next, and the next, and the next, till I found someone who'd let me swab decks or clean toilets just so I wouldn't have to take those checks.

"How the hell did *you* know about the job?" he asked. "The ad doesn't run till tomorrow in the *Times.*"

Well, what had happened was, there was an opening—not a *good* opening, as you'll see—but an opening nonetheless—and with the dumb luck that has sustained me all my life, I had by chance wandered into one of the few offices in New York that had a job. So he gave me the job, and said to report on Monday morning at 8:00, wearing a tie and jacket.

Two days later I showed up at the office building on W. 57th, and the line of applicants waiting for the job stretched from the elevator, through the lobby, and out onto the street. There was a lot of unemployment in New York during that period.

I shoved my way through, begging people's pardon, with secretarial and layabout types snarling at me, and when I got to the elevator, the operator looked at the note I'd been given on Saturday, and announced to the people, "Okay, you people, you can take off now. The job's filled."

I have never, before or since, felt such massed hatred and desire to slash my throat. Except once, at a science fiction convention in St. Louis, but that's *another* story.

The operator caged me and whipped me upstairs.

The office manager gave me over to a lady of sixty-five years, and told her to put me to work in the order room.

I was then taken into an enormous loft, about half the length of a football field, in which incredibly long zinc-top tables were lined up one after another, across the full distance from wall to wall. It was well-lit, by fluorescents hanging from the peeling ceiling. But the windows to the world outside were crusted over with filth, and were barred.

I was startled to see that even at a few minutes after eight in the ayem, the tables were being used by almost a hundred men and women, hunched over stacks of papers; their curved bodies were chaired a foot apart, like the visitors' room at a penal institution. And everyone was working, bent over and no one talking.

The old lady took me to an open chair in the middle of one of the tables, sat me down, and explained that the stack of bills of lading on my *left* had to be tallied with the invoice sheet on my *right*, that all I had to do was verify the number in red on the lading bill on my *left* with its corresponding number in blue on the invoice sheet to my *right*. Just check them off, that was all.

And she went away.

I looked around for a moment, before starting work. The room was dismal, cold and without atmosphere, somehow devoid of even ghosts or the warmth of days through which humans had lived. It was the compleat sweatshop. It was the distribution center for Capitol Records. Orders would come in from dealers and wholesalers all over the country, on the bills of lading, they would be verified, checked, authenticated, coordinated, and then sent out again to be filled by the various Capitol pressing plants such as the one in Gloversville, New York. My job was to paperwork that process by one small increment. Sighing, miserable . . . but *working* . . . holding down a steady, regular *job* . . . I set to my task.

It took me about six minutes to check off the numbers from the stack on the *left* with the invoice on the *right*.

I went quickly, it was monkeywork entailing no thought or imagination or even effort, really. The stack moved from my IN basket to my OUT basket.

I settled back for a moment of air, and—as if conjured up by the Demon God of Industry—a ferretlike little man popped out of nowhere, grabbed the stack from the OUT basket, and dumped another stack in my IN basket.

Then he was gone. Poof!

I shook my head, startled, and fell to the new batch of invoices and billings. Another six minutes.

IN basket empty, OUT basket full.

Poof! he reappeared, grabbed, dumped more stack, and Poof! was gone.

I did it again. Another six minutes.

Poof! grab dump Poof!

I did it again.

The process repeated itself about a dozen times in the first two hours. No variation, no break, no change, no thought. Then I realized the little old man sitting to my right was staring at me. I turned to him . . . covertly . . . I didn't want the Demon God of Industry to think I was dogging it.

"If you work so fast, they'll only dump more work on you,

young man," he said, in a thin, quavery voice. "And," he added, a little sheepishly, "it will make the rest of us look very bad."

He said it so gently, so meekly, so apologetically, I instantly perceived what the concept of "featherbedding" was all about, and why there are times when it isn't necessarily an evil work-practice. I nodded to him, smiled, and worked much *much* more slowly.

Shortly thereafter, we were given a ten minute break. Everyone else fled for coffee–and, but the little man sat there exhausted, so I sat with him. We talked.

He was a mouse of a creature; gray, balding, slump-shouldered, seemingly without visions or dreams or future. He told me his name but I don't remember it. I don't even remember his face. It was a face without hope, I remember *that*.

We talked about nothing in particular, until he asked me where I'd come from and what I'd done, and where I was going. He seemed almost unnaturally fascinated. When I asked him why his interest, he said it was because I seemed to be so alive, so filled with sharp cute moves and humor. I took it as one of the dearest, truest compliments I've ever received. And I told him about how I'd worked in a logging camp, and driven a dynamite truck, and gone to college briefly, and how I wanted to write. His eyes sparkled and a slow, shy grin came to sit on his lips. And when I paused for breath he said, "That's what I've always wanted to do . . . just go with the wind and do what-ever came to mind."

"Why don't you do it?"

"Oh, I couldn't. I'd lose my job here."

"How long have you been here?"

"Eleven years."

I paused. I was afraid to ask the next questions.

But I did, and he answered as horribly as I'd expected. He had come to Capitol Records's distribution center when he was thirty-seven, from an endless string of similar jobs, and he was now forty-eight. He looked seventy. He was making a terrific salary, though. Seventy-five bucks a week. I was making thirty-six bucks a week. Eleven years and he'd come to the magnifi-cent stage of existence where he was making seventy-five dollars, before deductions. Shit, that wasn't even enough to starve on, much less to derive any joy or enrichment from.

And I suddenly flashed on who he was, and what would happen to me if I sat there any longer. The terror that froze my soul cannot be put into words.

At that moment another stack of bills was dumped in my empty IN basket.

The rest of the room was back at work.

I looked at the withered little gray man beside me, divested of chances, stripped of dreams, flensed of hope or direction, set irrevocably on a cubicled routine of pointless chores making money for Gods on far mountaintops . . . and I saw what my future would be if I left my life in the hands of those prepared only to dole out thirty-six dollars a week for another human being's existence.

Thirty years from that moment, *I* would be *him*!

With nothing to look forward to but a pension—if I were lucky and Capitol Records was feeling magnanimous—or old age compensation—if they weren't. A testimonial luncheon, a turnip watch, a pat on the hairless, withered old head, and a twilight life reading *Arizona Highways* in a $13-a-week cockroach hostelry.

I grabbed up that stack of bills, leaped out of my chair, sending it crashing to the floor, and with all my strength and lungpower flung them into the air, screaming, "FUCK IT!" Amid the bill of lading snowstorm, I fled shrieking from that madhouse of boredom and dead dreams on West 57th Street, never to return.

As far as I know, to this day, Capitol Records has an unclaimed check for one-half day's work, in the name of Harlan Ellison.

Which slides me right into story number two, a very quick, paradigmatic story, that makes the point you may have missed in story number one:

Years later. I was already doing well as a writer. I was on my way to realizing all my dreams. I was in an expensive barber shop in Beverly Hills. I was talking to Manny, who was my barber at the time, about being on the road, about moving fast and experiencing life and taking great chunks out of the years so one didn't die unmourned and unmoved by the universe.

Beside me, in the next chair, was a kid of about seventeen, also getting his hair styled. His eyes were big and round as he listened to me bullshit.

Finally, he said, "Boy! That's the way *I* want to live!"

And a surge of joy leaped in my chest. Not *all* the kids were apathetic, deadass leeches. There were still kids like *this* one willing to risk, willing to go the distance. I grinned at him, and he finished his remark . . .

"Yeah, just give me my old man's Corvette, those credit cards, and I'll *go!*"

At that moment, I died a little death.

This commercial has come to you through the sponsorship of what used to be called the Puritan Work Ethic.

Interim Memo

MARIANA WENT ON TO BETTER THINGS, I'M TOLD. STOPPED using Maxim, went to Kava for emergencies; but basically I've been grinding fresh beans for the last, oh, decade or so.

Can you believe this column was written just as Watergate was breaking? Seems like another universe, doesn't it?

Ah, where have the good times gone?

Pres. Bush is *so* different from Nixon and Reagan. As I write this, he's in Poland promising them 1.5 *billion* in aid if they'll allow us to put Kentucky Colonel and McDonald's in Gdansk . . . immediately after gutting all programs to feed and house the homeless in America, after vetoing the minimum wage bill that would have given sub-subsistence pay to all those incipient capitalists shoveling up the shit at Kentucky Colonel and McDonald's.

The apple doesn't fall far from the tree. Or the Bush. Or something.

In Which the Imp of Delight Tries to Make the World Smile

23 August 1973

*I*n my never-waning efforts to keep you all sane and productive, I find periods in which the Antichrist attempts of the World-At-Large to drive you bananas press me to even greater efforts. This is one of those periods. You poor, sad things . . . they're really trying to do you in, aren't they? As if it weren't enough that you're barely healing from a 23-year involvement with the Vietnam War (it went on so long, most of you blissfully forgot that we entered the fray on 27 June 1950, when Harry sent in a "a 35-man Military Assistance Advisory Group to advise the troops there in the use of American weapons"), they're hitting you with skyrocketing prices on *every*thing, the unnerving Watergate mess that's guaranteed to make you so paranoid you think your *Mother* is on the take, a total absence of meat from the markets, the demise of *Life* magazine, a return of awful Fifties music, Dr. Atkins's crazy new diet that pillories you for being comfortably overweight, a gas and energy crisis, higher personal and property taxes, a reeling sense that you're spinning back in time with the reappearance on tv of the NEW Perry Mason and the NEW Dr. Kildare, rotten mail delivery but a greater flood of junk mail, another Jacqueline Susann novel, Egg McMuffin, ersatz Vernor's ginger ale, the death of Bruce Lee, a tv Special starring Kate Smith doing rock music . . .

Now take it easy. Come on, now, stop whimpering like that. Uncle Harlan is here to soothe you. You remember, I *told* you I'd protect you, I wouldn't let all dem nastie old mans hurt oo. All it takes is realizing there are still areas in which we are all human, all subject to the same vagaries of Fate.

Look: I'll make it all better right now . . .

Think of this:

When you're done making ka-ka, you know how you check the paper to make sure everything is spiffy back there? Well, just consider *this*: Richard M. Nixon checks the paper, *too*!

There! Now doesn't that make it all a little easier to bear?

What's that you say? Nixon is too anal retentive even to *make* a ka-ka? Come on, now, you don't believe that, do you?

You do.

Well, then how about this:

Ehrlichman is up living in Seattle, right? Okay, so one night he's out driving up toward Vancouver on some dumb errand or other, trying to find a roadside stand that sells fresh vegetables for a decent price, and it gets very late, and he's miles from anywhere, and he blows his right front tire and manages to get the car stopped without hitting a tree, and he opens the trunk and finds the spare is soft, and he starts to cry. But he pulls himself together just as it begins to drizzle one of those hideous Washington state rains that soak through to your interbronchial lymph nodes and, pulling his collar up and hunching his bullethead down into his sopping shirt, he starts trudging down the road, looking for a telephone. Well, this is a section of countryside that has been purchased on the sly by a dummy corporation owned, on the q.t., by Bebe Rebozo, because he's gotten a tip from the Secretary of the Interior, Rogers Morton, that this whole stretch will soon be picked up by the Federal Government as the future site of a combination SST landing field and Chicano Internment Camp, and all the farmers have been badgered off their land, and all the farmhouses have been bulldozed into the ground like something out of THE GRAPES

OF WRATH, and there isn't a lit window for six miles. By the time he finds a commune where there's a dry spot to sit down, he's already well on the way to pneumonia, dropping into pleurisy. And the dropouts don't have a phone. But one of them kindly offers to take his bicycle and ride up the road to the next town, which is three miles off, and call the Automobile Club. So Ehrlichman sits down and waits, and while he's waiting they offer him some navy bean soup which is laced with peyote, but he doesn't know it, and he gets stoned out of his mind so that when the AAA truck finally arrives and picks him up, he's bagged and doesn't remember where the car is. But the AAA guy—who is pissed at having to come out in the rain, anyhow—figures he may make a buck or two selling this nerd a new spare tire, so he puts him in the truck and drives back up the road to the car, where a Washington State Highway Patrol car is stopped beside Ehrlichman's vehicle. The Trooper is busy writing out a citation because Ehrlichman half-blocked the road when he skidded to a stop after the tire blew. And Ehrlichman is so miffed, he stumbles out of the AAA truck, slips on the muddy road, falls on his ass and ruins a $300 Savile Row suit, but gets up and tries to pillory the Trooper, who, sensing Ehrlichman is stoned, throws him in the back of the meat wagon to take him in for questioning. Ehrlichman, desperate, tosses his wallet through the window to the AAA guy, screaming, "Call that number on the ID card and tell Dick I'm in trouble!" The Highway Patrol car takes off, even as the wallet hits a mud puddle and sinks half out of sight. The AAA repairman lifts it out with two fingers, flips it open, sees Ehrlichman has no Auto Club card, and drops it back into the puddle . . . and drives away. Ehrlichman is tossed into a cell and, the next day, at his arraignment on dope charges, makes such a screaming ass of himself that the judge, a canny rustic type wholly out-of-touch with the world and its vices, remands him to the custody of the local insane asylum.

Which is where he is to this day.

Now. Doesn't *that* make you feel better?

Come on, there are *still* a few things around that make it all worthwhile, that can keep you from opening your wrists. Just to prove it to you, I'll give you a few of the ones *I've* fallen back on recently to keep my spirits up:

Maxim freeze-dried coffee. It's a damned sight better tasting than 99% of the perc stuff I get when I go to friends' homes for dinner. Johnny Hart's *B.C.* and *The Wizard of Id*. Bette Midler. The new (and, sadly, last) Bruce Lee martial arts film, *Enter the Dragon*, which is, I grant you, mindless violence, but such ballet-like graceful and impressive in its depiction of how the human body can exceed its limitations that if you ignore the silliness of what the plot is, you can derive the same kind of joy one gets at a fine performance by Nureyev. The *Swamp Thing* comic book by Len Wein and Berni Wrightson. Eli Wallach. Pipes by Erickson. Print Mint T-shirts with Mercs and other neat stuff on them. Stevie Wonder's new album, *Innervisions*. *M*A*S*H*, which breaks me up every Sunday. The retrospective of 20th Century–Fox films now going on at the L.A. County Museum. My gardener Alfred Takeda's kids, Willie and Aileen, who are sensational. The return to the real world of Brian Kirby, now that *The Staff* has died and released him from his pathological dedication. Walter Koenig and the rediscovery of Big Little Books. The completion of two new stories, one of them a *Jewish* science fiction story.

These may all seem to be frivolous, but for God's sake, we have to take our joys where we find them. It's an ever-increasingly more complex and crushing world through which we are expected to move, and those who condemn others for "not working" or "not being productive" need only examine their *own* existences to see that there is far less pleasure and satisfaction than even ten years ago. So take your little pleasures where you find them, friends. And surround yourselves with joyful people. Downerfolk can kill you quicker than the bite of the asp.

For my part, I'm presently surrounded by nice people, for the most part, led in their upliftiness by my secretary, the incomparable Mariana Hernández.

I've had a batch of secretaries over the last six or seven

years, beginning with Crazy June Burakoff, whom you all remember from my frequent mentions in *The Glass Teat* columns. When Junie moved on to a high-paying job at Universal Studios I went through two or three temporary associates who either were too spacey to get the work done necessary to keeping my addlepated existence in order, or who frankly couldn't stand me, and then Sandy Nisbet came on the job and it was a perfect merger of personalities. But then, Sandy and her husband moved up to Tumwater, Washington when he got a new teaching assignment, and I was back to scrounging. Mona Vakil was here for a while, and though she was as deranged as me, she was conscientious and everything worked well till she had to return to Iran, or wherever it was, with *her* husband. Then I had a couple of bummers, whom shall go nameless whom, and then . . . ta ra! . . . in came the Chicana Queen of the *barrio*, Mariana the Wise.

When mh came to work for me, I was just getting rid of a secretary who had driven me berserk, and Mariana now confesses that the bestial way I treated that former secretary led her to believe she'd be back looking for a job in a week. But since the 24th of December 1972, when mh hove on the scene, we've been doing very nicely, thank you.

Mariana is a remarkable creature, folks. Not only is she slick and quick and intelligent and feisty, and takes no shit from me, but has a quite separate existence and career in that she is a perennial runner-for-office, having first attempted to get elected to the office of U.S. Senator from Texas (against the now-famous George Bush) in 1970. She lost. Then she ran for Mayor of Austin, Texas, and lost. Then she ran for Congress in L.A's 30th District, and lost. Then she ran for the Community College Board of Trustees in 1973, got 44,000 votes . . . and lost. Part of the problem may be that mh runs on the Socialist Workers Party ticket.

Not only does she run, but she delivers periodic lectures here in my home—not to mention in the world at large—on socialism, populism, feminism, humanism and acupuncture.

She even does a little typing, once in a while.

Most of all, she answers the door and snarls at those intent on stealing my writing time with their impositions. And if you want to keep sane, as I've said, you have to keep all that lunatic stuff on the other side of the door.

So, until you get *your* mh to keep *you* inviolate, I hope this week's good news column has cheered you sufficiently so you don't do yourself in . . . and can return next week, when we'll deal with The Ethical Structure of the Universe, or something else equally as lighthearted.

Interim Memo

LOOK: CUT ME SOME SLACK ON THIS NEXT ONE, OKAY? IT WAS A bad day. You've had them. You know what it's like. I'm feeling much better now.

Except that the only thing I know for absolutely sure in this life is this:

The two most common elements in the universe are hydrogen and stupidity.

I Go to Bed Angry Every Night, and Wake Up Angrier the Next Morning

30 August 1973

*L*ast week I mentioned my secretary, Mariana. mh to her friends and employer. I was going to talk, this week, about how difficult it is to get through the day-by-day bullshit of nickel&dime-death that society lays on us, without being surrounded by competent, helpful associates. I was going to talk about mailman, George O'Brien from the Sherman Oaks PO branch; about my dear friend and CPA, Eddie London; about my auto mechanic, John Wilkes; about my doctor, John Romm; my agents, Marty Shapiro and Mark Lichtman; my housekeeper, Eusona Parker; my attorney, Barry Bernstein; my travel agent, Linda Wolk; my bankers, Al Court and Syl Bunyevchev. That's what I *was* going to talk about. Another of my "Ain't life beautiful" columns, to try and cheer your asses up.

But today got a blight on it.

Today, the leaves withered and the bush turned black and fell to ashes.

So, instead, you get one of my "You stupid fucking bastard" columns. Maybe you'd be advised to pass me up this week, if you're feeling good. Or come back to this column when they dump bat guano on *your* parade.

Last week, a guy came to interview me for his Doctoral Thesis, and he was sharper than hell. He asked me questions light-years beyond the usual "Where do you get your story-ideas" questions. At one point he said I seemed to be dichotomous in my reactions to people: on the one hand my writing was clearly humanistic, and I cared about people . . . on the other I was always railing and cursing "the Common Man" and saying what swine and assholes they are. I couldn't answer him. It's true. I am *very* ambivalent about the human race. Sometimes I weep with joy at the nobility, grandeur and heroism of which individuals are capable . . . at other times, had I a gun in my hand, I would without compunction riddle the bodies of people who commit such awfulnesses against other humans that my mind and soul cannot contain the pain. So I asked Mariana if she would try and explain me to this guy. And when he re-ran the tape for me, Mariana said something (and I'm paraphrasing) about how I *really*, at core, was on the side of the People, as opposed to The Establishment, or Big Business, or The System. She didn't actually say I was a good guy at heart, but she tried to explain to him that my thinking wasn't *entirely* fucked. And finally, at the end of her discourse, she must have shrugged (it *sounded* like a shrug) and she said she didn't really understand me, either.

Well, here's another of those ambivalences, friends. Last week I did a number on how good life is, and this week I want to lay on you four things I heard about today that make me want to rush out into the street with bombs!

The CBS news gave me two of them. The first was a story out of South Africa, where they have apartheid . . . you know about apartheid, right? Blacks and whites are separated. Right?

Well, today, there was an auto accident on a road near Johannesburg, and a white kid got all stove in, and the guy who ran to call the ambulance told the hospital, "Hurry up, a boy was seriously hurt, he may be dying." Well, in South Africa, blacks are referred to as "boy" and what was sent was a *black* ambulance, and when it got to the scene of the crash, the dumb stupid eggsucking motherfucking asshole cop who was in charge refused to let them put the *white* kid in the *black* ambulance! And nobody did a goddam thing to stop the silly sonofabitchin' pig! And he sent someone to call a *white* ambulance, and by the time it got there a half hour later, and they loaded the kid into the meat wagon, he was DOA. That's dead fucking on arrival, may that cop's rotted stinking bigot soul fry in Hell forever!

The second, you've probably heard about. It's down to modern mythology already in just the couple days since it happened: a little kid, a diabetic, name of Wesley something, had his life-saving insulin taken away from him, somewhere here in beautiful enlighted Twentieth Century California, by his murderously stupid Bible-thumping parents who believed so devoutly in that crock of shit called a "Good Book" that they had decided he would "get well with the help of the Lord." So he died! Do any of you know how painful a death insulin shock and diabetic death can be? Think about it! Think about it the next time you run your beads, you blind ignorant moronic superstitious dark-ages bastards! And when he'd died, they *still* weren't convinced. They swore he'd rise from the dead, because the father of the kid had read in the Bible that it would happen.

They laid hands on him and . . . guess what . . . goshwow, folks . . . the kid was *still dead*! So the cocksucker told the newspapers he'd mis-read the Bible, had miscalculated how long it would take, and in four days the kid would rise up and walk and live again. And 200 similar shmucks went on down to the funeral today and they all wept and chanted and prayed and laid hands on the poor stiff in his coffin, and gee golly, nothing happened. But there's still two days to go. By the time you read this, I'll either be proved a doubting Antichrist fool without faith . . . or, more likely . . . that Mother and Father will be ripe for prison for having murdered an innocent child.

Item number three was one line from Mariana. "Don't forget the thirty years' illegal experimentation on blacks," she said, "using them to find a cure for syphilis."

Yeah. That's number three.

And number four is Mariana's own brother, who got the shit shot out of himself in 'Nam, so bad he's paralyzed from the waist down . . . and an Army sergeant came to the house to make Mariana and her family feel better by telling them what terrific medical treatment he'd get in an Army hospital.

What kind of a week has it been? Well, I'll tell you, gentle readers. It's been the kind of week that starts out on a Monday with wanting to scream till you fall down and black out. *That's* what kind of a week it's been.

And you can all go fuck yourselves!

INSTALLMENT 34

Interim Memo

A COUPLE OF TIMES I MADE THE MISTAKE OF TRYING TO READ this little essay at one of my lectures. Even years later, I'd fall apart. Please excuse the fuzziness of the photo. There are only two pictures of me with my dog, and the other one was used in another book. This one was taken when I lived in the treehouse on Bushrod Lane in Beverly Glen. Something like 1963 or '4, something like that.

Not a day passes I don't miss him. He was a swell guy.

Ahbhu

6 September 1973

*L*ast year, my dog died.

There's nothing more maudlin than reading someone's treacly and bathetic self-pity in the form of a lament for a pet. Nonetheless, the death of my dog, Ahbhu, did me in. And rather than drowning myself in the loneliness of it, I did what I usually do when I'm going through changes of sadness that I

Photo of Harlan Ellison with Ahbhu

can't handle. I put it into a story. The story was called "The Deathbird," and it appeared in *The Magazine of Fantasy and Science Fiction* for March.

It will be the title story of my Harper & Row collection, DEATHBIRD STORIES, in February or March of next year.

But that section about Ahbhu has brought some odd and

sympathetic reactions from large audiences, and so I thought I'd share it with you, here, seeing as how I've bared my soul in so many other ways.

I thought it might be nice if you saw—after last week's ugly tirade against humanity—that I *am* capable of love.

Yesterday my dog died. For eleven years Ahbhu was my closest friend. He was responsible for my writing a story about a boy and his dog that many people have read. He was not a pet, he was a person. It was impossible to anthropomorphize him, he wouldn't stand for it. But he was so much his own kind of creature, he had such a strongly formed personality, he was so determined to share his life with only those *he* chose, that it was also impossible to think of him as simply a dog. Apart from those canine characteristics into which he was locked by his species, he comported himself like one of a kind.

We met when I came to him at the West Los Angeles Animal Shelter. I'd wanted a dog because I was lonely and I'd remembered when I was a little boy how my dog had been a friend when I had no other friends. One summer I went away to camp and when I returned I found a rotten old neighbor lady from up the street had had my dog picked up and gassed while my father was at work. I crept into the woman's backyard that night and found a rug hanging on the clothesline. The rug beater was hanging from a post. I stole it and buried it.

At the Animal Shelter there was a man in line ahead of me. He had brought in a puppy only a week or so old. A Puli, a Hungarian sheep dog; it was a sad-looking little thing. He had too many in the litter and had brought in this one either to be taken by someone else, or to be put to sleep. They took the dog inside and the man behind the counter called my turn. I told him I wanted a dog and he took me back inside to walk down the line of cages.

In one of the cages the little Puli that had just been brought in was being assaulted by three larger dogs who had been earlier tenants. He was a little thing, and he was on the bottom, getting the stuffing knocked out of him. But he was struggling mightily.

"Get him out of there!" I yelled. "I'll take him, I'll take him, get him out of there!"

He cost two dollars. It was the best two bucks I ever spent.

Driving home with him, he was lying on the other side of the front seat, staring at me. I had had a vague idea what I'd name a pet, but as I stared at him, and he stared back at me, I suddenly was put in mind of the scene in Alexander Korda's 1939 film *The Thief of Bagdad*, where the evil vizier, played by Conrad Veidt, had changed Ahbhu, the little thief, played by Sabu, into a dog. The film had superimposed the human over the canine face for a moment so there was an extraordinary look of intelligence in the face of the dog. The little Puli was looking at me with that same expression. "Ahbhu," I said.

He didn't react to the name, but then he couldn't have cared less. But that was his name, from that time on.

No one who ever came into my house was unaffected by him. When he sensed someone with good vibrations, he was right there, lying at their feet. He loved to be scratched, and despite years of admonitions he refused to stop begging for scraps at table, because he found most of the people who had come to dinner at my house were patsies unable to escape his woebegone Jackie-Coogan-as-the-Kid look.

But he was a certain barometer of bums, as well. On any number of occasions when I found someone I liked, and Ahbhu would have nothing to do with him or her, it always turned out the person was a wrongo. I took to noting his attitude toward newcomers, and I must admit it influenced my own reactions. I was always wary of someone Ahbhu shunned.

Women with whom I had had unsatisfactory affairs would nonetheless return to the house from time to time—to visit the dog. He had an intimate circle of friends, many of whom had nothing to do with me, and numbering among their company some of the most beautiful actresses in Hollywood. One exquisite lady used to send her driver to pick him up for Sunday afternoon romps at the beach.

I never asked him what happened on those occasions. He didn't talk.

Last year he started going downhill, though I didn't realize it because he maintained the manner of a puppy almost to the end. But he began sleeping too much, and he couldn't hold down his food—not even the Hungarian meals prepared for him by the Magyars who lived up the street. And it became apparent to me something was wrong with him when he got scared during the big Los Angeles earthquake last year. Ahbhu wasn't afraid of anything. He attacked the Pacific Ocean and walked tall around vicious cats. But the quake terrified him and he jumped up in my bed and threw his forelegs around my neck. I was very nearly the only victim of the earthquake to die from animal strangulation.

He was in and out of the veterinarian's shop all through the early part of this year, and the idiot always said it was his diet.

Then one Sunday when he was out in the backyard, I found him lying at the foot of the stairs, covered with mud, vomiting so heavily all he could bring up was bile. He was matted with his own refuse and he was trying desperately to dig his nose into the earth for coolness. He was barely breathing. I took him to a different vet.

At first they thought it was just old age . . . that they could pull him through. But finally they took X-rays and saw the cancer had taken hold in his stomach and liver.

I put off the day as much as I could. Somehow I just couldn't conceive of a world that didn't have him in it. But yesterday I went to the vet's office and signed the euthanasia papers.

"I'd like to spend a little time with him, before," I said.

They brought him in and put him on the stainless steel examination table. He had grown so thin. He'd always had a pot belly and it was gone. The muscles in his hind legs were weak, flaccid. He came to me and put his head into the hollow of my armpit. He was trembling violently. I lifted his head and he looked at me with that comic face I'd always thought made him look like Lawrence Talbot, the Wolf Man. He knew. Sharp as hell right up to the end, hey old friend? He knew, and he was scared. He trembled all the way down to his spiderweb legs. This bouncing ball of hair that, when lying on a dark carpet, could be taken for a sheepskin rug, with no way to tell at which end head and which end tail. So thin. Shaking, knowing what was going to happen to him. But still a puppy.

I cried and my eyes closed as my nose swelled with the crying, and he buried his head in my arms because we hadn't done much crying at one another. I was ashamed of myself not to be taking it as well as he was.

"I *got* to, pup, because you're in pain and you can't eat. I *got* to." But he didn't want to know that.

The vet came in, then. He was a nice guy and he asked me if I wanted to go away and just let it be done.

Then Ahbhu came up out of there and *looked* at me.

There is a scene in Kazan's and Steinbeck's *Viva Zapata!* where a close friend of Zapata's, Brando's, has been condemned for conspiring with the *Federales*. A friend that had been with Zapata since the mountains, since the *revolución* had begun. And they come to the hut to take him to the firing squad, and Brando starts out, and his friend stops him with a hand on his arm, and he says to him with great friendship, "Emiliano, do it yourself."

Ahbhu looked at me and I know he was just a dog, but if he could have spoken with human tongue he could not have said more eloquently than he did with a look, *don't leave me with strangers*.

So I held him as they laid him down and the vet slipped the lanyard up around his right foreleg and drew it tight to bulge the vein, and I held his head and he turned it away from me as the needle went in. It was impossible to tell the moment he passed over from life to death. He simply laid his head on my hand, his eyes fluttered shut and he was gone.

I wrapped him in a sheet with the help of the vet and I drove home with Ahbhu on the seat beside me, just the way we had come home eleven years before. I took him out in the backyard and began digging his grave. I dug for hours, crying and mumbling to myself, talking to him in the sheet. It was a very neat, rectangular grave with smooth sides and all the loose dirt scooped out by hand.

I laid him down in the hole and he was so tiny in there for a dog who had seemed to be so big in life, so furry, so funny.

And I covered him over and when the hole was packed full of dirt I replaced the neat divot of grass I'd scalped off at the start. And that was all.

But I couldn't send him to strangers.

Interim Memo

IF YOU WERE TO ASK ME WHICH, AMONG THE FORTY-SOMETHING pieces in this strange diary, is my favorite, I would tell you that it is the essay made up of Installments 35 and 36. Looking back at this writing, after twenty years, I wince at much of what I wrote, and the high-pitched voice in which it was written.

But not the story of Ronald Fouquet, the story of my visit to a Damned Place.

Death Row, San Quentin, Part One

30 September 1973

Did I ever tell you about the time I visited Ronald Fouquet in the death cell at San Quentin?

It was one of the three or four most terrifying, chilling experiences of my life.

On the off-chance I missed hitting you with that one, I'll

tell you now, because this week I went to visit a girl I know, who got busted for dope that wasn't even hers, and she's in Sybil Brand at the moment, though she'll get sprung in less than a month, and it brought back all those monstrous memories of Q and Fouquet.

It was about three years ago. My attorney, Barry Bernstein, who is a genuine heavyweight at the bar of justice, called me and asked me if I wanted to see Death Row at the joint. I said certainly, and how was he intending to slip me past the security at Quentin; in his pocket? And if that was a snide and convoluted way of commenting on my 5'5" height, he could just go suck a tort.

But Barry had it all figured out. I was to dress very conservatively, bring a briefcase with legal pad and felt tips, and I would go in with him as his law clerk.

I accepted in a hot second.

We flew up to Oakland Airport early in the morning, and rented an Avis for the drive to Marin County. It was a brisk, snapping cool morning in September of 1970. The drive across from Richmond toward San Rafael was sweet and clear, with the forests and mountains just emerging from beneath a shroud of moist blue fog. Barry and I talked about the Fouquet case, which he had been involved with from the start of legal proceedings, and he filled me in with facts that cleared up holes in my memory of the newspaper reports I'd assiduously researched before the trip.

Ronald Fouquet (pronounced foo-KAY), in 1967, was already a loser. An oddjob janitorial maintenance man, unable to keep a steady gig, he was living with his common-law wife, Betty, and their five kids, several of whom were from Betty's previous arrangement. For whatever reasons—the papers postulated earning bread and beans for five kids was more than Fouquet could handle, others felt it was an ingrained psychopathic reaction—over a period of three weeks, Ronald Fouquet beat to death his five-year-old stepson, Jeffrey. Betty Fouquet sat passively and watched it happen. When the child was dead, they took the body to Sand Canyon and threw it far out in the desert.

Returning home, they found that only one of the remaining children remembered Jeffrey. Six-year-old Jody. She kept asking where her little brother was. Ronald and Betty grew more concerned about Jody's questions. They reasoned that as she grew older, her memories and curiosity would pose a dangerous situation. They decided to get rid of her, as well.

Over the next six or eight months they "reprogrammed" the little girl. They convinced her she was not named Jody, but was actually a little girl named Linda. They confused her as to her age. Was she five? Six? Seven? They hammered into her brain the story that Betty was not her mother, that her real Mother was out there somewhere, and one day they'd take her to that person. By 1969, feeling they had her so totally confused as to her real name, where she lived, who her parents were, that they could drive her up near Bakersfield in Kern County, dump her . . . and she would be unable to get back to them.

Driving around on that awful mission, they finally decided to leave her off on a freeway. They saw some lights in the distance that night, and told her to walk toward them, that her real Mother was there. Then they drove off.

The police found blonde little Jody, clinging to the hurricane fence in the center divider, trembling with fear, screaming for help. After difficulties, they managed to pry her loose. And after trying to make sense of her garbled story, it was released to the papers, and Jody's picture was flashed nationwide. She was human interest news. Who is this child? You may remember the stories.

Babysitters who had worked for the Fouquets saw the photos, and recognized Jody. They contacted the police who had, by this time, established from Jody that whatever her name was, and wherever she belonged, she had been premeditatedly abandoned. With the lead to Jody's parents, the police arrested Ronald and Betty Fouquet and charged them with endangering the life of a child.

Relatives from Betty's first liaison came to take care of the children, and started counting heads. Where was Jeffrey?

The story finally fell together, with Jody's help, and Betty decided to fink on Ronald. She spilled the story, threw herself on the mercy of the court, and Ronald Fouquet was indicted and tried and convicted of Murder One. Murder in the first degree. He was remanded to the authorities, sent to San Quentin, and was on a direct line for the gas chamber.

There was, of course, the appeal.

Which Barry was handling.

Fouquet had been in Q for six months, on Death Row, as Barry and I motored toward him that sweet September morning.

Driving across the Richmond–San Rafael Bridge, I could see the dark and already ominous bulk of Quentin, sitting out on the southwest curve of a spit of land jutting into San Pablo Bay, almost directly across the channel from Point Molate and the U.S. Naval Fuel Depot located there. San Quentin is the postal address; they call it Tamal.

"Jesus Christ," I said, in a hushed voice. "It looks like Bedlam."

San Quentin is sunk to its knees in the earth, set apart like a pariah from even the tiniest town, elevation 32 feet above sea level. The waters of the Bay rush toward the black rocks and then, as if wary, at the last minute merely slide in like oil. Gulls wheel above it, but they never seem to light. Surely it was my imagination, but as we drove over the bridge the sun seemed to vanish behind gray clouds, and there was a sudden chill.

We drove up to the guard gate, were cleared through and were directed to the parking lot. We walked back up to the security booth, were checked out, our briefcases examined, and then, in company with several other visitors, mostly women, we followed a guard to the reception building.

Once inside, we were checked again, gave our names and Fouquet's, and sat down on the benches to wait. The walls of the reception house were covered with paintings done by the inmates. They were for sale. None of them were particularly striking—a preponderance of pastoral scenes, clearly wish-fulfillment, and views of men behind bars—all were amateur-ish, save for a group by one man, working in charcoal, depicting perspective-rich impressions of life in a cell. They were similar in style to Munch in some cases, and in others, to the drawings of Kathe Kollwitz. They reminded me of the drawings I'd seen done by inmates of Bergen-Belsen and Auschwitz. I did not look at them for very long.

Barry was talking to an officer of the guard, and I wandered up to pass the time. They were on opposite sides of a glass case containing jewelry made for sale by the cons, and when I looked up from the rings and pendants I was staring straight at the chest of the guard. He wore a tie tack with a little silver pig on it.

I turned around and assayed the other visitors.

Almost all were women, mainly black and chicana. They were not, for the most part, lavishly or colorfully dressed. They sat stoically, waiting for their men. One or two small groups had formed, but everyone talked in hushed tones.

It was not the happiest place I've ever visited.

Finally, we were called, and a guard came to take us to the maximum security section. Most of the visitors were seeing the cons in a large conversation room that let off the display/reception area . . . but we had to go into the penitentiary itself to see Fouquet.

We went out the front door, past neatly-trimmed lawns and flowerbeds being tended by trusties, and followed the guard to a huge wooden door with an iron grate set into it. We were passed through into a tiny intermediate cubicle with a wood and iron door on the other side. Guards there frisked us again, and then we were passed through. We walked down a series of corridors and through another guarded door, and emerged into the central courtyard, the exercise yard, of San Quentin.

Shirley Jackson once wrote a book called THE HAUNTING OF HILL HOUSE. They made it into a film called *The Haunting*. It set forth the eerie proposition that there are houses that have been possessed by the evil spirits of the terrible acts that took place within their walls. Demon houses. As Richard Matheson called the one in his brilliant novel on the same theme, HELL HOUSE.

San Quentin is such a diseased house.

As I stepped out into the courtyard, the very *weight* of the cyclopean stones that formed Q's structure seemed to lean over and press on me. I found it difficult to breathe. My chest hurt.

Imprisoned in those stones and that ironwork were god knows how many years of pain and loneliness and brutality and evil that had seeped into the very pores of the prison, exuded by all the men who had lived and died there. I had been in jails before, many times, but this was something greater, more terrible. That place had a life of its own. It held, condemned within its borders, the raw naked hatred and violence of men for whom this was the living cloaca.

We walked slowly across the yard, and the most frightening thing that had ever happened to me, happened without warning. It was a moment in which an entire area of thoughts I had never thought came thundering in on me.

I was dressed simply, wearing a long dress jacket of brown corduroy, dark slacks and a shirt with an open collar. Hardly flamboyant . . . for anyplace but San Quentin.

As we walked, the barred windows that filled one entire wall of a dorm to our left began to show men staring out. They hung on the bars and watched, and then they began to whistle.

I have heard a sound like that only once before in my life. At a concert for the Rolling Stones that was mostly young boys. It was not the high-pitched screaming of female groupies, but a lower, throatier moan, pierced by whistling.

That was the wave of sound that washed over me.

Never having had, or having even been *approached* to have, a homosexual liaison, and thus never having thought of myself as fair game for other men . . . I suddenly realized the horror and dismay experienced by women for whom a walk past a hardhat's construction site is a degrading experience.

To those men, I was a sexual object, a potential catamite, what Hammett called a gunsel. My asshole was suddenly, for the first time in my life, something more than an orifice used to void my bowels. My mouth was being looked at in a very different way than ever before. I was frightened, and chilled, and wanted to turn and run.

But the leaning, pressing diseased walls of San Quentin held me, at that moment, as firmly as they held Ronald Fouquet, waiting on Death Row for our arrival.

Interim Memo

IN A 5-TO-4 DECISION ANNOUNCED ON 29 JUNE 1972, THE United States Supreme Court ruled (the cases considered were known by the lead case, *Furman v. Georgia*) that the death penalty was in defiance of the Eighth Amendment to the Constitution, the Bill of Rights' guarantee against "cruel and unusual punishment." The Burger Court's decision struck laws in 35 states.

But earlier—in February of 1972—the California Supreme Court had already decided that the state's death penalty violated the California constitution's prohibition against "cruel and unusual punishment."

At that time, there were approximately seven hundred men and women on Death Rows in America. Between the date of the California abolition of the death penalty, and the Supreme Court's decision, one hundred of those inmates had been removed from Death Rows in California. They were dispersed throughout the California Penal System, many still on appeal.

One of those (actually 107) prisoners was Ronald Fouquet. The Offender Information Branch of the Administrative Services Division of the Department of Corrections of the Youth and Adult Correctional Agency of the State of California in Sacramento has furnished me with a printout list of inmates on Death Row when the death penalty was overturned in 1972.

Item 72 on that list of 107 names identifies San Quentin prisoner B27954, Ronald Fouquet, as having been admitted to Death Row on 06/04/70. It shows that sometime between February of 1972 and 04/26/78 he was removed from the Row and was moved to another housing, either within Q or to another facility altogether.

Here's what happened, as best I've been able to ascertain:

Barry Bernstein's efforts in behalf of Ronald Fouquet's appeal were successful. His first degree murder verdict was reversed, 23 July 1973, as I reported near the end of this installment.

He was set for retrial, having served only three years and change at that point.

Fouquet was never retried. Bernstein managed to plea-bargain a deal in which Fouquet pled guilty to Murder Two, bringing with it a sentence of fifteen years to life. (Short of having a chum of mine in the DA's office spend valuable time rummaging through the stale-dated files in the warehouse, for the results of a case more than a decade old, something I wouldn't wish on someone I hate, much less a woman with whom I share pleasant memories, there is no way to pass along to you the *reasons* Fouquet wasn't retried and was allowed to bargain down to M2. My suspicion is that in the years intervening key witnesses died or were misplaced, and the case looked less winnable at the higher price-tag.)

By September of 1973, when I got around to writing these pieces, he was serving his time in the San Luis Obispo Men's Colony, a medium security installation. If he served the balance of his sentence there, or was moved again, I do not know.

But on 26 April 1978 he was paroled back into the community.

For the taking of a child's life, Ronald Fouquet had actually served less than eight years. And on 24 October 1979, he was wholly discharged from his Paroled state, becoming a completely free man who had, in the vernacular, "paid his debt to society."

Thereafter, only two bits of history are available to me. Early in 1980, Barry Bernstein received a call from Fouquet, from somewhere in California. He asked Bernstein to help find him a job. Bernstein, who had never been particularly comfortable with Fouquet, was unable or unwilling to accommodate, but suggested to the ex-con that given the intensity and widespread attention of publicity attendant on his case, that he would be smart to leave California entirely, to attempt a new life somewhere far away from the long memories of those for whom the name Fouquet was synonymous with *monster*. That—as best he can recall today—was the last Barry Bernstein heard of the man whose life he had saved.

One last ancillary twist to the story:

Barry practiced law for twenty years, was prominent and very successful. In 1988, an attorney in the San Fernando Valley named Barry S. Bernstein—no relation—was busted for insurance fraud. It hit the news and was big time on radio-tv and in the papers. But nobody bothered to make the distinction between Barry Bernstein and Barry S. Bernstein.

The day after the announcements, Barry's phone stopped ringing. He took out ads in the law journals, demanded clarification from the commentators, and tried in vain to get his clients to understand that this was another guy entirely.

Barry had promised himself that he'd retire after twenty years, but with a suddenness he probably would have eschewed, his bridges had been burned for him by Barry S. And so, by the start of 1989, Bernstein was no longer practicing. He is currently in the international fashion licensing and brand-name merchandising business, with contacts throughout the world, but principally in Japan. He is doing well.

For the last ten years, unless he's died, the subject of these two essays has lived and walked among us. He has no doubt changed his name. He could be working beside you right now. You might be married to him. What do you really know of the guy with whom you shared a beer last night? Fouquet and hundreds of others are out there right now; where, I do not know; under what names, I do not know.

Among penologists, the seven hundred released from Death Rows across America are known as The Class of '72.

Death Row, San Quentin, Part Two

27 September 1973

Crossing the yard of the joint. Q. San Quentin, September 1970. I was playing the role of legal clerk to my friend and attorney, Barry Bernstein; the only way I could get onto Death Row, to observe convicted child murderer Ronald Fouquet.

Crossing the yard, with the eyes of hundreds of cons on me. But not merely curious the way strangers in Milford, Pennsylvania, a small resort town, had been curious and disdainful when I'd walked into the best restaurant in the town in 1966, wearing long hair. Not with animosity, the way an audience of fans stared at me when I accepted their award for a piece of work that had been butchered, and told them they were idiots. No, I was being stared at the way women wearing pasties and G-strings are looked at in a thousand tank strip joints; the way secretaries on their way to lunch are looked at by high steel workers and riveters; the way gorgeous young girls fresh off the bus from Shawnee, Kansas, are looked at by the sleek sharks at the private clubs when they come in, wide-eyed and ready, on the arms of junior studio executives who've seen them having a BLT on rye at the commissary. I was meat, and I was being examined and whistled at and taught an ugly lesson.

If anyone ever asked me at what moment in my life I

perceived even *dimly* how awful it must be for women most of the time, I would tell them *that* was the moment. See yourself naked and bent over in the eyes of three hundred degraded human beings, and it is the death of sexism.

"Come on, let's move it," I said to the guard who was chaperoning us across the exercise yard to the building that housed the maximum security section, and Death Row.

He gave me a nasty, knowing smile. For maybe the millionth time since I was first arrested, at the age of ten in Painesville, Ohio, for stealing comic character pins from boxes of Kellogg's *Pep*, I realized I didn't much like cops.

At the same pace, without hurrying, the three of us went around the bulk of the main dormitory, thank god out of sight of the faces in the barred windows, the hands wrapped around iron.

Stones. Dark, weathered stones, striated with lines of shadow and black rock as colorless as old blood. Huge stones, set one atop the other, descending into the ground and rising up around us. There was no sky, no Earth beneath us, just the weight of the imponderable stones.

Approaching the high wall with the heavy door set into it, the blind multi-faceted eye of the wire-screened window in it, was a sequence from Hitchcock: that series of trucking shots approaching a supposedly deserted house, closer and closer, the hand-held camera rolling and bobbing, the tension building because you know something terrible waits on the other side of the door.

That building *screamed* with silent pain.

The guard reached the door, knocked, and the door was opened from inside. We stepped over a low sill, and the door was slammed and barred behind us. We were in twilight, and to my right was a green door of metal. It could have been painted wood. I think it was metal. There were rivet studs.

The inside guard who'd opened the door saw me staring at the green slab. "That's the gas chamber," he said. He said it with the disenfranchised pride of a slattern holding up her thalidomide baby, knowing it was being taken away at the end of the week.

Barry asked if we could see inside the chamber. The guard who'd walked us over said we'd have to check that out with Warden Nelson. I was just as glad he didn't push it; I remembered having been taken on a tour of Ohio State Penetentiary back in the Forties. The little green room where they kept that splendid piece of American furniture, the electric chair, had turned up in vagrant nightmares for twenty years.

It was time to see Fouquet, however.

We were taken up in a cramped, tight little elevator, gut-to-back with two guards. I saw no slim, trim, hardbelly turnkeys at Q. All I saw were men who liked their sweets and starches.

The elevator ground to a stop on the second or third floor. It's been three years, some details are blurred.

We emerged onto a metal-floored landing with identical doors on either side. One of the guards was wearing taps on his shoes, he made little clattering sounds as he walked to the door on our left and rapped on the window. Some details stick.

As we waited for the door to be opened to the cell block on our left, the other guard indicated the door on our right. "Sirhan Sirhan is in there," he said. "All alone in a cell by himself."

"How come by himself?" I asked.

The guard looked at me as though I was stupid. "If we put him in with the other cons they'd tear him to pieces in a day. He's too important. We can't take a chance."

Then the door on the left opened, and we went in.

As the door was being locked behind us, I looked around. We were in a corridor painted a pastel color. Light green. To our left were floor-to-ceiling bars, battleship gray, and several feet beyond the wall of bars a second floor-to-ceiling barred wall. In the space between sat a guard at a desk, reading a paperback. Beyond the second wall of bars was a cell block with an exercise area that separated cells running down both sides of the block. Several men were walking around in the tank, and they stopped and stared at Barry and myself as we waited for the guard in charge to talk to us. There were remarks and more whistles.

But this time, for what reason I can't say, there was none of the gut-tightening feeling I'd experienced in the yard. The men back there in the channel were something alien. There was a feeling about them, a look, a presence, that removed them from any identification with the human race. It was like looking at great languid subsea creatures propelling themselves through dark waters in an aquarium. I stared back at them.

On our right were rooms. One of them was the office. The guard responsible for the section came out and shook our hands, checked our passes. "Welcome to Death Row," he said, cheerily. I could see him standing at a crossroads, at midnight, swinging a dead cat by the tail.

"Bring Fouquet out," he said to the guard at the desk inside the dead-space. The guard made a tent of his paperback, got off his ass reluctantly, and went to the inner barred wall. I didn't see if he released the door of one of the cells in the block, or if Fouquet was one of the men walking in the exercise area, but I suspect the former, because of what Fouquet said later.

The guard in charge walked us down the corridor to a tiny open-fronted booth about the double-width of a phone booth, in which they'd placed three chairs and a small table. We sat and waited for the condemned man to appear. Barry winked at me, as if to say, "Well, I told you I'd get you onto Death Row, how do you like the entertainment so far?" It was a wink of camaraderie, and I didn't have the heart—nor would it have been prudent with guards all around the booth—to tell Barry how my guts were churning. (As tough as I like to think I am, and during moments of violence or danger or blood I've found I stay calm and functional, it's always been my feeling that to be a good lawyer—and take it from me, Bernstein is tops—one must be capable of an uncommon coldness of soul at times; so cold that passersby would get frostbite if they touched your hand. Barry's got that ability, which is perhaps why he's so damned good at what he does; but I decided he had turned himself off, emotionally, the way the surgeons in *M*A*S*H* turned themselves off to slaughter. I could never be an attorney.)

I looked around the little booth. On the floor by the back

wall was a cockroach. It had been stomped. A big one, it had left a messy corpse. Some details stick.

Then they brought Fouquet in.

I must be careful of what I now report. I heard things in that booth with Fouquet that I may not repeat. Though at the time I saw him he'd only been on Death Row six months, it has been three years since, and Fouquet's appeal hearing occurred just this past July 23rd. Because of the outcome of that hearing—which I'll tell you shortly—it would be in the nature of possibly prejudicing the man's rights, were I to repeat what he said.

But I *can* pass along impressions, for what they're worth.

He began talking almost before he sat down. A high-pitched, utterly terrified recitation of the terrors he was experiencing in the Death Row cell. He had not been out of his cell in months. He had demanded, and been granted, the right to take his exercise when everyone else was locked away. And when they were out in the tank, *he* was locked away so they couldn't get at him.

And why did "they" want to get at him?

He pointed to a huge shaggy man with the face of a Newcastle coalman. He called him, I believe, Jonah Something. He told us Jonah was scheduled for the cyanide sleep for having stomped a cop to death. It seems Jonah was salivating for an opportunity to penetrate Fouquet's virginal ass. Fouquet seemed less frightened of the gas chamber than of Jonah's depredations. He talked at great length of the horror of it, imparting in almost poetic terms his fear of the man and his penis. At one point he said in the dead of night, as he lay on his rack, he could sense Jonah's prick out there, across the exercise tank, like a great blind snake, risen up, poised to strike.

He begged Barry to get the Warden to have his cell designation changed to the empty block across the way, where Sirhan sat alone and thought of whatever it is Presidential Assassins think about. Barry said he would try.

Then they got down to the grounds for appeal. Like most death cell inmates, like much of the population of any big joint, Fouquet had become a jailhouse lawyer. He had read and re-read the transcripts of his trial. He went over in exhaustive detail with Barry, minute by minute, what this witness had said that was inaccurate, what the prosecuting attorney had concluded that was wrong, where his wife Betty had lied to throw the blame on him alone. It went on and on.

And all the while, the cons stared at us from thirty feet away through two walls of bars. The death penalty had not been revoked at that time. They were all scheduled to die within the foreseeable future.

My impression of Fouquet, as he talked—sallow, yellow-skinned, parchment face, beady little eyes, the look of the cracker about him—was one of total amorality. The court had judged him guilty, and I tried desperately not to make any value-judgments of my own, but I must admit that Ronald Fouquet left me with the feeling that, in isolated cases, the death penalty is not altogether a cruel and unusual prize to be won by some men for certain special deeds of evil.

Because of the visiting rules, we were required to stay in that booth for an hour or two—all sense of time's passage distorts in jail—I have no recollection of how long we actually spent with the man—and when there was nothing left to discuss about the case, Fouquet regaled us with stories of his fellow prisoners. He told the cheery tale of how two brothers who were in for murder had taken a dislike to another con in the cell block of Death Row, and had beaten him so badly with a three-legged stool from one of the cells that the man was in the hospital and wasn't expected to live.

And there was more talk of Jonah. Fouquet could not mention the man's name without swallowing dry with horror.

Finally, our time was up, and we watched as Fouquet was taken back to the Row, and locked in his cell.

We stopped to talk to the guard in charge, and Barry said, "Fouquet is frightened of one of the cons."

"Oh, yeah, sure, that's Jonah," the guard said, walking to a big board on one wall of the office. The board was laid out to duplicate the order of ranking of cells just beyond the bars, and a photo of each con was in a slot below the cell number. He tapped the photo of Jonah. "This one."

Barry and I were stunned. The guards knew all about it. "Well, if you know what's going on," Barry said, "why don't you do something about it?"

"Do what?" he replied. "Look: we can't move him, and we can't stop them. If they want to, they can do whatever they want in there before we can stop them." He mentioned the beating of the con by the brothers. "What'll have to happen is one day Jonah will get to Fouquet, and he'll either give him his ass . . . or get killed."

Nothing further was said about it.

We were waiting for a chaperon to come over from the main building, and Barry passed the time exchanging pleasantries with the guards. I said nothing. I merely watched and listened.

And realized again that the guards, like the cons, were in prison. They were all locked away together. And the difference between them was only the uniform.

Finally, our escort arrived, we left Death Row, and went back to the car. Driving back across the bridge, toward Oakland and the plane to return us to Los Angeles, I didn't say much to Barry beyond one comment.

"He'll be lucky if they deny his appeal and kill him."

Barry glanced at me, a little surprised. "Why?"

"There are worse ways to live than dying."

Barry didn't answer. He just gripped the steering wheel a little tighter.

Ronald Fouquet's appeal hearing was held on July 23rd, 1973. The judgment of Murder One was reversed. He is subject to retrial. Instead, Fouquet pleaded guilty to Murder in the Second Degree, a crime that commands fifteen years to life by California law. He is now in San Luis Obispo Men's Colony.

On a 15-to-Life, the prisoner is eligible for parole in three years. Ronald Fouquet has already served three years in San Quentin. That time is credited to his account.

Right now, at this moment, Ronald Fouquet, who pleaded guilty to beating to death a five year old child and warping the mind of another child under the age of ten, *that* Ronald Fouquet is eligible for parole.

There are worse ways to live than dying.

Interim Memo

THE GRACE NOTE OF THIS COLUMN DID NOT SOUND TILL YEARS and years later.

I cannot remember at which university I was speaking, but it chanced to pass that I recounted the story contained in this essay. Now that I think of it, I may again have been lecturing at Ohio State, where I'd first told this story twenty years after it went down. And a woman in the audience raised her hand to ask a question; and when I recognized her, she said, "I work in a B. Dalton bookstore in—" and she named a town, "—and I was at the checkout counter one day, reading one of your books, when a tall, elderly man came up to pay for his purchases with a credit card.

"I took his card, not looking at it," she went on, "and I laid your book down with the cover facing him, as I rang up the books he'd picked. He looked at your book, and asked me, 'Do you read this person's work much?' and I said, 'Yes, I like his writing quite a lot.' And he got a really hateful look on his face and mumbled something unpleasant, including a few mild curses like, 'Damn him,' and I was surprised, but he signed the credit card voucher, took his bag of books, and left."

She paused a moment, smiling up at me on the stage, and concluded, "It wasn't till that evening, when I was assembling the vouchers and the cash for deposit, that I finally saw the name on his slip. I was here the last time you spoke, and I remembered the story you told about that professor who told you that you had no talent, a Dr. Shedd. And the name on the voucher was Dr. Robert Shedd."

(Why do I now think, in 1989, that it may have been *James* Shedd—originally, and in the woman's story—rather than *Robert?* Well, it was one or the other.)

Apparently, Shedd was still an obscure teacher, now at an even less prestigious college than OSU. But *damn him* with a really hateful look was his persistent fate.

As Dorothy Parker said, "Living well is the best revenge."

This has been in aid of asserting that I am a self-made man . . . thereby demonstrating the horrors of unskilled labor.

College Days, Part One

25 October 1973

(P ant! Pant!) I'm back.

Okay, I apologize. It couldn't be helped. I was out on the road, lecturing in Ohio, a 21-day block-booked tour of ten colleges and universities, plus (momentary sanity lapse) a *Star Trek* convention in Detroit. And I had to drive an Avis an average of 200 miles a day, give a three-to-four-hour lecture every night (plus speak to a scattering of classes during the day at some schools), go back to whatever dorm or Holiday Inn at which I'd been billeted and write the rewrite of the treatment for an ABC Movie of the Week I'm doing, get what sleep I could, then get my ass up the next morning and motor another 200+ miles to my next gig . . . and start all over again.

So I missed my deadlines on the column. I apologize.

But I've come back with some new stories that I think will make the empty spaces acceptable.

The most significant story, I'll tell you now.

After my Father died in 1949, we moved from the little provincial enclave of Painesville, thirty miles northeast, and I finished high school in Cleveland. I did very badly in school. But my Mother wanted me to go to college, and I wanted to write, so it seemed the logical thing to do, to go to college. Bad grades: all we could afford was a state college. I was admitted to Ohio State University in September of 1953.

I was thrown out in January of 1955.

In the seventeen months of my "college career" some of the most pivotal and formative experiences of my life transpired, and I suspect for many of *you*, the same applies. So, in the noble and lofty pursuit of stirring the alluvial layers of your memory, and to reinforce my contention that revenge is an enriching act, the beginning—middle—and end of a collegiate tale of revenge that I'm sure will strike a sympathetic resonance in each of you.

At "State" (as its inmates refer to it), I was not terribly enthusiastic about football. Instantly, that made me an alien. Ohio State had, at that time, a student population of something over 33,000 . . . virtually all of whom were pigskin freako-devo-pervos. (Today they have 48,000 of whom most are the same types as in 1953. They killed the big DNA biochemistry program at State, but they built a bigger stadium. Sort of gets you right here, don't it, this lemming-like pursuit of the Amurrican Way.)

But I was rushed and pledged by Zeta Beta Tau (sometimes chucklingly called Zeta Beta Tomatah) (sometimes referred to as the ZBT baby powder fraternity), a gathering of Jewish gentlemen dedicated to the principles of fire engine red Caddy convertibles, torment of pledge "brothers" and the indiscriminate fucking of as many Tri-Delts as they could locate. My weird and *their* weird reasons for accepting me into ZBT will have to wait till next week, when I do the rap on my brief and unseemly fraternity days; but let it suffice for now, that I was only in the frat for a few months before being bounced as "not really fraternal material."

So I moved to a rooming house where I lived with a guy named Don Epstein—whose story I will tell in a later column, as well, when I get into the subject of Midwestern Ohio anti-Semitism. (Oh, there are *such* goodies upcoming in the next few installments!)

While living in the rooming house, in abject poverty, I worked at various menial jobs to supplement my Mother's support for tuition, books, pizza, etc.

But I couldn't afford luxuries . . . like music . . . and non-textbook reading material . . . and clothes. So I shoplifted. Under no circumstances am I advocating such a practice; but it seems to me that if your soul truly cries out for music and books, and you cannot afford them . . . steal them. And repay society later.

So I shoplifted.

And was arrested. For boosting a 45 rpm album of Oscar Peterson. It was an RCA album featuring Peterson doing "Poor Butterfly," a song that, even if I hear it today, sends chills of terror down my spine. I was sent to the Columbus, Ohio jail, where I languished for a time, till Don Epstein bailed my poor ass out.

That was reason one for my dismissal from OSU.

Reason two was that I punched a Professor. I don't even remember now why or who, but it was a happy foreshadowing of my reactions to this day when confronted with the arrogance and cavalier nature of many authority figures. Tv producers have, of late, become my prime martial arts targets. But, anyhow, that was the second nail in my collegiate career coffin.

Reason three was that one night, using the car I had borrowed from my Mother for a prom called The Military Ball, I drove up The Long Walk of the main campus, and directly onto the statue of William Oxley Thompson—a gentleman famed for some obscure deed years before my arrival—and with considerable difficulty circumnavigated the plinth. An aged and crepuscular security guard came after me on a scooter, if I recall correctly, and chased me off. We had a *French Connection* chase and I eluded him, but he got my license number.

That was reason number three.

But the *big* reason, number four, the one that altered my

life more assuredly than anything else before or since, was my encounter with the "teacher" of Creative Writing, one Professor Robert Shedd.

I was, even then, obsessed with the desire to be a writer. No, erase that: I was obsessed with *writing*. I felt talent and ideas and creativity bubbling in me like lava, and wrote relentlessly. Every story I submitted to Dr. Shedd was turned back with denigrating comments scrawled in an illegible hieroglyphic that would have been intelligible only to a medieval alchemist. Shedd should have been an apothecary. He ridiculed and demeaned my work mercilessly. But without the clear evidences of affection and caring that *good* teachers demonstrate when they perceive a student has talent and needs uncompromising, harsh criticism. Shedd's comments were merely exercises in viciousness.

Now, you must understand that in this student population of 33,000 inquisitive souls—all shrieking for the point after TD—there were only *four* people in Shedd's creative writing section. Two aged ladies who wrote astrological poetry, and over whom Shedd fawned with a sickening obsequiousness, a young and extremely attractive young lady who, to my certain knowledge, never spoke a word aloud and never submitted any work for criticism . . . and myself. Handing in one science fiction story after another.

Shedd obviously felt all that bullshit about flights to the Moon, manipulation of chromosomes, Malthusian overpopulation and studies of the interface between mankind and machines was drivel. He said as much. "Garbage," I recall he summed up one story I'd submitted for critical attention.

Finally, I felt pressed to confrontation.

As you may have gathered from your encounters with me, friends, I am a congenital confrontationist, not an avoidist.

"Dr. Shedd," I said, one morning after class, as he was gathering his papers into his satchel, "I get the feeling you don't like what I write. Would you care to expound on that position?"

(Now understand, also, that at this point I was neither Chekhov nor even Clarence Buddington Kelland, but as subsequent events proved, I was close to professional level in what

I was writing. Maybe not the reincarnation of Chas. Dickens, but certainly not a *total* dub.)

He mumbled something I couldn't understand. Something politic. He had, after all, only four students.

"Dr. Shedd," quoth I, "what I'm asking for is an honest appraisal of my worth as a writer." At that stage I had not yet learned that you don't ask those who can't write for shit themselves, how good *you* are.

"Mr. Ellison," he finally said, drawing himself up to his extremely heighty height, "you cannot write. You have no talent. No talent whatsoever. No discernible or even suggestible talent. Not the faintest scintilla of talent. Forget it. If you write, you will never finish what you write. If you finish it, you'll never submit it for publication. Should you submit it, no one will buy it. Should some deranged editor go thoroughly mad and publish it, no one will read it. If a miracle were to be passed and someone read it, no one would remember it. And even if, flouting all the laws of probability in the universe, someone should remember it, your miserable and demented work could not stand the test of time. I understand you are minoring in Geology. Why not go back to that . . . because obviously you have rocks in your head to begin with."

(I have enhanced the above diatribe considerably. Shedd was never capable of such outstanding rhythm and invention.)

I listened to all this, nodded soberly, smiled and said, "Dr. Shedd, why don't you go fuck yourself."

Thus, reason number four for my expulsion from OSU.

We won't even bother with reason number five, that I had the lowest point average in the history of the University: .086 out of a possible 4.00—an average never before or since equalled for minusculeness. It meant a total of four Fs, three Xs, two Incompletes . . . and a question mark.

I left OSU; standing out on North High Street in the wee hours after Midnight, my little cardboard mailing box of dirty laundry beside me; and I shook my fist at the silent institutional bulk of the school, and like Napoleon on Elba, I screamed, "I'll be back, you motherfuckers! I'll be back and make you sorry you ever told me I'd be a failure! I'll be back and make you pay for it!"

I then went back to Cleveland, and soon thereafter went to New York to commit myself to a full-time professional career writing. In the first year, I sold only two stories. In the second year I sold *one hundred* stories and my first novel.

It went on that way, without break, from that time to this. And that's almost twenty years.

But so enraged was I at Shedd's dismissal of my talent, that I sent him a copy of every single story that ever appeared in print. Every article. Every book. Every essay. Every film and tv script. And when I began getting good reviews, I had them Xeroxed and sent *them* to him. Every time I won an award I had a photo taken of me with it . . . and sent *that* to him. And when WHO's WHO listed me for the first time, I had a copy PermaPlaqued and sent *that* to him.

In my idle waking moments I would envision the Harlan Ellison Annex Shedd must have had to build to house all that material . . . a bulk of material that would one day develop a sentience of its own, like the Swamp Thing, and begin oozing and slithering and extending oily black tentacles that would slimily slip across the greensward to Shedd's home, crawl like ivy up the night-shadowed walls, insinuate themselves through the screens of his bedroom windows and, with a suitable and happily ironic verve, choke the cocksucker to death in his bed!

I never heard from him. He never responded. Whether he actually received what I sent, I don't know, though none of it was ever returned by the post office.

And still my revenge was incomplete. We are all the same: inside each of us walking tall and straight, is a crippled child. We carry the past on our backs like the chambered nautilus. I still wanted a physical revenge!

And two weeks ago, I got it.

The tour from which I just returned was booked by Creative Entertainment Associates. They booked it early in the year. Ohio, they said, and named the schools that wanted me. Quite an impressive list: Bowling Green, Findlay, Wilmington, Wooster, Steubenville, others. And Ohio State.

Dum de *dum* dum!

"Sure, Steve," I told my booking agent, "I'll speak at State, but they have to pay *more* for me than any other school on the circuit. Personal matter."

So they did, and on Thursday night, October 4th, 1973, almost twenty years later, I returned to Ohio State University. At the entrance to the Main Campus there was an *enormous* billboard that had been erected: COME HEAR HARLAN ELLISON SPEAK! it shouted. And that night, before a huge audience in Mershon Auditorium, I delivered a three-hour presentation that released all the pent-up hatred and frustration and desire for revenge that had been festering in my gut for two decades.

I was a hit. I have the clippings from the *Columbus Dispatch* to prove it. The headline in the OSU newspaper said: "Ellison Mocks OSU!"

One of the requests I made of State, when they booked me, was that they cut a series of cassettes of the evening's presentation. I have it here. You ought to hear it. It's eerie: I started out telling about Don Epstein. Not one single laugh. You'll understand why when you read that column in a week or two. Then I went through what I've set down here. A few laughs, but not many. Then I did a number on how the frat boys used to fuck a sad little townie girl who was a bit slow in the head. No laughs. Then random anger and viciousness. No laughs. Then pathetic and saddening stories. No laughs.

It was not my usual happy-go-lucky madhouse presentation.

And, as you can hear on the tape, suddenly, in the middle of it all . . . I was purged.

I listen to that tape, and I hear my voice break. I hear silence and a cough from the audience. An embarrassed, hushed expectancy as students who've come up from Wooster and down from Steubenville, who laughed and enjoyed my raps at their schools, realize they are getting something quite different. And then I hear myself, like a stranger, softly and much more sanely than at any other place on that tape, murmur, "Dear god, I'm freed."

And you know . . . I am.

Interim Memo

JUST ON THE OFF-CHANCE THAT THE TONE AND CONTENT OF this one strikes you as no more than a childish fit of pique, I urge you to recall how *you* felt the last time some shop, bank, state or government office, credit card representative, billing officer for the phone company, Civil Service slavey, college, or IRS agent gave you a hard time over some incredibly simple matter.

If, after you've gone through what I report here, you didn't feel like raping their cattle and sowing salt on their loved ones, then you deserved every bit of frustration and humiliation you got.

The American Film Theatre folded very quickly. If I recall correctly, it managed to float for only two seasons, and then sank without a trace, taking vast sums of debt with it.

Eventually, when it was released to television, I saw the AFT production of *The Iceman Cometh.* Jason Robards, Jr. was marvelous, as always. But the production was no more unusual than any of the many previous stagings of that O'Neill standard.

Hardly worth all the good intentions I expended in its behalf.

The Death-Wish of a Golden Idea

1 November 1973

*I*t was my intention this week to run that nostalgic Ohio State fraternity story, but something happened a few days ago that demands instant spleen-venting, because it's current, so I'll beg your indulgence and promise to import the promised intelligence in the next installment. But *this* time, I want to comment on the death-wish of a golden idea.

Half a bunch of years ago, here in Clown Town, we had the same spate of discothèques all major American cities endured. We had our bucket shops and our kiddie havens, we had our posheries and our High Exclusives. One of the last group was run by several well-known, well-connected gentlemen who sank sizeable chunks of their personal fortunes in the joint. Trembling with crystal and scintillant with chrome, the fruggery was instantly the in-spot at which to be seen. The *hoi* and the *polloi* came out five nights of the week just to show off their razor cuts, their silicone injections, their poorboy sweaters and their Dr. Parks noses. The money fled from their pockets with a life all its own, and the gentlemen who had funded this sanctuary as a prime example of social work among the very hip, began to see themselves as direct lineal descendants of Croesus.

They were momentarily raised to the level of guru by the slithering shadow of ennui always just abaft the cruising pattern of the Beautiful People. They were offering a 100% guaranteed, diamond-encrusted, for-dead-sure *in* spot, and no worry about maybe it is or maybe it ain't and maybe there's a superkickier scene on the next block: *this* was the place to be, where Rona Barrett would find her scabrous items for the next day's column. It was Valhalla, and the keepers of that swinging gate felt like something out of a late Thirties' Universal horrorflick, with the electricity running up out of their wallets, through their groins, down their arms and out their fingertips! They had The Power!

So they skinned away their Via Veneto pimp altarboy smiles like copperheads shedding their hides, like high-platform gigolos dumping one withered Topeka widow for a tonier one, and they became the rapacious creeps they had always been, but had never had the clout to be openly. They began saying no entrance to this one, no table on the dance floor to that one, do you have a reservation to another, only members allowed to yet another one. And the rumbles began sub-strata. The little annoyances of the rabble. But . . . what the hell . . . hey, fuck'm, what do they matter!

And one night, passing the joint, I heard a Pittsburgh matron scream from the sidewalk, from above her Emba Cerulean carapace, from the Outer Dark to which she'd been consigned with her balding hubby, the well-known advertised-on-tv credit orthodontist with five handy locations throughout Pittsburgh to serve your 24-hour chomper needs, I heard her shriek like an Arctic Tern seeking smorgasbord, "You snotty punk sonofabitch, you just wait till *you* need customers!"

Well, gentle readers, there *is* a God, and one day soon thereafter He wasn't busy backstopping the fortunes of the Mets and He dumped a load of poetic justice on them there glossy gentlemen, and another disco opened and, overnight, their *bôite* was as empty as an Egyptian threat.

The dance floor reflected back no forty dollar boots, the canapes went unscarfed, the noise level of The Grateful Dead served to deaden no semicircular canals save those of the *maître d'* and when Gay Talese came to Hollywood he went elsewhere.

Because the best those two nerds had to offer, at the height of their most golden moments, was nothing more than an upholstered box to hold the Chanel-sweating bodies of bubble-heads happily kept off the city streets for a few hours.

But the American Film Theatre has something truly lovely to offer, and for the Ely Landau Organization (who lie behind the AFT concept) to practice the same sort of arrogant, swinish, supercilious, cavalier, common garden variety rude behavior, is tantamount to a naked death-wish.

In case you haven't heard about the American Film Theatre and what it has laid on for this year, I'll summarize *very* briefly, because if there's one thing I *don't* want to do it's shill for them.

Mr. Landau—a man whose rep till now has been unbe-smirched—came up with the idea of subscription cinema, in much the same fashion as subscription or "hard ticket" theatre. He put together eight films that, in the pre-release publicity touted through American Express (which is where I first heard of it), promised eight evenings of superlative entertainment. Participating movie houses, on their traditionally slow nights, Monday and Tuesday, once a month from October to May, would show the specially-created films to pre-sold audiences. Three seventy-five a seat. Twenty-eight bucks for the series. And what films they are to be! Eugene O'Neill's *The Iceman Cometh* with Lee Marvin, Robert Ryan and Fredric March; Zero Mostel in *Rhinoceros* by Ionesco; Alan Bates in *Butley* . . . Hepburn, Albee, Scofield, Olivier, Keach, O'Horgan, Franken-heimer . . . the list of authors, stars and directors is stagger-ing. How could one not love such a golden idea.

Not I, shouted the Papa Bear, rushing in his check for fifty-six dollars so he could take Lynda to the Encino Theater on Tuesday nights once a month to get dosed up with culture and M*A*G*I*C!! This was a series I didn't want to have to be waiting for a screening invitation to see. No hoping to be on the reviewers' "A" list from the Motion Picture Producers Association. Hard cash on the barrelhead. This was a series I wanted to tout to the skies in these columns, without any worry about missing a single presentation. That'll teach me to be honest. A loathing of payola, and an equally fervent loathing of most of the deadbeats who pretend to be film critics so they can mooch freebie screening passes, motivated the act of support for what I took to be the hottest, most idealistic cinematic project since Welles announced he would make Kafka's *The Trial*. And I do not make comparisons with that turkey coincidentally.

Now, for those of you who may only know your faithful columnist from these pages, or from the books I write, or from the movies and tv I write, let me advise you that I have been a film critic for some many years, with *Cinema* magazine, with *The Staff*, and on a free-lance basis for over a dozen rather prestigious publications. I am, as they put it in Jan Dingilian's office, "accredited."

So. You can imagine my horror when I discovered that on Tuesday, October 30th, just two days ago, I was to be not in good old Sherman Oaks, spiffing myself to see *The Iceman Cometh* at the Encino Theater, but would be starting ten days as Writer-in-Residence at the University of Kansas in Lawrence.

Ohmigod, I thought, my flesh crawling, I've got to DO SOMETHING. So I checked out the list of member theaters and, yes, there was one in Lawrence. But how to get them to change my tickets? Mariana, my indefatigable assistant, did some phoning around and managed to get in touch with the Ely Landau Organization in New York. Check with Joyce Ingram in L.A., she was told by a nameless individual in New York.

So I called Joyce Ingram. "Oh God, not another one!" she said, a trifle hysterically, "not another critic who wants to go to a screening!"

"No, no," I hastened to advise her, "I'm a critic—I'm an *accredited* critic—but I've bought my own tickets, and all I want is to get them switched to Lawrence, Kansas."

Ms. Ingram, who turned out to be a dynamite lady who knows her PR as well as her Ps and Qs, said she had nothing to do with that end of the situation, but if I was a critic, an *accredited* critic, why then I should be going to a screening. Terrific, I said, is there a screening before I leave town?

There was an embarrassed silence as deep as the hush at Ultima Thule. "Ms. Ingram?" I said. I thought perhaps she had had a seizure. "Are you there?"

"I'm here. I wish I weren't."

"You mean they've already had the critics' screening."

"No. I don't mean that at all."

"There hasn't been a critics' screening."

"There hasn't been *any* screening."

"Oh. Well, when will there *be* a screening?"

"I don't know."

Now the hush was at *my* end.

I tried again. "But there will *be* a screening, won't there? I mean, the film goes next Tuesday. This is Wednesday. That's less than a week. There *will* be a screening, yes?"

"There will be a screening, no. I think. I mean, I *don't* think. I mean . . . I simply don't know."

I have never heard such frantic in someone's voice.

What that unfortunate human being, saddled with the West Coast publicity job, was trying to say, without once badrapping her employers, was that the Ely Landau Organization was playing the same game as those two nerds who ran the disco I was telling you about. They had scheduled *no* press or critics' screening. Not even the PR staff out here had seen the film. Nor was there any evidence forthcoming from New York that they *would* see the film. Now I don't know how that hits you, friends, but it seems to me mighty specious reasoning on the part of big-time entrepreneurs to expect their PR people to sell a highly rarefied product like the American Film Theatre's toney and intellectual product without having glommed the merchandise.

"But, listen," I said, hoping I'd misinterpreted the whole thing, "I don't need a screening, all I need is a change of venue. A screening would be *nice*, but I'm willing to pay my own way. Who do I contact to get them to shift me from L.A. to Lawrence, Kansas?"

She suggested I try the New York office again, because all decisions were coming from that sector. She suggested I try Ely Landau himself, and failing that route, I should try Joe Friedman, who was making all the important decisions about publicity from the New York office. I muttered something about the non-existence of Mr. Friedman's decision-making abilities, and thanked her.

I hung up, dialed New York, and asked to speak to Mr. Landau. I did not call collect. I was told Mr. Landau was in conference. Okay, then, Mr. Friedman. Mr. Friedman was in conference. Then who's in charge of Subscriber Relations, I asked. Mr. Walter Reilly, I was told. Okay, then, Mr. Walter Reilly, I said. I'm so easy to get along with I even disgust myself.

"Mr. Reilly's office," a dulcet voice said, finally. But he wasn't there, either. Nor was his assistant. But the young lady would be *glad* to help me, seeing as how my Charter Subscription Account number was 5738. (You'll never know how slavishly grateful I was that I'd gotten a lucky number.)

I told the operator I'd talk to the young lady, and when we were connected, I poured my heart out. "Accredited!" I kept stressing. She said there was nothing she could do, but if I was a critic, why didn't I just call Ms. Joyce Ingram in Los Angeles and have her add my name to the critics' screening list. I tried to tell her that list was on a reality par with Abominable Snowmen, UFOs, The Great Pumpkin and Spiro's innocence, but she poo-poohed my protestations and said she was sorry. We were abruptly cut off.

I called Joyce Ingram back. Her position had grown more untenable since last we'd talked, but by this time we were like old friends. "What's the matter, Joyce?" I asked. If I couldn't see my movie, at least I could get in a little practice as a lay therapist.

"I don't know what's happening," she said. "I'm being deluged with calls from the press, and I don't know what to tell them. New York won't say whether there'll be a press screening or not."

"What's the matter, are they afraid someone'll pan the film?"

"I don't know," she said.

I don't think I've ever felt sorrier for someone. They were clearly driving that poor woman bananas, and she was trying to do a job for which they'd erected roadblocks of incredible stupidity and ineptitude. I felt I should do something. For her and for me. "Look," I said, "I'll try Friedman again. It's too late today, but I'll call first thing tomorrow. Maybe if I get him personally, I can let him know how this situation is bumming out the L.A. press."

She didn't urge me to do it, but I could detect in her politeness a hope that *something* would pry Mr. Friedman's decision-maker loose from its freeze-up.

I tried for three hours to reach Friedman. Mr. Friedman is in conference. Mr. Friedman is in a screening. Mr. Friedman just had a coronary. Mr. Friedman is out having lunch with the Easter Bunny at The Four Seasons.

Finally, when I'd had enough bullshit from Mr. Friedman's obviously high-born secretary, a young woman who could give ugly lessons to a loggerhead shark, I told the operator I'd speak to anythehellbody, and I was connected once again with Priscilla Personality, Friedman's Cerberus, the only living creature who breathed ice crystals. "Mr. Friedman is in a screening," she said, apparently affronted that I was disturbing the peace and calm of her publicityless world.

"That's terrific," I said, unleashing my scathing wit, "I'm glad *some*body gets to go to screenings." That one sailed past her at 30,000 feet, heading out to sea. "But if you're trying to alienate a columnist who only wants to praise your damned series, you're doing a helluva job, Princess."

That gave her pause. Maybe she thought I was Rona Barrett. On smoggy days our voices are similar.

So she asked what she could do to help me, and I ran through my by-now-shopworn compendium of woes. She listened, and when I was done whimpering, she advised me that she had nothing to do with rearranging tickets, that was Mr. Walter Reilly's area of concern. I said I *knew* that, but at this point I figured my best bet to see the film and review it here in this column was to be put on a list for a screening, if such a list and such a screening existed, or was in the process of *coming* into existence. I added that I wrote for *Esquire*, *Playboy* and other sterling publications, as well as the newspaper you hold in your hands now. She said she'd have Mr. Friedman call me right back.

Suffused with my own self-importance, that I, miserable lowly Harlan Ellison, listed in WHO'S WHO and considered by no less an authority than *Time* magazine as an important writer, Force for Good in Our Times, snappy dresser, terrific dancer and credit to my race . . . was actually going to receive a call from *Joe Friedman*, a personage I'd begun to suspect was a fever-dream creation of the Ely Landau Storm Window and Movie Production Company.

"Call me right back" turned out to be a euphemism. Mr. Friedman not only didn't call me back, but it wasn't till the next day, when I called Joyce Ingram to tell her how successful I'd been, and that I'd straighten things out with her boss pronto, that she conveyed a message from the New York office.

"There will be a critics' screening, but they advised me that the reviewers for *Esquire*, *Playboy* and all the other magazines were, at the moment you called, seeing the film; and there is no room for you at the critics' screening."

I think I started screaming. I'm not sure. I blacked out and only came to minutes later with the mouse sounds of Joyce Ingram peeping on the other end of the line. She was concerned about my health. *I* was concerned about my health.

"All I want is to move my goddam tickets to bloody Kansas!" I shouted. She said she understood, but what could she do? "I'll write a column that'll make them look like the rude bastards they are," I promised. She said she understood, but what could she do? Are they *trying* to turn the press against the series? I asked. She said she didn't know what to tell me, I wasn't the only one, there were others, influential others, who were in the same boat, and they were screaming bloody murder. She said it was Friedman's decision.

I thanked her and hung up. Then I started thinking: perhaps Friedman's secretary, the Daughter of Lucrezia Borgia, had gotten it wrong. Maybe she thought I was a ripoff artist masquerading as an *Esquire* film critic. Not an unreasonable assumption. Bogdanovich has been doing it for some time.

So I call Friedman's office again. Person-to-person. He was on the phone. When would he be off? Five minutes. I'll call back. Five minutes later I tried again. Sorry, said Lizzie Borden, he just stepped into a meeting. Bullshit, I said. Give me Walter Reilly's office. So I got Reilly's office again, and got a different woman then the first time. This one said she was Reilly's assistant, so I told the operator I'd talk to her.

You must pause to perceive, at this point, that I'd totally forgotten *why* I was so crazy to see their fucking movie, but like a man who spends his entire life tracking the renegades who slew his mother and baby sister, I was obsessed.

I told this new voice my problem, including and adding to the barely-veiled threats of rampant bad publicity. She checked the theater in Lawrence and found they were not even showing *The Iceman Cometh* first. They were showing Pinter's *The Home-coming*, which I would see when I returned to L.A. where it's the series selection for November. No help. She suggested I talk to their Mr. Joe Friedman, a paragon of assistance in PR matters, the Young High Mogul of splendid press relations. I thanked her and slashed my wrists.

So, the point is, I missed *The Iceman Cometh*. And unless either a miracle is passed or I fall into a time-warp, he ain't gonna cometh for me noway nohow.

All of which brings me back to those two nerds who ran the disco with arrogance and lousy public relations, until the moment came when they needed some good karma, and found all they'd stored up was dried fruit and three-dollar bills.

There is an attitude on the part of those who have a hot thing going, that they can treat you and me and anybody they choose, like a pound and a half of dogmeat.

So I bring to your attention the American Film Theatre, and the Ely Landau Organization. I have a pretty good idea who reads this column, after all this time writing it for you, and I have a hunch many of you are the ones who'll be on Mr. Landau's subscription list, or reviewing his product. I don't ask that you indiscriminately run him off the road, but suggest merely that if you love me even a little bit, that you take a somewhat more critical look at what the AFT puts before you. And if it doesn't pleasure you with the proper degree of wonder to repay the adoration this golden idea drew unto itself, that you drop Mr. Landau a note.

Maybe he doesn't know what Mr. Friedman and his canni-
bal herd of toadies are doing. Maybe, if he ever gets out of that
screening to which *accredited* critics aren't invited, he might like
to know. I've done my part.

Or maybe I'll have more to say about it *next* month. And
the month after that . . . and the month after *that* . . .
and . . .

College Days, Part Two

8 November 1973

*T*wo weeks ago I talked about going back to Ohio State to purge my feelings of hatred and revenge against the academic Establishment that had so crippled my spirit as a young man. Another part of that experience, twenty years ago, was my brief and hardly salutary encounter with fraternity life.

As I said earlier, we are like the chambered nautilus: a snail that has a shell made up of small vaults. It moves from chamber to chamber as it matures, until finally it leaves its shell and dies. But throughout its life it literally carries its past on its back. Each of us is a nautilus: we never *really* rid ourselves of the adolescent spurs that drove us to become the people, the "adults" we are today. Whether it was living up to your parents' hopes or fears about your final fate, or getting over a crushing defeat in a love affair, or recouping from a cataclysmic financial setback . . . whatever it is, long long after the validity or the need of the original situation has been dissipated . . . still we play to that vanished audience. We carry our past on our backs.

But occasionally, as it was with my return to OSU to speak before the very Establishment that had valued me as less than rubbish, the Wheel turns and we find ourselves in one of those pivot-points of our existence, a point in space and time where things become very clear, where the trembling moment becomes a scenario, and we realize just how far we've come, how divorced *in fact* we've become from the vestigial fears and motivations that still haunt us.

One such was in relation to my fraternity days, even as brief, even as traumatic as they were.

I was hardly the fraternity boy type. I was out of a small Ohio town, I was poor, I was unmannered and awkward and covered these flaws with an arrogance and berserkness that, finally, came off as rank obnoxiousness. But my Mother subscribed to most of the myths and forms of what she thought it took to be a social animal, and she wanted very much that I join a frat. "To make good connections for the future." I won't even dwell on the foolishness and speciousness of that proposition.

Nonetheless, at that stage of life where many paths are tried in hopes of finding the main route, I was rushed by three or four fraternities at State, and finally pledged Zeta Beta Tau.

ZBT is a national fraternity, with strong chapters at the Big Ten universities. It is a Jewish fraternity, and at Ohio State it was reflective of what I find to be most offensive in the moneyed Jewish community. It was a Shaker Heights mentality fraternity, with the emphases on social position, material manifestations of position—most prominently the fire engine red Cadillac convertible—on a Sunday morning you could see all the scungy pledges out Turtle-waxing the actives' trash-wagons—and the membership demonstrated acute attitudes of anti-gentile feeling, outrageous sexism (with special attention given to *goyishe* sorority girls, especially the stunning ladies of Delta Delta Delta, who were the most amazing gathering of incredible beauties on the campus), and the no-neck disrespect for intellectualism I've found rampant among Hollywood producers, many of whom are ex-frat men.

It was not, to be precise, the most enriching setting in which to place the rough jewel of my personality.

But I pledged. My reasons were a need to belong to something, to *any*thing at that point, to bulwark my fears against being adrift on a monster campus with a population of over 38,000 students . . . and to satisfy my Mother. You all know what that's about. I had been on my own since I'd been thirteen, and I was in no respect a momma's boy or even notably strong on family relationships. But I felt a need to *do* something for her, to say thank you and pay some dues. In an inarticulate way, joining ZBT assuaged that need.

For *their* part, they pledged me on the most indefensible grounds imaginable. First, I was working on the Ohio State *Sundial*, the humor magazine (which at that time was one of the leading college humor magazines in the nation), and though the chapter was heavy on members who had money, or who were affiliated with the football team, or whose fathers could contribute Scotty freezers for beer busts, they needed to insure their standing on the campus both scholastically and in the area of student activities. I was only a freshman, but already I was writing for the *Sundial*, and everyone knew what clever, witty people those *Sundial* bohemians were . . . so, ergo, I had to be a heavyweight in the grade department, thereby aiding them in pulling up the house average lowered by the Cro-Magnons or the scions of wealthy families. (Little did they realize what a downer I was to be in *that* department; lowest grades in the history of the school.)

The other reason they pledged me was a peculiar talent I've always had . . . that of being able to "read" people from their walk or speech or mannerisms . . . a kind of primitive body language thing that is in no way ESP or occult or . . . I'll talk about that in another column some time, but for the nonce let it suffice that one manifestation of that talent was, and is, the ability to tell if a woman is a virgin or not. I always had that "talent" (if such it can be called) and it never seemed like a big deal to me; just something I knew. But *they* thought it was very rare metal, trace element stuff, a valuable property. So they pledged me.

Right from the git-go, I was less than a satisfactory pledge. I'd been on my own, making my own living since I was thirteen years old, and I was used to a degree of personal freedom and personal pride that did not square with the essentially demeaning, dehumanizing, disgusting treatment accorded pledges by actives. Some brain damage case from Sandusky would come up to me, extend his Bass Weejuns and tell me to polish them, and I'd look confused and bemused and annoyed and say, "Do *what*?" And when he'd repeat the order—never request, always order—I would politely suggest he remove the pennies from the slots on the shoes and jam the leathers up his ass, horizontally.

This made for some small pique on the part of the ZBT superstructure.

They attempted to break my spirit (to what end I have never understood, but then I've never been able really to perceive what value fraternities had from the outset, save as enclaves to buffer the timorous and snobbish from having to rub elbows with the common herd). Their attempts to whip me into shape were doomed, of course. Nothing worked. Not the thousand chickenshit barbs to which I was heir, not the hell sessions late at night, not the ugly pranks, not the crummy errands I was ordered to run, not the unveiled attacks on my coarse and hardly fraternal manners, not even the night one winter when a BMOC named Gene Somethingorother demanded milk (during a meat meal at which milk was omitted as a weak-wristed gesture toward keeping kosher), and shrieked for me to go get it, when he knew there was none in the entire house; and I slipped and slid through the snow to the Protestant fraternity house next down the line; and brought the dumb fucker a ten-gallon can and dumped it on him at the head of his table. No, I was a hard punk to break.

So they slipped into high gear.

During mid-term week, during which I was having problems studying, during which I was coming to the realization that I was a lousy student, they came at me with pranks that tested my patience sorely.

I would study till three or four in the morning, then crawl wearily into my bunk-bed to get a few hours' sleep till my first class and/or mid-term test. No sooner had I crashed, then one of their number would come and roust my exhausted ass from slumber . . . to clean the garbage shed down behind the house.

The first night it happened, I was too exhausted even to argue. In my pajamas I half-fell down the three flights of fire escape stairs on the side of the ZBT house, and shoveled orange peels and eggshells into garbage cans, and swept the metal walls and slab floor clean. It took about an hour, the active assigned to the ordeal supervising my efforts, heaven forfend I should miss a milk carton or blob of spaghetti. When I'd finished, he let me go back to bed.

The next day, I slept through my biology mid-term.

The following night, they did it again. I'd studied till around midnight, then collapsed. Fifteen minutes after I'd dropped off . . . fully-dressed . . . lights still burning . . . another active came to roust me.

Comatose, I stumbled ahead of him, down the third floor corridor to the fire door at the end of the hall. I pushed open the door and stood on the landing, chilled by the December wind. In December, Ohio is not a terribly hospitable environment. I started down the stairs, and stumbled. The active shoved me. "Get your ass in gear!" That was his second mistake.

He was wearing a jacket and tie. I half-turned, reached over my shoulder, and grabbed the tie. I jerked him forward sharply and he sailed past me, went over the fire escape railing, and fell three floors through the roof of the garbage shed.

I went back to bed.

That incident, coupled with one other, melded to bring about my expulsion from ZBT during my first quarter at Ohio State. I never went active.

They called me down to the office of the President of the fraternity, and there they sat (in jackets and ties): the President, the Vice-President, the Treasurer, the Recording Secretary and the Strawboss of Pledges, or whatever dumb title it was that he held with such honor. And they suggested I move out at once. My behavior, they said, was something less than fraternal. They cited the two big incidents that had happily driven them to this expulsion. And, though he was grievously wounded, they told me, the noble active who had done the Brodie off the fire escape was prepared not to sue me for assault and battery, if I'd get the hell out within the hour and keep my mouth shut about the whole thing. Apparently, the garbage had cushioned the clown's impact, and they'd prevailed on him not to have me wiped out . . . in the good name of Zeta Beta Tomatah.

So I moved out, following the route taken by Don Epstein, who had pledged with me briefly. I'll tell you about Don next week. About how we lived in the same rooming house at Ohio State, and about the special tragedy that Don Epstein came to represent to me.

But that's next week. Right now, I'll finish the fraternity story, and make the point how the Wheel turns, and how we sometimes are accorded the luxury of knowing the moment when the past is dead and we need not lug it around with us like a millstone.

That moment came five years ago, in 1969, fifteen years after the morning in the office of the President of the Nu Chapter of Zeta Beta Tau; the morning during which one of those grand officials of that grand Greek organization told me I was, strictly between us, a bum, a creep, a hick, and a guy who was destined for the toilet.

Fifteen years later, that noble Greek called me, here in Los Angeles. Said he was in town for a convention. Said he was with his wife. Said he'd followed my career. Said he was proud to have been such a close friend of mine. Said he wanted to drop by and strike up acquaintances. Said he might be moving to Los Angeles. Said a lot of bullshit.

I confess to the cheap desire. I wanted to flaunt my success. I invited him and his wife to drop by.

When he arrived, his first words as he stepped through the inlaid wood art treasure by Mabel and Milon Hutchinson that serves as my door were, "Damn! It's good to see one of our guys has made it so big!" My gorge became buoyant.

It was a ghastly few hours. He was the same age as I, thirty-five, and he looked fifty. He had "made the right connections" in the fraternity. He had married the daughter of the boss and moved into the company, they had 3.6 children, he was in debt up to his ass, and she tried to proposition me as I showed her around the house, telling me what a wimp he was. I advised her that no matter what a loser her old man was, she wasn't about to make any points with me by badrapping him. For his part, he could not take his eyes off my lady friend, who was polite to him, but had the eerie feeling he might shed his skin and slither after her at any moment. My visitors were a pair who deserved each other.

Finally, they left, and with the same feeling of release I mentioned two weeks ago when I talked about having returned to Ohio State to lecture at the school that had bounced me, I felt free at last, free at last, gawd a'mighty, free at last.

It was very clear that the Wheel had come around, and what I'd believed about the insular and debilitating nature of fraternities had served me in good stead. I had gone my own way, and I was a happy (though flawed, even as you and you and you) individual, doing what I wanted to do, living the life that enriched me. And there was no need to seek any cheap revenge on that poor sonofabitch: there was nothing I could do to him half as terrible as what his own false gods, cheap goals and debased ideals had done to him. Time had taken care of him in a way I'd have had to be a monster to attempt.

But he was an object lesson. From that moment on, I never felt hatred for the time I spent in ZBT. I wouldn't mention it now, save to add a penultimate brick of memory in the final monument to my school days, occasioned by that final purge at OSU early last month. I mention it for that reason, and to tell *you* that you're grown up now, you're a different human being . . . you're free. Honest you are.

So smile, hey!

Interim Memo

THEY PAID. I'D MET AN EXTREMELY ATTRACTIVE WOMAN DURING that stopover in Columbus, Ohio; a reporter for the *Dispatch*. We liked each other, and we spent time together. After I'd returned to Los Angeles, and she got wind that OSU was refusing to pay for the appearance, she called me and told me she'd be delighted to do a follow-up story on their perfidious behavior.

I thanked her and said perhaps merely the threat of public disclosure would do the job. I called the comptroller or whoever it was who'd said I could whistle for my fee, and I advised him that I was on the other line with a reporter who wanted to do such an article, and did he want to interdict the process by some salutary action? He raged for about thirty seconds, and promised the check would be in my hands by special delivery the next day. I thanked him prettily, and assured him if the check *wasn't* in my hands in a day or two—and I made it clear it had damned well better be a certified cashier's check, not an OSU check they could stop-pay—that I had the reporter's number and would take up where we'd left off.

I thanked Cynthia, and two days later OSU had paid off.

Living well is the best revenge. And making them eat it ain't bad, either.

College Days, Part Three

15 November 1973

*D*on Epstein is out there somewhere, but *you'll* never find him. Shit, he can't even find him*self* any more. And you know who got him lost? The Pope got him lost. Not the current one, the nut who says everybody ought to keep having babies; the one who died in 1963, the good one, John XXIII. Good John got Don Epstein lost because he didn't tell all them terribly christian Christians sooner that we Jews didn't nail up the Son of God. I mean, if John had gotten it on a little sooner, say around 1954, or even 1953 (1952 would have been best), Don Epstein would not be lost today.

What's that you say? I'm babbling again? Well, hell, friends, you should know by now that I'll make it all *ugly* clear before I say goodbye, so just hang in there with me and let me play my nasty word-games.

You see, Don Epstein was just about my only friend in college, and since I've been telling college days stories in this column for the past month, I thought I'd tag them off with the story of my pretty-much-only-friend at Ohio State, Don Epstein, and what happened to him, and how he wound up getting so lost he'll never be found.

It's not one of my happy stories. You may not smile even once. But then, that's only fair: Don Epstein went a *lotta* days without smiling.

I met Don when I pledged ZBT. Well, Don was too dynamite a guy to put up with Greek bullshit very long, and he checked out about a month before I got booted. He moved into a rooming house across from Ohio State, but during the few weeks we knew each other in the fraternity, we became friends, so when I got the axe, I moved into the same rooming house, and the friendship flourished.

Don was a tall, good-looking guy with a gentle nature and a marvelous wry sense of humor. He was also literate, had a fine ear for classical music and jazz, and he was a marvelous dresser. He also looked *very* Semitic. That means something, so remember it.

Don was signed up for pre-med. He had a 4.00 average, which for those of you who don't know how they graded students in those dim, dead days before students graded themselves, was as high as you could get. It was a four-point, gentle readers, a bloody beautiful four-point, which was straight A's. What I'm trying to tell you, was that Don Epstein was a *brain*. And he wanted to be a doctor. Worse than anydamnthing, he wanted to be a doctor. What kind, I don't remember now. It's been twenty years. Things blur.

But what doesn't blur is that I learned so many things from Don that I could never repay him if I started now and kept on paying till 2001.

He turned me on to jazz. Mulligan, Brubeck, Chet Baker, Lennie Tristano, Kenton, Manne, Shorty Rogers—the whole West Coast jazz scene that was so exuberant during the mid-Fifties. It was like getting a whole new set of ears.

He introduced me to classical music. Hell, I'd been a dumbass Ohio kid who'd thought Spike Jones was the height of creativity and Perry Como and the Four Freshmen the pinnacle of vocal interpretation. Through Don I heard my first Bach, Scarlatti, Monteverdi, Buxtehude, Grieg, Holst . . . the list is endless. I listened to the imperishable sounds of genius and began to grow as a human being.

He taught me how to dress. Oh, shit, you should have seen me before Epstein wrinkled his brow and said, "Yellow socks and a green tie don't go with a charcoal-gray-and-pink sport jacket, Harlan." He showed me what shoes to buy, helped me pick out slacks and jackets that didn't make me look like a munchkin dressed up for a rat shoot. You might not think learning how to wear clothes was important—today I suppose it isn't all that important—but in the Fifties, what you looked like predicated what others thought of you. And I was so damned insecure that anything that helped make me look less like a nerd was a godsend.

He hipped me to Jean Shepherd, to Salinger, to pizza, to puns, to dinner table etiquette, to talking to girls, to how to do research in a library . . . he opened doors for me that I never even knew existed.

In a very special way, Don Epstein was a mentor and a guru for me. And man did I love him. He was beautiful.

So. It is with considerable sadness that I report what happened to Don Epstein. And I can do it quickly, briefly, shortly, succinctly . . . just the way it happened to him . . . and just this fast a superterrific person gets so lost he can't be found again.

Don wanted to be a doctor. But Ohio State had a "Jewish quota." Only so many yids per year. And Don came from a family of modest circumstances. They didn't have the clout or the money to buy him into the quota. So even with his straight A four-point, Don could not get into Medical School. So he plugged on, making straight A's, and he signed up for pre-dental. Same story. Quota. He couldn't make it there, either. No connections, no heavy sugar to squeeze the juice it took to get lesser lads admitted.

That was the way it went for several semesters, with Don growing more and more bitter, more and more cynical, more and more morose. He hit the books harder, didn't go out, sat for long hours in dark depression.

My last semester before I was booted out of State, Don dropped even lower in his goals. He registered for veterinarian school. I didn't find out till years later that he hadn't been able to score that one, either.

I ran away from OSU and started writing, started selling, got married the first time, got drafted, did my time, got discharged, went to Chicago to work on *Rogue* magazine, split Chicago when my marriage crumbled and I got divorced, went back to New York, wrote some more, got married again, and returned to Chicago in 1961. While living in Evanston with my second wife, I got a call from Don.

Except it wasn't Don Epstein any more. Now it was Don Forrester. He told me he'd gotten the name off a bottle of booze. Gentile booze.

I invited him to come over, and he did. With his wife.

When he came through the door, I hardly recognized him.

Don had changed. A lot. Because of the Pope.

You see, he had missed out on vet school and then gone to the last place a guy who wanted to be a doctor and had the brains and skill to *be* a doctor could go: he had entered the school of undertaking.

And there he was, seven years later, in my living room in Evanston, Illinois. Don Forrester. He had had a nose job. He didn't look even remotely Semitic now. And he had a Protestant wife. And he had a WASP name. And he looked like a man crushed by a pylon-sinking machine.

I helped him find a place to live. He was moving to Chicago for some reason or other, I don't remember why at this point. But we talked a few times. Not much. The Don I'd known was lost. Gone somewhere; where the wry dynamite guys go when history and compassionless forces over which they have no control make them ashamed of their heritage, make them ashamed of what they look like and who they are. Forrester (as opposed to Epstein) was a nice-enough guy, I suppose. But in my sad eyes he was a loser. A sad, beaten guy who had fought as hard as he could . . . but had lost.

It was painful to be in the same room with him.

Anyhow, I like to tell myself, I was too deep in my own grief at that time, and I didn't have much pity left for anyone but myself. I left Chicago soon after, went through another divorce, wound up here in Los Angeles. That's thirteen years ago, almost.

And when some asshole asks me if I've changed my name, I tell him, no, Harlan Ellison is my name, and if it'd been Ira Finkelstein, it'd *still* be my name, and my nose is my own, and I'm a Jew, and if I ever gave it a moment's thought that changing any of those things would make the slide smoother, all I have to do is pass a liquor store and see a bottle of Forrester, or Old Forrester, or whatever the fuck it's called, and I know all the bloody noses in the world aren't worth changing one Semitic syllable of monicker or one Yiddish inch of snout.

And as a period point to all of this purgative about Ohio State, and my return there after twenty years, be advised things don't change much, they only get a glossy new skin:

I did my lecture at State last month, and I told the fraternity story, and the getting-thrown-out story, and the Don Epstein story, from the stage of Mershon Auditorium . . . and the audience loved it. I've got it on tape, I *know* they loved it. But the Administration refuses to pay my fee. My lecture agent tells me the only school that hasn't paid what it owed me is Ohio State, that the Administration was upset that I spent only *part* of the three hours I did my number, talking about nice safe shit like science fiction and what a sweet world it is. They're pissed because I "harangued" OSU from the sanctity of the stage of good old Mershon.

They don't like to hear the truth, friends. But you know that. They like to pretend it's all pom-pons and high scholastic honors. They don't like to be reminded that they were, and probably still are, bigots and racists and anti-Semites and creeps.

They don't think they're going to pay me.

Well. Let me *assure* you, if not for my own greed and desire for revenge, they'll *pay*. They'll pay high. If not for me, then sure as Hell for Don Epstein.

Interim Memo

SADLY, THE GOLDEN CHINA IS NO MORE. MAYBE IT'S AGE SPEAK-
ing, and the miles taking their toll, but somewhichways the
world doesn't seem to be nearly as interesting a place as it used
to was been.

The Last of Three Culinary
Comments, Gonzo-Style

22 November 1973

O ver dinner the other night
with Dostoevsky and Kafka, I said, "Fyodor, have you read
Huck Barkin's new book, WHEN DO THE GOOD TIMES START?"
　　Dostoevsky looked up from his bowl of lentil soup and
mumbled something I couldn't make out. He had his cheeks
stuffed with soup-soggy pumpernickel. I turned to Kafka.
"Franz, how about you? Have you read it? Marvelous funny
book."

"Time ravages and memory seldom heals," he replied.

I turned back to Dostoevsky. That damned Kafka, always obtuse. "C'mon, Ferdy, did Huck let you look at the manuscript?"

"Da."

"And did you like it?"

"Let me borrow two hundred rubles and I'll tell you."

"Forget it," I said, "you still owe me a thousand from that weekend in Vegas last April. Just answer the question, did you like the book?"

"Good book. It was to laugh."

I gave up. Those guys are fun around the pool, but for a serious discussion they're the shits. So I called up Haskell Barkin, known to those of us who adore him as Huckleberry, and invited him over. He came a-visiting, and lectured me for three straight hours on one of my character flaws. If he'd had a couple of more hours free he'd have gone on to a second one, I'm sure.

Then he said, "You're always recommending sensational small inexpensive restaurants in your column . . . come on, I'm going to introduce *you* to a great place to eat." He wound his pure silk aviator's scarf around his neck and leaped for the door. On the pad just outside my house I could hear his Sopwith Camel revving.

"Hold it!" I yelled. "I just *ate* dinner, with Fyodor and Franz."

He stopped and fixed me with a piercing stare. It was Lamont Cranston as The Shadow, all over again. "Admit it," he said, "half an hour after eating with them . . . you're intellectually hungry again . . . aren't you?"

Sheepishly, I nodded. He chuckled with that devil-may-care Rafael Sabatini Sea Hawk Errol Flynn laugh of his, turned, and flung open the door. The whine of the Arctic Tundra wind whipped through the house. In a bound he was in the cockpit of the Camel, waving me to join him.

I buttoned the Bombay door of my Dr. Dentons, grabbed my Thesaurus, kissed Diana Hyland goodbye, and scuttled after him.

It seemed only moments later that we were winging
through the saddle between the mountains, spiraling down on
Van Nuys. Huck screamed, "Hang on!" against the shriek of the
180 hp Clerget engine, and performed an exquisite immel-
mann. We altered direction and swooshed over Ventura Boulevard. Huck pointed over the portside and I saw a group of
people milling around the Joe Namson Union 76 station on the
corner of Ventura and Van Nuys Boulevards. They were
carrying placards. "Reagan/Nixon supporters," he screamed.
"Dupes who believe all that 'energy crisis' crap Dickie's using for
political misdirection."

He threw the joystick forward. "Hang on!"

He dove with all the grace of a tern going after a seafood
cocktail and just as he pulled out and leveled, he opened up on
the mob of Imperialist lackey degenerate pawns of the Oil
Monopoly with his twin Vickers'. Huck ran the most beautiful
strafing run I've ever seen.

Then, laughing gaily, he pulled up, did a barrel roll at a
dangerous altitude, and we streaked away over Van Nuys
Boulevard.

He finally touched down in a perfect three-point in a
parking space right in front of Sid Fine Bail Bonds, in Van
Nuys and, leaping from the cockpit, he removed his Captain
Midnight secret decoder badge. He put it in the glove compart-
ment of the Camel. "No sense advertising who we *really* are," he
said. I nodded dumbly. I'm always awed by Barkin's worldly
ways. Debonair, that's what he is, fucking debonair!

"Where we going?" I asked. The last time Huck'd taken me
off on one of those cavalier adventures, I'd wound up fighting
for my life at Ft. Zinderneuf with the Geste brothers.

"An inscrutable Oriental restaurant," he said, smiling wick-
edly. Oh, God, I thought, not Fu Manchu again!

We turned onto Van Nuys Boulevard and crossed the
street. I saw the marquee. It said: GOLDEN CHINA RESTAU-
RANT.

"Is that it?"

Huck merely nodded. His ice-chip eyes were narrowed
down, watching for the enemy that always lurked in his trail. It

was scary, traveling in company with a Living Legend, there was always danger and excitement when with Huck Barkin, but there was also the risk of grievous bodily harm . . . or even death.

"Who are we afraid of tonight?" I asked, softly, very softly.

"The Circle of the Serpent," he said, enigmatically, and then shushed me to silence with a wave of his kung fu–calloused hand.

As we came abaft the restaurant, he indicated I should memorize the address. 6209 Van Nuys Boulevard. I marked it in my memory banks for future reference.

When we entered, I was struck first by the perfectly ordinary look of the place. Had I not been in Huck's company, and had I not had ample reason to know that such innocent lairs always masked nefarious goings-on, I would have thought it merely a quaint, charming dining spot: booths, tables, Muzak. "Careful," Huck hissed under his breath. He flexed his shoulders and the bulge of the .357 Magnum in its breakaway shoulder rig showed for only a moment. Then he relaxed and his tuxedo fell back into its elegant lines of composure. That's another thing about Huck: he really knows how to wear clothes!

We slid opposite one another in a booth, Huck watching the door to the kitchen with steely scrutiny. "Do you hear that unearthly sound?" he asked.

"'Poor Butterfly' by Oscar Peterson, isn't it?"

"Not the Muzak, stupid. The sound of ungodly resonances, drawn from Cyclopean depths by nameless sources."

I listened carefully. "Sounds like 'Poor Butterfly' to me," I said. Huck looked away. I hate it when I disappoint him.

The door to the kitchen swung open and a svelte, almond-eyed beauty in a skintight satin dress slit to her thigh came slithering toward us. "That's Jade," Huck murmured, "one of their best agents. On your guard now, Watson."

"Are you sure it isn't 'Poor Butterfly'?" I said, then realized he'd called me Watson. For a nanosecond I thought Huck was slipping toward the Banana Works, but then I realized he'd cleverly tipped me to my code-name. "Right, Holmes," I replied.

"I thought I told you never to call me that?!" he snapped.

"Menus, venerable sirs," Jade said, handing us the bill of fares.

With chagrin at Huck's rebuke still stinging me, I took the menu and scanned it quickly. Thunderstruck, I whispered, "Doc, this is incredible! Black mushroom chicken for only $2.50 . . . Kung-Pao beef at $2.45 . . . prawns sautéed with hot spicy sauce only $2.95! Mongolian beef only $2.35 . . . Moo-Shi pork for $2.50! No one can sell Mandarin cooking at these ridiculously low prices. Why, the prices weren't even this good at Ting Ho before they sold out and a lousy cook took over their kitchen."

Huck was staring at me with scintillae of light in his glacier eyes. I realized what I'd done. I'd called him "Doc." If the booth was bugged, now the Circle of the Serpent would know the real identity of this mild-mannered cabinetmaker and brilliant novelist. Clark Savage, Jr. Doc Savage! Scourge of the underworld. *What had I done!*

"Now we're in for it, motormouth," he said.

And just then, as Jade brought the five entrees I'd whispered—the booth *was* bugged—the henchmen of the Circle of the Serpent attacked.

They came up from the floor. One of the tables revolved, an elevator cleverly concealed beneath the linoleum rose, and seventeen screaming thugs of that most devilish of Oriental murder societies lunged toward Huck Barkin and myself.

"Defend yourself!" Huck howled and leaped from the booth. As I used my chopsticks to snag one of the delicious pan-fried dumplings, Huck met the first wave of assassins with a savate kick that sent two of them crashing through the showcase. "Hieeee!" he screamed, whirling a reverse crescent kick into the face of a 350 lb. sumo wrestler carrying a battering ram. I sipped at the delicate essences of the three flavor sizzling rice soup.

"Use your wrist radio!" Huck yelled at me, whipping out the .357 Magnum and cutting in half an opium-crazed Serpent worshipper. "Call Blackhawk, tell him we need help! And have him bring Terry!"

"How about the Pirates?" I asked, chewing on some sensational crackling shrimp.

It went that way for the better part of an hour. Finally, they brought him down. The radioactive asp was the final blow.

He lay there beside the booth, staring up at me as I polished off the last of Golden China's special dessert, the unforgettable candied apple, and he managed to gasp, "Why, Friday? Why didn't you call for help?"

I stared down at him, my mind half with his fading glower of disenchantment and disappointment, half with memorizing the phone number of The Society for the Abolishment of MSG.

"Sorry, Huck," I said. "A friend is just a friend . . . but the best goddam Mandarin restaurant in town is a treasure."

He died, then. Quietly, sadly, without having eaten a morsel. I wiped my chin and paid the check. "Was he a friend of yours?" Jade said, looking at me carefully.

"Who? That scrutable Occidental? Hell, no," I said, and waddled toward the door, burping happily.

I'll always remember that roguish laugh and those sparkling eyes. And as I flew home, swerving slightly to run Jonathan Livingston Seagull through the propellor of my Sopwith Camel, I thought to myself, "You just can't *beat* odds like those, Huck."

But I knew when next I returned to the Golden China, I would be a man in search of revenge . . . they'd been all out of Tang Tang noodles.

Interim Memo

THERE WAS ACTUALLY MORE TO THIS COLUMN THAN WHAT you're getting here. Another, oh, page or so. Dull stuff. And very much out of date. This'n'that about books of mine that were soon to be published (all of which, except TLDV, came forth), titles of stories I was writing or had just sold . . . that sort of twaddle. You know, the "what are you up to these days" items that are really a bore twenty years later.

So I cut them.

Trust me; you're not missing a thing.

Out of the Mail Bag

29 November 1973

*I*t's mail-answering time around the old column this week.

You know, actually you're a sensational audience. I don't know whether it's due to your gestalt cleverness and perceptivity, or to my essentially cranky nature, but the kind of mail this column draws from you is just exactly right. There's very little of that time-wasting bullshit mail I get from science fiction fans who want me to read their 186,000 word novel, THE BLUE SLIME-DEGENERATES FROM PLUTONIAN DEPTHS, critique it, rewrite it, market it, and sell it to the movies. There's hardly ever one of those imposing maneuvers by some college sophomore who has been assigned me as a report and wants me to answer nine thousand intimate questions about the creative process. Seldom do I receive lunatic communiques from religious fanatics. And I *never* get those depressing notes that tell me how much the reader loves my work . . . but cannot find my books on the newsstand. (*Nothing* frustrates a writer more than being told his books are being distributed lousily.)

No, you *Hornbook* readers are dolls, all of you.

When I get mail from you, either you say nice things about the column or take me to task (usually with cause) and you advise me that it isn't necessary to reply; merely to correct my mistake is happiness enough for you. For a writer backed up with deadlines and overloads of work, that is a consummate joy. You don't steal my time, you just keep in touch like good friends.

So, to repay the kindnesses, I'm taking time out this week to respond to some of the questions and stuff you've laid on me these past 42 weeks of column.

First, I appreciate the newspaper items some of you clip for my attention. For instance, Fred Cropper out in Altadena sent me a terrifying clipping from the 18 November edition of the *Pasadena Star-News' Parade* magazine section. In Pamela Swift's *Keeping Up with Youth* column, there's a brief takeout on the John Birch Society summer camps in Minnesota, Michigan, California, Washington, Colorado, and Tennessee. Apparently, more than 1000 innocent young minds were exposed to the crazed and paranoid opinions of the Birch-barkers while a captive audience at some remote woodsy site. Mr. Cropper asked me to comment on these camps . . . clearly he, along with Ms. Swift who wrote the piece, was appalled at the persistence of the Birch idiom, and he drew an inescapable parallel with the Hitler Youth Camps of the Thirties. Well, I'd comment on it, but what's the use . . . ?

The simple truth of lunacies like the Birch summer camps, is that adults continue to feel that their beliefs *must* be inculcated into their children at all costs. It's not just tunnel-visioned views of the world like the Bircher concept of an octopoidal Communist conspiracy or the historically arid racisms of nigger-haters and anti-Semites and Catholic-baiters, it's *any* ingrained belief that serves one person but may not serve another. Hell, I've seen dying mothers and fathers quite literally reach up with clawed hands to grasp the wrists of their children, even as they lay gasping on their deathbeds, and with their final breaths extract a promise from their offspring that they'd read the bible every day or go to church every Sunday or raise the grandchildren as good Whatevers . . .

It's all of a piece. The forcing upon others of personal beliefs is a terrible thing. It's Hoffer's "true believers" going down in flames and taking as many with them as possible. And I'd comment on it, but what's to say? The Birch summer camps are certainly evil, but then so is your Daddy or Mommy telling you that voting Republican or Democrat or Whatever They Ain't is wrong, is evil. Fred, I'd spend time babbling about it, but life's too short. Let them corrupt their kids, and let them do their number. They'll never succeed. Time and history are against them. It's one of the few things about human beings that gives me hope for tomorrow: in the final ticking moment, sufficient rationality surges to the fore and saves the day. I mean, if Hitler couldn't pull it off with *his* organization, how the hell are piddlers like the Birch nuts gonna do it? Take it easy, Fred. Have a cup of coffee and relax.

Next on the catch-up agenda is a response to Marcie Ferguson in Green Haven, Maryland, who was curious about my hobbies or outside interests. Most of what I'm into is related in some way with writing, of course, but when I'm not here behind the word-machine I like to shoot pool (and do not too badly with a breakdown elephantwood cue I bought some years ago), I make plastic models of airplanes and monster figures, I collect philatelic first day covers, I read a lot, go to as many movies as humanly possible, search&find sensational small restaurants such as the Golden China, do my best to bug David Gerrold just to keep him humble, play gin rummy, collect comic books, buy modern art, worry if my '67 Camaro can make it to 90,000 miles without falling apart, commiserate with Walter Koenig over his having to act in three more episodes of *The Starlost*, and putter around my house. My hobbies include Royal Doulton figures and toby jugs, the works of Edward Gorey, finding jobs for my indigent friends, supporting an ever-decreasing number of social causes, posters, comic character buttons (like from Kellogg's *Pep*), Big Little Books, cartography, the literature of Latin America, mystery novels, collecting and smoking pipes, and friends.

By the way, if you're tooling around Los Angeles and you see a bronze-toned 1967 Camaro with a black landau top and the license plate HE, honk if you love Zoroaster.

I'll probably turn around and give you the finger.

(Or haven't you ever noticed that when you see a car with one of those dumb bumperstickers that says HONK IF YOU LOVE JESUS or HONK IF YOU'RE HORNY, and you *do* honk, the driver—ostensibly a purveyor of love in the most casual form—never realizes what you're doing and, with a display of love unparalleled since the Spanish Inquisition, turns around in his or her seat and curses you out for honking.)

Ah, well, so it goes.

Interim Memo

JUST WHEN YOU THOUGHT IT WAS SAFE TO HANG YOUR BALLS again . . .

Remember Installment 9, in which I offended both heaven and earth with my "Fuck Xmas" screed? Well, by the time I'd been doing the *Hornbook* for a year, that column had become, er, uh, sorta infamous. Art Kunkin, publisher of the *L.A. Weekly News,* to which the column had been moved from the *Freep,* decided it would be a big seller, so he featured it on the front page (on bilious green newsprint) and called it "Harlan Ellison's Famous Christmas Carol," accompanied by a rough line-drawing of Scrooge and the words (of course) "Bah! Humbug!"

Now you may think this is a cheap way to include yet another column, when in fact all we're doing is reproducing the first one—like an Andy Warhol painting—but it isn't a cheap dodge, it is a *semi*-cheap dodge. I actually wrote a new introduction to this second appearance of what was intended as an annual event; and there was one paragraph changed that updated it in relation to the Watergate mess, then fully in blossom. So the two installments are not the same. Close, but not exactly.

And besides, think how annoyed you'd be if you got to the second page of this piece, found a lot of blank space, and the command to turn back to page such-and-such. This becomes the lesser of two conundra.

There is, however, a perplexment pursuant to this column. This was the last piece I wrote for the *L.A. Weekly News.* The

Hornbook abruptly ends in that journal, without announcement of termination, or explanation. I don't remember why.

Between this installment and the next, three years elapsed; and the last three essays would never have been written had not I received a call from John Heidenry, an excellent writer and editor, then living in Missouri, who was contemplating starting a monthly tabloid-style review of literature, politics, and the arts. He asked if I'd be interested in reviving the *Hornbook* on a monthly basis, and for reasons that now elude me, I agreed to undertake the chore.

But *why* had I stopped writing the column for Kunkin?

I called Art today, in aid of jogging his/my memory, but good old Kunkin is living way up in Topanga, and he hadn't bothered to pick up his messages by the time it was necessary to send this manuscript to Jack and Otto. So your guess is as good as mine. The best I can recall, is that I simply grew weary of exploding in print every week. I was working on a number of books, a movie, a tv series . . . the workload was starting to get to me . . . and though I didn't know it at the time, I had begun to develop the progressively more pronounced symptoms of a malaise now known as Chronic Fatigue Syndrome (formerly the Chronic Epstein–Barr Virus). It was getting harder and harder for me to work the twenty hour days I'd put in since I was in my teens. But that's another, by-now-boring, story.

(Although it goes right to the heart of why it took twenty years to get these columns into hardcovers.)

And so, the *Hornbook* ended its second incarnation, and there were only three more essays to come.

Oh, Dear, He's Not Going to Do Xmas Again, Is He?

13 December 1973

*L*ast year, in the ninth install-
ment of this column (when it was appearing in another newspaper), I did a long essay on my true feelings about Christmas
as a holiday institution. It was in the H. L. Mencken–Alexander
Woollcott–Oscar Levant stream of curdled curmudgeonry. I
don't like Christmas. No, strike that, I *loathe* Christmas. It is an
utter phony, as removed from the hypocritical lip-service of
paying homage to Christ and fellowship as George Wallace's
blattings of state's rights is removed from the simple reality of
his being a racist.

Frankly, I anticipated that column's drawing terrible hell-
fire down on me. To my amazement, hundreds of people felt
the same way. They had been nursing hatred of Xmas equally
as strong as mine own. Some of them were even *more* violent
about the senseless proliferation of expensive cards whose
massed cost could feed starving children or build schools. (And
don't give me none of that shit about hearing from people once
a year and ain't that sweet . . . I didn't want to hear from most
of those dips anyhow, and if they *really* had something to say to
me, they should have sent me a postcard for 6¢ that said I'm
dying of Leukemia, or Your undershorts are on fire, or
whatever the hell it was that was relative to me, instead of some
nonsensical Hallmark copywriter's effusions. I got one today

THE HARLAN ELLISON HORNBOOK

that measured 10″ x 7″ and almost made me snow-blind with the gold raised lettering and the silver globes on it. The only thing that keeps me from going over and punching the sender of that embossed abomination is that he's a sweet, dear man and I admire both him and his wife. But he only lives across town, and we talk twice a week, and if I didn't already know he loves me and wishes me well without a "Happy Holiday" the size of a Foster & Kleiser billboard, I'd be a pretty damned insensitive friend to begin with, in which case he should know better than to send me a card at all!)

The violence from my correspondents re Xmas encompassed the moral blackmail of having to buy gifts they couldn't afford; the way greeting cards fucked up the mail deliveries of *important* communiques; the toadying false camaraderie of salespeople working on commission; the ripoff of businessmen who spend all year selling borax furniture to blacks and at holiday time suddenly burst into ho ho ho's of goodwill, with a 22% markup on shit merchandise; the senselessness of cutting down trees that wind up in the gutter on January 2nd, lying there with their tinsel spaghetti twined among brown pine needles, like the skirts of a rape victim bunched up around her hips; the cost of hauling away all that garbage . . .

And this year we can add to it the energy drain from Santa Clause Lane parades, tree lights burning throughout the night, outdoor decorations in neighborhoods with "display" contests, the high cost of everything and . . . worst of all . . . the multiplied feelings of have-not burned into the breasts of the poor, who couldn't afford *last* year's frivolities, when we *didn't* have a recession and an energy crisis.

So I'm re-running my column from last year. I've decided to make it an annual event.

But add to it, this year, that I also despise the concept of the Christmas Bonus, a filthy extortion that ennobles neither the giver nor the taker. Bonus for what? For being there when Christmas rolls around? For having done a job one was hired to do? That's bullshit! My secretary Mariana got her bonus in August. She got a raise. She got it for doing such a fine job that she was *worth* more money, not because she's a Christian.

There'll be no bonuses around here. And for all of you con artists out there waiting to see what kind of freebie ripoff you can expect in your pay envelope from the boss, consider that *you* ought to give *him* a bonus at Christmas—for providing you with a job all year.

No bonuses, no false spirits, not even a wassail. And if you send me a greeting card, I'll only roundfile it and call you an asshole. Save your money. Send it to The Salvation Army or the American Civil Liberties Union or some worthy charity. Or go get drunk on it. But don't lumber me with your artificial emotion.

And, for your reading pleasure, here's the annual FUCK CHRISTMAS column of your old friend, Scrooge Ellison.

First of all, let's exclude the Prince of Peace. None of what I'm about this week has anything to do with him. From what I've read, he was an okay sort of guy on whom has been laid more superhero tripe than any one social malcontent should have to cope with.

What I'm concerned with here is how much I, and most of you, whether you will cop to it or not, come to hate, loathe, despise and revile Christmas.

Not even the obvious cliché Scrooge anti-commercialized Christmas denigration that berates greedy shopkeepers for stringing plastic holly in the middle of August, that castigates even worthwhile charities for their shameless whipguilt hustling for funds, that chides average citizens for falling for the okeydoke and going in hock to BankAmericard to buy gifts they can't afford for people they don't give a damn about. *That* facet of the problem is so much an obviousness that everyone has learned to live with it, pays it lip-service the way lip-service is paid to horrors such as "everyone knows politicians are crooked," and does nothing to revise the situation. Amazing how much shit folks can learn to eat.

No, I'm finally going to come out of the closet and openly state in print how much the entire concept of the "holiday" horrifies me. If I touch a shuddering chord here that resonates in tone with what you've been concealing in your heart of hearts, then consider me only as the fatmouth willing to suffer the brickbats of Jesus Freaks, et al., who'll surely burn a cross on my lawn for putting down their be-all/end all's natal day. I'm willing to stand the gaff, gentle readers, if you will merely turn to the East and say to the sunset, "God forgive me, I've had the same thoughts."

Consider: the following items came over the news on December 24th and 25th: four men in San Francisco abducted two young girls off the streets in broad daylight; a young woman whose estranged husband showed up at her door with presents for their kids was shot to death by the wife, who then put the pistol in her mouth and blew her head off; a 65-year-old man in Manhattan threw himself off the Brooklyn Bridge with a note (apparently written with a ballpoint so it wouldn't smudge in the water, which is really forethought of a high order) saying he couldn't make it through another Christmas alone and unloved; a sniper in downtown Chicago knocked off four people on Christmas Eve, and was never located; a noted psychologist released a statement that suicide rates go up to triple normal during the holidays; police in Los Angeles and San Francisco agreed, with some consternation, that crime doubles during Christmas. There's more, much more, but why belabor the point? The only *good* news during Christmas this year is that they may impeach Nixon after all.

Christmas is an awfulness that compares favorably with the great London plague and fire of 1665–66. No one escapes the feelings of mortal dejection, inadequacy, frustration, loneliness, guilt and pity. No one escapes feeling used by society, by religion, by friends and relatives, by the utterly artificial responsibilities of extending false greetings, sending banal cards, reciprocating unsolicited gifts, going to dull parties, putting up with acquaintances and family one avoids all the rest of the year . . . in short, of being brutalized by a "holiday" that has lost virtually all of its original meanings and has become a merchandising ploy for color tv set manufacturers and ravagers of the woodlands.

Look: I dig my privacy. 364 days out of the year I can think of nothing more pleasant than being left alone of an evening, working at writing a story, watching some television, making a small meal, smoking my pipe, just swimming along softly behind an ambience of aloneness. There is nothing of *loneliness* in all that, but *aloneness*, which is something else altogether, something fine and rewarding and filled with restoking the internal fires, coming to grips with myself, perceiving my directions and my place in the universe.

But on Christmas Eve I was alone, and I wanted to slash my carotid artery. (And when I read the foregoing to the two young ladies who are secretarying for me, they stared at me with undisguised loathing for my rottenness and countered with the arguments that a *lot* of people *like* Christmas a bagful, and they offered as their reasons that many people dig it because they don't have to work, and others adore it because they get bonuses.

(Had I the sense of a maggot, I'd rest my case right there.

(But for the sanctimonious few who would revile the ladies for their opinions, only slightly less than they will me for mine, I press forward, bearing in mind Dickens's remark that ". . . every idiot who goes about with 'Merry Christmas' on his lips should be boiled with his own pudding, and buried with a stake of holly through his heart."

(And did you ever notice, the only one in A CHRISTMAS CAROL with any character is Scrooge? Marley is a whiner who fucked over the world and then hadn't the spine to pay his dues quietly; Belle, Scrooge's ex-girlfriend deserted him when he needed her most; Bob Crachit is a gutless toady without enough get-up-and-go to assert himself; and the less said about that little treacle-mouth, Tiny Tim, the better. No, Dickens knew what he was doing when he made Scrooge the focus of the story. My only disappointment in him is that he let himself be savaged by those three dumb Ghosts. God Bless Us, Every One *indeed*! Not even at Christmas would I God Bless Nixon or the terrorists who machine-gunned the Olympic athletes or the monkey-trial reactionary fundamentalists who blud-geoned the California State Board of Education into stating in all future textbooks that Darwin's Theory is an "unproved theory" as valid as the "special creation" nonsense. Bless 'em?

I'd like to boil them in their own pudding and bury them . . . but you know.)

Christmas is constructed and promulgated in such a way that to defy it or ignore it makes one a monster. To refuse to send cards, to toss the ones received in the wastebasket, to refuse to accept gifts and refuse to give them, to walk untouched through the consumer-crowds and never feel the urge to buy Aunt Martha that *lovely* combination rotisserie-&-bidet, to maintain one's sanity staunchly through the berserk days of year's end makes one, in the eyes of those who lack the courage to eschew hypocrisy, an awful heretic, a slug, a vile and contemptible thug.

But consider the millions who are alone on Christmas. All the divorcees, all the kids on the road, all the septuagenarians in the Fairfax retirement homes, all the parents who lost kids in 'Nam, all the truck drivers who take Christmas schedules so they won't have to sit around and brood on how miserable they are. Think of the poor sonofabitch glimpsed through the front windows of an Automat, sitting there by himself eating the $1.79 Xmas Special w/giblet gravy.

And don't give me any of that bullshit about how we must take these poor unfortunates to our Christian bosoms and make them welcome at this wonderful time of the year.

Half of them are rapists and ax murderers, and they'll eat your dinner, knock you in the head with a candlestick and steal all the presents from under your tree.

What they want, flat truth, is to be left well alone, to get through this horrendous sorrow-show as quickly as possible.

And when I read all *that* to one of my secretaries—the other having resigned and stalked out of the house muttering *Antichrist*—she snottily advised me she didn't mind anyone's not liking Christmas, what she resented were loudmouths like me who *talked* about it. Which is a terrific Silent Majority attitude, paralleling the Administration's attitudes about civil disobedience and vocal dissent. They don't mind your *thinking* it (at the moment), but god forbid you should try to *do* something about it.

It never occurs to her that the pro-Christmas lackeys

bombard the rest of us through every possible medium of mass communication from Muzak wassail wassails in the elevators to *White Christmas* and *Miracle on 34th Street* all over the tube for two weeks prior and a week post. That every nit one encounters in banks or bakeries, who snorted and snarled and dealt you inept service all the rest of the year suddenly blossoms forth with a phony "Merrrrry Christmas" in hopes of a Yuletide giftiepoo. That even the blasphemy blasphemy curse blasphemy telephone company answers its phones with, "Merry Christmas, may I help you?"

"Yes, I'd like you to check out an address for me, please."

"Merry Christmas, we are not permitted to check addresses."

"Yes, but, er, I'm a paraplegic cancer victim in an iron lung and the house is on fire and I'd like you to check out my address because I'm blind and the fire department needs it to locate me before I'm incinerated."

"Merry Christmas, I'm sorry, sir, but you'd better fuck off."

"Thanks. And a Merry Christmas to you."

What I'm saying, in sum, dear friends, is that it is all hopelessly artificial. That people are no better at Xmas time than any other time, and by spouting platitudes in the name of a scrawny prophet who got hammered in place for saying stuff a lot more radical than what I'm saying here, none of those Yule-nuts become brighter or more sanctified or even a tot kinder.

And weighed against the people who suicide out of loneliness and misery, all the sales of Timex watches don't mean a goddam thing.

So next year, to all my friends, and particularly to my enemies, take your pointless and money-wasting Hallmarks and jam them up your pantyhose.

Next year, time and finances permitting, I will cause to have erected on the roof of my home, a ten foot high neon sign that blinks on and off in blood-red and cash-green, BAH! HUMBUG! and any little clown who comes caroling at my door is going to have boiling pitch dumped on him.

And fuck you, Tiny Tim!

Interim Memo

JOHN HEIDENRY—JACK TO HIS FRIENDS—CAME TO MY KEN early in the 1970s, when he submitted a short story to the then-in-progress anthology I was editing, AGAIN, DANGEROUS VISIONS. He wrote a wonderful piece that I used as the opening of that elegant and still-in-print sequel to 1967's DANGEROUS VISIONS, labeling it the "keynote entry."

Over the next few years, after A,DV was released in 1972, I exchanged a few letters with Jack; and when he asked me to resume writing the *Hornbook* for his fledgling *Saint Louis Literary Supplement* (first issue dated November 1976) I resolved to write the essays in a more structured way. Not so much consciously "literary" in style, but with greater care and at more substantial length. These were, in fact, the training ground pieces I wrote that informed the technique I would later apply to my film essays in *The Magazine of Fantasy and Science Fiction*. (Those film critiques are collected, with the balance of twenty-five years' worth of film criticism, in a volume called HARLAN ELLISON'S WATCHING.) The three final columns of the actual *Hornbook* cycle were watershed writings for me.

The *Supplement* didn't last very long, as I recall, but for its brief life it was a superlative journal. Jack Heidenry, last time we talked, was working for the Penthouse International organization in New York.

As for this first of the final trio, well, it has a very special place in my heart. As you will understand.

Photo of Serita Ellison

The Death of My Mother, Serita R. Ellison

11 October 1976

On Sunday the 10th of October, I committed the final outrage against my family. I spoke the eulogy at my Mother's funeral. The family will never speak to me again. I can handle that.

When I say "my family," I mean, mostly, my Mother's side. The Rosenthals. Who resemble in more ways than the mind can readily support, the brutalizing members of the Sproul clan in Jerrold Mundis's current and brilliant novel, GERHARDT'S CHILDREN. They remind me of the first line from Tolstoy's ANNA KARENINA: "Happy families are all alike; every unhappy family is unhappy in its own way."

And prime among that unhappy family's myths was the one that Harlan, Serita and Doc's kid, Beverly's brother, would wind up either dead in an alley somewhere, having come to a useless end . . . or rotting away his old age in a Federal penitentiary. That I became a writer of some repute and became the first member of either the Rosenthal or the Ellison family to get listed in WHO'S WHO IN AMERICA, confounds them to this day. To them, I am like the snail known as the chambered nautilus, that has a shell with rooms in it. As the nautilus lives its brief life it moves from room to room in its shell and finally emerges and dies; thus, it literally carries its past on its back. To the family, I am still a nine-year-old hellion who took a hammer to Uncle Morrie's piano. (The fact that this never happened, that Morrie never owned a piano, does not in any way invalidate for them the essence, the canonical truth of the legend.)

It is probably no different for anyone reading these words. All families form their opinions of the children early, and so we spend the rest of our lives in large part paying obeisance to shadows who neither care nor *in fact* have any power over our reality. It is thus for all of us, no matter how sophisticated and cut-loose we may be from the familial spiderweb.

To them, I am a nine-year-old chambered nautilus; even though I ran away from home at the age of thirteen, grew up, and have barely spoken a dozen words to my sister in the past ten years.

But there was still my Mother, whom I supported in large part during the last years of her life, picking up the burden when I was financially able, from my Uncle Lew and my Uncle Morrie and from Beverly's husband, Jerold.

My Mother had been terribly ill for many years. To my way of thinking, she wanted to die on May 1st, 1949, when my Father had his coronary thrombosis and died in front of both of us. He was her life, her happier aspect, and she became—in any sensible not even exquisite sense—almost somnambulistic.

In August she had the latest of an uncountable number of strokes, followed it with a full-sized heart attack, and was taken into the Miami Heart Institute. She knew the end was on her and she let me know that was the sum of it when we talked long distance.

She lay there getting worse and worse, and finally, forty-five days before the green blips went to a flat line on the monitor, she was down from one hundred and twenty pounds to forty-one pounds, her lungs were filled with fluid, her brain had swollen so her face was terribly twisted, her leg was filled with blood clots, her blood sugar had risen to an impossible level, she ran a temperature in excess of 102° constantly, she was blind, paralyzed, and no oxygen was going to the brain.

Blessedly, she was in deep coma.

She never recovered consciousness. They kept her on the

IV and the monitoring for a month and a half. She was a vegetable and had she ever come out of it would have been an empty shell. I begged them to pull the plug, but they wouldn't.

The greatest fear my Mother ever had was that some day she would wind up in a nursing home. She thought of them as hellholes, as repositories for discarded loved ones, as the very apotheosis of rejection. She begged us never to put her there.

Shortly before she died, the Miami Heart Institute held one of their "status meetings" and decided she was "stable," that is, she needed custodial care. And so they wanted her out. They suggested we get her booked into an old folks' home. They used another phrase. They always do. But it was a hellhole, an old folks' home.

Beverly, my sister, who had gone through the anguish of the last six weeks down there, was forced reluctantly to find such a place. On Friday, October 8th, 1976, the day my Mother was to be removed from Miami Heart and carted by ambulance to the hellhole, though she was in deep coma and could not possibly have known what was intended for her dead but still-breathing husk, she chose to expire at 5:15 A.M.

In some arcane way, I'm sure she knew.

When my brother-in-law Jerold called to tell me Beverly had just advised him of Mom's death, he asked if there were any arrangements I particularly wanted.

"Only two," I said. "Closed casket, and I want to read the eulogy."

From that moment till Sunday at the funeral services, my family trembled in fear of what I would say. They knew I was no great lover of the clan, and they were terrified I would make a scene, depart from protocol in a way that would humiliate them in front of friends and relatives. They gave very little thought to my feelings about my Mother. But that's the way it always is, I'm sure, with all families, with all deaths.

I flew all night Saturday and got into Cleveland (where my Mother's body had been taken, so she could be buried beside my Father) at 6:30 in the morning. I drove to Beverly and Jerold's house and when Jerold asked to see the eulogy I'd written, which was almost the first thing he said to me, thus indicating the obsessiveness of their concern about "crazy" Harlan and what he might do, I lied and said I hadn't written anything, that it was to be extemporaneous, from the heart.

The relatives began arriving, and with the exception of my Uncle Lew, who has always been the coolest and the most understanding of the clan, they all circled me warily as if I were a jackal that might at any moment leap for their throats.

At the funeral home, Rabbi Rosenthal seemed equally uneasy about my participation in the ceremonies. It was Succoth, the Jewish harvest holiday, and just a week after Yom Kippur, the holiest of the holies. Thus, certain prayers that are usually spoken at funeral services could not be spoken; alternate words were permissable, but few, so very few.

Rabbi Rosenthal is no relation to my family. His name and my mother's maiden name being Rosenthal is just coincidence. Like Smith. Or Jones. Or Hayakawa. Or Goetz. Or Piazza. He's a fine man, the Rabbi Emeritus of Cleveland Jewry, a strong and familiar voice in Cleveland Heights and environs. He has been for many years. But he didn't know my Mother.

My family felt themselves honored to have pulled off the coup of Rabbi Rosenthal attending to the services. My family thinks in those terms: what looks good . . . social coups . . . fine form and attention to protocol. As you may have gathered, I am not concerned with shadow, merely reality.

Nonetheless, he advised me he would speak the opening words and then would call on me.

Before the main room with the pink anodized aluminum casket was opened to the attendees, the immediate family mourners and their spouses and children and grandchildren were taken to a family sitting room to the right of the main chamber. Jane Bubis, Beverly's best friend, bustled around. Morrie met old chums from Cleveland. My nephew Loren and I insisted on seeing Mom. Everyone told us not to look, that she had withered terribly, that we should "remember her as she had been." They always tell you to "remember" someone as "they were." Bear that phrase in mind. The nature of the outrage I committed against my family is contained in my pursuit of that admonition.

Loren and I insisted.

It didn't look like my Mother. It was a cleverly constructed mannequin intended for some minor wax museum in an amusement park. The embalmers and cosmeticians had done as good a job as could be done, I'm sure; but it wasn't my Mom. She was already gone. This was a stranger. But I cried. Pain that clotted my chest and made me gasp for breath. But it wasn't my Mom.

The service began, and when Rabbi Rosenthal called on me, I walked up to the lectern, trailing my hand across the casket foolishly to establish some last rapport with her.

I pulled the pages I'd written from my inside jacket pocket and though there was no appreciable movement in the people sitting in front of me in the main chamber, the agitation I caught with peripheral vision, from the family seated in the side viewing room, was considerable: the frenzied trembling of small fish perceiving a predator in their pool.

Understand something: my sister and I have never been friends. Eight years older than I, she was *always* distressed at who I was, what I was, what I did. (I have long harbored the fantasy that I was actually a gypsy baby, stolen from the Romany caravan by an attacking horde of Jewish ladies with shopping bags.) Beverly is no doubt an estimable human being, filled to the brimming with love and charity and compassion. I have never been able to discern these qualities in her, but she has many loyal friends and if an election were to be held among the relatives, as to which of us could safely be taken into polite society of an evening without worry about a "scene," my sister Beverly would win in a walk. Though they take a (to me) somewhat hypocritical pride in my achievements and the low level of fame I've achieved for the Ellison family, it is a public pride, not to be confused with actually having to get near me. I can handle that, too.

As I began to read, my sister began to fall apart. I'm not sure if it was the "inappropriateness" (to her mind) of what I was saying, or the fact that I was crying and having difficulty reading the words, or that the torture she had undergone for six weeks had finally broken her, but she began writhing in

Jerold's grasp, and in a voice that could be heard throughout the funeral home hoarsely cried for Jerold to "make him stop, make him stop! Stop him!" Beside her, her daughter, Lisa, my niece, snarled, "Shut up, Mother!" but Beverly never heard her. She was manipulating her environment, and her lunatic brother Harlan was doing another of his disgusting numbers, desecrating the funeral of her Mother. They finally manhandled her into another room, where her cries could still be heard. And I went on, with difficulty. And this is what I said:

> My Mother died three days ago. Her name was Serita R. Ellison. The R stood for Rosenthal, her maiden name. I'll tell you everything I know about her.
>
> My Mother told me only one joke in her entire life. She probably knew a lot of others, but she never told them to me. I'll tell you the one she told me.
>
> It's about these two Jewish fellows who meet on a street in Buffalo, New York. They are related, see, but not close; something like in-laws once removed. And Herschel doesn't care much of Solly, because Solly is always trying to sell him some crazy thing or get him involved in some shtumie business deal. But Herschel gets trapped coming out of the butcher shop and Solly says to him, "Have I got a deal for you!" And Herschel says, "If it's as good as that last deal, this time we'll go to the bankruptcy court hand-in-hand."
>
> And Solly says, "Listen, you can't pass this one up. It's terrific! A friend of mine is having an affair with a woman whose second husband's brother is married to a girl whose father is in business with a guy whose son is a merchandising agent for circuses, and I can get for you, for a mere three thousand dollars, a guaranteed fully-grown, two-ton Ringling Bros. Barnum & Bailey elephant."
>
> So Herschel looks at him like he's sprouted another head, and he says, "You know, you've gotta be out of your mind. I live in a fifth floor walkup apartment with a wife and four kids, and one of them is sleeping in the sink we got so little room. What the hell am I gonna do with an elephant, you dummy?"
>
> And Solly says, "Listen, only because you're married to Gert, I'm gonna make this a special. You can have the elephant for two thousand five hundred."

Herschel starts screaming. "Listen you yotz, what is it with you, are you deaf or something. I'm telling you I don't want, I don't need, I have no use for a two-ton elephant, not for twenty-five hundred, not for nothing. How the hell am I supposed to get the thing up the stairs? What do I feed it? You could die just from the body heat of a thing like that in a four room apartment. Get away from me, you moron!"

And they argue back and forth, with Solly constantly reducing the price, till finally he says, as a last resort, "Okay, okay, you momser! You want to bleed me, a relative, you got no heart? Okay! My last and final offer. For you . . . not one . . . but two! Two two-ton Ringling Bros. Barnum & Bailey elephants for five hundred dollars!"

And Herschel says, real quick, "Now you're talking business!"

When Momma told me that joke she was laughing. She laughed *very long and very hard, and I did, too. Not because the joke was so funny, although it's not bad and she told it well, but because* she was laughing. I never saw my Mother laugh very much.

From May of 1949 on, I never saw her laugh at all.

That was when my Father died.

It's impossible to talk about Serita without talking about Doc. Of course I never knew them when they were young and running around the way young people do, but from what I'm told by members of the Rosenthal family, they were some kind of short, Jewish equivalent of Scott Fitzgerald and Zelda. They were in love, and they were nuts together.

When my Father died, I think my Mother's life stopped. It was twenty-seven years of shadows for her. Just marking time. Waiting to join Doc. If there's anything good about death, and anything that even remotely lightens the pain of my Mother's death, it is that finally, after twenty-seven years, she came up lucky and went to meet my Dad, to take up where they got cut off in 1949.

I'd tell you how old my Mother was when she died, but as anyone who knew her for more than an hour can tell you, she would rather have had bamboo shoots thrust under her fingernails than reveal her age. She was like that.

She was a good woman, and a decent woman, and had all the right instincts about life, all the usual things people say at funerals; she was also opinionated, stubborn beyond belief, a frequent pain in the ass, and capable of a dudgeon so high it would put the Queen Mother to shame. But God, how she worked for her kids. I don't remember a time when she wasn't working. Either beside my Dad in the jewelry stores, or in the B'nai B'rith Thrift Shop, or somewhere. And no matter how much we took, she always came up with what we needed.

I remember once when I was a very little kid—and I was not the world's most tractable youngster—when I did something grotesque and awful; and Mom said, "You're going to get it when your Father comes home." No doubt I deserved it. I usually did. And when my Dad got back from work, exhausted and anxious to simply sit down and relax, Mom told him what I'd done and that I needed a good strapping.

Now understand: my family wasn't that big on corporal punishment. But my Dad took me down in the basement of our house on Harmon Drive in Painesville, and he took off his belt and he did a good job on me.

After a while, I came upstairs, and Mom and Dad were nowhere to be seen. I climbed the stairs to the second floor and through the closed door of their bedroom I could hear my Dad crying. The licking had devastated him much more than it had me. And my Mom was crying, too. She was consoling him, telling him it was the only thing he could do, and together they were solacing each other.

The Rosenthals were a family with a capacity for unhappiness that was awesome to behold, and Mom was a Rosenthal to her shoetops. There was the endless ganging-up of brothers and sisters in ever-changing permutations of the familial equation, with my Mom sometimes allied with Alice and Lew against Morrie, and sometimes associated with Morrie and Dorothy against Martin, and sometimes the hookups were so Machiavellian it was impossible to tell who was mad at whom. But throughout, no matter how affronted she thought she should be, my Mother was a Rosenthal, who would take fire and axe to anyone who tried to harm one hair on the head of her kin. The Russian soul of the Rosenthals, which was so intimately a part of my Mother's makeup, kept her from tasting unlimited joy in her later years—my niece Lisa was the great exception—they were in no way like grandchild and grandmother: they were best friends, chums, and the love between them so enriched both their lives that I think Mom's death is more crushing for

Lisa than for any of us—but even so my Mother managed to live to see Beverly well-married and the mother of two good kids, and me safely beyond any possibility of spending my life in jail. She took that to be treasure indeed.

I wish I could tell you more about Serita Ellison, but the sad, sorry fact is that we lived our lives as shadows to one another. We never really understood each other, the dreams never realized, the hopes set aside, the hungers that made us alien to one another. And so at final moments, as I speak of her, I try to hold the important memories; and the one that is richest, most recent is the picture of her in New Haven, Connecticut, in February of last year. I was invited to speak at the Yale Political Union, at Yale University, and I brought Mom up for the prestigious event. She was like a twenty year old girl. She was, as she used to put it, "in Seventh Heaven." Her kid was lecturing at Yale! How she did kvell! What naches! Radiant, like all the suns of the universe. It was snowing so hard in New Haven, and the drifts were so deep, and it was so bitterly cold, I was terrified that a woman in her condition would suffer damage. But she strode around like a cossack, I had to run to keep up with her.

And at my lecture, when I introduced her, she stood up and nodded so regally to all the Yalies that I thought I'd burst from pleasure. And when they brought over my books for her to autograph, she wrote, "Thank you for liking my son's books."

Near the end, when she was clearly in pain and knew she was going away, we talked several times a day long distance, and I kept saying, "I'll come down there." And she kept saying, "No, I don't want you to see me like this. Beverly and Lisa are here, and I'm all right." She was more lucid than she'd been in years; I guess she knew it was all over; and she said to me during what I guess was the last time we talked, though it might not have been the last time, "You turned out all right and I love you."

And now she's gone, and there's nothing much to say about the death of an old woman, any old woman, except that she's dead and everyone who knew her now has a finite number of days and nights to lament never having said all the things that should have been said.

She was my Mother, and I miss her.

* * *

By the time I stepped off the platform and returned to the family room at the side of the main chamber, Beverly had been returned to her seat. I'm not sure she even heard the eulogy beyond the telling of the "joke." After the ceremony was completed—so briefly, so awfully briefly—no one would speak to me. No one came up and said, "That was beautiful, what you said about your Mother." My nephew Loren shook my hand and we hugged, because he was crying, too, and he said, very softly, "You did good." Much later, Jerold took me aside and said, "Serita would have been proud of you." But other than those two remarks, I was shunned. Beverly, the uncles and aunts, they didn't stone me, but they made sure they didn't even brush my shoulder. One holds oneself aloof from pariahs and other uncleans. And their outrage frees me of them forever.

My Mother is gone, and I did what I wanted to do for her: she always enjoyed listening to me read, so I did it one last time for her. I know damned well she never heard it, but it's an innocent conceit. And they wanted to put her down too quickly, with too few words being spoken. I would have read my eulogy and then asked Beverly and Lisa and Lew and anyone else who had something to say, to come up and say it. She deserved that much at least.

Eulogies are never for the dead. They are always for the living; to pay off debts; to say goodbye formally one last time. But no one should be sent down into darkness with two few words.

Interim Memo

THIS IS THE ONLY SIGNIFICANT PIECE OF FILM CRITICISM THAT I've written, that wasn't included in HARLAN ELLISON'S WATCHING. It was omitted on purpose, for inclusion here. That rather irked Gil Lamont, who served as shadow-editor, amanuensis, skilled factotum, indexer and all-around general *nuhdz* on that hefty volume. Irked him—and in that irkability revealed his secret trepidation—because deep down I believe he—like Jack Chalker and the thousands of demented dipsticks who chivvied him over the years—always thought this book would not be carried to term.

Now understand something:

Jack Chalker, for twenty years, did not belabor me with calumny about my dilatory behavior. He was, he says, sanguine in the knowledge that when it was Hornbook Time, I would produce the *Hornbook* for him. But like the many contributors to THE LAST DANGEROUS VISIONS, as months grew into years and they waited for their stories to appear, a dolorous fatality about the project *had* to grow in Jack. Yet he maintained. He waited, becoming a prolific and bestselling author just to pass the time; and in large measure specifically *because* of Jack's faith and rectitude, I resolved to get this book to him.

In lesser degree—because he's only been affiliated with this project for three years—Otto Penzler also kept the lamp burning. I was to have gotten the manuscript to him within ninety days (as I recall) of his sending me an advance payment check for the trade hardcover edition . . . and it's been three years. But apart from the usual verbal bamboo shoots under my fingernails that form a necessary part of our peculiar friendship—for Otto and I are as dissimilar an Odd Couple as has come down the pike since Burke & Hare—Otto has been nothing but supportive. (Granted, Otto's support occasionally resembles the support Long John Silver visited on Jim Hawkins, nonetheless, he is a Prince.)

And it was this column that assuaged Otto's irk about a year ago. He saw a note of advance publicity for publication of HARLAN ELLISON'S WATCHING, and called to inquire (ever so quietly, sweetly, politely) as to why I was having this *other* book published when he was sitting on an unfulfilled contract from two years earlier.

I explained it all so logically, so thoroughly, and so simply that Otto fell into a paroxysm of apologia, offering me even more money to tide me over till I could get the *Hornbook* assembled. (Those who know Otto will vouch for this sort of philanthropic, effusive behavior. Largesse, as a common practice.)

But I could not, in conscience, permit such an extension of friendship. And to return the favor I promised Otto I would not include this *Hornbook* installment of film criticism in that other book. So it is (as I write this) the only chunk of movie comment to be found outside HARLAN ELLISON'S WATCHING.

One must keep faith with one's friends.

Enormous Dumb

Feb-March 1977

Several months of *angst*, death, and betrayal forming the loci of pain, I was driven from the path of wisdom and philosophy, from contemplations of the richness of the world around me. Surcease! I cried. Respite! Gimme a break. Let me find momentary oblivion. Breathing space. So I embarked on an endless movie crawl.

Thus, refurbished, comes to you the ellisonian moviegoer, emerging breathing freely again; emerging from the sweet dark cavern of celluloid dreams; blinking in the mid-afternoon effulgence; tummy rumbling from too many Milky Ways (that no longer are made with real chocolate) and popcorn (that is drizzled with something redolently reminiscent of butter, but which ain't). This here now cute little fellow, bold of wit and perceptive of analysis, snappy dresser and terrific dancer, altogether a credit to his race (not to mention his species, genus and phylum), stands on the sidewalk in front of the theater and asks no one in particular, "Why did they make that movie?" He speaks to the uncaring universe, asking, "Why would anyone *want* to make that movie?" But in its silence, the universe says *Hey, go sit on it, willya, Ellison; I got problems of my own!*

And so, the greater problems of morality and ethic, time and space, art and commerce being handled by everyone from Buckminster Fuller on airport populations to Zsa Zsa Gabor on fiscal responsibility, I address myself to one of the lesser burning topics of our troubled times:

I would speak of simple-minded movies.

* * *

It does not confuse me in the slightest that someone would make *The Shootist* as a film. It came from quite a good commercial western genre novel by Glendon Swarthout and, though John Wayne grievously diluted the moral imperatives by rewriting one of the main characters and the ending of the film in the traditional Wayneian bullshit manner that cannot bear to deal with reality if a bit of cliché fantasy is handy, it is a strongly mythic story that gave Wayne his best chance actually to create a character in many years. I can understand the thinking that preceded the scripting of such a film.

Likewise, it does not stretch credulity that such a group of once-blacklisted talents as Martin Ritt, Zero Mostel and their compatriots chose to cast Woody Allen as *The Front* and proffered a serio-comic indictment of the McCarthy Fifties. Nor that Altman would find impressive material in the stage production of Kopit's "Indians" and turn it into *Buffalo Bill and the Indians*. And *Shoot*, *The Bingo Long Traveling All-Star and Motor Kings* and even a simple, direct action adventure like *Sky Riders* make their *raisons d'êtres* known within the first twenty minutes of exposure.

But what kind of dingbat thinking leads apparently rational human beings to think that *aloha, bobby and rose* or *Car Wash* or *The Ritz* or *Murder by Death* have any value beyond being cut up for use as mandolin picks?

Not to mention a genuinely evil movie like *Lipstick*, a mindless melange like *The Gumball Rally*, a flat-out moronic cheat like *Obsession*, an icky piece of terminal tackiness like *The Duchess and the Dirtwater Fox* or a card-carrying stupidity like *The Big Bus*—all of which are such dogs they ought to be led out of the theaters on leashes.

These are motion pictures so wrongheaded, so utterly without cerebrating substance, so adolescent and clownish, that they quite literally compel the viewer to scratch his or her head and wonder *Why?*

These films I mention with such vehement denigration are only the most recent in memory. There have been endless others over the past two years—and I hasten to clarify by saying

I'm not referring only to "bad" films such as *The Hindenburg*, which simply turned out to be a turkey.

Let me thumbnail sketch the plots of a few of these films, in the event you've been fortunate enough to escape them. Bearing in mind, of course, that *any* story, capsulized in one sentence, is going to sound as stupid as MOBY DICK if one were to summarize it as the tale of a one-legged nut chasing a big fish. But the point is, I think, in large part, that excellences such as *Taxi Driver* or *Lifeguard cannot* be thematically summarized in one sentence, and these films can.

aloha, bobby and rose takes two thoroughly dull young people, cobbles up an illogical sociopathic situation for them, and then sends them on the run for no particular good reason; the young man gets shot to death, again illogically and conveniently, and the film ends with the girl crying over his corpse in the Los Angeles rain. Yes, indeed, we does have Los Angeles rain.) (And you'd just adore our Los Angeles lava flow.)

Car Wash has some funny moments and some interesting performances, most notably by the young black comic Franklin Ajaye and by Ivan Dixon, who ought to take off some weight. But. There is virtually no plot. It's all about a bunch of very flip-talking black dudes working in a car wash, and it's like a non-singing Cotton Club Revue of the Seventies: sight gags, running shticks, vignettes, and an almost obstinately hyper need to seem "hip" (or hep or hap or hop or whichever is supposed to be the pronunciation of the moment).

The Ritz is a bore. Based on the Broadway farce of the same name, it concerns itself with the hysterically senseless (and always loud, never under 180 decibel) activities of a straight slob from Cleveland hiding out from his *mafioso* brother-in-law who wants to kill him, in a gay hotel/baths vaudeville set in New York. Reviewers have lauded this bit of dreariness, somehow forgetting how good *The Boys in the Band* was, and praising Rita Moreno's performance. Where were those critics when Ms. Moreno burned the screen with her brilliant performance in *The Night of the Following Day?*

The Gumball Rally and *Mother, Jugs & Speed* are chiefly concerned with the contemporary cinematic replacement for the templates of the shoot'm'up Western: the car crash. Much meat and metal is macerated in the course of what are intended as "funny" films about driving fast, flipping cops the bird, and practicing at being scofflaws.

Lipstick panders to the basest, vilest, lowest possible common denominators of urban fear and lynch logic. It is the sort of film that, if you see it in a ghetto theater filled with blacks, will scare the bejeezus out of you. The animal fury this film unleashes in an audience is terrifying to behold. It gives exploitation a bad name; and it has less to do with rape, which is the commercial hook on which they've hung the saleability of this bit of putrescence than it does with the cynicism of Joseph E. Levine, a man who probably has no trouble sleeping with a troubled conscience.

Murder by Death is one long, repetitive in-joke for subscribers to the Detective Book Club and members of the Mystery Writers of America. Neil Simon, who wrote the film, is a man whose universal acceptance as a major comedy talent escapes me. Like John Simon, I find this other Simon to be a superficial creative entity, more fitted to tickling the risibilities of Scarsdale women's club matinee audiences than to grappling—even humorously—with life in our times. It is, purely put, a *dumb* film.

As for *The Duchess and the Dirtwater Fox*, after I saw it in London, I rushed back to my hotel to take a shower. The sight of Goldie Hawn's stained underwear, and George Segal (one of my personal heroes) demeaning himself with pratfalls and moronic dialogue, made me feel as if I'd stayed overnight in one of those Lyons House fleabags on the Bowery. If this is the state to which the American Western film has fallen, we are in worse shape than even a decade of Nixon/Ford leads us to believe.

These are films that, in one or two cases, have bright moments in them. A funny gag or two in *The Big Bus*, some hilarious antics in *Car Wash*, the Rita Moreno performance in *The Ritz*. But that's not the point, good or bad film. The point is: *why?* For whom are these films slanted, to what end are they made, about what of consequence are they speaking? Nowhere in these films can one find a coherent theme or underlying philosophy. They are like the dancing madness of the Middle Ages: they simply dervish without rationale.

Yes, of course, we can assume they were made to make money. But what quirky self-delusion convinced backers to put up the money for films without bankable stars or scripts by big-name writers or directed by men or women whose work has drawn for them a loyal following? What auguries did they consult to convince themselves that there would be a ticket-buying market for a spoof of disaster films such as *The Big Bus* or a pointless exercise in violence like *aloha, bobby and rose?*

I take it as a bellwether of the condition of the film industry today. Thousands of dynamiters from other lines of work—parking lot owners, garment manufacturers, computer company magnates, stock analysts—need diversification; they need tax writeoffs, they need shelters and capital gains deals. Most movies lose money. That's terrific for their purposes. And so they become easy prey for the show-biz hangers-on who cling to the hull of Hollywood like barnacles to the underside of a barque. As a film scenarist myself, I have been approached well over a dozen times in just the last eight months to "participate" or "spec write" a treatment or script for juicy little guys with leisure suits and ice cube eyes who have found an angel and want to get up a project.

For them, the art is in the dealmaking, not the creation. For them it is always a project, not a piece of art. And they have no sense or understanding of the creative act, and therefore they are as gullible as yokels freshly fallen off the turnip truck. You can sell them any damned stupid idea if you can orally spin a storytelling web around them.

And the results, if the project goes beyond the talking and seed-money stages, are hideous to behold. They are like thalidomide babies, crippled and illogical and graceless.

The reason for dumb, mindless, simpleton movies is that the people behind them, usually, are not creators in any sense of the word. They are nouveaus but lately come to the state of grace where they think they understand how a story should be strung together, what an audience wants (and they always throw demographics at you), and the subtle truth of that most imbecile of concepts, the *auteur* theory . . . that the director is the author of the film. They are, as Pauline Kael has pointed out, businessmen in charge of an art form.

They are, at bottom line, men and women who have been not-so-subtly seduced by the philosophy Andy Warhol propounded as a gag, that we have such a lemminglike need for superstars that one day soon *everyone* will be a star . . . for fifteen minutes. And these are people who look with disdain on their lives as Dentists, CPAs, Hairdressers and Business Moguls. They wanna play with the stars. They wanna roll in the fields of Elysium. And so they offer their hoard in exchange for being able to have cocktails at the Polo Lounge, and the smooth little salamander people suck them into deals, and sometimes the deals come to fruition and we get . . .

Dumb movies.

It is so grotesque a period for motion pictures, with so much persiflage and imbecility being thrown out onto the screens of America, being four-walled in drive-ins, being hyped and pre-packaged to sucker the unwary, that it makes the despotic days of Louis B. Mayer and Jack Warner seem like The Golden Age.

Interim Memo

AND SO IT ENDED. THIS LAST ESSAY, CALCULATEDLY A CODA TO the television essays I'd written circa 1968–1972, collected in THE GLASS TEAT and THE OTHER GLASS TEAT, served as update and more-or-less final statement about the television medium. It appears as the introduction to my 1978 story collection, STRANGE WINE; and it is included here as part of the *Hornbook* cycle, in the spirit of completism.

Upon reflection—buttressed by rereading these forty-six pieces a decade and a half later—it becomes clear to me that what I was learning when I wrote the columns of "The Glass Teat" series, was put to effect in the *Hornbook* outings; and that the year I spent doing these commentaries was a transition phase, a bridge between the casual, peripatetic manner of the tv criticism, and the more structured writing in AN EDGE IN MY VOICE and HARLAN ELLISON'S WATCHING.

Throughout those years, my fiction and film/tv work was drawing most of the attention, and the non-fiction writing— perhaps because it was appearing in Southern California rather than in a national venue—was almost totally ignored. But when I insisted on including three essays in STALKING THE NIGHT-MARE (1982), suddenly an audience developed for the commentaries. Mike Burgess of Borgo Press solicited a collection of essays, and did so solely because of the three pieces in STALK-ING. It took me by surprise, to be honest. Though I'd been writing easily as much non-fiction as stories since I'd begun my career—and had done even more work as journalist, columnist and magazine article slavey during college and the first years of professionaldom than I had as a fictioneer—I'd always downgraded the importance of the non-fiction in my own mind. Have no idea why that was so. Perhaps because, when I was learning my craft, fiction was more highly considered by the Establishment, magazines published tons of fiction, and those who wrote non-fiction usually did it from some special knowledge.

But when Burgess asked for the book that became SLEEPLESS NIGHTS IN THE PROCRUSTEAN BED, that new audience appeared; and since that first venture—somehow the two TEAT books seemed out of contention—well, everything I've done in the essay form has found its way into print in hardcover. Now, with the publication of the HORNBOOK, the last large chunk of commentary is on the record.

As for this final word on television, written twelve years ago, the only comment that seems needful by way of updating is this:

Plus ça change, plus c'est la même chose.

Or, as we say in the teevee biz, "Whaddaya think, Bruce, can we recycle *Perry Mason* again? Howzabout we make him blind, quadraplegic, transvestite and miraculously remitted from AIDS? Whaddaya think?"

Revealed at Last! What Killed the Dinosaurs! And You Don't Look So Terrific Yourself.

June-July 1977

*I*t's all about drinking strange wine.

It seems disjointed and jumps around like water on a griddle, but it all comes together, so be patient.

At 9:38 A.M. on July 15th, 1974, about eight minutes into *Suncoast Digest*, a variety show on WXLT-TV in Sarasota, Florida, anchorwoman Chris Chubbuck, 30, looked straight at the camera and said, "In keeping with Channel 40's policy of bringing you the latest in blood and guts in living color, you're going to see another first—an attempt at suicide."

Whereupon, she pulled a gun out of a shopping bag and blew her brains out, on camera.

Paragraph 3, preceding, was taken verbatim from an article written by Daniel Schorr for *Rolling Stone*. I'd heard about the Chubbuck incident, of course, and I admit to filching Mr. Schorr's sixty concise words because it *is* concise, and why should I try to improve on precision? As the artist Mark Rothko once put it: "Silence is so accurate."

Further, Mr. Schorr perceived in the bizarre death of Chris Chubbuck exactly what I got out of it when I heard the news broadcast the day it happened. She was making a statement about television . . . *on television!*

The art-imitating-life resemblance to Paddy Chayefsky's film *Network* should not escape us. I'm sure it wouldn't have escaped Chris Chubbuck's attention. Obvious cliché; onward.

I used to know Dan Blocker, who played Hoss Cartwright on *Bonanza*. He was a wise and a kind man, and there are tens of dozens of people I would much rather see dead than Dan. One time, around lunchbreak at Paramount, when I was goofing off on writing a treatment for a Joe Levine film that never got made, and Dan was resting his ass from some dumb horsey number he'd been reshooting all morning, we sat on the steps of the weathered saloon that no doubt resembled in no way any saloon that had ever existed in Virginia City, Nevada, and we talked about reality versus fantasy. The reality of getting up at five in the morning to get to the studio in time for makeup call and the reality of how bloody much F.I.C.A. tax they took out of our paychecks and the reality of one of his kids being down with something or other . . . and the fantasy of not being Dan Blocker, but of being Hoss Cartwright.

And he told me a scary story. He laughed about it, but it was the laugh of butchers in a slaughterhouse who have to swing the mauls that brain the beeves and then go home to wash the stink out of their hair from the spattering.

He told me—and he said this happened *all* the time, not just in isolated cases—that he had been approached by a little old woman during one of his personal appearances at a rodeo, and the woman had said to him, dead seriously, "Now listen to me, Hoss: when you go home tonight, I want you to tell your daddy, Ben, to get rid of that Chinee fella who cooks for you all. What you need is to get yourself a good woman in there can cook up some decent food for you and your family."

So Dan said to her, very politely (because he was one of the most courteous people I've ever met), "Excuse me, ma'am, but my name is Dan Blocker. Hoss is just the character I play. When I go home I'll be going to my house in Los Angeles and my wife and children will be waiting."

And she went right on, just a bit affronted because she

knew all that, what was the matter with him, did he think she was simple or something, "Yes, I know . . . but when you go back to the Ponderosa, you just tell your daddy Ben that I said . . ."

For her, fantasy and reality were one and the same.

There was a woman who had the part of a home-wrecker on a daytime soap opera. One day as she was coming out of Lord & Taylor in New York, a viewer began bashing her with an umbrella, calling her filthy names and insisting she should leave that nice man and his wife alone!

One time during a college lecture, I idly mentioned that I actually *thought up* all the words Leonard Nimoy had spoken as Mr. Spock on the sole *Star Trek* segment I had written; and a young man leaped up in the audience, in tears, and began screaming that I was a liar. He actually thought the actors were living those roles as they came across the tube.

Chris Chubbuck perceived at a gut level that for too many Americans the only reality is what's on the box. That Johnny Carson and Don Rickles and Mary Tyler Moore are more real, more substantial, more immediately important than the members of their own family, or the people in their community. She knew that her death wouldn't be *real* unless it happened on television, unless it took place where life is lived, there in phosphor dot Never-Never Land. If she did it decently, in the privacy of her home, or in some late night bar, or in a deserted parking lot . . . it would never have happened. She would have been flensed from memory as casually as a popped pimple. Her suicide on camera was the supreme act of loathing and ridicule for the monkeymass that watched her.

When I was writing my television criticism for the *Los Angeles Free Press*, circa 1968–72, I used *The Glass Teat* columns to repeat my belief that those of us who cared, who had some ethics and some talent, dare not abandon to the Visigoths what was potentially the most powerful medium the world had ever known for the dissemination of education and knowledge. I truly believed that. And I said it again and again.

But it's been five years since I last wrote those words, and I've done so many college speaking engagements that Grand Forks, North Dakota, has blurred with Minneapolis, Minnesota, has blurred with Bethel, Maine, has blurred with Shreveport, Louisiana, and what I've come away with is a growing horror at what television has done to us.

I now believe that television itself, the medium of sitting in front of a magic box that pulses images at us endlessly, the act of watching tv, *per se*, is mind-crushing. It is soul-deadening, dehumanizing, soporific in a poisonous way, ultimately brutalizing. It is, simply put so you cannot mistake my meaning, *a bad thing*.

We need never fear Orwell's 1984, because it's here, with us now, nearly a decade ahead of schedule, and has been with us for quite a while already. Witness the power of television and the impact it has had on *you*.

Don't write me letters telling me how *you've* escaped the terror, how *you're* not a slave to the box, how *you* still read and listen to Brahms and carry on meaningful discussions with your equally-liberated friends. Stop and *really* take stock of how many hours last week you sat stunned before the tube, relaxing, just unwinding, just passing a little time between the demanding and excoriating life-interests that *really* command your energies. You will be stunned again, if you are honest. Because *I* did it, and it scared me, genuinely put a fright into me. It was far more time than I'd have considered feasible, knowing how much I despise television and how little there is I care to watch.

I rise, usually, between five and seven in the morning, depending how late I've worked the night before. I work like a lunatic all day . . . I'm a workaholic . . . pity me . . . and by five or six in the evening I have to unwind. So I lie down and turn on the set. Where before I might have picked up a book of light fiction, or dozed, or just sighed and stared at the ceiling, now I turn on the carnivorous coaxial creature.

And I watch.

Here in Los Angeles between five and eight, when "Prime Time" begins (oh, how I *love* that semantically twisted phrase) we have the same drivel you have in your city. Time that was taken from the networks to program material of local interest and edification. Like reruns of *Adam-12*, *The Price is Right*, *The Joker's Wild*, *Name That Tune*, *I Dream of Jeannie*, *Bewitched*,

Concentration and *Match Game P.M.* I lie there like the quadruple amputee viewpoint character of Dalton Trumbo's JOHNNY GOT HIS GUN, never speaking, breathing shallowly, seeing only what flashes before my eyes, reduced to a ganglial image receptor, a raw nerve end taking in whatever banalities and incredible stupidities they care to throw at me in the name of "giving the audience what they want."

If functional illiterates failing such mind-challenging questions as, "What was the name of the character Robert Stack played on *The Untouchables*?" is an accurate representation of "what the audience wants," then my point is solidly made . . .

. . . and it goes directly to the solution to the question of what killed the dinosaurs and you don't look so terrific yourself!

But I wander. So. I lie there, until my low bullshit threshold is reached, either through the zombie mannerisms of the *Adam-12* cops—dehumanized paragons of a virtue never known by L.A.'s lunatic Chief of Police, Weirdo Ed Davis—or because of some yotz on *The Price is Right* having an orgasm at winning a thirty year supply of rectal suppositories. And then I curse, snap off the set and realize I've been lying there for ninety minutes.

And when I take stock of how much time I'm spending in front of that set, either at the five-to-eight break or around eleven o'clock when I fall into bed for another break and turn on the *CBS Late Movie*, I become aware of five hours spent in mindless sucking at the glass teat.

If you're honest, you'll cop to that much time televiewing, too. Maybe more. Maybe a little less. But you spend from three to eight hours a day at it. And you're not alone. Nor am I. The college gigs I do have clearly demonstrated that to me. Clearly. I take show-of-hands polls in the audience; and after badgering them to cop to the truth, the vast bulk of the audience admits it, and I see the stunned looks of concern and dawning awareness.

They never realized it was that much, nor did I.

And the effect it has had on them, on you, young people and old alike; black and white and Hispanic and Oriental and Amerind; male and female; wealthy and impoverished; WASPs and Jews and Shintoists and Buddhists and Catholics and even Scientologists. All of us, all of you, swamped day after day by stereotypes and jingoism and "accepted" life-styles. So that after a while you come to believe doctors are all wise and noble and one with Marcus Welby and they could cure you of *any*thing if only you'd stop being so cranky and irrational; that cops never abuse their power and are somehow Solomonic in their judgments; that in the final extreme violence—as represented by that eloquent vocabulary of a punch in the mouth—solves problems; that women are either cute and cuddly and need a strong hand to keep them in line or defeminize themselves if they have successful careers; and that eating McDonald's prefab food is actually *better* for you than *Foie de Veau Sauté aux Fines Herbes* . . . and tastier, too.

I see this zombiatic response in college audiences. It manifests itself most prominently in the kinds of questions that are asked. Here I stand before them, perhaps neither Melville nor Twain, but nonetheless a man with a substantial body of work behind him, books that express the artist's view of the world (and after all, isn't that why they paid me two grand or better a night to come and speak? surely it can't be my winsome manner!), and they persist in asking me what it was like to work on *Star Trek* or what Jimmy Caan is *really* like and why did Tom Snyder keep cutting me off on the *Tomorrow Show*. I get angry with them. I make myself lots less antic and entertaining. I tell them what I'm telling you here. And they don't like me for it. As long as I'm running down the military-industrial complex, or the fat money cats who play sneaky panther games with our lives, they give me many "Right on, brother!" ovations. But when I tell them how shallow and programmed television is making them, there is a clear lynch tenor in the mob. (It isn't just college kids, gentle reader. I was recently rewarded with sullen animosity when I spoke to a dinner gathering of Southern California Book Publicists, and instead of blowing smoke up their asses about what a wonderful thing book publicity through the *Johnny Carson Show* is—because there isn't one of them who wouldn't sacrifice several quarts of blood to get a client on that detestable viewing ground for banal conversationalists—I quoted them the recent illiteracy figures released by HEW. I pointed out that only 8% of the 220,000,000 population of this country buy books, and of that 8% only 2% buy more than a single book a year. I pointed out that 6% of that measly 8% were no doubt buying, as their single enriching literary experience each year, JAWS or OLIVER'S STORY or the latest Harold Robbins ghastliness, rather than, say, REMEMBRANCE OF THINGS PAST or the Durants's THE LESSONS OF HISTORY or even the latest Nabokov or Lessing novel. So that meant they were hustling books to only 2% of the population of this country, while the other 98% sank deeper and deeper into illiteracy and functional illiteracy, their heads being shoved under by the pressure of television, to which they were slavishly making obeisance. They were, in effect, sharpening the blade for their executioner, assisting in their own extinction. They *really* didn't want to hear that. Nor do college audiences.)

A *bad* thing. Watching television. Not rationalizing it so that it comes out reading thus: "Television is *potentially* a good thing; it can educate and stimulate and inform us; we've just permitted it to be badly used; but if we could get some *good* stuff on the tube . . ." No, I'm afraid I've gone beyond that rationalization, to an extreme position. The *act* of watching television for protracted periods (and there's no way to insure the narcotic effects won't take you over) is deleterious to the human animal. The medium itself insists you sit there quietly and cease thinking.

The dinosaurs. How they died.

Television, quite the opposite of books or even old-time radio that presented drama and comedy and talk shows (unlike Top Fifty radio programming today, which is merely tv without moving parts), is systemically oriented toward stunning the use of individual imagination. It puts everything out there, *right there*, so you don't have to dream even a little bit. When they would broadcast a segment of, say, *Inner Sanctum* in the Forties, and you heard the creaking door of a haunted house, the mind was forced to *create the picture* of that haunted house . . . a terrifying place so detailed and terrifying that if Universal

Studios wanted to build such an edifice for a tv movie, it would cost them millions of dollars and it *still* wouldn't be one one-millionth as frightening as the one your own imagination had cobbled up.

A book is a participatory adventure. It involves a creative act at its inception, and a creative act when its purpose is fulfilled. The writer dreams the dream and sets it down; the reader reinterprets the dream in personal terms, with personal vision when he or she reads it. Each creates a world. The template is the book.

At risk of repeating myself, and of once again cribbing from another writer's perfection of expression (in this case, my friend Dr. Isaac Asimov), here is a bit I wrote on this subject for an essay on the "craft" of writing teleplays:

Unlike television, films, football games, the roller derby, wars in underdeveloped nations and Watergate hearings, which are spectator sports, a book requires the activation of its words by the eyes and the intellect of a reader. As Isaac Asimov said recently in an article postulating the perfect entertainment cassette, "A cassette as ordinarily viewed makes sound and casts light. That is its purpose, of course, but must sound and light obtrude on others who are not involved or interested? The ideal cassette would be visible and audible only to the person using it. . . . We could imagine a cassette that is always in perfect adjustment; that starts automatically when you look at it; that stops automatically when you cease to look at it; that can play forward or backward, quickly or slowly, by skips or with repetitions, entirely at your pleasure. . . . Surely, that's the ultimate dream device—a cassette that may deal with any of an infinite number of subjects, fictional or non-fictional, that is self-contained, portable, non–energy-consuming, perfectly private and largely under the control of the will. . . . Must this remain only a dream? Can we expect to have such a cassette some day? . . . We not only have it now, we have had it for many centuries. The ideal I have described is the printed word, the book, the object you now hold—light, private, and manipulable at will. . . . Does it seem to you that the book, unlike the cassette I have been describing, does not produce sound and

images? It certainly does. . . . You cannot read without hearing the words in your mind and seeing the images to which they
give rise. In fact, they are *your* sounds and images, not those
invented for you by others, and are therefore better. . . . The
printed word presents minimum information, however. Everything but that minimum must be provided by the reader—the
intonation of words, the expressions on faces, the actions, the
scenery, the background, must all be drawn out of that long line
of black-on-white symbols."

Quite clearly, if one but looks around to assess the irrefutable evidence of reality, books strengthen the dreaming facility,
and television numbs it. Atrophy soon follows.

Shelley Torgeson, who is the director of the spoken word
records I've cut for Alternate World Recordings, is also a mass
media teacher at Harrison High School in Westchester. She tells
me some things that buttress my position.

1) A fifteen year old student summarily rejected the reading of
books because it "wasn't real." Because it was your imagination,
and your imagination isn't real. So Shelley asked her what was
"real" and the student responded instantly, "Television." Because you could see it. Then, by pressing the conversation,
Shelley discovered that though the student was in the tenth
grade, when she read she didn't understand the words and was
making up words and their meanings all through the text; far
beyond the usual practice in which we all indulge, of gleaning
an *approximate* meaning of an unfamiliar word from its context.
With television, she had no such problems. They didn't use
words. It was real. Thus—and quite logically in a kind of
Alice-Down-the-Rabbit-Hole manner—the books *weren't* real,
because she was making them up as she went along, not actually
reading the book. If you know what I mean.
2) An important school function was woefully underattended
one night, and the next day Shelley (suspecting the reason)
confirmed that the absence of so many students was due to
their being at home watching part two of the tv movie based on
the Manson murder spree, *Helter Skelter*. Well, that *was* a bit of
a special event in itself, and a terrifying program; but the

interesting aspect of their watching the show emerged when a student responded to Shelley's comparison of watching something that "wasn't real" with a living event that "was real." The student contended it *was* real, he had seen it. No, Shelley, insisted, it wasn't real, it was just a show. Hell no, the kid kept saying, it *was* real: he had *seen* it. Reasoning slowly and steadily, it took Shelley fifteen or twenty minutes to convince him (if she actually managed) that he had not seen the authentic, living, real historical event—because he had not been in Los Angeles in August of 1969 when the murders had happened. Though he was seventeen years old, the student was incapable of perceiving, *unaided*, the difference between a dramatization and real life.

3) In each classroom of another school at which Shelley taught, there was a tv set, mostly unused save for an occasional administrative announcement; the sets had been originally installed in conjunction with a Ford Foundation grant to be used for visual training. Now they're blank and silent. When Shelley had trouble controlling the class, getting them quiet, she would turn on the set and they would settle down. The screen contained nothing, just snow; but they grew as fascinated as cobras at a mongoose rally, and fell silent, watching nothing. Shelley says she could keep them that way for extended periods.

Interestingly, as a footnote, when Shelley mentioned this device at lunch, a chemistry professor said he used something similar. When his students were unruly he would place a beaker of water on a Bunsen burner. When the water began to boil, the students grew silent and mesmerized, watching the water bubbling.

And as a sub-footnote, I'm reminded of a news story I read. A burglar broke into a suburban home in Detroit or some similar city (it's been a while since I read the item and unimportant details have blurred in my mind) and proceeded to terrorize and rob the housewife alone there with her seven year old son. As the attacker stripped the clothes off the woman at knife-point, the child wandered into the room. The burglar told the child to go in the bedroom and watch television till he was told to come out. The child watched the tube for six straight hours, never once returning to the room where his mother had been raped repeatedly, tied and bound to a chair with tape over her mouth, and beaten mercilessly. The burglar had had free access to the entire home, had stripped it of all valuables, and had left unimpeded. The tape, incidentally, had been added when the burglar/rapist was done enjoying himself. All through the assault the woman had been calling for help. But the child had been watching the set and didn't come out to see what was happening. For six hours.

Roy Torgeson, Shelley's husband and producer of my records, reminded us of a classroom experiment reported by the novelist Jerzy Kosinski, in which a teacher was set to speaking at one side of the front of a classroom, and a television monitor was set up on the other side of the room, showing the teacher speaking. The students had unobstructed vision of both. They watched the monitor. They watched what was real.

Tom Snyder, of the NBC *Tomorrow Show*, was telling me that he receives letters from people apologizing for their having gone away on vacation or visiting with their grandchildren, or otherwise not having been at home so he could do his show . . . but now that they're back, and the set is on, he can start doing his show again. Their delusion is a strange reversal of the ones I've noted previously. For them, Snyder (and by extension other newscasters and actors) aren't there, aren't happening, unless *they* are watching. They think the actors can see into *their* living rooms, and they dress as if for company, they always make sure the room is clean, and in one case there is a report of an elderly woman who dresses for luncheon with "her friends" and sets up the table and prepares luncheon and then, at one o'clock, turns on the set for a soap opera. Those are her friends: she thinks they can see into her house, and she is one with them in their problems.

To those of us who conceive of ourselves as rational and grounded in reality (yes, friends, even though I write fantasy, I live in the real world, my feet sunk to the ankles in pragmatism), all of this may seem like isolated, delusionary behavior. I assure you it isn't. A study group that rates high school populations recently advised one large school district that the "good behavior" of the kids in its classes was very likely something more than just normal quiet and good manners. They were *too* quiet, *too* tranquilized, and the study group called it "dangerous." I submit that the endless watching of tv by kids produces this blank, dead, unimaginative manner.

It is widespread, and cannot possibly be countered by the minimal level of reading that currently exists in this country. Young people have been systematically bastardized in their ability to seek out quality material—books, films, food, life-styles, life-goals, enriching relationships.

Books cannot combat the spiderwebbing effect of television because kids simply cannot read. It is on a par with their inability to hear music that isn't rock: turn the car radio dial from one end to another when you're riding with young people (up to the age of fifty); you will perceive that they whip past classical music as if it were "white noise," simply static to their ears. The same goes for books. The printed word has no value to them, and carries no possibility of knowledge or message that relates to *their* real world.

If one chooses to say, as one idiot I faced on the *90 Minutes Live* talk show over the Canadian Broadcasting Corporation said, people don't need to read, that people don't like books, that they want to be "entertained" (as if reading were something hideous, something other than *also* entertainment), then we come to an impasse. But if, like me, you believe that books preserve the past, illuminate the present, and point the way to the future . . . then you can understand why I seem to be upset at the ramifications of this epiphany I've had.

Do not expect—as I once did because I saw Senator Joseph McCarthy of Wisconsin unmasked on television—that tv will reveal the culprits. Nixon lied without even the faintest sign of embarassment or disingenuousness on tv, time after time, for years. He told lies, flat out and outrageously; monstrous lies that bore no relation to the truth. But well over half the population of this country, tuning him in, believed him. Not just that they *wanted* to believe him for political or personal reasons, or because it was easier than having waves made . . . they believed him because he stared right at them and spoke softly and they could *tell* he was telling the truth. Tv did not unmask him. Television played no part in the revelations of Watergate. In point of fact, television prevented the unmasking, because Nixon used tv to keep public opinion tremblingly on his side. It was only when the real world, the irrefutable facts, were slammed home again and again, that the hold was loosened on public sentiment.

Nor did television show what a bumbler Gerald Ford was. He was as chummy and friendly and familiar as Andy Griffith or Captain Kangaroo when he came before us on the tube. Television does not show us the duplicitous smirk, the dull mentality, the self-serving truth behind the noncommittal statement of administration policy. It does not deal in reality, it does not proffer honesty, it only serves up non-judgmental images and allows thugs like Nixon to make themselves as acceptable as Reverend Ike.

And on the *Johnny Carson Show* they have a seven minute "author's spot," gouged out of ninety minutes festooned with Charo's quivering buttocks, Zsa Zsa Gabor's feelings about fiscal responsibility, John Davidson on recombinant DNA and Don Rickles insulting Carson's tie. Then, in the last ten minutes they invite on Carl Sagan or Buckminster Fuller or John Lilley to explain the Ethical Structure of the Universe. And they contend this is a rebirth of the art of conversation. Authors of books are seldom invited on the show unless they have a new diet, a new sex theory, or a non-fiction gimmick that will make an interesting demonstration in which Johnny can take part . . . like wrestling a puma, spinning a hula hoop or baking lasagna with solar heat.

All this programs the death of reading.

And reading is the drinking of strange wine.

Like water on a hot griddle, I have bounced around, but the unification of the thesis is at hand.

Drinking strange wine pours strength into the imagination.

The dinosaurs had no strange wine.

They had no imagination. They lived 130,000,000 years and vanished. Why? Because they had no imagination. Unlike human beings who have it and use it and build their future rather than merely passing through their lives as if they were spectators. Spectators watching television, one might say.

The saurians had no strange wine, no imagination, and they became extinct. And you don't look so terrific yourself.

APPENDIXES

Interim Memo to Appendixes

THE SIX FULL-LENGTH ESSAYS THAT FOLLOW WERE NOT A PART of the cycle now gathered as THE HARLAN ELLISON HORN-BOOK. Two were written for *Los Angeles* magazine, two for *Playboy*, one for ALL IN COLOR FOR A DIME, a long out-of-print volume about comic books, and the last an unpublished piece written for the defunct *Show* magazine. They total about 27,000 words of non-fiction.

They represent the level of "serious" at which I work, as parallel to the level of "serious" when I'm doing fiction.

They are included here to show the fruits of the *Hornbook* labors, and for several other imperatives. Only "Comic of the Absurd," written in 1969 and published in 1970, and "Dogging It in the Great American Heartland" (1970), predate these columns.

While it is not strictly echoic of the *Hornbook* metier, "Comic of the Absurd" informs and links with the herein-included longer piece I did last year on comic books for *Playboy*. And I don't want it lost in the files; Geo. Carlson deserves *at least* this much attention.

As for "Dogging It . . ." being included, well, I always like to include something in every book that has never been published. There aren't many of those, so I usually wind up writing something brand-new. In this case, the article extended the range of what I wanted to exhibit as subjects that drew my attention during the general period of the years of the *Hornbook* columns. Also, the essay fleshes out background to oblique references in several of the installments.

But the other four articles tie in directly with what I did in the *Hornbook* columns. They are the adults that grew from the children who present themselves in forty-six installments. What I learned from writing the *Hornbook* manifests itself in the later, more exhaustive pieces. Three of them were written only last year, and they are (at least in my view) Major Work.

They are included as lagniappe. A little something extra.

They serve to advise the curious reader what the Author is up to right now, how the talent fares; an updated interim memo.

Appendix A

Interim Memo

GEORGE CARLSON IS DEAD, HE APPARENTLY DIED SOME YEARS even before this piece appeared. But when it was published—the first piece on this extraordinary "lost American original"—I heard from his daughters, who were in their early forties. They were pleased, as you might imagine, that their father was not wholly forgotten. They sent me many pieces of his work, in hopes that I might find a museum or archive that would preserve them (oh, how I tried, and tried, and tried . . . unsuccessfully). And if I had been impressed by Carlson strictly by way of "The Pie-Face Prince of Pretzleburg" and the "Jingle Jangle Tales," I was stunned by the range and importance of work he had done *outside* the world of comics.

Did you know that George Carlson did the booklet that was issued to everyone on the maiden voyage of the Queen Mary?

Did you know that George Carlson did the original dust jacket art for GONE WITH THE WIND?

Did you know that George Carlson was the first illustrator of the *Uncle Wiggily* books written by Howard R. Garis, a series among the most famous and longest-extant of children's standards? And though the publishers, Platt & Munk, have kept these books in print since the Thirties, nowhere on the books is George Carlson given credit (unless one scrutinizes the corners of the art and sees his name neatly printed, or finds the initials G.C.), leading the casual to believe Garis did the art, as well. And if one compares the tone and style of the *Uncle Wiggily* stories (which almost always end something like this: "And, if the loaf of bread doesn't get a toothache and jump out of the oven into the dishpan I'll tell you about Uncle Wiggily Learns to Dance"), to the tone and style of the inspiredly whacky *Jingle Jangle Tales*

("The Sea-Going Rajah and the Milk-Fed Fraction"

("The Musical Wifflesnort and the Red-Hot Music Roll"

("The Self-Winding Organ-Gander and the Overstuffed Bull-Fiddle"

("The Sea-Seasoned Sea-Cook and the Heroic Pancake"

("The Toothless Scarecrow and the Tamed Wildflower"

("The Very Fair Weatherman and the Clock-Less Cuckoo"),

you may surely be convinced—as I am, thoroughly—that the absurdist touches in the Garis stories (so unlike the mundane stories themselves), the touches that have made these books perennials, were the unsung contribution of Carlson's miraculous mind, and not those of Garis, who got rich off the books.

A few years ago, an art gallery owner in New England called, saying he knew of my admiration for the work of Geo. Carlson, and recently into his possession had come three splendid watercolors Carlson had done for some long-forgotten children's book. Would I be interested in purchasing them? Would I?!? They hang in my home now, and I tell you truly that no one can pass those lovely animals dressed as pirates, framed as a triptych, without pausing and smiling.

I've lost touch with Carlson's daughters. The artwork was all returned. Some years later a "middleman" of dubious credentials surfaced, offering for sale the original *Jingle Jangle Comics* pages, at exorbitant prices, with questionable provenance. Several of us tried to get the two Museums of Comic Art, one on the East Coast, the other in care of Bill Blackbeard in San Francisco, to purchase these priceless artifacts, so they could be preserved. For one reason or another, no sale was effected; and those originals have, likewise, vanished.

And though my little essay on Carlson circa 1970 raised the prices of the original comics in the Overstreet Guide from pennies to many dollars (*Jingle Jangle* #1, February 1942, goes for $141.00 as of Overstreet's 19th edition), when Arlington

House published "Comic of the Absurd" in hardcover—as a selection of ALL IN COLOR FOR A DIME, edited by Richard Lupoff and Don Thompson— and Ace reprinted it in paperback, almost twenty years ago, they didn't even bother to reproduce a page of Carlson. They picked a cover at random from the forty-two issue run of the magazine, and it was a cover by Dave Tendlar. Aaaarghhh! Also, grrrr!

Not even when his name had a scintilla of chance of being saved from utter obscurity, did Geo. Carlson catch a break.

And so, in this book, for the first time in more than forty years, you can read a complete Carlson *Jingle Jangle Tale*.

That is, for the first time in forty years, unless you happen to own the prestigious volume, A SMITHSONIAN BOOK OF COMIC-BOOK COMICS, edited by Michael Barrier and Martin Williams (Harry N. Abrams, Inc., 1981), in which Carlson is elevated to classic stature by inclusion as one of the "greats" with such few as Carl Barks, Walt Kelly, Basil Wolverton, Jack Cole and C. C. Beck.

When Barrier contacted me late in the '70s, and told me that the Smithsonian had elected to preserve the names and work of these few—Sheldon Mayer, and the creators of Superman and Batman—and that Carlson shouted to be among the Best of the Best, I thought it might serve to draw the work of this wonderful, lost satirist to the attention of an art world so easily dazzled by the derivative swipes of the Lichtensteins and Warhols.

But it didn't happen.

Somewhere out there, hundreds and hundreds of Geo. Carlson originals lie moldering, while gallery owners and the heirs of the estates of fripperish Pop artists grow fat selling the transitory fad-pieces of lesser lights to Museums of Fine Art that pay lip-service to "the preservation of American artists."

Excuse my grrrr. But now, for certain, you understand why I stretched the parameters to include this little essay. If we must remember Dachau and the Palmer Raids and John Fante and The Book of Kells, because to forget them costs us more than merely ignorance, then we must remember and honor George Carlson, as well. We need the light of his buoyant spirit.

Comic of the Absurd

(1969/1970)

When the aliens come from Tau Ceti in 2755 A.D. and begin scrabbling like dogs digging bones, in the rubble that is left of Civilization As We Know It, they will surely unearth the finest works of the geniuses of Art. They will discover Bosch, and van Gogh, and Vermeer, and Monet, and Dali, and Wyeth, and Rembrandt, and Picasso. They will also discover George Carlson.

Beg your pardon? Who?

I said: George Carlson.

I sense your outrage. This unknown, in company with these undisputed greats. I hear your question. I see your sullen, reproachful mien. You want to know, *who the hell is George Carlson?* And, *by what right do you presume to link him with the greatest masters of Art?*

Who is George Carlson? I'm glad you asked. It's about time someone did.

George Carlson is Samuel Beckett in a clever plastic disguise. He is Harold Pinter scrubbed clean of the adolescent fear and obscurity, decked out in popcorn balls and confetti. He is Ionesco with a giggle. He is Genet without hangups. He is Pirandello buttered with dreamdust and wearing water wings. He is Santa Claus and Peter Pan and the Great Pumpkin and the Genie in the Jug and what Walt Disney started out to be and never quite made.

George Carlson is . . .

Or, rather, he was. He's still alive; I have it on good authority, though I've been unable to track him down. (And in a way, am rather glad. I once received a letter from Edward Gorey, and considered going to meet him, but decided it was better to let gods live in their Valhallas, and not muck them about with the realities of acquaintanceship. The same goes for George Carlson.) But Carlson is no longer an "is". He's a "was". He doesn't do *that* any more.

Again, I hear you: what *that* is it he don't do no more?

Well, he don't chronicle the adventures of the youthful yodler and the zig-zag zither; he don't tell what happened to the toothless scarecrow and the tamed wildflower; he don't reveal the startling tale of the fashionable fireman and the soft-boiled collar-button; he don't hip you to the extra-salty sailor and the flat-footed dragon; he don't regale you with the facts in the contretemps of the coffee-eyed hermit and the unprisoned princess; he don't . . . well, he just *doesn't*, not any more. And that, woeful folks, is terrible sad-making.

Because the man known as George Carlson, the incredible artist who—for forty-two issues of *Jingle Jangle Comics*—scripted and drew a series of unparalleled contemporary fables called "Jingle Jangle Tales," no longer draws. *Jingle Jangle Comics* is long-since gone. It died in December 1949. At Christmastime. During a season of joy and colored lights and children's laughter, George Carlson went away, taking with him one of those rare and marvelous gifts we had been joyously allowed to savor from March of 1943 till that emptiest of Christmases. He went away, and he took the "Jingle Jangle Tales," and most of all he took "The Pie-Face Prince of Pretzleburg."

It won't mean much to kids today—surfeited as they are with this week's post–puberty sex-symbol—but back in 1943 when I was nine years old, Dimwitri (The Pie-Face Prince) was a very special person in my world.

Sitting here now, writing about Carlson and his mad brood of improbable characters (was there ever a more convulsive duo than the self-winding organ-gander and the overstuffed bull-fiddle?), I find it barely short of incredible that he happened as he did. Carlson was easily thirty years ahead of his time. He was

one of the first cartoonists of the absurd, on a par with Winsor
McCay, Geo. McManus, Rube Goldberg or Bill Holman. Without the rampant sex, he was the progenitor of R. Crumb and
Gorey and Tomi Ungerer and Ronald Searle and even Row-
land Emmett. And how a) he came to develop his style in a time
when cuddly animals were the going thing, b) a publishing
house like Famous Funnies that trafficked in cuddly animals
employed him, and c) kids like myself who really couldn't have
understood what he was about, were wild about him . . . are
improbabilities too staggering to deal with.

His drawing was neither simple nor retarded as was the
bulk of the line-work being done. His style was one of pre-*Mad*
goodies secreted here and there in the panels; of jumbled and
overlapping shapes that delightfully bedevilled the reader; of
fats and thins that gamboled and bumbled everywhichway; of
plot-lines surfeited with double-level puns and plays on words
as Oscar Levant would have treasured. Carlson was a *rara avis*.
One of a kind. His like had never been seen before, and since
him it has all been the sincerest form of flattery.

I suppose pedants would find his little flummeries filled
with examinations of Man and His Times, of the eternal
struggle between Reality and Fantasy, of the Essential Absurdity of Existence. They're probably all there, replete with
literary and allegorical allusions. But what a snore. Dissection of
Carlson's work would merely leave lying about a great many
rocketeering doodle-bugs and non-skid dickys, with no world-
view or *weltweisheit* obtained.

Carlson, you see, was like cotton candy. Very sweet, very
good for you, and totally unclassifiable. Tearing him apart
would have served no end, and serves no end now. And like
cotton candy, he was ephemeral, dissolving even as you tried to
grasp him. His meanings were about as obvious as "Waiting for
Godot," and to those who seek meanings (in either) a Kaf-
kaesque exercise.

What he had (and what these cartoon fables have even
now, in the crackling, brittle pages of comic books nearly forty
years old) was magic. Come on, I'll show you.

We can begin with the incredible adventure of the Colly-

Flowered Walrus and the Woggle-Eyed Carpenter, from *Jingle Jangle Comics* #39. June, 1949.

Once, long ago (Carlson begins), there lived a near-wealthy but colly-flowered walrus. His favorite three-tune radio, now of age, had come down with a razz-berry fever on the very day he was going to sell it to the king. So he took it to his dumbest friend, a busy woggle-eyed carpenter, saying, "Look, ole top! The king wants a snappy unwatered concert t'day. Fix th'goofus on this radio so it works, and bring it to him, and I'll pay you when I get that royal job as royal TRIPE INSPECTOR!"

(The panel shows the walrus, a rotund tusky chap with albino fur more like a sheep dog than a walrus, wearing a pink flowered vest, a green morning coat, huge floppy red shoes— certainly inadequate for ballet—white gloves, and bearing a battered radio with three birthday candles stuck in it. It also shows the carpenter who, over a fire composed of a burning firecracker, is boring a hole with chisel and bit in an alarm clock resting awkwardly in a frying pan. I don't interpret these things, I just tell you how they look to me.)

In the next panel, the carpenter is dashing off bearing the radio, saying, "Wait! All it needs is a new grimmick! And I know where to get one . . . almost."

In the next panel, the walrus, whose crimson bowler has just blown off his head in consternation, is saying, "Oh-oh, I forgot! I left my triple-best sneezing powder inside that radio! An' if the king gets a whiff of *that*—oh, I must get it out before he finds it!" In the far distance, the carpenter can be seen streaking away down an exceedingly twisty road. (By the side of the road there is a gold-colored mushroom, smiling insipidly, for no discernible reason.)

In due time, says the next panel, the carpenter came to a very, very cross road. "Hmmm! Seems I smell something spice-like from this here radio." He sits down under a tree that is wearing a trunk-expression like a pregnant woman who has just been led on a guided tour through a slaughter-house. "Well, I'll sit down to think . . . anyway, I'll sit down." From behind the tree suddenly appears a yellow foot and the word AHEM! "Uh, what's that?" asks the carpenter. And since he is alone, we must assume it is the radio to whom he is speaking.

In the next panel the visitor has stepped around the tree, and in a story-panel (on which is perched a weird-looking bird wearing a blue top hat) tacked to the tree, Carlson informs us: There stood a late weather report who had on hand all the best and cheapest brands of weather as he warned the carpenter. In big red letters: WAIT! (It behooves me, really, to describe this late weather report. He stands about six three, wearing a Mother Hubbard in blue, with pink pantaloons showing underneath. On a generally humanoid body rests his head, which is a large round circle in which the words "fair & warmer" are printed. The buttons on the Mother Hubbard say R-A-I-N. Like I said, I don't explain 'em, I only describe 'em.)

At this moment the walrus knew just what to do! (For a wonder.) Hustling down the twisty road past a way-sign reading "To the Very Royal Castle," the walrus looks like a hirsute Zero Mostel, and he's saying, "Yessir! I'm goin' right smack to th' king! There's no time t'lose. Any minute now that sneezin' stuff will get ripe and his concert will be sour!"

In the next panel, labeled: While the carpenter—, our secondary hero is being chased like a muthuh down the road toward the Very Royal Castle by the late weather report, still bearing the radio, and screaming, "No—I haven't time to wait for YOU! I must get to this nice dark gloomy castle an' SOON!"

BUT (says the next panel) at the very doorway a sign (reading: Rooms to Let—See Janitor), coming down on his head, stopped him. That was all he knew just then. CRACK!

Overleaf, a large wide guard picked up the drowsy carpenter. It was a grade A, but rough, welcome. "In y'come," says the guard. In the lower left corner of the panel, the radio also looks bonked.

In the next panel, the carpenter, clutching his head, is incarcerated in a cell that looks like the interior of a boiler (save that the barred window has curtains on it, and a lopsided stove in the corner sports a dripping old coffee pot). Through the barred door comes the voice of the large wide guard, "An' here's y'r cell. A lovely view an' three kinds of heat—steam, gas, an' midsummer!" The carpenter is groaning, "Ooo! Th' radio!" Which really seems dissociated, but then what can one expect when one has fled a late weather report, been zonked by a rooms to let sign, and thrown up under a jail, all in the space of three panels? (The radio is saying, forlornly, "Lissen, boss, when do I get fed?")

Now the plot takes on a genuinely helter-skelter pace as we see in the next panel a Rube Goldberg locomotive pulling something that looks like a cast-iron baby's crib. The explanatory panel tells us: meantime, the walrus boarded a well-buttoned unlocal train headed direct to the castle. Hay was cheap, so the scenery was changed daily.

The late weather report (whose face now says "hot") is engineering the loco (which also has curtained windows . . . on the outside), and on the back deck of the baby crib, the walrus is staring out and intoning, "Oh me! Night is falling with nice neat patches, an' look who is the *engineer*! I don't like that guy! I'm leavin'!" From the sky, needless to add, there are nice neat patches falling.

Next panel, the report (with a face that says "rain") is saying, "Now's your chance," and the walrus has one leg over the rail, ready to dive, saying, "Okay, here I go!" As the loco dashes tracklessly away in the next panel, a delicate "tweet!" lofting back on the breeze, the walrus lands flat on his ass in the middle of a PLOP!

And in the castle the guard reported to the king, "Yep, he's in the guest cell AND he has a three-tune RADIO with him!" Before the king could answer—a loud whistle sounded outside. TWEET! (Accompanied by a C-note.)

The king stalks to the balcony, saying, "Can it be that UNLOCAL on time again? I'll go out on my 98 cent balcony and look." Two steps out, the balcony rips away from the outer wall, and the king plunges forward, screaming, "OOOPS! This cheap balcony! It's loose—an' HERE I go!"

The king landed right on the little flat-car (right on his face). The late weather report—now reading "fair & hotter"—

says, rather maliciously, I feel, "Hah! Th' king! Long may it reign! And it WILL rain tomorrow, too!"

After they had gone a few miles . . . the sneaky late weather report unhooks the loco, and chortling, "Guess I'll pull up the hook and leave you, ole bean!" he boils away, his face reading "snow."

Meanwhile, the walrus was now walking up to the royal front door. He spies the broken sign that clonked the carpenter. "Huh . . . a piece of a sign or something!"

(Held upside the down, the "rooms to let" reads: 137 01 51×10071.)

Reading the sign in pure arithmetic, he rang the bell at the same time, saying, "137=07+51×100=71. 137=07+51×÷97 ÷ 7000000×0÷1=?"

I particularly like the pluses and divided-bys.

The heavy guard of course opened the door. He looks at the walrus holding the broken sign, and making reference to the pure arithmetic says, "It's a good thing you had the password. Where's th' rest of it?" "Over there," says the walrus, pointing with his cane. Did I mention the cane? Yeah, well, somewhere along the line he acquired a cane.

As the guard stepped out to look, the walrus sneaked in, slammed the door shut and turned the key, muttering, "Stupid oaf!"

Next panel, a big round one, the wide heavy guard is blamming on the door with ten thousand fists, shouting, "Hey! Y'big hairy baboon! Whatsa idea of lockin' me OUT? Hey you, open up!"

Now . . . down a treacly staircase in the sub-basement of the very royal castle, the walrus approaches the door of the cell wherein the carpenter lies in durance vile. "Heh, heh, heh! I locked that sap out for good! Now I'm alone in here and I can find out where this smell comes from. It's just like my SNEEZE-STUFF! I'll open this door with its very correct doorknob an'—"

Then, suddenly, from within the cell comes an explosive, atomic AH-CHOO! and the door is blown outward, once again knocking the woggle-eyed walrus on his woolly west end. Out comes the carpenter, all smiles, holding the three-tune radio which now looks *much* healthier. The radio is sending and the candles have somehow become pink, phallus-like tubes. "Look-it," says the carpenter, holding the radio aloft, "it's FIXED! I found a grimmick in that—er—cell . . . and with that sneeze stuff it's sending out a BEAM, too!"

Then, in a long shot of the countryside, in which we see the *most* peculiar shape of the castle (with a nightshirt hanging out to dry and an extremely satiated sun sinking in the East . . . the *East*!?!) we read the panel that says: YES, a strange beam came out of the castle. And there it is, humble as little green peas, a jaggedy bolt of something or other that stretches across to the next panel where the legend reads, "Suddenly the king (alone on the flat car) felt something hit the high tip of his crown." It is, *naturellement*, the jaggedy bolt of castle-beam. "OW!" shouts the king, "what was that? And the car! It's beginning to move!" Yes, so it was! And soon it was moving fast, guided by the beam, and direct to the king's castle.

While, inside the castle, the walrus and the carpenter stride toward the front door. "I know what we will do," says the carpenter, reaching for the doorknob, "let's take it outside and see how it works!"

As he opened the door, the car, with the king on it, whizzed right inside. "Th' king!" ejaculated the carpenter. "Yep! Here I come!" said the king humbly. The walrus says nothing in that panel.

Now, only two panels from the end, the king leans over the flat-car rail, the lightning-rod in his crown still a-quiver, and as the carpenter presents him with the radio, he makes the longest speech of the story, a veritable *tour de force*. "WONDERFUL! You indeed have it! A radio with a super-schmaltz-beam! You should have a super-schmaltz reward—both of you—you, Mr. Walrus, will become my most royal TRIPE INSPECTOR at an almost salary! And *you*, my friend," addressing the carpenter, not the radio, "shall be my ROYAL CARPENTER . . . and clean up the mess around here."

And so, in the last panel, a silhouette square, they both had jobs to keep them busy ever after!

As for the guard and the weather report, they were certainly never heard of again!

THE END.

The epic poem died a lingering death when the form of the sonnet came into vogue. When the narrative style was introduced, poetry began a decline that is evident even today. And even before the poem can vanish, we see both the short story and the novel taking a back seat in importance to the kinetic forms of motion pictures and the other visual media. Comic books were the precursor of this change. And I find it not strange at all that a Carlson should have managed to spin his fantasy webs for so short a time. He was too far in advance of himself.

What he did was miraculous and happens only once in a particular art-form. We will never see his like again.

Thank god he passed this way at least once.

It was a richer world for George Carlson, from '43 to '49. And have you noticed . . . it's been a lot sadder since.

CONTINUED NEXT PAGE

CONTINUED NEXT PAGE

CONTINUED NEXT PAGE

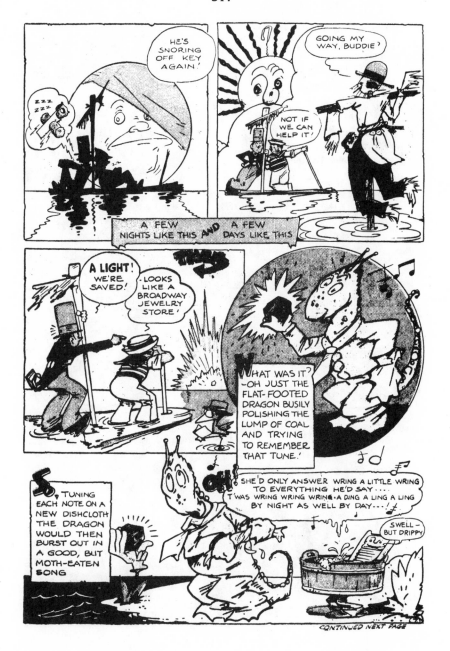

CONTINUED NEXT PAGE

Appendix B

Interim Memo

IN SEVERAL OF THE *HORNBOOK* ESSAYS I MADE PASSING MENTION of being out on the road, touring with a then-popular rock group called Three Dog Night. It was not the first, or only, time I'd been thrust into liaison with musicians. Many years ago I made a brief, and precarious, living as a singer; and off'n'on I've been a music critic—mostly jazz—for about thirty years.

But during the Sixties and Seventies it chanced that I was called on either to write an article about the rock scene for some magazine, or was solicited to write a movie for some musical entity. (Did you know there's a rock group named after your humble columnist? They call themselves *Harlin*; and it may be the source of their name that has denied them stardom.) Auracle, The Rolling Stones, Vikki Carr, Kenny Rogers . . . yes, all of them crossed my auctorial path.

The weeks I spent with Three Dog Night in 1970, however, were particularly invigorating. I liked the group, I liked the guys who made up the group, and I liked the feeling of imminent damnation that came with running alongside them.

How it came to pass, was not all that extraordinary. What happened *during* the tour, and what happened *after* . . . ah . . . those were pitted prunes of another variety.

In 1970, the billionaire Huntington Hartford decided to start a magazine called *Show*. Big, glossy, very chi-chi magazine, filled with writing on the arts and entertainment by the top wordsmiths in the country. The editor was Dick Adler (until its demise last year, with the *Los Angeles Herald-Examiner*). He called one day, and asked me if I wanted to write a piece on science fiction movies. He offered me what was, in 1970, enough lucre to purchase several fair-sized islands in the Comoros chain. I counted to seven, just to let him know I was an independent kind of guy, and to Dick I said yes. That was a 10,000 word article succinctly titled "Lurching Down Memory Lane with It, Them, The Thing, Godzilla, Hal 9000 . . . That Whole Crowd."

When they ran it, they retitled it *"Them* or Us."

Ah, me. Where hath fled the opulence of yore?

Anyhow, the piece made a bit of a splash, Huntington Hartford hisself—a man who liked to play at being an editor—took notice of the scads of letters (well, perhaps only half a scad), and advised Dick Adler to keep me working for them. Almost before *"Them* or Us" (yechhh) appeared in print, I was put onto a piece about Sal Mineo. That was March, 1970; six years before Sal was murdered. We became good friends, and I began writing an extended essay-interview based on about twenty hours of taped conversations we held over a period of many weeks. The tapes are here, the article remains one-third written . . . maybe some day I'll finish it. Not that it'll do Sal any good now.

But Sal got a gig in Italy on some potboiler that never got made, and because I couldn't go further with it till he got back, I called Adler and asked him if there was something quick and now that I could do to fill the dead time.

He told me they were interested in Three Dog Night—very hot at the time—because Mr. Hartford had attended one of their concerts and was impressed. Was I interested in doing a rock-oriented piece? Was I knowledgeable about the rock scene? Did I have something already in print that might establish credential in that area?

I sent him a copy of my 1961 rock novel, SPIDER KISS.

The one Elvis's people had had under option for a while.

Dick called a few days later and said, "It's a go." And arrangements were made to send me out on the road, Texas and Louisiana, with the group. I've written some about that trip, in one of the GLASS TEAT books.

But I didn't write about what happened in Lubbock, Texas. That's a helluva story. How I leveled Lubbock with a tornado. Maybe some time I'll tell you that one.

Anyhow, I got back in one piece, sat down and wrote the article at 4200 words, and sent it off to Dick. Unfortunately, Dick was out of there. *Show* was a bit of a nuthouse operation, and Adler washed his hands of it, and split. Hartford brought in a couple of editorial bag-men from Back East, and decided he could edit as well as anyone, himself. And I waited and waited, but no check arrived; and I called and called, but "Mr. Hartford is in conference." Finally, a month or two later, the bag-men got around to sending back the article with the advisement that they were no longer interested in doing a piece on anything as tacky as rock'n'roll. "Fine, jes fine," I told them, "but you commissioned me to write this thing, I spent many bucks traveling with them, and you are into my pocket for about three grand; hey, so pony up."

They told me, in effete bag-man parlance, to go take a flyin' leap at a rolling doughnut. I said to them, grasping at the last vestige of rational behavior, "I have a letter of commission, stating terms of this assignment. You *owe* me this money." They chuckled and hung up on me, with the parting shot, "Tough titty . . . sue us!"

Well. I've heard that line before. And I've sued. And I've always won. But there are *other* situations in which suing them into oblivion would be letting them off too easily. There are other ways of adjusting the balance of justice in the universe. (In such matters, I take as my role-model Dr. Doom. Today Latveria, tomorrow . . .)

On Vine Street, midway between Hollywood and Sunset Boulevards, in 1970, flourished The Huntington Hartford Theatre. A nice little legitimate theater where elegant stage productions were mounted, for the predilection of the public, the amusement of the glitterati, and to the greater wealth and grandeur of Huntington Hartford. Every evening (save when dark) limos would sweep up to the curb, and emergent from same would be all those personalities whose exotic lives were chronicled in *TV Guide* and *People* . . . and *Show.*

My picket sign read something like:

HUNTINGTON HARTFORD IS A CHEAPO
WHO STIFFS HIS WRITERS!

About a week of that, strolling up and down, perfectly within my Constitutional "rights of peaceable assembly and petition," not to mention exercise of my rights under the First Amendment, and the word got back to Mr. Huntington Hartford, the great editor, philanthropist, doer of good works, endower of museums (and maybe even attendee of stage productions at the elegant Huntington Hartford Theatre). Sue you? Hell, no, I'd rather embarrass you. Tought titty, indeed, Mr. Huntington Hartford, employer of snotty bag-men.

The check was hand-delivered by a messenger to my home.

Thereby keeping my record for getting stiffed (see *Hornbook* Installment 5) at Artists 2, Lions 0.

So now, with the exception of what happened in Lubbock, you know it all; and for the first time ever, that essay on Three Dog Night reaches print.

Dogging It in the Great American Heartland

(1970)

*T*he heat in the Warehouse can kill you, fry your eyeballs and turn your brains to prune-whip yogurt. It's bad enough in the middle of the day, bad enough standing empty when there's no one there. But put 4500 screaming kids, all sweating out Patchouli at the same time, put them belly-to-back in that hundred and twenty-five year old cotton&coffee shell, and it's instant sauna city.

New Orleans, 1970.

And there's the writer, way out of his depth doing an article about a rock group on tour in the Deep South. The writer makes no bones about it, he ain't that fond of rock music. He'd much rather sit and smoke his pipe and listen to Kipnis rendering a Bach Fughetta on the clavichord. But Huntington Hartford and *Show* magazine have said, "There's something happening out there with this weird-named rock group and we will lay on you B*I*G M*O*N*E*Y if you travel the tour with them for a week and report back what it is that's happening." So the writer, who cannot be bought but certainly can be rented, is standing in his own sweat in the middle of a converted warehouse, in the middle of New Orleans, in the middle of 1970, cranky as hell and not loving that rock group a whole lot.

New Orleans. An uptight city where rock music is a definite threat; a threat to the tourist trade, to the heritage of jazz, to the landed order of things. New Orleans never *actively* tries to keep rock out, but it just happens there's no place to hold a rock concert. The halls and the auditoriums just somehow don't get available.

So in 1968 Bill Johnston decided to bring rock to New Orleans. To provide for the hordes who buy all those albums, a place to go to hear something more innervating than Al Hirt. He found the Warehouse, and proceeded to get stiffed by every big-name outfit in the country. "Sure," they tell him via long distance, "you can have Mountain, but you gotta book the opening act from us, too." But Bill Johnston wants to put on Poco, not some mickeymouse no-draw what you couldn't sell if you were giving triple S&H green stamps as a bonus. So he tells them to pick it and stick it, because tonight, just tonight, he's golden.

Because tonight he's not getting a lousy 1400 soft-ticket advance. Tonight, just tonight, he's sold out.

SRO, and the scalpers are getting so fine they'll be able to feed their jones for a month.

Three Dog Night is booked, and at three-thirty in the sweaty afternoon the crowd is already *marabunta* swarming the sticky sidewalks on Tchoupitoulas Street. The gig isn't until nine tonight, but at three-thirty they're already lying up against the walls, hanging out, waiting. Waiting out the heat, waiting out the prowling gumball wagons, waiting out the crowds to come, waiting out the time. The kids who somehow aren't imbued with the roots and the nobility of Dixieland Jass, who've been musically starving in the delta lands . . . they're out there on folded-up denim jackets, cooling it, hanging out till nine o'clock comes, bringing a Three Dog Night.

And the writer sees *that look* on their faces, and he begins to understand. Seven days later he's back in the Real World and writing about it, and the stereo behind him is banging "Mama Told Me" and Igor Kipnis has some potent competition. Bach doesn't venture an opinion.

The abos of Australia, who dig holes in the earth, in which they sleep—rather than building huts or highrises or bomb shelters where thermostats are turned down to 68°—use their dingo dogs to keep them warm on bitter nights. When the nights get terribly cold, they may need as much as three dogs' body-heat. A three-dog night is considered a very heavy night indeed.

June Fairchild, who was Danny Hutton's lady friend, found the group's name in an issue of *Mankind* magazine. Danny Hutton is 31, is so thin he looks like a reject from Auschwitz, has the disposition and inherent temperament of a borstal boy, and he co-founded the group that bears the name Three Dog Night. He is one of the three lead singers with the group.

The second singer, co-founder with Hutton, is Cory Wells, 33. He started singing when he was sixteen, for free, in Lulubelle's Bar & Grill in Buffalo, with dynamite big name groups like The Peelers and The Gear Grinders. When he wasn't working a set, he was out boosting hubcaps and breaking into boxcars. Typical Horatio Alger success story: music saved him. 1959, he went into the Air Force straight out of High

School. 1960, a hardship discharge so he could help support this three sisters and his brother. His stepfather had gone out for a pack of cigarettes and didn't bother to come back. Back to Lulubelle's and working in a furniture factory till a little man with a big cigar told him he could make him a star.

The star was about as impressive as Kohoutek: Wells wound up gigging with The Enemies as the house band at the Whisky on the Strip for a year. He met Hutton while on tour with Sonny & Cher, he made a few movies, split for Phoenix in '67, worked a topless joint called the Satin Doll as Cory Wells' Blues Band, and hungered to get back to L.A.

He made it in 1968 and, during the fifteen minute breaks between sets he was playing at The Haunted House, he sat in the car in the parking lot, planning Three Dog Night with that crazy Irishman out of Buncrana, County Donegal, Danny Hutton.

Still dancing for dimes, the two big dreamers came up with their third lead singer, Chuck Negron, now 32, through Tim Alvarado who had produced Danny at MGM Records.

Negron should never have become a singer, he had it made as a basketball star. Born in Manhattan and brought up in the Bronx, Chuck Negron made the All-City All-Star basketball team while still in PS 22 Jordan L. Mott Junior High. And even though he was hated by every Jewish daddy who hated the good-looking goy for dating his daughter, it didn't slow Negron's dribble and he played in the high school basketball finals in Madison Square Garden. Let Elton John match *that* one!

Bobby Pittari, a friend of Negron's, entered him in a school talent show without Chuck's knowledge. When Negron rehearsed for the first time, he was so twitchy he fainted. Tried it again, made it, and began singing around. When he was in the 9th grade, fourteen years old, nothing more than a little pisher, he and Bobby cut a demo for fifteen bucks—"Dream," the old Everly Bros. number. He went down to the Brill Building at 1650 Broadway and sang in the halls. Some wiseass handed him a mop. Somehow, he wangled a managerial contract and began playing black dances, black clubs. Was he good? Had to be.

Negron is white. At fourteen, he was singing on the same bill at the Apollo with Jackie Wilson.

Time passed, calendar pages flipping over in a Warner Bros. film, and he went to college, continued singing, kept dribbling, cut some sides for small labels and Columbia heard him in 1963. Irving Townsend signed him to a contract. In mid-1965 they got around to releasing his first cut, a single called "Speak for Yourself, John." Chuck calls it a flat, grooved piece of cow flop. More calendar pages. Went to Hollywood and bummed around, met Danny, went away on a three week Job Corps gig, came back just in time to save Hutton from a coronary: "Where the hell you been, man, I've been trying to reach you for *days*! We've got a sneak audition." Fah-*joomp*, as Lenny used to say before he got planted . . . Three Dog Night had its front line and they were moving. Three years later they made one and a half million bucks, between twenty and twenty-seven thou a night, and grossed $90,000 in one evening at The Forum.

You wouldn't think three bums like that could do so fine, would you?

For the purchasers of Three Dog music (who number sufficient to have garnered for the group 10 gold LPs and 9 gold singles) it is a cold and naked fact of life that the group is a musical entity of unquestioned excellence. Yet to read the maunderings of Olympian ingroup critics, one might never perceive that cold and naked fact of life. One might never realize Three Dog Night has been a top-of-the-charts, top-of-the-draw, top-of-the-heap group for over six years. Virtually the same personnel, never a layoff season to bind up the knife wounds, same front line all the way, a viable gestalt . . . for six years. If you've got all your fingers on one hand *maybe* you can fill out the pinkies naming the other four groups with records of continuity as long or longer.

And if you've never seen them in person, live, turning a cow barn amphitheater of fifty thousand individual souls into one enormous epiphany with celebration humming in its synapses, you are the poorer for it. The writer saw it, and understanding of *why* Three Dog Night has been so damned popular for so damned long came flooding in like a moment of satori.

That was a night in Houston. I've got it sharp and clear in the storage banks of my brain; it was a spectacular night. But here's how a nerd from the *Houston Post*, who couldn't keep his dinner table companions awake through a single anecdote reported it: "They're tight, flashy and commercial and the kids ate 'em up at Hofheinz Pavilion Wednesday night. Three Dog Night, that is, freaked-out Monkees with a little talent thrown in.

"It's essentially a stage act, even in the studio. The barber-shop trio—Chuck Negron, Danny Hutton and Cory Wells—do Top 40 arrangements of songs by the better composers, add a standard four-piece backup band and wait for the gold records to roll in.

"Negron . . . sounds like he's working, but he's not. . . . In between numbers, and often during them, the gang horsed around and goofed off. Kid stuff. . . . Everything ran on time, smoothly and, so long as I was there, peacefully."

Let me tell you, in this life filled with ogres and Furies and shadows, there are few things I despise as much as lousy reportage, and a sterile imagination making points off his betters. I'll forego any comments about the aridity of prose, the banality of perception, the stupidity of viewpoint or even the reactionary Fascistic attitudes indicated in the final sentence of that pickaxe job. I'll merely tell you what that evening at Hofheinz Pavilion was *really* like:

Three Dog Night is a highly physical act, carefully and professionally mounted to produce a seamless, sparkling stage presentation. As the *Post*'s resident brain damage case clearly stated, the audience for god's sake *belonged* to the group that night. From the first emergence on stage to the final moments of their third curtain call, not one kid in that auditorium would have traded his or her seat for a front row center at even something as spectacular as The Coming Impeachment. They laughed, they clapped, they sang and, during the cresting wave high point of the concert's final number, "Eli's Coming," they did something I've *never* seen a rock audience do.

I've been in audiences of Stones, Beatles, Grand Funk and Elton John concerts; Joe Cocker, Chicago, Bob Dylan and Leon Russell concerts; Blood, Sweat & Tears, Simon and Garfunkel, Buddy Miles and Stevie Wonder concerts; and I have seen entire Visigoth hordes break and run, swarming over the wheelchair cases used as barriers down front, climbing to the stage over the broken backs of screamies fallen into the orchestra pit; I've seen them overwhelm the stage like *marabunta* army ants devouring a laggardly ibex, raging into a backstage from which the group itself had departed seconds before, abandoning their instruments to the looters and pillagers. But at Hofheinz Pavilion that night I saw fourteen thousand adoring Three Dog fans swarm toward the stage . . . *and stop.*

They wanted to be close, they wanted to suck up all that joy and music right through their pores. But they *respected* the group. They would do nothing to halt the sound, to panic the musicians. I was on that stage, right beside drummer Floyd Sneed, and I had visions of that cute little writer being trampled to green mint jelly. But they came up to within mere *inches* of Sneed's machinegun paradiddle *and stopped.*

The purest loving tribute a musical act could receive.

They stood there and moved like a field of winter wheat. God, you should have seen those faces! For a few glorious minutes kids who couldn't believe in family, government, religion, authority . . . hip and cynical and wise beyond their years from a decade of civil unrest and being lied to . . . for a few minutes they were home. While that music possessed them, Three Dog Night had a backup group of not *four* . . . they had fourteen *thousand*, and it was a jubilant thing to behold.

And *that* was what happened that night. *That* was what the arrogant and tunnel-visioned self-styled authority of the *Houston Post* missed by splitting early. And even had he seen it, would it have altered his concretized view of Three Dog Night? Probably not. He was one with the wrecking crew who still feel it infra-hip to badmouth one of the most musically successful groups ever to come out of rock.

The question asks itself unbidden, why do they do it? What brings out the assassin in the cult critics' manner when confronted by a new Three Dog Night album? These same dynamiters grow charitable and ameliorative when they confront a second-rate album by a talent then-currently fashionable. "He'll do better next time," they say, spin around widdershins and hit a solid Three Dog album with, "Another big, brassy, overproduced Three Dog Night set by the Ringling Bros. Barnum & Bailey's of pop music." Why? Come *on*, fer chrissakes, *why*?

For the cataclysmic answer to this soul-shattering question stay tuned for the Further Adventures of Captain Rationale and His Cartesian Coordinates!

They don't strike the correct socio-economic postures. They are not into politics or revolution or moral or spiritual uplift. They are into rock. As Fred Astaire is into dancing, as Bob Griese is into the long bomb, as Wanda Landowska is into fugues, as George C. Scott is into the expansion of acting space, Three Dog Night is into rock. They are not one of the "artificial" produced studio groups hyped with horns and string sections, they chart and choose and play all the cuts on their albums.

But because they are utterly professional and musically adept, and dare to be arrogant about it ("When you got it baby, flaunt it!"), and because they have not taken public stands on the burning topics of our times—because they are merely into making special music with a cohesive sound—and because they play *other people's music* (remember what the banana from the *Post* said?) they are continually bumrapped by the third world magazines and their lint-examining critics. Because Three Dog Night has the taste and perceptivity and reputation for making hits out of songs that might otherwise languish unnoticed, the underground press calls them simply entertainers. What a terrible slur! And while you're in that place, add the names of Al Jolson, Frank Sinatra, Barbra Streisand and Nat King Cole as *simply* entertainers who made millions for composers and lyricists no one would have paid a dollar to hear sing and play their own songs.

Simply entertainers? It is to boggle.

The Paul Whiteman Orchestra, The Mills Bros., Bing Crosby, Diana Ross and the Supremes, Mary Martin, Alfred Drake, Gene Kelly, Elvis Presley. They were *all* performers whose status and accessibility to audiences drew to them the best writers of their days. No one ever dumped a Mosler safe on Crosby's head because he didn't write "White Christmas." The rigid, uncompromising and infantile attitude that merit only resides in musicians who write the material they record is a fairly recent aberration. For ten thousand years of the performing arts no one would have conceived of such a ludicrous concept as being viable. But the pop music industry is often a nasty, incestuous, daisy-chain little universe, and if I had a quarter for every yo-yo with a typewriter who wanted to make a rep as a critic by bandwagoning badmouth interpretations of stars, I'd have at least enough funds to launch a Saturn rocket.

Apparently the only redeeming qualities possessed by Three Dog Night are such nebulosities as a) everything they record becomes enormously popular (but hell, what do the record buyers know? they can be stampeded into buying *any* sorta crap, right? look at how successful Terry Knight's *Faith* was, right? how many hundreds of thousands did United Artists lose on *that* superhyped fizzle?), b) other estimable musicians—such as B. B. King and Elton John—consider *them* sensational musicians (see the quotes on the next page), and c) they are one of the three or four top American rock groups of *all time*.

Three Dog Night serves the not inconsiderable commonweal of allowing fresh writing talent to ride their coattails to public attention. By serving as scintillant figureheads whose every recording gets massive attention, they keep the lifeblood of the rock idiom red and rich and flowing. They aren't alone. Carole King might not be such a hot number today had it not been for James Taylor. Burt Bacharach might today be only a legman for his father's gossip column if it hadn't been for Dionne Warwick. Leon Russell's top hat would likely be a tam today if Joe Cocker had never existed. It's a symbiotic relationship, and why the effete snob critics cannot perceive that is one of the great unsolved conundrums of the Modern World.

The painstakingly evolved popular appeal of Three Dog Night is used to lend clout to the careers of other young talents. Anyone doubting the foregoing need only consider how much notoriety and money has been garnered for talents like Laura Nyro, Randy Newman, Hoyt Axton, Harry Nilsson, Paul Williams, Danny Moore, David Arkin, David Loggins, Alex Harvey, and a pressboxload of others via the express route of a Three Dog Night interpretation. Consider the common good, if you will: while a McCartney writes and sings his own work and draws down the adoration of the critical gurus on crystal mountainpeaks, Three Dog Night juice the careers of twelve different creators per album. Nothing at all wrong with an artist self-serving, but who the hell has the *chutzpah* to put down a group that carries so many others with them as they rake in the goodies?

ALEX HARVEY: "I've long admired Three Dog Night as an outstanding and entertaining musical group. But it was not till they cut my *Tulsa Turnaround* that I realized how much they could add to a song with their unique interpretations. In fact, I liked their version so much I copped it for my own act."

RANDY NEWMAN: "What can I say about them that their music doesn't say better? They have great taste, they work hard, they're at core *musicians*. Anyone who questions that should stop to consider how big they've been, and for how long . . .

"*Mama Told Me* would not have been a hit if they hadn't recorded it; it's that simple. When I heard it was going to be a single, I thought they'd bomb with it. I'm glad I left them alone; what they did for that song is going to put my son through college."

BRIAN WILSON: "Why don't you ask who I think is better,

Danny Hutton or Frank Sinatra? I'd tell you Danny Hutton. Wow! Wow! Three Dog Night! Wow!"

DANNY MOORE: "Three Dog Night is really a workhorse group . . . music is a serious business with them. They've helped my career enormously. I was ecstatic when they recorded *Shambala*: to date it's sold over one million two hundred thousand copies. They can do that for a song because they keep going for perfection in their performances, and so they appeal to such a broad range of audiences. There just aren't many groups that can do something as difficult as that."

And if you think this largesse is extended only to the favored few composers whose names are now common currency, consider that Gary Itri, who wrote "Midnight Runaway" (on the *Seven Separate Fools* album), was the cleanup janitor in the recording studio where they were cutting that album. He took his time sweeping up the rancid coffee cups and dropped chunks of cheese danish the night of the session, and when Chuck Negron stumbled off wearily into a corner to get a breath of untainted air, Itri braced him to listen to a song he'd written. Negron, head sunk into his neck like a Galapagos tortoise from the endless hours of sifting tunes and rehearsing, might just as easily have pleaded exhaustion or disinterest, or simply told the eager young guy to take a push-broom walk for himself. But he didn't. Itri got an acoustical guitar, played the song and fah-*joomp*, instant success. If Itri had been Mickey Rooney, MGM could have gotten Judy Garland to play the lead girl singer and made it into one of those loverly implausible musicals.

Ask Gary Itri how worthless is Three Dog's stock as *merely* entertainers.

Look: this writer has been paid to put this article together. I'm hardly an altruist. But I don't write flack. What you find in these pages is what I came away with from a week on tour with Three Dog Night. I started out cynical and very Missouri "show me." What they showed me is contained herein. As flack for the group, it may not satisfy. Hell, it doesn't even satisfy the group itself; I've related personal data they never even knew I'd glommed eavesdropping, I haven't devoted appropriate lineage to the other members of the group—Jimmy Greenspoon, Floyd Sneed, Mike Allsup, Jack Ryland and the new keyboard guy, Skip Konte—and I haven't even said what a wonderful human being and credit to his race is Jay Lasker, the President of ABC/Dunhill, who release the group's albums. I'm not a rock critic and I can't abide about 98% of what I hear on records these days. But I *buy*—not get freebie for review, I *buy*—every Three Dog Night album, and I take an almost pathological delight in what they do on records.

And I was approached to do this piece probably for those reasons. And because I won't buy the bullshit that artists who don't write what they record are dismissable.

For me, Three Dog Night appears to be an entity suffering the perils of a double-edged sword. They cut clean in promoting other people's music in a way few other groups could . . . or would. But the backswing leaves bloody marks on them because they aren't The Rolling Stones.

Appendix C

Darkness Falls in the City of the Angels

(1988)

P hone rang about five-thirty in the morning. I was already up, making my coffee. I said the effword and made a grab for the receiver before it screamed again and woke my wife. Said the effword because I knew the call was from some imbecile on the East Coast who, like most of those shell-shocked New Yorkers, hadn't yet assimilated the fact that two-thirds of the continent ain't on Manhattan time.

Ethnocentrism at an ungodly hour. It may be eight-thirty where *you* are, dork, but it's still dark out here in the civilized world! Have an effword, dork!

It was a buddy of mine I'd left behind when I fled New York in 1961. A buddy who takes great pride in having four deadbolts and a Fox police-bar lock on his apartment door. A buddy who's been burgled six times in the past nine years, been mugged three times in the past five years, and can survive only by living in a high-rise as fortified as Hitler's bunker. Two ex-cop doormen, two rent-a-cop security wardens, full-range tv monitors, coded entry, and laser-scan security check at the front desk.

For the privilege of thus living in a battle-zone with "peace of mind," my buddy exists in his two-and-a-half room cave high up in that co-op mountain paying out each month an amount only slightly less than the combined budgets of Bosnia and Herzegovina.

He'd called to gloat.

"Heard the news this morning," he said, with a nasty chuckle. "Heard a couple of Crips with AK-47s took out a whole restaurant full of nutburger vegetarians. Just wanted to check you out, make sure nobody'd stapled you to a wall."

"In your ear," I said.

Then followed a charming chat about how he figured I might be considering moving back to New York, where life was safer. I used the effword a lot, told him at least we weren't as dopey as Gothamites who went for the Tawana Brawley scam, and assured him Los Angeles was still Paradise.

Then I hung up and turned on KNX-AM for the news.

In Venice, a drive-by shooter unloaded from a van at a bunch of people standing around talking, and killed a nine-year-old boy playing in his front yard.

A family in Willowbrook, just south of Watts, broke up a gang dope deal going down on the sidewalk at 1:00 A.M. outside their house, shoo'ed off the creeps who returned later and pumped some shots through the windows. The father of the household fired back, wounding one of them. Their car was, thereafter, vandalized and stolen, the house broken into, ransacked, trashed and, finally, set afire with Molotov Cocktails. House and the one next door burned to the ground. But the Fuentes family didn't find out till this morning, because they'd already fled in terror.

The last thing my buddy had said to me, before I'd hung up on him, was a little street-rap currently fashionable in New York, as admonition to California-bound travelers:

> In L.A. town, a warning true.
> Don't wear red, and don't wear blue.
> Some vato loco will shoot at you.

I turned off the radio. It was too early in the day to be reminded that Paradise has been paved over and the Uzi is the calling card of choice. It was too early in the day to be scared. I waited for the darkness to lift, and drank my coffee, and thought about what's happened to my town.

You don't need me to tell you what this place was like when I got here just after New Year's Day 1962. If you're under thirty it'd be like trying to describe Atlantis to a Visigoth: most of you think concrete is a natural state, that the peak of Western Civilization is gelato, that you're *supposed* to pay fifty cents when you call information for a phone number, and the more Caucasoid Bill Cosby gets, the cuddlier he is to you. If you're under twenty, then for most of you nostalgia is breakfast. If you're over forty, only an idiot would insist that the condition of life in Los Angeles is better now than it was even twenty-five years ago.

So telling you that this was the best goddam town in the world, that smart and witty and educated people chose to live here rather than London or Paris or New York, that one felt every day like Ali Baba in magical Baghdad . . . is a pointless exercise.

And stating flat-out that darkness has fallen in our beloved town is something we all know, from the most frightened homeless bag lady camping under a freeway overpass to the best-protected estate owner in San Marino Mesa. We're scared. We're scared in so many different ways that even trying to put it in coherent form, simply attempting to codify it, makes the reason reel and the words get hysterical. We're so goddam scared we don't even know where to begin . . .

Scared. You used to be able to drive anywhere in the Los Angeles area and not worry about it. You could take off on a Sunday afternoon with out-of-town visitors or your kids or just a bunch of friends, and go over to South Central to admire the Watts Towers. You had to use a Thomas Guide to worm your way between the railroad tracks down around Willowbrook Avenue, to find that little dead-end street where Rodia's magnificent gift to us stands, and you'd always get lost, but you had no fear of pulling in to the curb anywhere in that neighborhood to ask a resident how to thread a way through the labyrinth. Now you're too scared even to go to Watts to see those Gaudi-like wonders. Scared.

Scared. To drive down La Cienega to a Creole restaurant was as easy as going to a neighborhood grocery to pick up a pint of whipping cream. Now there are damned few neighborhood groceries left, having been squeezed out of existence by the chain supermarkets as methodically as Crown Books has squeezed out of existence so many independent bookstores . . . and you don't drive *anywhere* without looking constantly at every car moving alongside, to see if some roadway shooter has a 9mm Parabellum aimed at your head because you inadvertently cut him off. Scared.

Scared. If you're a man, you don't understand why women are frightened of elevators. Think about it. You're a woman, and you enter an elevator, and you're all alone, and a man gets in with you. And you're in an enclosed space where no one can hear your moans if that particular man is one of the thousand loose-cannon crazies in Los Angeles, who gets his jollies raping and robbing. Paranoia? If you're a man, ask the nearest woman. Scared.

Scared. Because we can't leave our doors open or unlocked on those days when the Santa Anas blow in hot and humid off the inland deserts. Because if you're old and slow-moving, there are street specialists in mugging senior citizens for the welfare check or the food stamps. Because if you're a kid, you know someone will be bracing you for your lunch money in exchange for not beating the crap out of you. Because you can't park your new car on a city street and not be worried all through dinner and the movie that when you return it'll be there; or if it's still there, if your tape deck and spiffy aluminum wheels will be there. Scared because your neighborhood is changing so fast you go to sleep at night with the tremor that you're living on the edge of the slide area. Scared because you've got to have a security system and bars on the windows, and if they fire-bomb your house you'll probably fry inside before you can get through those bars. Scared because everybody's got a gun, and only half your worries are about the stereotypical nine-foot-tall black man who wants to rob you; the other half of your worry is that your own kid will get pissed at you and shoot you, or your neighbor will run amuck because your friends are making too much noise at your party, and *he'll* shoot you. Scared because no place is safe, no place is quiet, no place is free of the developers, no place has the peace and ease it had when you first came to live in that area.

You've been scared for quite a while now. But it didn't affect you as much, because you had a safe haven away from *them*. And that's the way you thought of all those people in the Projects, in the ghetto, in Watts, in the *barrio. Them*. But now the gangs are everywhere. Your fears are no longer ephemeral, vague, omnipresent and disquieting. The gangs rule.

And not all of the pronunciamentos of Chief Daryl Gates, not one example of Action News posturing on his part, can cover the fact that no matter how much money we give him for more cops on the street, no matter how many sweeps and special task forces he deploys, no matter how many tiger tank battering rams he unleashes, *nothing* he does can contain the atrocities and depredations of the 70,000 kids currently estimated to be gang members.

We're enjoying a death a day, on the average, from gang warfare. And for the fat, happy, self-deluding yups safe in their Beverly Hills or Malibu or Pacific Palisades enclaves, it has even passed the point at which they could dismiss the darkness, on the theory that, "Well, let them kill each other, what has that to do with us?" That cheerily racist point was passed when a gang kid smoked a member of Our Kind in warm, cheery, well-lit Westwood one collegiate weekend recently.

We have long been reaping what was sown in Los Angeles; even farther back than 1966 when Reagan was elected Governor, and proceeded to dismantle the best educational system in the nation. All the way back to the days of the theft of the Owens Valley water and the greening of the San Fernando Valley and the making of illicit millions by the forefathers of some of the richest movers and shakers in our community today. All the way back to the conspiracy that tore up the streetcar tracks of one of the best urban transportation systems in America, killed off the Big Red Cars, and made us smog-slaves of the automobile, for the greater enrichment of the road-building lobby, the auto manufacturers, the tire and gas companies. A long way back before 1966 and Reagan those seeds were sown . . . but something happened to us a little more than twenty years ago that accelerated the decay. Something that began to show its evil fruition in the flaming blossoms of the Watts Riots in '65. And we learned *nothing* from that terrible warning.

Something happened to us at that nexus point.

Something that told the rest of the world that Los Angeles was getting fat and complacent under the vanilla sun, that it was Xanadu for the high-rollers and the blue-sky merchants and all the corporate entities with floating ethics. That we were a city so intent on building swimming pools and having a good time that we turned a blind eye to what we were creating—the Under-classes. Cities like Detroit and Pittsburgh and Cleveland, and even New York, took note of the days and nights of bloody civil rioting, and they moved to rectify their awful situations. But L.A. went back to sleep in front of the tv set, learning nothing from the message of the Watts Riots. Went back to feeding its face, feeding its ego, feeding its coffers as if we'd never come to the equivalent of New York's sickness.

Something happened in Watts that should have scared us sufficiently in 1965 to avert the darkness under which we now tremble.

Something that foreshadowed eight years of Reagan's America and the Me Decade that spawned the yuppies, and the slaughter of our ethics.

More than twenty years of "benign neglect" and of unre-stricted "progress" that has left us with our hillsides ravaged by million-dollar-a-unit crackerbox builders and the Underclasses condemned to the Projects. Twenty years of Reagan/Deukme-jian law'n'order horse puckey and no urban revitalization worth a spit in the wind. Twenty years of slapdash, if any, coordination among federal, state, county and city agencies to address what was going on among the *people*, to mitigate Nixon's 1973 cutoff of federal funds for gang rehabilitation.

The streets are filled with litter, there's hardly a vertical surface that hasn't been "tagged" by illiterate thugs puffing up their withered egos with spray cans, six hundred different gangs have turned the schools into gulags where the dropout rates for blacks and latinos is pushing sixty percent, and the leading cause of death for black men between the ages of sixteen and thirty-four isn't cancer or heart attack or even dope overdose.

It's murder.

Crack is everywhere; driven in, flown in, trained in, floated in, backpacked in, and as easy to score as a McDonald's toadburger. This week a couple of UCLA scientists released a report based on their tracking of 700 students for eight years, the point of which was that kids who have a heavy dope habit in school fare far worse later in life, than kids who don't. Gee, honestly!?! Would you believe that those of us out here in the darkness kinda figured that one a while ago? Dope is a trillion-dollar business, and the repeat market is the key to a fat p&l bottom line. And of all those pontificating, well-groomed politicos who appeared on KCBS's evening-long preemptive special on gangs, a month or so ago, not one of those who paid lip-service to this bogus "war on drugs" seemed to understand that the big business of drugs is what we are reaping for twenty years of self-serving greed.

What do I mean? What fascinating, obscurantist theory am I pushing here? Well, I'm as scared as the rest of you, out there in the darkness, but being scared hasn't turned my common sense into spinach. I can still figure it out as easily as Jesse Jackson, who points out quite rationally that we're a self-indulgent species and if we weren't wrecking ourselves with dope it would be something else. That if there weren't vast fortunes being made from selling dope, if there weren't *jefes* and Generalissimos getting rich off the trade, it would be better policed. So the theory is that L.A. has long been a model of greedyguts slum lords and pols on the pad and middlemen who are living on velvet from the circulation of dope.

And why shouldn't the kids in the *barrio* and the Projects pick up on that? They see it on television every day. They see the choice between coming home after a shift at the Burger King, reeking of grease, with a few miserable bucks in their pocket, and buying a BMW and a nice home in Orange County from a few days of "slippin'" and moving some crack.

The Underclasses, the ghetto blacks, the latinos, the Asian refugees, they see the results of twenty years of gimme gimme gimme; and they want theirs!

It's about jobs, and it's about big money; and it's about the turf where those street jobs and that big money are all that matter. It's about people learning the lessons Los Angeles has been teaching for more than twenty years, and doing it outside the rules of the game set up by the Old Boys' Network, and doing it in a violent manner that has the rest of us so scared that it's made security systems the fastest growing industry in Southern California.

And, of course, it's just lovely for the gun merchants. The NRA *loves* it! Get everyone so witless with terror that their distributors can't keep up with the demand. Play on all that racist fear, and get guns into the hands of everyone. *That's* the new L.A. way!

And the damned ugliest part of all this, is that nobody can talk about it in realistic terms without sounding like a racist or an apostate Liberal. If someone gets right down into it and says that a large part of the gang warfare problem, for instance, is the insane Latin adoration of the macho mystique, someone else (who's usually making a buck from keeping his people paranoid) jumps up and yells racism.

But *machismo*, and its brutish effect on men and women alike, is not the sole property of the *vatos locos*. We're *all* paying the price for that John Wayne posture. White folks demonstrate it with the need to fight wars all over the world, trumpeting that "God is on Our Side," with Reagan blustering that even if we shot down a passenger plane by mistake, however inadvertently snuffing out 290 lives, it's a "closed matter" because he's the high-steppin' brass-balled big-mothuh' President of the Yew Ess, and those Shiites had damned well better listen up! It's Wally George in the White House, and we can see how effective such posturing has been in the past.

But that's how Whitey does it. The Black, Chicano and Asian Underclasses we've watched develop have learned the lesson. And those kids, untutored, poor, burning with hate and anger, they strut and blow smoke the same way. They think of "community" as the gang, R60s, Southsides, Crips, Bloods, it doesn't matter: *that's* family. And no one in authority, least of all Daryl Gates, seems to understand that sweeps and busts and arraignments won't bring us back the daylight. Because for every hundred kids picked up on a big-PR weekend for the LAPD, there will be five hundred replacements out there on Sunday morning, dealing and shooting and tossing Molotov Cocktails. Because it ain't macho to pay any attention to the cops; it's like a pit bull curring out and humiliating its owner when it won't fight. But if someone suggests that a *part* of the answer is somehow burning that machismo crap out of the consciousness of thirteen and fourteen year old kids, sure as hell someone will leap up and denounce the observation as racist.

Yeah, racist. Like suggesting that before you can civilize crackers and rednecks you've got to get them off believing blacks are inferior, that Jews rule the world on the sly, that Catholics all pay obeisance to the Vatican, or that women have been put here just to keep men fed and happy.

But such a partial answer won't put a dime into the budget of the LAPD, and offering kids who can get rich moving crack a part-time job at the Burger King won't convince one Blood to shuck his colors, and Eddie Murphy bragging to Barbara Walters on-camera that he never reads won't make one admiring black kid believe there's any point in getting an education.

And until you've come face to face with just what we've allowed the Underclasses to turn into, here in the City of the Lost Angels, you'll never know how *truly* scared you can be.

We live in darkness. And in that never-ending night the roaming madmen burn the libraries, the slumlords debase whole families, freeway shooters pack shotguns to revenge themselves for someone shooting them the finger; and every weekend hundreds attend barbaric pit bull contests, synagogues are defaced by neo-Nazis, Cotton Mather religious fanatics vandalize family medical centers; trigger-happy cops go more steadily buggy, families are broken and merchants terrorized, lottery tickets replace baby's milk, and now we can even be treated to one of our ever-so-responsible tv stations offering us *The Morton Downey, Jr. Show* from the East Coast, just in case we haven't had our share of deranged bigotry and vigilante justice by way of Wally and his slavering idiot audience of pinheaded fruit-bats.

Why are we scared? Because when one tries to talk about it, as I have here, one thing leads to another, and one ends up raving. And there is oh so little consolation in the apologia offered by the Pollyannas: "Things have *always* seemed bad, *always* seemed on the edge of the abyss. It's no different now. You're just getting hysterical."

No one in a right mind can go for that okeydoke any longer. Darkness has fallen, and we *do* grow hysterical. So we look around for a simple sociological scapegoat. It's *them*, they've got polluted genes. It's some other *them*, they don't have the accepted Good Ole 'Murican Values. It's not enough money from the State or Federal honeycomb. It's lousy teachers. It's not enough cops, and let's get them cops out of the prowl cars and back on foot patrolling the neighborhoods. It's this, and it's that.

But the truth is, *we* let it happen!

We lied to ourselves that Los Angeles would be Baghdad forever, and to hell with *them* over there in BBQ rib and taco land. Hysteria finally wanes, and we admit that it is us, the readers of this very magazine, who distract ourselves with glossy liposuction and plastic surgery ads, with articles about the ten wealthiest people in town, with fashion spreads featuring clothes *they* couldn't afford if they worked for a hundred years. We didn't want this magazine to run articles on the 10 WORST SLUM LORDS or WHY HAS THE BLACK MIDDLE CLASS DESERTED ITS UNDERCLASS. We didn't have time or interest for that. We had time for the latest designer pizza and the newest disposable clothing shop on Melrose. But we didn't want to admit that the darkness was falling.

And so now, we're scared. Even the dullest, most lock-

and-bar secure, glossiest and silliest of us: scared. And in the words of Bertolt Brecht, "He who laughs has simply not heard the terrible news."

From high above what was once the City of the Angels, one can look down through the smog and delude oneself that we do not live in the darkness. But even from on high one hears the message of the Uzi. Is anybody listening?

Appendix D

Lenny Bruce Is Dead

(1986)

*L*enny died in 1966. Gee, how time flies when they're busy bumping off the good guys.

It came over the 11:00 news, and they ran some film clips. The usual sort of flaming-stick-in-the-eye sensationalism: Lenny in a wheelchair after his 1965 window-falling accident; clips from one of his college gigs, with Lenny satirizing a cop at one of his nightclub performances trying to take notes about his act for an upcoming obscenity trial, while roaring with laughter; some random photos of mother Sally and daughter Kitty.

And then they ran a seventeen-second interview with one of the cops who was on the scene of his death. A swell human being named Vausbinder. He could as easily have been talking about a garbage bucket or a side of beef as one of the sharpest social critics this country ever produced. "Lenny Bruce, whose *real* name was Leonard Schneider, died at 6:10 tonight. There was evidence of narcotics on the premises and—"

—and they couldn't even let him die with a little dignity. We learned later, years later, that they had gone in, found him dead, and propped him up on the toilet with the spike sticking out of his arm. They hounded him and stole his days and they crippled his humor, turning him into a pudgy bore worrying court transcripts like a withered old man with prayer beads, and they broke him financially supporting lawyers, and they wasted his life in courts for "offenses" that were as substantial as fog, and then the creeps rearranged his limbs and wouldn't even let him die without calling him filthy names.

He was surely the most moral man I ever knew.

He saw clearly enough to know it was a terrible world, filled with hypocrisy and casual, random viciousness; and he talked about it. Because he was a comedian, a nightclub comic, a *shtickmeister,* and not Eric Hoffer or William Buckley, his mercilessly accurate social criticism was labeled "sick," and his lampooning of the powerful and pious was impermissible of entry as "philosophy." He talked about what was wrong with us in the Fifties and Sixties in the language of the hipsters and the poor Jews and the showoffs. The language that made you sit and laugh till you thought you'd drop from an infarct. He talked about the most serious concerns of decent men and women the way the guys on the corner talk—honestly, slyly, phonographically reproducing the way people *really* talk about such concerns, rather than in the simpering, mealy-mouthed "at this point in time" corruption of language employed by frauds and thugs and those shining the seats of power with their pants.

His was the humor of painful truth; and he was driven by the sheer absurdity of it all—or fearless beyond a sense of his own survival—so that he kept talking; never able or willing to back off, even when they told him they would drive him, chivvy and harass him, harry him to a nuthouse or to the grave. He persisted, nonetheless. He was in the American grain of great humorists: Chaplin, Twain, Benchley, Thurber, W. C. Fields. He told them more than they wanted to hear. And they killed him for it, as they had promised. Then they propped him up on the can, and stuck the spike in his arm.

What was his crime? As the creator of *archy & mehitabel,* the journalist Don Marquis put it: "If you make people think they're thinking, they'll love you; but if you *really* make them think, they'll hate you."

And rearrange your limbs in death.

I never knew him as awfully well as many others did. But we had a special liaison in that I was the guy who got him to write some of his material for magazines, and who edited and arranged those higgledy-piggledy columns of prose, and published them in a magazine called *Rogue* from 1959 through 1961.

I met him in Chicago soon after I started editing for *Rogue*. I was fresh out of the Army, and Lenny was the hottest new comedian in the country. He was the darling of Rush Street, and having heard a couple of his albums for Fantasy Records, I was determined to get him to do a regular humor column for the magazine. It was a time when men's magazines were emerging as more than publications displaying the naked female form, a time when *Playboy* was publishing better and more daring material than any other periodical in America, and *Rogue*'s publisher wanted a similar claim to legitimacy. So, though he'd never even heard of Lenny Bruce, the publisher gave me the go-ahead to try and snare him for the book.

He was working Mr. Kelly's on Rush when I connived an introduction, and we hit it off. I'd been doing standup comedy on one coast while Lenny was working similar material on the other coast, and we spent many nights prowling and dunking doughnuts in coffee. He was friendly (and always funny) and outgoing; and even then near the beginning, a little wary of how people wanted to use him, then revile him in print.

He had cause to be wary: already they had started in on him, the Catholic Church, the politicos, the big, Irish cops of Chicago who were coming to scope his act so they could go back to their superiors and report that that motherf—— Bruce was using awful words like motherf—— right from a public stage and wasn't it a motherf—— shame that a filthy blue comedian like him was littering up motherf—— Rush Street with his foul mouth!

His columns for me were always brilliant. Sometimes they were disjointed and rambling, the way his rap on stage was; sometimes he mailed them in to me from somewhere on the road, scribbled on menus and cocktail napkins; sometimes he'd call me and dictate the copy, and I'd sit there at three in the morning writing furiously, trying to capture the cadence and inflection that made the material work. But they were always pertinent. They were funny and sharp and insightful . . . and they hurt. Which is what good satire is supposed to do. He knew how to write, even if it was verbal writing off the stage; he wrote a swell book, even if it was ghosted; he produced great American humor. Human and universal . . . and dangerous.

His records are for always. They capture only a small corner of the arena he ruled, but even they, incomplete as they are, will last. Because he talked of his times, and the dishonesty of his times, and the absurdity that he saw in the most loathsome lies his times could tell.

It is now twenty years since Lenny went down. They don't have him to harass any longer; they've gone on to other poor bastards who believe in crazy stuff like the First Amendment. They got their heart's desire: the junkie, the pervert, the foul-mouthed Lenny Bruce is dead.

And they made a movie about him, because even in rearranged, disreputable death, legends do not die if they're played by Dustin Hoffman. That's called irony. Gee, how time flies when Hollywood's having a bout of conscience, particularly if there's a kopek to be made from it.

Sticks and stones did not break his bones, names never really hurt him. But they broke his heart and they silenced his voice, a voice we needed so urgently, then *and* now, and the malicious, stupid motherf——s still don't realize that they killed one of our few heroes.

Appendix E

Did *Your* Mother Throw *Yours* Out?

(1988)

Joe Tobul's mother ruined my life. Under another name, Joe Tobul's mother blighted your life, as well. For the past fifty years, all the Joe Tobul's mothers of America—kind and decent women who kept kitchens so clean you could eat off the floor, and who wouldn't harm a fly—blighted the lives of boys and girls with absolute innocence. They did it, as Joe Tobul's mother did it to me, by tossing out all those kid's funny books.

Stand in one of the hundreds of direct-sales comic book stores that have sprung up across the country in the last decade, challenging the hegemony of traditional newsstand distribution, and listen to that fifty-year-old man accompanying his twelve-year-old grandson rummaging through this month's various X-Men comics. Mr. Fifty stares into the triple-locked display case at the unnumbered first issue of *Captain Marvel Adventures*, dated 1941, and he says oh-so-conversationally, "I had that comic. How much is it?" And the clerk smiles benignly, because he's had this conversation a hundred times, because he knows the guy remembers paying 10¢ for it when it was new, because he knows what's coming, and he replies: "It's only in fine condition, not near mint. It goes for $2700. Shame it's got a little spine roll to it, or we could've called it very fine; that'd be about six grand." Pale, very pale, goes Mr. Fifty.

And he says (make book on it), "My mother threw out all my comics."

And that's why this guy's kids never got to go to college. Because Joe Tobul's mother threw out all those comics that would have become an annuity. Guy could have been living on the Riviera today. Could own a controlling interest in AT&T.

But that's the way it was. Because comics were kid stuff. They were "bad" for kids, the way a Red Ryder B-B gun was "bad" for kids. The rifle would put your eye out (as Jean Shepherd has told us), and comics would rot your brain. And if you didn't believe it, along came the 1950s' own Cotton Mather, the late Dr. Frederic Wertham, in a book called SEDUCTION OF THE INNOCENT, who could give you chapter and verse, gore and protuberant nipples, on how mind-rotting those evil comics were. So all the Joe Tobul's mothers in this great nation, meaning well or just cleaning out the closet when you went to college, saved their kids from a fate worse than enlightenment, and thereby blighted millions of lives.

(In Torrington, Connecticut, there is a shop called *My Mother Threw Mine Away*. Just thought I'd mention that.)

Yeah, that's the way it *was*. Today, following the lead of the rest of the world, coming to awareness behind the eye-opening and groundbreaking achievements of a handful of comics writers and artists who have snared critical and flash-media attention, this great nation is coming to understand that it's been a long time since comics were only kid stuff, that comics need no longer be a secret "guilty pleasure" for adults, that a vast treasure trove of wonders has been lost, forgotten, mishandled and ignored while its creators have been kept in artistic chains and actual poverty like poor beanfield hands, and that comic books not only have a claim to Posterity, but are one of only five native American art-forms that we've given the world: Jazz, of course. Musical comedy as we know it today. The detective story as created by Poe. The banjo. And comic books.

Yet every time some parvenu publication "discovers" comics, only twenty or thirty years late, untutored and ham-handed editorial twits invariably present the material under idiot headlines of the BANG! SOCKO! WHACK! ilk, reinforcing subliterate stereotypes of a genre that has delighted the rest of the world with our cleverness for three generations.

Every other year in Lucca, Italy, comes October and the town turns into a comic book festival. The whole town. Guests stream in from around the world. They even issue postage stamps with Prince Valiant and Steve Canyon and Little Nemo on them. In Japan, as common as *sashimi* are the millions of copies of comic books—called *manga*—sold every week; some as thick as the annotated Kobo Abé, read by more adults than children in that most literate of nations, and read as seriously as novels and financial reports. In parts of Africa, Marvel's ebony superhero, The Black Panther, is looked on as a significant myth figure, in the way Spaniards revere El Cid. In France, comics are held in such high esteem that *Metal Hurlant*, the graphic magazine, is a bestselling periodical, and the artist Moebius is considered a national treasure.

Ah, but in America, venal televangelists as crazy as fruitbats hold up copies of Miller's and Sienkiewicz's *Elektra: Assassin* and scare a video congregation slavering for fresh Satanic menaces (having long-since grown bored with the red herring of alleged demonic messages badly-recorded backwards on heavymetal albums nobody would listen to without a gun at their head anyway) with assurances that this here now comical book is filled, nay riddled, nay *festooned* with demonology, bestiality, rampant sexuality and even—whisper the dreaded word—humanism! Yeah, sure; and Mighty Mouse sniffs cocaine . . . if your head is loose on its bolts.

Everywhere but in the place of its birth, the phenomenon of comics, like the prophet noted in apparently the *only* book the fanatics can read without the scent of brimstone filling their nostrils, "is not without honor, save in his own country." For more than a half century comics in America have been kept adolescent, considered throwaway trash, beneath the notice of "serious" critics of art; paid heed only when the Warhols and Lichtensteins plunder the treasurehouse, self-consciously recasting the innocent and innovative work of creative intellects whose names are unknown to all but an underground of readers, specialty hucksters, Pop Culture academics and wave after wave of bright-eyed naïfs come to work in that slaughterhouse of talent, the comics industry. Their names are unknown to those who stock the Frick and MOMA and the Guggenheim, but not to Fellini, Truffaut and Resnais who constantly pay *hommage* to the images of Stan Lee, Jack Kirby, Jerry Siegel, Joe Shuster, Jack Cole, C. C. Beck, Will Eisner, Bob Kane and Bill Finger.

If those names do not resonate even as clearly as those of Norman Rockwell, Maxfield Parrish, or N. C. Wyeth—great American illustrators who worked in mediums popularly accepted and not considered disreputable—then how about *these* names: Captain America, the Silver Surfer, the Hulk, Superman, Plastic Man, Captain Marvel, The Spirit and Batman?

While your back was turned, while you were busy growing body parts and learning to "interface" with your PC, busy fighting wars and codifying the rise'n'fall of the Yuppie Empire, comic books went whistling past adolescence and reached puberty. They gained adulthood, even as you and I.

In a recent issue of *The Hulk*, an up-and-coming young writer named Peter David did one of the most powerful battered wife stories you'll encounter outside *60 Minutes*. Yes, the story featured the tormented Dr. Bruce Banner, whose exposure to gamma rays turns him into the ravening Hulk when he gets angry, but the spur to triggering his transformation was a mainstream examination of *machismo*, the tyranny of small town bullies, and the brutalization of women.

In the first issue of a marvelous new comic titled *The Big Prize*, the talented Gerard Jones recasts the Walter Mitty idiom by taking nearsighted, plain-as-soda-water Willis Austerlitz into the wish-fulfillment world each of us has yearned to know: he wins the big prize . . . a time-traveler from a tv show of the future makes a mistake, lands in our today and awards him the right to visit the past. He goes back to a gentler, more interesting time, the 1930s. Except it isn't the idyllic dream our memories deliver. It is a time of poverty, racism, the Iowa Farm

Strikes, red-baiting. It is the *real* '30s, not an adolescent recollection of "good times."

Antic comedy as rich as *Pogo* or the best of *Dudley Do-Right* roils and gushes and overflows the pages of William Van Horn's *Nervous Rex*, the primordial saga of a henpecked tiny Tyrannosaurus, whose behemoth of a wife devils his every moment, whose world is filled with mud-flies that deliver one-liners in a Mexican accent, with the saurians determined to debase him, with a world very much like our own, in which we find ourselves often unwittingly acting like Caspar Milquetoast when we know inside ourselves that we are capable of courage and heroism.

Doesn't sound much like what was going on in comic books even ten years ago, does it?

Those are a mere handful of the creations of a cadre of some of the most innovative, wildly imaginative artists and writers this country has ever produced. Work-for-hire talents who have created a vast body of popular art that constantly struggled against Philistine ignorance and marketplace brutality toward High Art. But Siegel and Shuster's Superman does not hang in the Museum of Modern Art, and the imitations of Warhol and Lichtenstein do. But the former is persiflage, you might say, as the culture mavens at *Art Forum* would agree, while the latter has solid claim to posterity.

But consider this: if one of the unarguable criterions for literary greatness is universal recognition, in all of the history of literature, there are only five fictional creations known to every man, woman and child on the planet.

The urchin in Irkutsk may never have heard of Hamlet, the peon in Pernambuco may not know who Raskolnikov is; the widow in Jakarta may stare blankly at the mention of Don Quixote or Micawber or Jay Gatsby. But every man, woman and child on the planet knows Mickey Mouse, Sherlock Holmes, Tarzan, Robin Hood . . . and Superman.

This fanciful creation—in 1933—of a pair of seventeen-year-old Cleveland schoolboys, has remained center-stage in the American mythos for more than fifty years. The orphan from Krypton has appeared in animated cartoons for theatrical exhibition, in live-action movie serials, in a radio series, television series, cartoons for television, novels, hundreds of thousands of comic books, Broadway musicals, appeared on lunch boxes, bedsheets, drinking glasses, as Halloween costumes, dolls, plastic models, and made a star of Christopher Reeve.

But Superman is more than just the fanciful daydream of a couple of kids who wanted to break into comics. He is the 20th century archetype of mankind at its finest. He is courage and humanity, steadfastness and decency, responsibility and ethic. He is our universal longing for perfection, for wisdom and power used in the service of the human race.

Of all the literary creations of American fiction, out there riding solely on the ability to touch people of all ages and all sympathies, Huck Finn and Ahab, Yossarian and Slothrop, Charles Foster Kane and Scarlett O'Hara, none seems more certain of permanence than Superman. After all these years, born of a "disreputable, dispensable" genre, this Jungian archetype of the hero cannot but get posterity's nod. And that is because, simply put, he is our highest aspirations in human form. He, and the uncounted thousands of creations in comic books have taught more than fifty years of young people about the eternal verities: courage and ethics, right from wrong, good from evil, the values of friendship and leading a productive life.

The comic books have been the *McGuffey's Primers* of the masses. The picture books of our strange society. And at last, in just the past six years, it has become clear: intelligent adults, lovers of art, discriminating readers, observers of the forces that shape our culture are rediscovering the comic book. At their best, the new work of Alan Moore, Paul Chadwick, Peter David, Frank Miller, the Hernandez Brothers, Dave Gibbons and Steve Moncuse—and a rage of others—are creating a superior library of serious, entertaining, important reflections of our times, our dreams, our nobility and our depravity.

As the science fiction movies of the Fifties reflected Cold War paranoia, so do the comic books of the Eighties mirror and interpret our contemporary fears and obsessions. In *Concrete* we deal with individual identity, the cult of celebrity, the venality of the common man and woman; in *Batman: The Dark*

Knight Returns we suffer the terrors of urban blight, random street violence, and the alleged impotence of the average citizen; in *The Watchmen* and *V for Vendetta* we are permitted to extrapolate the menace of multinationals running amuck, government by secrecy, the instability of society in the nuclear age . . .

But that's getting ahead of the story. It's only been since November of 1981, and the appearance of the premiere issue of *Captain Victory*—the first creator-owned superhero comic in the history of the industry—written and drawn by the legendary Jack Kirby—that the exploitative "plantation mentality" of the traditional comics publishers was challenged. A mere seven years since the emergence of the independents, the kick-in of a royalty concept, the advent of the direct sales market (brainchild of an unsung hero, the late Phil Seuling), and the greening of a creative arena that permitted the newest crop of talents to flourish, to get comics into print that have swept the medium into the mainstream.

But if you would understand the nature of the chains that are being shattered, come back in time to the days in which those chains were first shackled on. Come back to the origins of the Gulag.

1933. Since the turn of the century, the closest thing to modern comics have been compilations of previously-published newspaper strips. Now a New York printing company, Eastern Color, one of perhaps a dozen firms engaged in producing newspaper comic sections as Sunday color supplements, begins issuing books in the modern format—slick covers, newsprint-paper guts in crude color, roughly seven by ten inches in size—as premiums: giveaways for retailers and manufacturers.

A salesman at Eastern named M. C. Gaines notices how popular the loss-leaders seem to be. Gaines is a colorful character: ex-haberdasher, ex-bootlegger, ex–munitions factory worker; a man who marketed *We Want Beer!* neckties during Prohibition; and the father of *Mad* magazine's Bill Gaines. But beyond his flamboyance, he's canny: he sees how kids seem to clamor for these eight-page tabloids folded down to 32 pages. He tests the market by putting ten-cent price stickers on a few copies and leaves them at two newsstands, just to see what happens. They're snapped up instantly. So Eastern publishes the first modern comic book, *Funnies on Parade*; and follows it with *Famous Funnies* later that year; and sensing they are on to something hot, still later that year go to one hundred pages in *Century of Comics*.

But these are still reprint books. It isn't until February of 1935 that the first comic book comprised entirely of original material and continuing characters is published. It is titled *New Fun Comics* and its parent company is an offshoot of a healthy printing company owned by Maj. Malcolm Wheeler-Nicholson; he names it DC, short for Detective Comics. You can soon forget the Major, because late in '37 he folds, and sells some of the DC properties to Harry Donenfeld, who comes to the business with the attitudes of the garment industry—piecework, sweatshop, assembly line—and Donenfeld takes on as an operating partner a savvy accountant, Jacob Liebowitz, who functions as publisher.

I say *soon* forget, but not *immediately* forget, the Major, because he plays one additional role in the creation of this eventually multimillion-dollar industry. By 1936, he is using comic strips with titles like "Dr. Occult" and "Slam Bradley" in *New Fun*, *New Adventure* and *Detective Comics*; features written and drawn by Siegel and Shuster. The Major has given the break to the two men who are most responsible for the popular appeal of comic books. Now he passes into the mists of minutiae and we follow Jerry and Joe, those two ex–Cleveland high school boys who, three years earlier, came up with the concept of Superman.

They'd been shopping the strip. Unsuccessfully. The Major wanted it, but Jerry and Joe were finding him slow-pay and often intrusive artistically. So as early as 1935 Superman was being sent around, even to Dell, the house that eventually would make its biggest splash publishing the Walt Disney comics. And at Dell it was seen by—here he comes again—M. C. Gaines, who gave it a pass. But now it's December 4th, 1937, the Major is gone, and Jerry Siegel meets in New York with the new

DC publisher, Liebowitz. Heed this meeting. It sets the tone for all labor-management relations in the comic book medium for fifty years.

According to historian Steve Gerber (who incidentally is the creator of Howard the Duck): "That meeting resulted in a contract agreement which stipulated that Siegel and Shuster would continue to produce 'Slam Bradley' and 'The Spy' exclusively for Detective for two years, that Detective would be sole owner of the material, that the creators would be paid ten dollars a page (of story and finished art) for their efforts, and that Detective would have first option on acceptance of any new comics features that Siegel and Shuster might originate."

Now it's 1938, Gaines has come over to help Donenfeld get the DC line moving; *Superman* has grown tattered being shunted around for possible daily strip syndication, but has been universally rejected; Siegel takes it in to DC where Gaines, Donenfeld and Liebowitz look it over and decide to buy the feature and to use it as the lead in their new book, *Action Comics*.

Liebowitz then sends a release form to the boys that reads as follows:

I, the undersigned, am an artist or author and have performed work for strip entitled 'SUPERMAN.'

In consideration of $130.00 agreed to be paid to me by you, I hereby sell and transfer such work and strip, all good will attached thereto, and exclusive right to use the characters and story, continuity and title of strip contained therein, to you and your assigns to have and hold forever and to be your exclusive property and I agree not to employ said characters or said story in any other strips or sell any like strip or story containing the same characters by their names contained therein or under any other names at any time hereafter to any other person, firm or corporation, or permit the use thereof by said other parties without obtaining your written consent therefor. The intent hereof is to give you exclusive right to use and acknowledge that you own said characters or story and the use thereof, exclusively. I have received the above sum of money.

The garment center sweatshop work-for-hire mentality comes early and ferociously to the new land, AKA, the Gulag.

On March 3rd, 1938, Jerry and Joe sign the release and lose, for all time, any and all claim to whole or partial ownership of Superman, the creation on which they've pinned most of their hopes and dreams for five years.

To forestall any Yuppie denigration of Siegel and Shuster's acceptance of such ludicrous terms for a property that has netted for DC (by conservative estimates) more than a *billion* dollars (it is impossible to arrive at even a ballpark figure, even for DC, but a knowledgeable source who continues to work in the field suggests that in just the twenty years from 1960 to 1980, more than 250 million dollars was logged by DC for royalties accruing from Superman geegaws, collectables and *tchatchkes*), remember that we're talking about 1938. The Depression was in full swing. Gasoline cost 15¢ a gallon. A loaf of bread was 7¢. If you bought a house and spent $5000, you owned a mansion. In today's currency, that $130 would be equivalent to two thousand dollars. And don't forget: these were two naïve, hungry Ohio kids, trying to make a living in a fledgling industry. *No one* could have imagined what Superman was to become.

In a 1975 press release on the occasion of the purchase of rights to *Superman* by Ilya Salkind and Pierre Spengler for the first Man of Steel motion picture, a film originally budgeted at fifteen million dollars (eventually fifty-five million), a deal from which Siegel and Shuster never realized a cent, Jerry Siegel wrote, "I can't stand to look at a *Superman* comic book. It makes me physically ill. I love Superman, and yet, in my mind, he's been twisted around into some kind of alien thing." And that was more than a decade before DC unleashed the arrogant revisionism of John Byrne on the character.

At the time of that press release, Siegel and Shuster were 61 years old. Siegel was working in a mail room in Los Angeles, making $7000 a year. Shuster was legally blind, unemployed, and being supported by his brother. They lived in what historian Gerber reported as "a shabby apartment in Forest Hills, Queens, from which he ventures out only occasionally."

Today they both live in Los Angeles, and DC Comics, now a division of Warner Communications, sends them an annual stipend . . . as long as they make no public statements about their history with DC, their feelings about the last fifty years, or contribute to the perpetuation of said sordid history. Needless to say, I was unable to obtain any statements from Siegel or Shuster during the preparation of this article. As their seventy-fifth birthdays approach, fear of retaliation insures that Siegel and Shuster, whose work does not hang in the Guggenheim, will not add to DC's ongoing weight of albatross guilt.

Nor is there, without verification from Siegel, any way to prove the truth or falsity of the long-standing story that the infamous $130 for the buy-out on *Superman* was actually money *owed* to Siegel and Shuster by DC for work previously done; money that was withheld as an extortive spur to their signing the release. This bit of ugliness has circulated in the industry forever, but remains unverifiable, because DC has that press blackout clause in the annuity deal with two elderly, no-doubt-weary gentlemen.

But for those who dote on stories that wallop you in the heart, here are a couple that have been authenticated in the New York *Times*, the Washington *Star*, by the Associated Press and on NBC's *Tomorrow* program:

On March 29th, 1966, opening night of the Broadway musical "It's a Bird It's a Plane It's Superman" directed by Harold Prince, with book by David Newman and Robert Benton, music and lyrics by Charles Strouse and Lee Adams, among the crowd milling about in front of the Alvin Theater on West 52nd Street was a shabby old man. Tear your heart out just to see him. Right. But it would more cause anger than knee-jerk sympathy to learn that it was Joe Shuster, the guy who first drew Superman, standing there without the money to buy a ticket to his own creation.

Shuster was working as a messenger. Broke, going blind, unable to get work in the industry he had helped bring into being, he was delivering parcels to midtown offices. Which brings us to story number two, guaranteed to cap the Siegel and

Shuster anguish with an anecdote emblematic of the way the comics business has treated its best talents:

Joe found himself making a delivery to DC. He walked in with the parcel, and no one knew who he was. He started to leave—so the tale goes—and Liebowitz, the guy who'd gotten the boys to sign over Superman for $130, came out of his office. He recognized Joe. Frayed cuffs, old jacket, looking gray and destitute. They confronted each other after all those years.

One version has it that Liebowitz gave him money to buy a new suit. Another version says the millionaire publisher pulled a fistful of money from his pocket, thrust it at Shuster, and told him never to come back. A third version says it was ten bucks. A fourth telling ups the amount to a hundred bucks. But all versions concur that the messenger service received a call from DC later that day, insisting that the old geezer who'd done the delivery that day never be given that run again.

Who the hell knows what the truth is? Time and the failing memory of the principals blurs the facts. And like those families that go to Watergate lengths to conceal the skeletons, corporate unity and maintaining a pleasant image for an industry that sells reading matter to kids smothers the gasps and smooths the jagged edges.

But what happened to Siegel and Shuster is not uncommon. Wally Wood, whose extraordinary art was showcased in the EC comics and *Mad* for more than a decade, worn out and alcoholic, unable to draw after a lifetime at the board, worked so hard he has migraines not even a Dexedrine addiction can ease, returns from his doctor in Los Angeles, having learned that he'll be hooked up to a dialysis machine for the rest of his days, puts a Saturday Night Special to his head and blows his brains out. They don't find his body for three days, there in that squalid little room.

Joe Maneely, Atlas Comics artist who drew more than half of the covers for the seventy comics a month the company was producing in the Fifties, having gone days without sleep to complete work unceasingly thrown at him by a publisher, rides a commuter train out to Jersey. He steps between cars to clear his head—some say he'd been drinking, but so the hell what—

the train takes a sharp curve, the cars jostle him, and he slips between them, and is crushed to death.

Jack Kirby, whose thousands of pages of brilliant art for Marvel made Thor, the Fantastic Four and The Avengers such stars that Marvel now commands almost 60% of the market, only recently, after a public crusade, has managed to regain a fraction of his originals, hundreds of pages of which have been given away as convention auction items, have been ripped-off by office personnel, have been tendered to fans visiting the publication offices in New York, have been sold and resold by dealers for a tidy fortune over the years. And to this day he receives no co-credit line for characters he helped to create.

Jack Cole, who created Midnight and Plastic Man, whose cartoons illuminated the pages of *Playboy* in the Fifties, after twenty years of backbreaking labor in the comics Gulag, pulled the trigger, in effect saying ah to hell with it.

Reed Crandall, whose stylish renditions of Blackhawk remain a pinnacle of comic art that newcomers still struggle to reach, died broke and legally blind, a night watchman in Kansas City, not one cent of pension or royalty coming to him from the uncounted pages of exemplary art that made millions for half a dozen funnybook companies.

And that's the way it was. Till 1981, till Kirby's *Captain Victory* and Sergio Aragonés's *Groo the Wanderer* started making money in the direct sales market, and comics creators were able, at last, to break out of the beanfields of the two major publishers to begin controlling their own destinies.

And at that point, the pressure to keep comics a childish, introverted, essentially frivolous commercial product, began to ease. Once there were alternatives, the maturity that had always been there, stunted and ridiculed, censored by the Comics Code Authority and the strictures of the publishers, burst loose.

By 1986, with the blasting open of the medium by Frank Miller and his *Dark Knight Returns* version of Batman was an aging, more-than-slightly-psychotic crimefighter coming back from retirement, comic books began to achieve the mainstream notice that aficionados always knew was potentially possible.

If Siegel and Shuster were the artistic and imaginative

godfathers of the field, if Neal Adams was the champion who shamed DC into giving them a yearly nibble at the profit pie, if Stan Lee and Jack Kirby were the first major talents to reduce the level of silliness in comics characters and show them as real people with unreal powers, then Frank Miller has been the ass-kicking, indefatigable spokesman for a new, adult outlook on funnybooks.

The last two years in the world of comics has been a real toad-strangler. Censorship, duplicity, heroes and Quislings, mountebanks and arrogant *poseurs*. The Gulag has turned into a feeding frenzy, and from the melee has come a banquet of tasty tidbits.

Here's the line of logic, for those who think it's been a long journey: if comics are so worthy, howzacum Joe Tobul's mother tossed out the books I loaned Joe back in 1946 when we were both twelve years old in Painesville, Ohio?

Because Joe's mother, who was a nice lady, thought they were trash. And why did she think they were trash?

Because those who ran the industry had a vested interest in keeping the material childish and narrowly focused. They were men of limited artistic vision, and their commercial view of the medium was equally as tunnel-visioned. And how did they keep the unpredictable artists and writers who aspired to nobler ends in line?

They did it by holding both copyrights and trademarks on every last creation. If they owned Superman and Spider-Man lock, stock and longjohns, they could always fire those who threatened their policies, even if the one getting the sack was the talent who thought up the character in the first place. So we study the Siegel and Shuster case at length, not only because *Superman* was the feature that made comics as popular as they've become, but because what happened to Siegel and Shuster is the same scenario for virtually everyone who had come into the field.

And that is why it took over fifty years for Superman to appear on the cover of *Time*; fifty years for journals like the New York *Times*, *The Village Voice*, *The New Yorker*, *Rolling Stone*,

Seventeen, and *The Atlantic* to publish essays that said, "Wow! Look what we've discovered!"; fifty years for magazines like *Spin* (intended principally, one assumes, for MTV refugees who had the misfortune to learn to read) to write, "These days, comics stores are infinitely more exciting than record stores, even if you aren't a dweeb in highwater pants."

Because for fifty years what could have been, was prevented from being. But six years ago the creator-owned comic came into existence, and the all-powerful interests that ran the Gulag found that the best talents were cleaning up with offbeat and original work for the independent, smaller houses. In a matter of months, direct-sales comics shops were springing up all over the country, selling many times the units that were being sold by traditional newsstand distribution methods.

Companies like Comico, Kitchen Sink, Eclipse, First Comics, Quality, and Vortex were stealing away the artists and writers who were producing the books that made them the most money. They still had Superman and the X-Men, Batman and Daredevil, but Mike Grell had gone to First where he created Jon Sable, Sergio Aragonés and Mark Evanier had gone to Pacific where *Groo the Wanderer* was pulling down big numbers, and Chuck Dixon was writing the revived 1940s character Airboy for Eclipse. Even more significantly, Dave Sim, up in Canada, was self-publishing the astonishing *Cerebus the Aardvark*, and copies of the first issue were selling for huge sums through dealer ads in the weekly tabloid of the funnybook world, *Comics Buyer's Guide*; Steve Moncuse in Richmond, California was self-publishing *The Fish Police* and copping reams of critical praise; Eastman and Laird had started publishing *Teenage Mutant Ninja Turtles* in Sharon, Connecticut, as a gag parody of the profusion of *X-Men* comics flooding the market, and suddenly their Mirage Studios was a thriving company.

So Marvel and DC, who had outlasted the hundreds of comics companies that had flourished in the Forties and been destroyed by the likes of Dr. Wertham in the Fifties, who had blossomed anew in the Sixties and Seventies, now saw the empire at peril. For fifty years the giants had stonewalled the concept of author royalties, vowing *Over our dead bodies!* But Frank Miller, who had blown breath back into Marvel's *Daredevil*, wouldn't produce for anyone simply with a work-for-hire contract any more, so DC lured him away with a royalty deal, and he created the astonishing, multi-leveled six-book "graphic novel" *Ronin*; and then *The Dark Knight Returns* . . . and it was all over for the plantation mentality.

Rolling Stone did a major takeout on Miller and his gritty, surreal, *film noir* vision of the myth of superheroes, set against mean streets filled with vicious mad-dog *vatos* and SWAT-crazy fascistic authorities. Batman, middle-aged, wracked with guilt over the death of the young man who had been Robin, lost in memories of his caped crusader career but retired for a decade, goes back to the shadowy alleys and rooftops of Gotham City, a half-crazed vigilante prowling in a nighttime world dolorous under the threat of imminent global nuclear warfare. Superman works for the government. The Catwoman is a madam. The Joker, now a media celebrity, shrills at us from the set of *The David Letterman Show*, having at last found his proper venue.

And suddenly the UPI and Associated Press start blowing kisses and urging their adult audience to *get a load of this!* Not yet thirty, Miller found himself riding the wave of serious attention. The evening news shows interview him, treating him like a modern poet of urban society. Like Fulton, Chaplin, Kerouac or Nader, Miller has been in the right place at the right time, with the deliverable goods and an enormous talent, and he becomes the point-man for the entire comics industry. He opened the door and, because there are now alternatives to work-for-hire, work-at-command, other restless creators kick that door off its hinges and the Gulag begins to empty.

Now an adult reader who makes no snob distinctions between the value of a Jim Thompson or Harold Adams suspense novel and the work of Pynchon, Jim Harrison or Joyce Carol Oates, considered "serious" writing, can go to the nearest comics shop and find magazines and graphic novels that—in this different medium of presentation—have as much emotional and intellectual clout as the best movies, the best novels, and one or two items on television. Here are a few of the best:

- *Omaha, the Cat Dancer*: a spunky, sexy, cleanly-drawn contemporary soap opera about the life and loves of a nude terpsichorean who happens to be a, er, uh, a cat. Reed Waller is the intelligence guiding this fable. It is a magazine that has the religious Right crazed. It is wonderful.
- *Lone Wolf and Cub*: a series of squarebound, stiff-cover reprints of the Japanese *manga* on which the "baby cart" films were based. The episodic story of a masterless samurai and his infant son, wandering through blood and shogunate Nippon, staying one jump ahead of the assassins sent to slay them. Kazuo Koike and Goseki Kojima tell the tales.
- *The Spirit*: masterworks month after month by Will Eisner. Denny Colt, residing under Wildwood Cemetery, a cross between the young Jimmy Stewart and the Steve McQueen of *The Great Escape*, helps Inspector Dolan battle crime and usually gets the shit kicked out of him in the process. Stories of character and human foible, tragic and funny and illustrated by a man whose work is simply cinematic.
- *John Constantine, Hellblazer*: a sublimely deranged view of present-day England and America as a black-and-white battle between the grotty, amoral survivor Constantine and all the demons of Hell that darken our lives, be they religious crusaders or violence-drenched street thugs. Jamie Delano is the deliciously perverse talent who dreams this stuff up every month. If Rimbaud and Baudelaire were writing comics today, they would acknowledge Delano as their superior in portraying decadence.
- *The Watchmen*: a twelve-issue graphic novel that is what experts mean when they talk about science fiction doing what no other genre of literature can do. From Alan Moore and Dave Gibbons, a pair of olympian English talents, this milestone saga is nothing less than an illustrated alternate-universe novel postulating a world in which Nixon still reigns, in which superheroes have been outlawed because the common man fears them, in which a complex murder

mystery is the core of a study of our times and our tenuous grasp on sanity. It was *The Watchmen*, following the *Dark Knight* opus, that kicked the Gulag's door off its hinges. As exciting as Hammett, as intricate as Proust, as socially insightful as Auchincloss, if comics have approached Literature, it is here.

- *Concrete*: probably the best comic being published today, by anyone, anywhere. Trying to describe the down-to-earth humanity and sheer dearness of Paul Chadwick's creation requires more than words or pictures. Ronald Lithgow, ex–Senatorial speechwriter, has been, er, uh, *altered* by alien forces. His brain now lives in a rock-hard monstrously-ponderous body. And he visits Tibet; and he swims oceans; and he saves a family farm; and he performs at kiddie birthday parties; and none of this casts even a scintilla of light on the magnificence of what Chadwick is doing, issue after issue.

- *The Fish Police*: another idea that turns to gibberish when one attempts to codify it. There's this cop, Inspector Gill, who is a fish. Except he keeps thinking about something called "ankles." He is obviously some other being, from some other place where people breathe air and "walk." It is Chandler and Willeford and the antic parts of Hammett, told as an aquatic allegory. It takes Steve Moncuse to conceive it . . . and to explain it.

If one now gets the sense that trying to encapsulate these ribald fantasies in mere narrative is akin to summarizing *Moby Dick* as a long story about a crazy one-legged guy trying to kill a big white fish or *Citizen Kane* as a biography of a guy whose life got fucked up because he lost his Flexible Flyer . . . one has put one's little paw on the problem.

Comics are a different medium. They combine film, animation, the novel form, the succinct joy of the short story, the mystery of the haiku, and the visual punch of great paintings. They are their own yardstick. Parallels fail. They must be seen to be enjoyed.

And trying to sum up the hundred different wonders of a

genre this various would fill (and *has* filled) copious volumes. There are the exquisite reprint books of *Steve Canyon, Li'l Abner, Terry & the Pirates, Popeye* and Shel Dorf's meticulous reissuing of *Dick Tracy*. The English reprint comics of *Judge Dredd, Miracleman, Halo Jones*; the frequently-dangerous stories of a war over which we still anguish, *The 'Nam*; Gerard Jones's and Will Jacobs's *The Trouble with Girls*, that stands James Bond on his ear; the satire on '50s bomb-shelter Cold War paranoia, *The Silent Invasion*; and Eric Shanower's gorgeous Oz graphic novels, and *Nexus* and *Zot!* and The Hernandez Bros. constantly enriching *Love and Rockets*, and . . . and . . .

It goes on. It goes on without drawing a breath or relaxing its grip on imagination. Volumes can be filled with praise for the treasures these last six years have given us.

In the pages of a new newsletter called WAP! (for Words and Pictures), for the first time in the history of the Gulag, comics professionals are speaking out. Endless recountings of the screwings and hamstringings of their work in a field that was purposely held at an adolescent level. In the pages of WAP! and in the pages of *Comics Buyer's Guide*, the new, strong voice of an art-form coming to maturity can be heard. The censors tremble, the moguls fret, the occasional jumped-up fan turned editor of critical journal (in the same way that *The National Enquirer* is a critical journal) spits bile, but after a half century the *talent* is finally speaking out.

(WAP!—twelve times a year for $25—can be obtained from RFH Publications, 1879 East Orange Blvd., Pasadena, CA 91104; *Comics Buyer's Guide*—free copy on request, available from Krause Publications, 700 E. State St., Iola, WI 54990. The former gives the inside, the latter gives the outside.)

Television wearies. Films pander to the sophomoric, to the knife-kill crazies. Novelists write smaller and smaller about less and less. Fast food gives you zits. But from the rubble of the Gulag the song of imagination is heard. And there is an insistent rapping on the sanctified portals of the Frick and MOMA. Those who survived come with *Zot!* and *Swamp Thing* to demand that at last attention, attention must be paid.

That's truth, justice, and the American way.

Appendix F

The Song the Sixties Sang

(1987/1988)

Seven-league strides have been made driving the words nigger, kike, spick, wop and broad back to the darkness from which they shambled. (Which is not to say there is any less bigotry and racism in the chopped liver; it's just that even the most slope-browed trog knows it ain't cool to use such catchy appellations in *nouvelle* society.)

Consigning those words to the dust-heaps is one of the small benefits we derived from the heightened social consciousness of the Sixties. One of the uncountable number of good things the Sixties and its action handed down to us struggling through the Eighties.

How ironic, then, that we now have a *new* epithet to replace the old derogatories used to dismiss those we hold in contempt; a freshly-minted replacement for *beatnik, old Wobbly, longhair* and *burnout*: now, from the pens and mouths of Sixties-bashers, we discover that those who fought, and in some terrible instances died, for those benefits are "refugees from the Sixties." And the stereotype is a hairy, unkempt, ponytailed buffoon in either tie-dyed jeans or a Nehru jacket, mumbling like Shirley MacLaine about cosmic oneness, and offering flowers on a street corner in the Haight.

Last night, on an ABC sitcom called *Head of the Class*, the character of Charlie Moore, teacher of a group of high-IQ honors students in a New York high school, played by Howard Hesseman, is summed up by one of his smug, computer-linked nerds as a "refugee from the Sixties." Charlie Moore lives in Greenwich Village, wears his hair with a slave-tail lock hanging over his collar, tries to imbue his charges with the subtleties and personalities behind the cold dates of historical events, is humane and passionate and bemusedly dedicated to the nobility of teaching with excellence.

He *is* a refugee from the Sixties . . .

As opposed to the prototypical yuppie-in-training we see around us as the paradigm of the Eighties, the icon movies and television proffer as the billboard ideal for us all: the self-serving, essentially hollow, mass-consuming, fad-following, cowardly, afraid to speak up refugee of the Me Decade.

It has become Accepted Wisdom that those who were "active" in the Sixties (actually the decade roughly beginning with the inauguration of JFK in 1961 and ending with the disgrace of Nixon in 1973) gave us nothing of value. That it was a twelve-year carnival of clowns. A time of folderol and flapping jaws. That it was a cultural aberration, from which the rich and prosperous Eighties, in all its somnambulistic grandeur, derives no noble legacy.

The phrase *horse puckey* leaps to mind.

Strap me in the chair, turn on the juice, and fry my fruit salad: I remember a *different* Sixties. One the bashers labor mightily to discredit. A Sixties that kids weaned on the drumbox and frozen waffles cannot find in their parents' scrapbooks among the shots of blissed-out flower children and vegetable-dye tattoo'd Deadheads at Altamont. The Sixties *I* remember was a time of life being lived at the edge of the skin, one filled with an entire nation of concerned, active Americans throwing off the restrictions of two hundred years of cultural hypocrisy and repression, challenging authority, refusing to believe the advertising-promoted lies about life and ethics that had been the hallmark of John Wayne's Fifties.

There was music in this land during the Sixties. Not just the sound of The Beatles or Dylan or Motown, but a song that spoke of human involvement. A melody of strength and commitment, to responsibility and giving a damn about the condition of life for everyone, not just those who could make the best bottom-line showing on the year-end annual report.

The horn-tooter pauses.

I was not a kid during the Sixties. I was born in 1934 (also not a terrific year). I was on the cusp of thirty when it all started, just about at that Never Trust Anyone Over age. But I was a kid in the Forties and I managed to live through the Fifties, if one uses the broadest definition of "living." And therein lies the core of why the Sixties were, and remain, so important. The Fifties. Anyone who forgets or never knew what this country was like during those years of the military draft, the war in Korea, the resurgence of the Klan, the free and blithe testing of nuclear weapons, the miasma of fear produced by the McCarthy hearings, the blacklists, the Cold War hysteria, the selling of handy backyard atomic bomb shelters . . . simply does not remember, if ever known, just what an uptight, terrified place this place was. A young Hefner knew (said the horn-tooter, knowing which side his essay was buttered on). And he got a jump on the Sixties with this very magazine, that by the Sixties had already become a powerful anti-Fifties-sensibility pry-bar in dislodging a bogus and self-deluding image of The American Way.

In the Fifties, anyone who did not subscribe to the idea that going to war was nobler than opting out, emptying bedpans in a hospital, and coming on as a Conscientious Objector . . . was looked on as subversive, suspect, cowardly and unAmerican.

In the Fifties, schools had dress codes.

In the Fifties, there were "good" girls; or "tramps" who did it in the back seats of Edsels. Those were the available categories. Women prepared meals, bore babies, fetched the coffee in offices and asserted their interest in serving the commonweal by rolling bandages at the hospital two afternoons a week. Norman Rockwell painted the family unit for the cover of *The Saturday Evening Post*; and in those paintings Mom was always smiling . . . no doubt as she looked forward to the load of dirty laundry waiting just offstage.

In the Fifties the voices of America were Pat Boone, Patti Page and Connie Francis. Perry Como was the voice that resided in the perfection of the egg at the center of the universe.

In the Fifties the lies that had sustained America through the Thirties and Forties began to crumble from ethical dryrot. We began to understand that we could not continue to delude ourselves that we were a nation formed in the melting-pot like some crazed Hollywood concept of the typical B-17 crew: 1 wop, 1 spick, 1 kike, 1 mick . . . but never any blacks. The supporting roles were all the same, all loveable in a harmless character actor way; and save for that one stereotyped ethnic difference, they were interchangeable. In the Fifties, if you wanted to be a star of the first magnitude, you changed your name from Julius Garfinkle to John Garfield, from Margarita Carmen Cansino to Rita Hayworth, from Walter Matasschanskayasky to Walter Matthau; you didn't even conceive of the possibility of getting a studio to make a picture starring anyone as "unbankable" as someone named Arnold Schwarzenegger, Meryl Streep or Emilio Estevez.

In the Fifties, if your name was Eddie Murphy, you played an Irish cop.

(Look at *It's A Wonderful Life,* emblematic of all that was good in our view of ourselves—and as subtext, what was bad—the celluloid embodiment of all the attributes of earlier decades. The immigrants were all noble, all eager to lose their funny accents and foreign ways and stinky cooking, to be Just Plain Folks, melded and invisible with Whitebread WASPdom.)

But by the late Fifties this attitude was seriously mildewed, thanks to McCarthyism, television, juvenile delinquency, an alcoholism rate soaring heavenward, Korea, and the rapid deterioration of the small communities within great cities that were once called "neighborhoods." We snarled in our chains, and the Sixties waited, poised, to blow it all away.

But I was no kid as the Sixties came rattling its changes. I do not look back on those times with blinders and sigh for the good old days. Though I was a part of much of it—the civil rights wars, the rise of the feminist movement, the breakouts in Arts and Letters, the anti-nuclear protests, the restructuring of political attitudes—I was *in* it, but not *of* it. Though I marched with King and Cesar Chavez, got myself on Governor Reagan's subversives list, wrote columns for the *L.A. Free Press,* and lectured in hundreds of universities about the changes a new generation was happily forcing on us, I never accepted the bullshit and mickeymouse, the okeydoke and flummery of much of what individuals were doing; the gaffes and peccadilloes that the bashers now use to dismiss *everything* of consequence in that twelve-year decade.

Like them, I snicker at Mellow Yellow banana-smoking as the drug of choice; wince at the self-consciousness of protest folksingers; revile the irresponsibility of Leary turning so many dips onto LSD; question the efficacy of Allen Ginsberg trying to levitate the Pentagon; and am simply reduced to porridge at the memory of a Woodstock audience believing if it chanted in unison it could stop the rain pissing on its holy ceremony. I praised the song of the Sixties, but I haven't preserved my bell-bottom Levis with the appliquéd butterfly in misty adoration of a halcyon era softened by memory, or in expectation of its return, no matter *how* big a resurgence paisley is having.

And who gives a shit that the campaign to eat natural fiber breakfast cereals was led in the Sixties by Euell Gibbons, with John Denver munching along behind?

The bashers can correctly ridicule a brainless philosophy like Don't Trust Anyone Over Thirty, but the song of the Sixties was also No War Toys, and I'd hate to lose that baby with the bathwater of triviality. One truth remains: you judge, at your peril, an entire decade and its activists by the worst of its adherents. All but those who have a secret agenda for making us ashamed of our past, understand that a time and a movement are evaluated on the basis of the *best,* not the dumbest.

* * *

Nothin' happened in the Sixties? You really think comedians like Sam Kinison and Richard Pryor and Eddie Murphy and Robin Williams and Franklin Ajaye and George Carlin and Bobcat Goldthwaite would be working the material they're laying down in comedy clubs and on HBO if there hadn't been shrapnel-catchers like Lenny Bruce, Mort Sahl, The Firesign Theatre, the Smothers Brothers, and Harry Shearer and David Landers with The Credibility Gap? Remember, if you will: the Pythons got going in the Sixties. If it hadn't been for jokers like Lenny, Elaine Boozler wouldn't be telling us today that she's picking up CB messages on her IUD; we'd still be picking bits of old Bob Hope routines out of our teeth and spuds like Buddy Hackett would still be running loose instead of being institutionalized in Vegas lounges.

In the pre–social consciousness days of Disneyland, kids with long hair were forbidden entrance to The Magic Kingdom and those who jammed their hair up under caps and slipped through often found themselves patted down for marijuana by the security staff. By the end of the Sixties rock bands had replaced Grinning Young Americans groups in Walt's domain, and attempts to exclude gay couples from the park were knocked back so fast it made Tinker Bell's tummy ache.

In the Sixties there arose a reverence for our artistic past: major studios sold their film catalogues to television, and motion pictures that had been left to fade and decay in vaults were rediscovered. *The Wizard of Oz*, never a commercial success, became an annual national event. *It's a Wonderful Life* suddenly started appearing on Best of All Time lists.

In 1961 the first real awareness that television was turning us into a nation of functional illiterates, that it wasn't universally a swell thing, was voiced by FCC Chairman Newton Minow, who told a National Association of Broadcasters convention, "I invite you to sit down in front of your television set when your station goes on the air, *and stay there*. You will see a vast wasteland—a procession of game shows, violence, audience participation shows, formula comedies about totally unbelievable families . . . blood and thunder . . . mayhem, sadism, murder . . . private eyes, more violence, and cartoons . . . and, endlessly, commercials—many screaming, cajoling, and offending . . ."

Did it have an effect for us here in the Eighties?

The networks didn't hear the song Minow was singing; and today they've lost almost half their audience. As Santayana told us, "Those who cannot remember the past are condemned to repeat it." The bashers of the Sixties, for their own reasons, want us to forget the Sixties. Perhaps because the strengths that emerged from that time are counterproductive to their ends here in the Eighties.

Nothin' happened in the Sixties? The rise of black consciousness, black pride, opening channels for all the black versions of Albert Einstein and Marie Curie and William Faulkner who had been denied to us for two hundred years. The rise of the feminist movement, for all its *Bitch Manifesto*s and bra-burnings, unleased a tsunami of cultural change by that half of our population previously kept barefoot and pregnant.

We got:

Credit cards and credit banking; oral contraceptives that demolished thousands of years of male fiat where who would get screwed and by whom was concerned; space program technology that gave us not only desktop computers and medical lasers and weather & communications satellites, but Teflon coating for pans and Tang. (Okay, so *every*thing wasn't laudable.)

Producer Edward Lewis broke the Hollywood blacklist by defying the conspiracy of silence, and hired Dalton Trumbo to write *Spartacus* . . . and gave him credit onscreen.

A fascination for the youth culture that has remained undimmed, prompted by the thorough domination of rock'-n'roll, the Beatles and their haircuts, mod fashions, and total cross-country mobility. And all because the baby boomers' demographic bulge swelled into late adolescence and young adulthood. This does not mean I can listen to the Beastie Boys or Prince. But then, that too, shall pass.

On the plus side, we got Ralph Nader. How many of you out there are alive today because of his *kvetching* about auto safety that resulted in the redesigning of cars, seat belts, frequent recalls of deathtraps, and consumer protection laws. Truth in packaging. Truth in Lending. Childproof caps on cleansers, drugs, paint thinners. On the minus side, we got terrorism and skyjacketing.

All through the Forties and Fifties we were told that rampant urban development was *progress!* Pave it over, tear it down, plow it under. In the Sixties we learned that we are all part of the planetary chain—remember *The Whole Earth Catalog* and Frank Herbert founding Earth Day?—and a magical environmental awareness blossomed. The EPA was created in 1970, the same time America celebrated that first Earth Day.

But by 1966 the Department of the Interior—operating off a saner philosophy of life than that offered by our recently-deposed sweetie James Watt, who told us it didn't matter if he sold off the forests for McDonald's packaging because the Apocalypse is coming and we won't be here to enjoy them anyway—had already gotten the rare and endangered species list to Congress, and in 1967 the Act was passed. Millions of acres of watershed land were purchased by the government for parks and preservation. Tough smog standards were clamped on a heretofore unchecked heavy industry still trying to convince us (as Coolidge had said) that "The business of America . . . is Business." Leading the environmental movement was the state of California with higher emissions standards than anywhere else in the nation. From the land of the flower children, the Sixties bashers seem to forget, came the desire to breathe more healthily.

In the Sixties women got "equal pay for equal work" from the 1963 Congress; the beginnings of success in sexual harassment lawsuits; Betty Friedan founded the National Organization for Women; the removal of "women's menus" sans prices; the topless bathing suit introduced by Rudi Gernreich that led to a general abandonment by young women of brassieres staved with metal that produced breast cancer; and by 1969 pantyhose had replaced girdles, garterbelts and nylons save for those who chose to use them in the privacy of the sexual arena. Martina Navratilova would not today be a millionaire several times over, had not Billie Jean King perceived that whipping the crap out of Bobby Riggs was an object lesson for the sons of *machismo,* and not just a cheap show filled with megabucks.

Nothin' happened in the Sixties, oh my bashers?

Well, howzabout in addition to the Civil Rights Act of 1965, we got the Gideon decision in 1963, providing legal counsel for indigent defendants, or Miranda in 1966, with its right to remain silent, right to have an attorney present during questioning, right to have your brains left unscrambled by cops straight out of a Spillane novel. Don't say it hasn't had an effect on the Eighties: in addition to turning arresting officers into crybabies because they can't use the truncheon as freely as they might wish, it has made the writing of cop shows on tv much harder. They actually have to resemble the real world now. Sure.

The first community for older citizens, Del Webb's Sun City, opened outside Phoenix, 1960. LBJ signed the first MediCare bill, 1965. The Gray Panthers were founded, 1970. That's what the old folks got from the Sixties. And homosexuals fought back in the late Sixties, chiefly as a result of the constant police harassment of the Stonewall, a gay bar in New York; that led directly to the formation of Gay Rights groups, lobbies, newspapers, a forceful movement. Now that may not be a very positive result of the Sixties sensibility, in the view of the bashers; but as one who had a good friend, one of the best men and best editors I've ever known, blow his brains out because he'd been driven nuts living in the closet most of his life, I submit the freedom of choice championed in that twelve-year decade has resulted in hundreds of thousands of decent men and women being able to live in the Eighties in a somewhat saner atmosphere, Falwell and his "wrath of God" interpretation of AIDS notwithstanding.

Now we're on a roll. Kids became a subject of concern in the Sixties. Not just leaving the tots to the tender mercies of parents who used them as cheap labor and whipping posts, but beginning to consider them as *people,* with rights. In 1969 they got *Sesame Street.* Prayer was banned in schools in 1963. Traditional restrictive images of "little boys" and "little girls," and what was acceptable for a boy or girl to aspire to, were thrown up for grabs. Child brutality laws became a prime concern of city and federal courts.

You want to talk responsibility? Consider something as trivial as celebrity. Apart from those who, in any era, would be frivolous dips even if we were sloughing through a Nuclear Winter, in the Forties and Fifties the "social involvement" of celebrities was largely manifested by their narking on one another in front of the House UnAmerican Activities Committee or Tail-gunner Joe's All-Purpose CommieSymp Inquisition. In the Sixties we saw a dawning awareness of the power of celebrity, coupled with a sense of personal worth and responsibility on the part of show biz personalities, sports figures, and even the kind of "names" who appear on *Hollywood Squares* bearing with them the enigma of precisely *why* they are famous. Muhammad Ali laid it all on the line rather than serve in a war he felt was wrong, a war he had the nerve, the gall, the *chutzpah* to point out was dedicated to killing his people, and people *like* his people. They busted him, jailed him, and stripped him of his title. And some schmucks were so dopey on JohnWayneism that they suggested he was *afraid* to go. Tell that to Joe Frazier. And the faces we knew from the covers of the *National Enquirer* and *TV Guide* were the faces we saw in daily newscasts, marching through Alabama under the gunsights of rednecks and state troopers, being schlepped across the pavement like sacks of millet during anti-war protests, working for Greenpeace and Native American rights and the Southern Poverty Law Center. Brando, Fonda, Newman, Baez, Lancaster, Cleveland Amory, and even Vanessa Redgrave (like her position or not) demonstrated that merely taking the gravy and giving nothing back was a Fifties aberration.

In 1968, Paul Ehrlich founded Zero Population Growth and for the first time a great many fast-breeding Americans learned the ultimate horror of the Malthusian theory of geometrical population increase. Pave it over, tear it down, plow it under: filing cabinets for humans, color-coded structures for cars, and brother, can you spare a maggot sandwich?

Does it all jumble, one fact over another, one event atop the next? Does it have a breathless, crazy-quilt quality that leaps years and squinches history into a bewildering cube like something burped out of a car-compacter? Paraphrasing Whitman, "Do I jumble? Very well, then I jumble. The Sixties were large, they contained multitudes." It all happened at once, so it now seems. Not a day passed that the fabric of American society did not get redraped on a general consciousness being raised from its Quasimodo-like bestial slouch. Nice image, that.

Nothin' much happened in the Sixties that influences us in the Eighties? Countries granted or claiming independence in the Sixties, with which we now have to deal, as part of the universal economic chain, include: Somalia, Ghana, Upper Volta, Senegal, Nigeria, Rwanda, Syria, Algeria, Jamaica, Uganda, Malawi, Zambia, Biafra, Guyana and Botswana, not to mention the other twenty-five I don't need to make the point. The bashers seem unable to make any connection between the rise of black power in this country at the time, the riots, the demands for an equal share of that mythical American Dream that blacks saw on television every day, and the assumption of responsibility for their own destinies of black people in far places. It took the French thirteen years after America fought and won its independence to get the message. But then, maybe black folks ain't as slow as Prof. Shockley or Al Campanis think they are. Maybe there was one of those sudden biological leaps in intellect; after all, *Amos 'n Andy* had been pulled from syndication in 1965, and there's no telling what *that* did for universal black intelligence. It certainly did a lot for their self-image.

Even our obese citizens benefited from the Sixties: Weight Watchers was founded in 1963. The same year gourmets realized Hydrox were better than Oreos.

We came to learn, in the Sixties, that one person *could* make a difference: Mario Savio's stand in defense of free speech that began campus unrest at UC Berkeley in 1964 and culminated in the Kent State massacre of 1970, thereby bringing to full, hideous circle an object lesson we needed desperately to learn, that the cost of civil disobedience in the service of the commonweal can end up being tragically more than a failing grade in civics; Martin Luther King, Jr. dedicating, and finally giving up his life that half a nation might see out of the eyes of the other half; Rachel Carson almost singlehandedly raising the alarm that we are killing the earth beneath our feet, alerting a generation to its responsibility to something as arcane as a planet; John Kennedy, for good or bad as the youngest President we ever elected, killed papist bigotry where the highest office in the land was concerned, and brought to his constituency a love of literature and the arts that not even Reagan can wholly flense from our priorities, try though he may; Ralph Nader, going at the corporations again and again, like some mad Quixote, till they clapped their hands over their ears and screamed, "Enough already! We'll make it safer, cheaper, better, saner!" Those were the positive icons. We had, as well, the classic Jungian archetype of the trickster; madcaps like Ken Kesey and Hunter Thompson and Paul Krassner and looney Abbie; and that nameless vigilante who called himself The Fox, who appeared in bright sunlight to dump garbage in the pristine lobbies of Dow Chemical and the Rand Corporation, to bring the public's displeasure with war games to the very doorsteps of the sightless masters on far glass mountaintops.

And we had our negative images. Men and women who gave us pause at the depth and inventiveness of their ability to make the world a drearier, deadlier place: Charlie Manson, Anita Bryant, Mayor Richard Daley, Spiro Agnew, John Mitchell, Lt. William Calley, the mad bombers of the Weather Underground, Lee Harvey Oswald, Jack Ruby, James Earl Ray, Judge Julius Hoffman. Forget their names. They made us feel bad, and many of them are now, thankfully, worm-food. They were that part of the learning experience of the Sixties that produced in us the occasional unworthy thought that maybe we ought simply to pack it in and let the cockroaches take over the ballgame. But they had their place: they showed us what we'd be like if we continued to operate off the *status quo*.

The jumble coalesces. The great Bayeux tapestry of the Sixties, from JFK's joyous inauguration to Nixon's ignominious fall from power, solidifies into one unseamed memory. The good times and the bad times, the rivers of blood and the brave winds of change. All the names that mostly mean nothing to high school kids today, as distant and chill as the Norman Conquest. But definitely not the revisionist horse puckey of the bashers.

Is the current prevalence of reactionary attitudes a product of the baby boomers' hardening of the liberal arteries? Where did all the passion go? What happened to the great starts made in the Sixties, now backslid with erosion of civil rights, feminist imperatives, environmental concerns, humanistic philosophies?

After all, even *Rolling Stone* has sold out. Consider their Summer '86 glossy folio insert in *Advertising Age*. In a ten page, slick paper explication of the magazine's stance as a journal oh so *au courant*, they said, "If your idea of a Rolling Stone reader looks like a holdout from the '60s, welcome to the '80s." And on the left we see a hippie in jeans and Mexican wedding shirt, festooned with love beads, an elephant hair bracelet on his wrist, auburn locks fit for a biblical prophet hanging to his elbows, the beatific look only enhanced by the beard and the poached-egg eyes. Above the photo is the single concept: PERCEPTION. On the facing page is the gently smiling, self-assured photo of a clean-shaven, neatly-coiffed yuppie in linen slacks, pinstripe buttondown shirt, loose-fitting Giorgio Armani jacket and a look of such consummate smugness that we know with the certainty of those who were never invited to pledge his frat, that this demographic rep of the 18–34 wedge is wondering whether there'll be a ticket on the windshield of his Porsche when he gets finished with this photo sitting. Over his head is the word: REALITY.

On succeeding spreads we get as PERCEPTION the day-glo painted hippie VW bus; and as REALITY that smirking yuppie's burgundy-toned, mag-wheeled import with the rear deck spoiler and the back seat only Billy Barty could love . . . a funky aluminum beer keg tapped with a vacuum pumper; as against a dozen lightly bedewed bottles of the Now brews, Erlanger, Bud, Dos Equis and imported Guinness extra stout (we are told *Rolling Stone*'s readers consumed 33,607,000 glasses of these socially-relevant elixirs in just the preceding seven days) . . . on the left we get as PERCEPTION a handful of spare change, the kind kids in the Hashbury used to panhandle, total 48¢; and on the right the REALITY is a stack of credit cards, American Express on top (at least they opted for suave good taste: the AmEx is a standard green, not a gold card) . . . and on the final spread the PERCEPTION is that weary disappointment George McGovern, arms outspread as he makes his speech, his hands open and a trifle pathetically imploring; on the right (oh yeah, on the *right*) we done got the REALITY: Ronald Reagan, a grin as wide and as deep as the Cayman Trench, arms lifted and thumbs up in his best Gipperwin gesture.

All this little appeal to *Miami Vice*–manqués lacks is a left-hand shot of backyard-grown marijuana as PERCEPTION with a dozen fat lines on glass of the best unstepped Peruvian nose candy as REALITY.

What a sorry pass it all seems to have come to. Technology pioneered in the Sixties, to better our condition of life, has been coopted by the recidivist Eighties not only to abet the Me Decade selfishness and lethargy of an increasingly conscience-dulled electorate—pocket calculators so no one has to be able to add or subtract, digital watches so no one has to figure out what it means when Mickey's big hand is over his head and his little hand is in his crotch, cable tv and videocassettes so no one has to read a book that ain't interactive or a newspaper that doesn't sport a headline informing us that 300 LB. MOTHER TRADES TWINS FOR COOKIES—but that same technology has totemized the post–Me Decade sensibility. It has given the semiliterate, smug know-nothing a cachet. To rely entirely on the purchasable gadget is the mark of *homo superior*. And since the President himself is all style and no content, a man who may not be a know-nothing but who doesn't seem to know what he knows, or when he did or didn't know it . . . that cachet looms large as reflected in the top man of the U.S.

How did it happen? No big secret. No codex needed to fathom it. Activists got weary after twelve years on the barricades. Took a breather. The whole country took a breather. Out went Nixon, and we thought we'd bought some surcease. But as we keep forgetting, the price of freedom is eternal vigilance, and in that vacuum of power, with the balming hum of Gerald Ford's motor in neutral, Torquemada returned with Reagan, Meese, Schlafly, Watt, Falwell, Ollie North and all that little gang of knuckle-brushing shamblers from the 15th century. We snoozed a few years too long.

Now we have the sorry spectacle of that Brightest Hope for the Future, the young of his nation, littering in a way that would have been unthinkable in the Sixties, spazzing out for the benefit of MTV exploiters during Spring Break in Ft. Lauderdale and Palm Springs, coming out of school only slavering to work in airless cubicles for a corporate pension; we have Rambo-ism, vigilantism, racism redux, Bernard Goetz as Zorro, inhumane tv interviews with people saying of murderers who've drawn life sentences, "He should oughtta burn in Hell forever"; we have millions gulled in every aspect of their lives by televangelists who tell them everything they do is wrong or dirty, movies geared to the mentality of a twelve-year-old (a *retarded* twelve-year-old); and we have the bashers of the Sixties. A time, we are told, not worthy or our respect.

There is a scene in *The Big Chill*, written by Lawrence Kasdan and Barbara Benedek, a famous dinner scene, that is the perfect example of Newspeak about the Sixties. In that scene we have seven characters who have gathered to attend the funeral of one of their '60s group. The time is more or less today. These seven are: Sam, a successful tv actor know for his popular *Magnum*-like series; Sarah, a successful doctor; Michael, a successful *People*-style gossip journalist; Nick, a successful drug dealer; Harold, a successful manufacturer of running shoes; Meg, a successful lawyer; and Karen, a successful suburban wife and mother.

At the funeral, a disingenuous pecksniffian minister who didn't even know Alex, the dear departed, lays down the first paradiddle of the song of revisionism sung by the Eighties about the Sixties: "A brilliant physics student at the University of Michigan who, paradoxically, chose to turn his back on science, and taste of life through a seemingly random series of occupations."

Let us rewrite history through the innocent medium of the nostalgic movie. Let us dismiss the symbols and the reality will scintillate into nothingness, for the oxen are slow, but the earth is patient. And memory fades. And youth knows not.

They sit at the dinner table, these seven (and Alex's Now Generation girlfriend, a model of pragmatic sensibility and sweetness, not a mean bone in her body, but also not a passionate one, either), remembering what Harold said at the service: "Alex brought us together from the beginning; now he brings us together again." Alex as symbol of the Sixties. Time gone by, and the bashers have told us friendships were transitory, so we know it now by these seven; they have grown apart. Alex as symbol of the fruitless Sixties—lost hope, misspent life, protracted irresponsibility, frustration, self-loathing, suicide.

The song Karen played at the funeral: the Stones' *You Can't Always Get What You Want (You Get What You Need)*.

And here is the dialogue:

The Doctor: "I feel I was at my best when I was with you people."

The TV Star: "When I lost touch with this group, I lost my idea of what I should be."

The Journalist: "Maybe there was something in me then, that made me want to go to Harlem and teach those ghetto kids."

The Lawyer: "And I was going to help the scum, as I now so compassionately refer to them."

The Doctor: "I hate to think it was all just fashion; no commitment."

The Lawyer: "Sometimes I think I put that time down, pretended it wasn't real, so I could live with how I am now."

And the running-shoe magnate sums it up: "Great then; shit now."

How sad if Larry Kasdan and Barbara Benedek really believe that ready-made tract for the bashers. They portray these seven "refugees from the Sixties" as cynically hollow, confused, ambivalent, duplicitous, betraying, distrusting, self-absorbed, settling for mediocrity, overly analytical but at heart simply shallow . . . profligates, has-beens, dopers, figures better suited to Hemingway's Lost Generation than to the activist Sixties.

But that's the bashers' view. That's the revisionism proffered by people who have settled into way-over-age-thirty guilt at having become part of Reagan's America, the yuppie generation, the survivors of the Me Decade. And like those who drink till they puke on your shoes at a party, they cannot stand to see those who came out of the Sixties with their souls and humanity intact not drinking. So they will ridicule sobriety. Rambo teaches us that going to war in 'Nam was somehow morally superior to staying out. Environmentalists are fuzzy-headed idiots who care more for the snail-darter than they do the sensible development of watershed land for a new shopping mall. Anybody who ain't looking out for #1 is simply a wuss whom we will not see lodged in upper management.

They pose the question: was it all just fashion?

And they reassure themselves that they've made the right choice, joined the winning side, played it smart, outgrown all that kid stuff, by answering, negatively, with the skepticism swamping Reagan right now. Like *Rolling Stone,* in for the ride when it was fashionable to follow the dissenters (from a safe distance behind the typewriter), they try to convince us that the Sexual Revolution ended up in herpes, and AIDS, that the creative ferment, questioning of authority, and outpouring of simple concern for others was a Big Chill.

But we *live* with the benefits of the Sixties, the large and small treasures enumerated here. In the din of the bashing to justify personal moral flaccidity and floating ethics, they try to drown out the song the Sixties sang.

They despise themselves, and what they have settled for;

and so they seek to make us join their zombie death march to the nearest point of purchase.

But here are the vocals accompanying the song, remastered and digitalized, pure in their melody:

Martin Luther King, Jr.: "I have a dream. I have a dream that one day, on the red hills of Georgia, sons of former slaves and the sons of former slaveowners will be able to sit down together at the table of brotherhood . . ."

Ronald Reagan: "If you've seen one redwood, you've seen them all."

Muhammad Ali: "No Viet Cong ever called me nigger."

Barry Goldwater: "Extremism in the defense of liberty is no vice . . . moderation in the pursuit of justice is no virtue."

Eldridge Cleaver: "You're either part of the solution or part of the problem."

Neil Armstrong: "That's one small step for [a] man, one giant leap for mankind."

Richard Nixon: "I'm not a crook."

Anonymous, 1965: "Save water: shower with a friend."

Bob Dylan: "Don't follow leaders; watch the parking meters."

Pogo: "We have met the enemy and they are us."

Martin again, and last, and always: "Free at last! Free at last! Great God a-mighty, I'm free at last!"

I thought I'd buy it at age fourteen, but I've done the Thirties, the Forties, the Fifties, the Seventies and most of the Eighties. And though the sky is no darker, and though the friends have gone to dust, and though the killers of the word are still with us, I must tell you that those who bash the Sixties out of present shame and self-loathing flummox you about a time that this country can be proud of. They are merely trying to devalue Boardwalk and Park Place so they can get you to like living in one of their hotels on Baltic or Mediterranean.

Hotels in which every room is numbered 101.

Screw'm. The Sixties were *exactly* as good as you remember them. The Eighties suck because viewers couldn't handle *Buffalo Bill.* And God don't hear the prayer of the Swaggart.

Cup your hand behind your ear. Listen hard. The song is still being sung. Not as loud, perhaps, but just as sweetly. It'll all be better in the morning, kiddo.

Appendix G

The Dingbat Appendix

Installment 5 (page 32)

Goodness knows why, but my Publisher bristled at my description of publishers as creatures whose ancestors, when their fossilized remains have been dredged out of primordial ooze, sported tails with rattles on them. He assured me he wasn't taking it personally, but he *did* bristle. He did not rattle. He is, in fact, a good friend and a fine publisher. And as should be painfully clear, this far along in the book, he is long-suffering with your Humble Author. So let me say this:

I wrote those words of asperity in 1972.

In those days one dealt with a very different kind of publisher than clogs the landscape today. I'm not sure things are *better* because of this difference in template, but they sure are different.

When I started writing as a professional in 1955, the great multinational epicures had not yet recognized what a banquet could be enjoyed at the groaning board of the American Publishing Industry. Nothing like Michael Milken, junk bonds, leveraged buyouts, greenmail or entrepreneurs who reside in

Hokkaido owning the Statue of Liberty existed. Publishing today is a bookkeeper comptroller bottom-line lawyer-festooned forest of conglomerate redwoods, heterogeneous and arrogant, captious and greedy, with its guiding intellects as far from Maxwell Perkins or Alfred Knopf as Paula Abdul is from Bessie Smith.

It is, in brief, a nightmare. For publishers of the sort we revere because of their obstinate adherence to the standards of responsibility and literature-nurturing that was *de rigueur* in times past. (And you may assume the publisher of this book is one such, for I would not otherwise be with him in this venture.) For agents who care more about a writer-client's future and art than for how much can be gouged in a cattle-call manuscript auction. For the book-buying public, that has been so often stampeded into buying trash by blanket-bombing hype that it now turns to the tabloids and tv for "quality entertainment"—a cynical statement that speaks for itself. And for authors, who now deal with obdurate, faceless entities who proffer contracts as complex and as heteronomous as the Treaty of Versailles.

Yes, things are different now; and I do not envy in the tiniest degree any writer starting his or her career as the new decade rises from the dust-heap of the Nixon and Reagan years.

These moguls and their representatives are not the sort of whom I wrote in 1972. They are on a moral plane of commerce where terms like "crook" and "schlockmeister" are no more than archaic white noise. The marketplace is all, for them; and such a chill sensibility of amorality obtains that they truly seem astonished when they are brought to the bar for their actions.

But like the passel of mooks of whom I wrote in that 1972 essay, they are just a part of the publishing world. A large part, but not the totality.

My friend, my Publisher, had every right to feel I was blowing hard with hyperbole. There were decent publishers back then, and there are men and women I trust implicitly in the business today. Yet one expects—however foolishly—one takes as the norm, the righteous. It is the encounters with the thugs and the arrogantly stupid and the cavalier that make the deepest, most hurtful impressions. And so, perhaps too often, and too flamboyantly, we who do the work out here report only of the barbarians, and insufficiently extol the virtues of the ladies and gentlemen who struggle against the system as hard as some writers.

This has been an update from the battlefield.

🎓 Installment 8 (Page 61)

"Begin with either a Chi-Chi cocktail or a marguerita," I wrote. But a page earlier I remarked, "There's a bar, though beer and wine are all you can get." It has been pointed out to me that these are incompatible realities. I have been asked to explain.

I wish I could. But I can't.

Not being a drinker, I have never had a marguerita, but I do know that the potable is made with 2 oz. of tequila, 2 tsp. of Cointreau, 1 tbs. of lime juice and ½ a lime, combined and shaken well, strained and served straight up.

I'm sure there's a simple explanation for this seeming incongruity. I would give at least half a buck to be able to present that explanation to you here. Unfortunately, it's an answer almost twenty years and a defunct restaurant lost in the mists of time and memory. I doubt that I got it wrong, because I sent the column over to Roberto Rivera for fact-checking, and he never called me on it. Nor did anyone remark on this "error" when the column appeared. So there has to be a fact missing, such as, maybe, that Los Angeles liquor licensing authorities permitted tequila as a liqueur back in 1972. The Chi-Chi cocktail was probably made with wine, and maybe possibly dining establishments waiting for their liquor license—as was the case early on with El Palenque—managed to slip tequila through. Or maybe it was some kind of weird hybrid marguerita made with something *other* than tequila, though when I suggested that to one of my tosspot friends, he winced and left the room.

Thus, I cannot reconcile the anomaly. But at least you know we didn't ignore the problem. Big fat consolation.

🎓 Installment 10 (page 74)

Here's where a picky picky editor can make you nuts. On this page I said, "I've never been one for cooking for myself." In the preceding installment I wrote, "I can think of nothing more pleasant than being left alone of an evening, working at writing a story, watching some television, making a small meal . . ." One of the editors who worked on this manuscript felt that was inconsistent. Okay. It's inconsistent. (I am large, I contain multitudes.)

In fact, it parses. I *don't* like cooking for myself. That doesn't mean I'm incapable of doing it. And doing it once in a while, on an otherwise unstressful, pleasant evening, is hardly traumatic. I was a bachelor for the greater part of my life, and I do know how to dine elegantly; but preparing a full meal for myself is a pain in the ass, and I'd sooner go without or simply fling together a grilled salami sandwich on corn rye. Bachelors will understand.

Nag, nag, nag. You'd think with the world in the state it's in, that some pecksniffian editor could find better things to do with his time, wouldn't you?

🎓 Installments 11 through 20 (Page 78)

In late 1972 and early 1973 I was engaged in the writing of a screenplay for a man named Marvin Schwartz. He was a terrific guy, and a wonderful motion picture producer; and he is the *only* film executive in my almost thirty years as a screenwriter to give me full and total freedom to write what *I* wanted to write, no interference. Consultation, yes; guidance when sought, yes; harsh criticism when he thought it appropriate, yes. But mostly the respect one gives to a laborer when one trusts his abilities and inventiveness. Marvin insisted we call it HARLAN EL-

LISON'S MOVIE. We both knew it wouldn't hold that title if it ever got made, but what the hell . . . it was fun while it lasted.

Because I was hip-deep in that primary project, all those long months, my newspaper column became a problem. So with Marvin's approval—an unheard-of act of courtesy and friendship—he let me serialize the entire screenplay in the *Hornbook*. Ten columns, smack in the middle of the run.

That screenplay, those columns, do not appear in this book.

Before you start screaming, "I been robbed!" let me assure you it is only because of my stupidity and lousy memory that you have been denied that stretch of *Hornbook* entries.

What happened was this:

I sold this book to Jack Chalker twenty years ago, as I've reported any number of times in these pages. At that time it was the kind of book no mainstream publisher would touch. It wasn't a book of my stories, it wasn't a novel, and it was off-the-wall comment by a writer unknown as an essayist. So I jumped like a hammerhead shark at a severed leg when Jack offered to publish the *Hornbook* as a small press specialty item under his Mirage Press imprint. The pay was not large, but that was then, and we both figured if the book did well in the limited edition market, well, we'd both be recompensed.

Two decades passed. I finished the book. And because, during those intervening years, I had almost always sold a limited edition right to books intended for trade distribution to a larger, general market, I sold the *Hornbook* to Otto Penzler, thus fulfilling a promise to do something for him that had existed between us for almost ten years.

I didn't bother to go back and check that ancient contract with Jack. Careless. Just stupid.

Otto purchased the trade rights for a lot of money. He knew Jack was doing a signed/numbered limited edition prior to the Penzler Books release of the *Hornbook* in the larger general market. Jack thought Otto was going to do a trade paperback. He assumed—because he had it in his twenty year old contract—that he had the right to do both the limited and the trade editions.

By the time we were into early production, I realized what a schmuck I'd been. It was a very nasty situation.

Jack and Otto bailed me out.

I didn't deserve it, but when I said in a previous dingbat footnote that my Publisher is a gentleman, I wasn't just whistlin' *Dixie*. Otto suggested that we yank out the only part of this book that could be withdrawn comfortably and still not short the readers of the trade edition, and let Jack use it in his limited edition. A large and interesting chuck that would give Mirage Press something they could make a buck with, while not impeding the flow of material in the trade edition.

Most of you won't miss it.

It was long, and it wasn't written in straight narrative form. It was a screenplay, and most of you don't read those, don't ask me why. You didn't avoid TRISTRAM SHANDY or ULYSSES because it was written in a different format . . . but screenplays somehow seem to daunt so many of you.

For those who feel the unearthly itch to Get It All, the signed, limited edition of the *Hornbook* is available from Mirage Press. Here is the address to write for information:

The Mirage Press, Ltd.
P.O. Box 1689
Westminster, Maryland 21157

It's a gorgeous volume, with HARLAN ELLISON'S MOVIE scrupulously reproduced in screenplay form printed as a separate chapbook, both volumes slipcased together. And expensive. By the time you see this trade edition from Penzler Books, there may not be any copies of the limited left, but drop a line. If you are the sort of reader who collects First Editions, or one who wishes to read one of the great, lost, unproduced screenplays of all time, I can only suggest with humility that you get in touch with Jack Chalker at Mirage.

And all posturing aside, you are reading the words of one lucky chap. I committed a publishing crime that usually results in the fumblefooted author hoist lithely on his own petard, or by the nape of the neck, whichever is handier. Otto and Jack acted like a pair of *mensches*, and I escaped with my skin intact. My composure is somewhat frazzled, but then, from the resigned sighs issuing from the Publishers, I suspect they chalk it up to the occupational hazards of working with an *extremely* flawed fella.

When I offered to make it up to them by doing *another* book with each of them, imagine my surprise when they bolted and dove through closed windows.

🎓 Installment 22 (Page 90)

In 1973, in those halcyon days before people like Judith Krantz began getting multimillion-dollar contracts for utter twaddle, the kind of advances for a book that Herb Kastle was pulling in were considered heavy sugar. Today, it's chump change. Which says a great deal about what has happened to American publishing with the taking-over of the cathedral by the Trump Tisch Helmsley mentality. I could have upgraded the amounts in that installment to make them consistent with the equivalents today, but every word of these columns has been left *in situ*, as they appeared originally.

🎓 Installment 24 (Page 114)

"Somehow, even if they suicide, everyone survives." This epigraphic sentence seems to have troubled some readers.

Perhaps it's because I didn't write it as "commit suicide." Or perhaps it's because I'm suggesting that there might be a case made for snuffing oneself as an acceptable survival answer to anguish so profound that continued life becomes the act of suicide. It's intended as a surreal remark. I don't recommend it.

🎓 Installment 25 (Page 121)

Devotees of the best work of Kurt Vonnegut, Jr. will instantly recognize the word *foma* as one of the delightful concepts to be found in CAT'S CRADLE, Kurt's best book in my opinion (with THE SIRENS OF TITAN, MOTHER NIGHT and the out-of-print paperback collection originally titled CANARY IN A CATHOUSE close behind). Kurt explained that "foma" are harmless untruths. Little lies or embellishments or exaggerations used to make life smoother, warmer, moister and generally more susceptible to smiles. Santa Claus is a foma. So is the Loch Ness Monster. So is the saying, Every Cloud Has a Silver Lining. They don't hurt anyone.

Installment 37 (Page 210)

One of the problems of living past the absolute outside time in which you can have a zit, is that you know a lot of stuff all the johnny&jill-come-latelies never even heard of, much less remember.

Go try to convince some hotshot baby-boomer stocking up on CDs that there was a time before the LP was devised in which one went out and bought a packet of ten needles for one's Victrola, and if you were flush they were steel needles, good for maybe a dozen plays before getting dull; but if you were a poor kid who had only a buck or two for the whole week, the proceeds of your paper route or selling *Grit* or working a shoeshine spot on the corner of State and Main on a Saturday night, then you laid out a nickel or a dime for a packet of phonograph needles made from either wood or cactus needle, and they were serviceable only for two or three plays. Take a poll, and see how many yuppies can identify the Burma Surgeon or Laird Cregar or Senator Bilbo. Suggest to the average product of the American Educational System that the word "bazooka" wasn't invented by a bubblegum company, that it didn't originate with the World War II weapon, and that it had something to do with a bucolic radio and film personality named Bob Burns, who made *music* on an instrument of his own devising, that he dubbed the *bazooka*, and clock the look s/he whips on you.

A younger person, working on this manuscript, appended via Post-it the following observation:

> Manuscript p. 422, par. 5: A "45 rpm *album*"?
> I think he means an LP, which is 33 rpm.

Gee, and I'll bet next you'll be trying to convince me the Earth is round, right?

Well, kiddo, I mean just exactly what I said. A 45 rpm album. They had such things back there in the old days, when we only got a chance to listen to our moldy-fig music when we weren't trying to escape the fangs of the stray dire wolf or *Smilodon*.

As I write this, I am looking at a 45 rpm *album*, containing eight cuts on a two-record double-sleeve package. Shorty Rogers and His Giants. *Cool and Crazy*, it's called. West Coast jazz. Reissued later on an LP. Or how about this single-sleeve *album*, one disc (with that big hole in the middle) with four tracks, two to a side: Harry James and his Orchestra, featuring Helen Forrest singing "Skylark" (the best rendition ever cut, after Jackie Paris's version on an old Wing Records release) (Wing was a subsidiary label of Mercury, back there when we had to watch out for invasions from Atlantis or Lemuria) and also singing "I Don't Want to Walk Without You" and . . . well, you get the idea.

File this one under: Don't try to teach your old granny how to suck eggs, kiddo. Play your cards right, and maybe I'll let you listen to all those swell Bobby Sherman sides I've got put away till the day they're collector's items.

Index

Only matter from page 1 on is indexed.